JONNY THOMPSON

Atlantis

For my Family.

1

Clive stared thoughtfully at the entirety of his life's possessions, which consisted of a neatly packed single duffel bag, as he tried his best to ignore the throbbing pain in his swelling right hand. He glanced around the recently acquired one-bedroom apartment that a friend was kind enough to lend him and tried to figure out exactly where he'd gone wrong.

This relocation was not by choice. It had been, more or less, mandatory after coming home from a short, albeit adventurous, assignment in Istanbul to find his previous apartment occupied by his now-ex-girlfriend and her spindly armed PhD advisor, who apparently found it easier to discuss marine biology while in bed, naked, drinking red wine.

Clive had always imagined himself to be cool and collected in difficult situations. He'd been in more than a few of them over the years during his time as a Joint Task Force (JTF) 2 operative. But something about the way Gregory had tried to play off the situation, like it was somehow Clive's fault, drove Clive's fist into his face.

Needless to say, Lara wasn't happy. The bottle of chianti earlier consumed was doing Gregory no favours. His nose was spouting blood like a bilge pump and it was making a mess of the beige carpet—the carpet they'd put in before Clive's last tour. Not that it bothered him.

After that, the conversation disintegrated, as Lara screamed an endless torrent of cliches, like, "You did this to yourself", "If you cared more about me than you do your work …", and so on, as Clive tried to explain to them both that Gregory's nose "probably wasn't even broken". *It was.*

In the end it settled itself and they were able to find a compromise. Lara wouldn't call the cops and Clive would find a new place to live.

The speed with which all of this went down was quick even by Clive's standards. This made it all the more unnerving when he heard a knock at the front door.

"Master Sailor Davies," Commander Dale Hammond said, his formalities never dropping even during an impromptu, off-duty appearance. "Having fun being home?" He glanced at the bag of peas wrapped tightly around Clive's hand with a dirty T-shirt.

"You could say that," Clive said as he moved inside, leaving the door open for his boss and mentor to follow him in.

"Beer?" Clive called back as he walked toward the kitchen.

"It's not even noon, Davies."

"Is that a no?" Clive opened the fridge and was happy to find a couple Olands in the door.

"I think I'll pass."

"Suit yourself," Clive said as he twisted the cap off, wincing as his swollen knuckles tightened awkwardly with the movement. "So," he asked, collapsing into one of the plush chairs occupying the open-space living room, "how the hell did you find me?"

"Does it matter? The point is I'm here," Hammond said, sitting down in the centre of decent-sized sectional.

"Navy news seems to travel a little too fast sometimes." Clive took a swig of his beer. "Let me guess. You think that, since I asked for leave to be with Lara, and Lara is no longer …"

"I'm not here to try and bring you back, if that's what you think," Hammond said, though Clive had a feeling that was a lie.

"You think I'm lying." Hammond smirked.

"I've known you a long time. You've told me a lot of things."

"Like what?"

"Ummm," Clive said, tapping a finger to his chin as he pretended to think, "like that Nova Scotia was just as good as BC."

"And it is."

"Minus the mountains."

"Give me Cape Breton over 193 days of rain." Hammond shrugged.

"Umbrellas!" Clive retorted.

"Look, you told me you left Toronto to find adventure. Did I or did I not give you adventures?"

"You did," Clive said, tilting his head in a half nod before taking another sip of beer.

"Good. Now can we stop this damn debate? It's been ten years and you're starting to sound like a broken record." Hammond let out a rare laugh. "I missed you, Son."

"I missed you too, Boss," Clive said, taking a sip. "So, why are you here? You have an update on the Iran investigation? I haven't heard anything about it since before the last assignment I would have thought something—"

"I'm not here about the investigation. I told you, I've got that handled." Hammond sighed. "Is it really so hard to imagine I just wanted to check in on you?"

Clive narrowed his eyes and began rocking side to side, feigning deep thought.

"Yes," he said with a toothy grin.

"Ditch the peas and get dressed." Hammond stood and started brushing the wrinkles out of his brown khakis.

"I just opened a beer," Clive said, tapping the brown bottle with a fingernail.

"I'm taking you for breakfast. That's an order, Son," Hammond said in an authoritative voice usually reserved for the base. "On me," he added when Clive didn't budge.

"Why didn't you say so?" Clive said, downing the nearly full beer. "But I would like to point out that you can't actually give me orders on my personal time."

Clive disappeared and returned a few moments later in a white T-shirt and brown cargo shorts.

"Isn't that the same outfit you just had on?" Hammond asked, eyeing him suspiciously.

"Yes, but this one doesn't have blood on it," Clive said, slipping on a pair of Crocs.

"What the hell are those?" Hammond pointed at the black, holed shoes.

"Comfortable and practical."

"Practical?" Hammond asked as a brow rose quizzically.

"They float. Now, can you stop judging my personal wear? Let's go, I'm starving." Clive shooed Hammond out the door and locked it up behind them.

Commander Hammond chose the Armview, which in Clive's opinion was a little out of the way, seeing as his apartment was right downtown. But as he wasn't the one paying, he was happy to oblige.

"What can I get you fellas?" A young woman, no older then twenty-two, greeted both men with a warm smile. "An ice pack, perhaps?" she asked, glancing down at Clive's swollen hand.

Clive shrugged it off, but an ice pack would have been wondrous.

"Just the standard breakfast, with rye bread, hash browns, eggs over easy, and bacon," Clive said, before looking at Commander Hammond thoughtfully as he tapped the plastic menu. "I'll also have a side sausage, a coffee, and an orange juice, please."

"Hungry, are we?" the waitress replied as she jotted down the order.

"I think it helps that I'm the one paying," Hammond said with a grin.

"In that case," she said to Clive, "would you like to see our pie selection?"

"Maybe after we find out what he wants from me," Clive said with a smirk.

"Sounds good. And you?" she said, looking at Hammond.

"I'll do the standard, eggs over easy, rye, and sausage. I'll also have a coffee, please." He slipped the menu back behind the condiments against the wall.

"Coming right up, fellas," the waitress replied, before hurrying behind the counter to pour a couple coffees.

Clive waited, letting the silence between him and his commander grow.

After taking a sip of his coffee, Commander Hammond reached down into his leather satchel and pulled up a copy of *The Globe and Mail.*

"Hadn't realized they still did print," Clive said, poking the folded paper in front of him.

"Not all the old ways are dead." Hammond slid the paper towards him. "How much do you know about this?" He pointed to the front headline: "Tech Genius and Heiress Billionaire Builds Atlantis." Clive glanced the headline and didn't need to read too much further.

"Grace Alice, acting CEO of Alice Industries, dropped off the map a few years back to build Atlantis, the worlds most advanced technological city, currently semi-operational somewhere in the Atlantic Ocean." Clive slid the paper back across the table. "Not many people these days don't know a little about Grace Alice."

"Well, according to our intelligence at Five Eyes, they are a little further along than semi-operational," Hammond said as he poured some sugar in his coffee and stirred, and was surprised by Clive's sudden laughter.

"Why would Five Eyes be monitoring Alice Industries?" Clive said, sipping his own black coffee.

"You know we monitor everything we find a threat," Hammond said without a hint of irony in his voice.

"And what sort of threat does a high-tech city floating in the middle of the Atlantic Ocean possibly pose to Canada, or anyone else for that matter?" Clive asked skeptically.

The waitress swung in, efficiently placing the two meals, a side plate of sausage, and an orange juice in front of the two men.

"Condiments are in the tray. Can I get you gentleman anything else?" She was already on her toes, ready to hop to the next table.

"Excuse me, " Clive said, preventing her hasty escape. He caught a glimpse of her name tag as she turned back around. "Renée. Have you ever heard of Grace Alice?" He sent a sideways glance to Commander Hammond, who was peppering his eggs, pretending not to be interested.

"Right, yeah. She's the billionaire building that floating city. I've had a few friends apply for their residency program. Apparently, it's some new tech mecca or something. Why?" she asked, glancing between the two men.

"Are you worried about this city?" Clive asked, trying to throw the question away.

"Worried? Why would I be worried?" Renée asked, her weight shifting from one foot to the other.

"I don't know? Tech billionaire doing a mysterious project in the middle of the ocean somewhere isn't weird to you?" Clive asked, and Renée looked thoughtful for a moment.

"Honestly?" she asked, looking between the two men. Clive gave her an encouraging nod. "I'd hardly say she's been secretive about what she's doing. And I'm no tech person, but my friends seemed pretty impressed by the levels of advancement they're making. So, I guess it hardly seems weirder than some other things."

"Other things?" Clive prodded. Renée eyes shifted nervously, holding a little longer on Commander Hammond before she continued.

"Well, I guess projects like the companies who do government contracts. There's enough money being spent in Halifax that I have no idea about. As far as I can tell, Atlantis doesn't seem to have an agenda."

"You don't think money is an agenda?" Hammond chimed in.

"Sure it is. But who isn't trying to make money?" Renée said with a light laugh. The table fell silent for a second. "Anything else?"

Clive shook his head, and she bounced off to the next table.

"I'm not sure what you were trying to prove there, Clive," Hammond said, cutting into his sausage. "You know better than most the difference between what the general public knows and what's really going on."

"So, what's really going on?" Clive asked, as he placed an egg on a piece of toast and bit into it.

"The details are … vague."

"Off cors hey re," Clive said, his mouth full of food. He finished chewing and took a sip of juice. "Stop pissing about and tell me what you're thinking," he said, before taking another bite of toast.

"Fine. We have strong evidence that suggests Grace Alice is building a weapon. A weapon that could destroy our way of life," Hammond said bluntly. Clive sat still for a moment before he began to laugh.

"You mean to tell me that Five Eyes has been monitoring a tech company because they think they're developing a weapon to destroy us? Who the hell thinks this? America? She's one of theirs, for Christ's sake."

"She operates in international waters. That little residence program our waitress referred to is open to anyone from any country. She's gathered some of the brightest minds on the planet in one place and we have no idea what they are doing there." Hammond set down his utensils and let out a deep sigh. "Look, I'm not going to lie to you. Our intelligence is thin. Whatever software they have is … it's good. We need to send someone in to gather more information. Find out what the threat is, and neutralize it before god knows what happens."

Clive leaned back in his chair, chewing on a piece of bacon, as the realization of what was being proposed settled into his brain. He sat patiently, unwilling to be the first to speak.

"I know you just got home," Hammond said, his voice soft and low. "And I wouldn't ask you to do this if it wasn't important."

"Which it is?" Clive asked skeptically.

"Very," Hammond said, leaning under the desk to grab a brown folder and sliding it across to Clive as he leaned in. "Whatever Atlantis is," he whispered, "it's not a business. It is a threat."

Clive grabbed the folder and a black USB drive slipped out from between its pages. He picked it up and rolled it around between his fingers.

"We need you to get that into the main server so we can access their files," Hammond said, gesturing to the USB drive. "It contains a program that will download all files linked to a series of keywords."

"Since when did the Canadian government condone corporate espionage?" Clive asked, sliding the USB to the centre of the table.

"Our role has been and always will be to do what's best for the Canadian people," Hammond said, leaning back in his chair.

"How very political of you, Commander."

"Open the folder," Hammond said, nodding down to the file. The topmost paper was a redacted document, most of which had been blacked out.

"Sasha Keen, twenty-eight years old. US Marine sent undercover to Atlantis. Her last communication suggested she found the weapon and was in the process of collecting the data."

"And?" Clive asked, scanning the document.

"And no one has heard from her since. That was over a week ago. Currently presumed captured or dead." Clive sat there for a long moment, reading over the document. He moved on to the next piece of paper.

"Who's this?" he said, looking down at the face of an older man, roughly fifty-five, with gray stubble and short balding hair.

"Dr. Jakub Nowak," Hammond said with a sigh.

"Why do I know that name?" Clive asked, using his fork to stab a sausage off his side plate.

"Dr. Nowak is a Polish scientist who worked with the US military for 15 years on some sort of new project."

"Weapons?" Clive's brow lifted as he chewed the sausage.

"Something that absorbs the heat of the sun and yes, finds alternative uses for it," Hammond said in hushed tones.

"Sounds theoretical," Clive said with a laugh.

"Right, 'cause our friends down south only deal in the theoretical," Hammond said.

"So, you said worked? I'm going to assume he left." Hammond gave a curt nod. "And let me guess, he's not returned to Poland."

"One year ago, he joined Grace Alice's team on Atlantis. One week ago, Sasha Keen went missing, and as of this morning we have reason to believe that whatever they are planning is going to happen in thirty days," Hammond said to a confused-looking Clive.

"Thirty days?" Clive asked, as Hammond pulled out a second newspaper.

"This morning's paper." He pointed to the front-page

headline: "Grace Alice Stuns the World Again with Unknown Countdown, Leaving the World to Wonder—What Will Happen in Thirty Days?"

"Ominous. Okay, fine, I'll bite. Why JTF 2? Why me? I'd imagine the Americans must be ready to blow the damn thing up," Clive said.

"They are. Or they would be if it weren't for public opinion. Let's just say our waitress isn't the only one who thinks Grace Alice is some sort of folk hero. Someone untainted by the big bad political state. If the US were to act without evidence, all hell would break loose," Hammond said casually. "But they're on her radar now; Canada, for the moment, isn't. As for you," he said, picking up his knife and fork and cutting into an egg, "your skill set would be an asset for this particular mission. Not to mention your recent change in relationship status—"

"That only just happened," Clive interjected.

"One man's loss and all that." Hammond shrugged.

"Well, I appreciate your confidence in my love life," Clive said, picking up a crispy slice of bacon and taking a big bite. "Wait, is all this you *not* trying to get me to come back in? 'Cause I would hate to see what it looks like when you try."

"You'll be gone, off the radar," Hammond said, ignoring Clive's remarks.

"For how long?" Clive shook his head as he looked back down at the paper. "Stupid question. Look, I've only just got home and, in case you hadn't noticed, the last tour might have destroyed what little hope I ever had in having a relationship."

"I'm not here to force you to do anything," Hammond said, his palms up in defence. "Honestly, I was just checking in on you. This only came across my desk this morning"—Clive raised a finger to jump in, but Hammond barreled through—

"and of course I thought of you for it. You're my number one, not to mention the specs for it scream your name. But I honestly hadn't planned on showing you." His voice was so calm, Clive almost believed it.

"Right, you expect me to believe you didn't plan this?" Clive said, his tone harsh.

"That you'd catch your girlfriend sleeping with her professor? How on earth would I have done that?" Hammond began to chuckle. Clive shrank down in his seat and folded his arms. The act seemed a little too childish for a man his age and yet it felt oddly comfortable.

"Look," Hammond said, as he slid the USB and the file back across the table to Clive. "The reality is, we don't know what this woman is doing out there on the ocean and I, for one, hope she's not a hopped-up sociopath with too much money." He let out a little sigh. "But if she is, the last thing any of us needs is to be caught back on our heels."

Clive stared at the file, his hand tapping the table just beside it, like touching it would burn him. *Maybe it would.*

"Have a look through the operation. You may be pleasantly surprised by what you find. I wasn't joking. This Op seems to be tailored to you," Hammond said with a sly grin.

"Say I was to take the Op; wouldn't they be a little suspicious about a JTF 2 operative coming aboard?" Clive added skeptically.

"Your record would be wiped, showing only some basic training and early Navy work. Just enough to make you seem interesting," Hammond said lightly. "For all intents and purposes, you are a kid from the city who wants to get out."

"So, the truth," Clive added ruefully.

"Take the file. I can give you a day to think about it. But that's all. You know where to find me." Hammond got up, pulling out a red fifty-dollar note from his pocket and placed it on the table for the food. He grabbed his bag and made his way to the door.

"Thanks for breakfast," Clive called out, getting a simple nod in response, and just like that he was alone with his thoughts and half a plate of food. Taking a swig of coffee, he began tapping the file. Renée stepped up to the table and looked down at him.

"More coffee?" she said sweetly.

"Sure," Clive said absently, setting his mug on the end of the table.

"Everything alright?" Renée asked. When Clive turned to look up at her, she gestured to the bruised hand again. "Seems like you've had a rough morning."

"You could say that." Clive laughed as he took hold of the mug. "Out of curiosity," Clive began, looking up at Renée, "if you could do anything you wanted, what would you do?"

The questioned caught Renée off guard, but she recovered quickly.

"I guess travel, have some sort of adventures" she said simply.

"You don't like being here?" Clive asked, genuinely curious.

"In the diner?" Renée tilted her head at him, narrowing her eyes.

"No." Clive laughed. "Not the diner. Halifax. Having a home, being … here," he said, looking out the window and noticing the inlet of the northwest arm beyond the busy rotary filling up with cars.

"I mean, I like it here, sure. But I don't know, shouldn't life be … exciting?" Renée said, looking off somewhere beyond the diner.

"Sometimes excitement isn't all it's cracked up to be," Clive said, more to himself than to her. "This is for you by the way," he said, sliding the fifty across to Renée, "from our friend." He winked. Renée giggled and ran off to refill coffees, leaving Clive alone in his booth.

He opened the folder and began to read.

2

The rest of the day was utterly uneventful. Clive had hoped that something, anything would happen to convince him not to take the operation. Instead, he sat lazily in his apartment, unable to even unpack his one bag, and not finding a single reason to stay.

He'd gone over the file twice. Each time, he understood more of the logic behind the operation. Intel was vague and it was difficult to understand the depths of what they were trying to do on Atlantis.

To the public, it was a safe haven for inventors, scientists, artists—anyone who shared a common goal of free development. And they did it all from the safety of their ocean city somewhere in the Atlantic.

From what Clive could tell, they were completely forthcoming about their defences, claiming they had a small onsite security team, along with anti-air and marine defence. All this was understandable given the fact they were in open waters, having to deal with pirates and the like.

As for the program, Hammond had been right. It was clear they didn't prevent anyone from applying to live in their city. Just skimming through some of the pages, Clive found a botanist from Holland, marine biologists from Canada, Japan,

Australia, scientists from Israel, China, India. Overall, they had more nationalities on their ship than the UN, not to mention all of their families. *How big is this place?*

But the information that worried Clive, and, as it would seem, Five Eyes, was the chatter from the city of a hushed project with limited access.

According to Sasha Keen's intel before she'd disappeared, she'd learned of an internal project, headed by Grace Alice herself, called Blue Crest. Only her internal team had been working on it, but Corporal Keen had overheard discussions from some of programmers, who used phrases like *life changing, dismantle everything, shatter society as we know it.*

Clive knew from experience that those were not phrases that Five Eyes, or the American government, would be inclined to ignore.

He set the file aside. He'd read enough to pique his interest, though he was still trying to figure out what the catch was.

He looked around the empty apartment. He currently had no home and no partner. But if he left, all he would have was his work. *Is that what I want?*

He laid across the couch and turned on his TV. *Hell of a first day home.*

...

"I have to admit I'm a little surprised to see you," Commander Hammond said, as Clive stepped into his office the next morning. He was wearing more formal attire today, in white pants, a black belt, and a white button-down shirt. Other than his badge showing his official rank as Master Sailor, he kept his uniform free of the various decorations he'd been awarded. "At ease, Son. You're looking good," he added with a nod.

"I look like a knob," Clive said stiffly, his hat tucked firmly under his left arm. "Sir."

"You'd look a hell of a lot better if you wore your decorations," Hammond said, lifting a brow.

"Wearing medals for assignments I'm not allowed to discuss hardly seemed worth it. Like buying a beer I can only look at," Clive said with a sideways smile.

"People don't need to know what you've done, just that you've done it."

"I know what I did." *Everything I did*, he thought.

"I take it this means you're in?" Hammond said, gesturing for Clive to have a seat.

"I want to know some of the details first," Clive said stubbornly, taking a seat in front of Hammonds large oak desk. Atop it sat an IBM laptop, a monitor, and a picture of Hammond's family. Clive had met them a handful of times. Commander Hammond sat down and finished jotting down a note in his little black book.

"Still writing in that thing?"

"Since I was ten. It shows—"

"Discipline. Yeah, you've told me. About, umm …" Clive pretended to count. "A million times."

"Then I'm not sure why I have to keep telling you," Hammond said with a smile, before closing the book. "So, what do you want to know?" He placed the book on a shelf behind his desk, next to a few encased medals and a hockey puck signed by Sidney Crosby.

"I need to see the rest of the files."

"There are none. Everything we have was in the folder I gave you," Hammond said, swinging back around in his chair to face Clive.

"That can't be everything," Clive said, a little stunned. "There were almost no details."

"So, you understand why we need someone on the ground."

"Bullshit."

"Easy, Son. You're in my house now," Hammond said, narrowing his eyes.

"Sorry, Sir. Too much time away."

"Look, that's the beauty of this operation, Clive. It will be like a vacation compared to what you're used to," Hammond said, smiling. Clive gave him a hesitant look. "Did you read the breakdown?"

"Yes, Sir."

"Then you know why I thought of you." He pulled out his own copy of the file from his desk drawer and opened it up. "Maritime engineer, deep-sea diving, underwater welding. You can do this stuff in your sleep."

"I haven't been a hull tech in years, I'm not even sure—"

"Bullshit," Hammond said with a grin. "You always told me you would have been happy drinking wine with the dive teams and fixing up boats. What was it you used to call yourself?"

"A glorified plumber, with a decent government pension." Clive laughed.

"Look, you do this, you won't be getting shot at or sneaking into hostile territory. You will be in a new city in the middle of the ocean, diving every day. It will practically be a vacation for you. Then, when you get back, you can do whatever you want."

"I can do whatever I want now," Clive interjected.

"True. And you deserve that."

"This some kind of penance for what happened in Iran?"

"Iran was a mistake. I can see that now. But no, this operation," he said, jabbing a finger into the beige folder, "this is what you need right now."

"What I need? Or what you need?"

"I'm not going to lie to you and pretend that having you onboard wouldn't put my mind at ease more than a little. But I'm serious. At this point you are simply going in for surveillance, to gather intel and let us know if anything is actually going on over there. As you said yourself, the evidence is vague." He let out a sigh when Clive didn't look convinced. "We believe there is a strong credible threat. It's better to be prepared," he said with a shrug. "You know how it is. But honestly, I just need someone I trust there to get what we need."

"Your USB downloads," Clive said cautiously.

"That's it. Other than that, you'll be a civilian, your service record will be tucked away. You're just a deep-sea welder with a background in marine engineering."

"A civilian." Clive was liking the sound of the operation more and more. But something still seemed off, and he couldn't put his finger on it. "What's the catch?" Clive asked, relaxing back into his chair.

"No catch," Hammond said with a shrug. "Your paperwork has been set up, and the moment you agree, we wait for approval."

"And if I don't get approval?"

"Then we find someone else, and you have three months' leave as previously arranged. But I have no doubt your application will be accepted," Hammond said coolly.

"So, what? I just go home and wait?"

"Do you accept?" Hammond asked.

"I accept."

Hammond stood. Clive jumped up to meet him and accepted his proffered hand.

"Great news, Son. Now, before you get angry with me, this was rather time sensitive, so I already took the liberty of submitting you for a position on Atlantis."

"You've already submitted me for the Op?" Clive asked indignantly.

"Yes. And no. Yes, I had you submitted for a position at Atlantis. No," he said, putting a finger up to stop Clive's obvious reply, "I didn't know you would agree to any of this. But I needed to be prepared."

"You really can be a bastard, you know that?" Clive tossed the words out with mild annoyance.

"Be mad at me when you get home."

"I've been accepted?" Clive tried to sound angry, but his excitement was getting the better of him.

"You leave in twenty-four hours," Hammond said, his authority coming out.

Clive had a sudden urge to punch his boss on the nose for lying to him, but seeing as it wouldn't have changed anything and would likely result in being detained, he opted for a curt nod instead.

He'd never actually unpacked anything, so Clive didn't have much to do to get ready to leave, save a little laundry. Which meant he passed the better part of the day lounging around the house, trying to decide if he was doing the right thing.

After hour four, he decided it didn't matter; he'd already agreed, and it was too late to say no. So, after grabbing the folder and stuffing it into a knapsack, he made his way down to the waterfront.

It was packed, understandable on such a beautiful day. Between the ships docking at the port, foot traffic, and, although the year was nearly out, a quieting mass of university students, Halifax teemed with enthusiastic travelers making the most of the boardwalk.

Which meant it shouldn't have been a surprise when he spotted a couple from his former unit walking towards him. He was thinking about ducking behind the immortalized giant blue wave just as a group of young children scrambled up the crest of the wave in a sudden burst of energy. Only a handful made it to the top triumphantly, and their enthusiastic cries drew the attention of his friends.

"Clive?" Lyla said, doing a double take, as if Clive might disappear as easily as he had appeared. He wished he could have.

"Lyla." Clive stepped in to embrace his old friend, her broad shoulders and long arms from her days as a swimmer wrapping him in a tight hug, as her blonde ponytail whacked him in the face.

"I didn't realize you were home." She let him go but kept her hands firmly on his shoulders.

"I'd heard a couple rumours," Charlie said, with a smile that let Clive know the story of the promiscuous professor had already made its rounds. Charlie's physique was enough on its own to make Clive feel like a toddler in his arms, but he also stood at whooping six-foot-six and practically cocooned anyone he embraced. The toggle of his navy-blue Tilley hat rested on the top of Clive's head as he squeezed.

"Sorry I missed your wedding," Clive said, his voice muffled from inside his friend's embrace.

"Forget that. You were on assignment. What can you do?"

Charlie said, releasing Clive from his hold.

"Why didn't you tell us you were home?" Lyla asked.

"I was going to but—"

"When you off?" Charlie asked, cutting him off.

Clive sighed. "Twenty-four hours."

"You just got back! What about … ummm … shit."

"Lara. We apparently decided to start seeing other people."

"Rough." Lyla grimaced.

"I see you took it well." Charlie said, glancing down at Clive's fist.

"You didn't! Clive!" Lyla laughed, shaking her head, as Clive gave a cool shrug.

"Gregory will bounce back," Clive said, and Charlie started laughing before Lyla smacked her hand against his chest.

"So, we have you for twenty-four hours," she said, smiling, as her eyes narrowed in on him. "And don't you dare try to run off on us." She put a finger to his chest.

"Fine. But I have to take it easy. I just came down to read over the file and get some food. That's it." He said this last part looking directly at Charlie, who'd already began rubbing his hands together and giving Clive a crooked smile. "I'm serious, Charlie."

"As a heart attack, buddy."

"We can play by your rules, Clive. Where were you thinking?" Lyla asked. "The Goat?"

"The boardwalk is packed, and I'm not walking up that damn hill again until we're heading home," Charlie said, gesturing to the unreasonably steep slope the entire city was built on.

"Your legs are still sore from this morning, pumpkin," Lyla said, jutting out her bottom lip in a pout.

"Yes," Charlie said, rubbing his thighs for emphasis. "Thank you for your concern. What about McKelvies? Good food, and the street's shut down for their patio."

"You mean the patio they share with the Old Triangle?" Clive asked suspiciously.

"Do they? I had no idea." Charlie stuck his massive palms up in the air, feigning disbelief.

"I'm serious, Charlie, I can't." But Charlie was already off, heading down the street towards the restaurant.

"Can't what, Clive? Have a good meal with friends?" Lyla tucked her arm through his as she pulled him to catch up with Charlie, whose long legs had already made some good headway.

Clive forced them to take one of the more secluded tables at the back of the patio, where they would be a far away from the band that would most certainly begin to play from the tavern beside them.

"Well, you're no fun," Charlie said, sliding the plastic chair out from under the table.

"I know you, man. I know where this night goes if I give you an inch," Clive said.

"Three Galaxies," said the server, setting down the beers before Clive had even taken a seat.

"How?" He said looking at Charlie who put his hands up in defence. "He's corrupted you, Lyla!" Clive said, shaking his head, as she pretended to not understand.

"You missed our wedding!"

"What happened to *you were on assignment?*" Clive laughed as she gave him a shrug.

"Cheers," she said, and the three clinked their glasses.

A few minutes later, the server was back, and Clive ordered

the seafood platter, deciding he would be treating himself and his friends, since he likely wouldn't be back for a while to do it again.

"So, you going to tell us about the assignment?" Lyla asked, after she'd put in her own order of fish and chips.

"You know I can't."

"Oh, come on. Like we're not going to find out about it in a few days, anyway. Maybe we can help," Charlie said with a wink.

"I doubt it. Unless you know a lot about—" Clive paused while he pulled out the folder and looked up the names. "Dr. Jakub Nowak." Charlie shook his head.

"It's pronounced No-vak," Lyla corrected, hitting the Polish *V* sound instead of the English *W*. "Umm, he's a biochemist with a PhD in thermodynamics," Lyla said, as both men looked at her, wide-eyed. "What? You forgot I did my undergrad in biochemistry? I had to read his thesis on thermonuclear fusion when we were looking into alternative power supplies for one of our ships."

"Sounds fascinating." Charlie laughed.

"It was, dipshit," she chided. "He was doing some pretty wild work with the US military before he ..." She stopped and looked at Clive suspiciously.

"Before what?" Charlie asked.

"You sack of shit. Tell me you're not ... Why? ... How?"

"Would someone please tell me what the hell she's talking about?" Charlie said, taking a rather large gulp of his beer. Clive stayed quiet. He wasn't supposed to be talking about assignments with anyone, let alone people in his unit. *Then again, I've only said a name?*

"Clive's operation has something to do with Grace Alice,"

Lyla said, leaning in. "She's the tech billionaire who is building that city in the ocean. Atlantis," she added, when Charlie still looked confused.

"Oh, shit, yeah, I've heard of that. Is that what you're doing?" Charlie leaned in closer.

"You both know I can't talk about it," Clive said, shaking his head.

"Okay, you can't tell us why you're going, but you know we'll find out," Charlie said impatiently.

"Come on, Clive, don't be a wiener." Lyla laughed as the server dropped off another round of beers.

"How do you keep doing this?" Clive finished his pint and grabbed for the second beer. "This is my last one."

"Maybe, but only if you give us a little nugget of gossip," Charlie said, his eyes lingering on Clive.

"Truth? And then you won't pressure me into going out tonight?"

They both nodded.

"Okay. Honestly, I'm not doing anything. According to the breakdown, I'm just keeping an eye on what they are doing out there."

"This have anything to do with the countdown?" Lyla asked.

"Countdown?" Charlie said, taking a big gulp from his fresh beer and giving Clive a sly grin, making Clive a little nervous.

"Alice Industries announced that in twenty-nine days they will be making some big announcement. This have anything to do with the Americans?" she asked, looking to Clive, who was trying not to give anything away—and clearly failing. "Of course it does. Dr. Nowak was one of theirs."

"I thought he was Polish?" Charlie jumped in.

"He is, but he'd been working for the US military for the

better part of fifteen years before getting recruited by Grace Alice."

"You know a lot about this." Clive said.

"You mean, I know a lot about the woman who's likely the single most influential person existing in the world right now?"

"Those are some big words," Charlie said.

"Possibly the understatement of the year. She graduated from MIT at fifteen, worked for various humanitarian aid foundations for years. Then at twenty her father got sick, and she went to run his company till he passed away five years later. After that she disappeared all mysteriously to start this new project."

"Ooooo." Charlie laughed waving his hands in the air like a phantom.

"Mock her all you want, but she speaks seven languages and has more money than you and I could ever imagine."

"Why all the mystery behind the city?" Clive asked.

"No one knows. But then, four years ago, she started inviting different people from around the world to come live there, and she's been enlisting people ever since. The real question should be, why Dr. Nowak?"

"What do you mean?"

"Well, Grace Alice has some of the greatest minds in the world working for her, on projects that I'm sure every country in the world would want access to. But you have Dr. Nowak's name? Why?"

"Honestly, I have no idea, but I do know one thing."

"What's that?" Lyla said, leaning in.

"I won't have to read any of those boring-ass briefs with you here." He laughed, taking a sip of his beer as the server came with yet another round, and their food.

"I'll drink to my wife's brilliance," Charlie said, holding up his beer and giving Lyla a kiss on the cheek.

"You'll drink to anything," she said, wrinkling her nose at him.

"Maybe, but today, I'll drink to you."

"I can second that," Clive said, finishing his own beer. Lyla reluctantly followed suit.

The band began to play "Sonny's Dream" from the end of the lane next to the Old Triangle. Clive perked up. "I love this song."

"He's back, baby!" Charlie said, slapping the green plastic table.

. . .

Clive awoke to banging on his front door, wishing he hadn't had so much fun last night. The throbbing pain behind his eyes made it difficult to remember exactly what had happened the night before, but somewhere in his mind he recalled himself and his two accomplices slipping over the red nylon rope into the pit of Old Triangle patrons on the other side, where they screamed a rather enthusiastic ballad of "Barrett's Privateers."

"I'm coming!" Clive's voice cracked as he tried to shout from his bed after another round of knocks.

Agitated, he got up to see who it was, not bothering to put on a T-shirt.

"Be wary, I'm practically naked, in case that insults your sensitive nature!" he said, peering through the front window and letting out an audible sigh when he saw a young officer standing pristinely at his door.

The kid couldn't have been much older than nineteen and stood at attention as soon as Clive had opened the door. He wasn't wearing any military garb, but everything about the kid screamed fresh recruit.

"Sir, I'm Sailor 3rd Class, Irons, Sir. I'm here to take you in for your appointment back on base." He paused briefly before cautiously adding in another "Sir".

"First of all, that's too many sirs for this early in the morning," Clive said, rubbing his palms against his temples. "Second, I'm not going to the base. I'm supposed to be on a plane in less than twelve hours. In fact," Clive said, looking at his wrist for a watch that wasn't there, "I'm not supposed to be up for at least another three hours."

"I have orders to bring you in, Sir," Sailor Irons said, readjusting his stance before adding, "Immediately."

"So much for covert undercover," Clive said, stepping away from the door, leaving the young man unsure of what to do. "I'll be a minute, so you can either stand awkwardly outside, or come in. Your choice." After hesitating for a moment, Sailor Irons stepped inside and shut the door behind him.

Clive made his way slowly to the bathroom, grabbed his toothbrush, and loaded it with toothpaste, only just realizing how grimy his mouth was.

"Sir. We need—" Sailor Irons said from the front room.

"Clive," he interjected, the toothbrush between his teeth causing it to come out muffled.

"Sir?"

He removed the toothbrush from his mouth and poked his head out the bathroom door.

"If you're going to call me anything, call me Clive."

"Right, Clive," the young man said tentatively. "We need—"

"Who are you?" Clive shouted from the bathroom, spitting a particularly large glob of spittle and paste into the sink.

"Sailor 3rd Class, Irons, Sir, uh, Clive," he called back from the other room.

"Right, but it's a little long, so what's your first name?" Clive stepped into the hallway. He turned into the bedroom and grabbed a particularly comfy Hawaiian T-shirt from his bag, then came back out to meet the silent stare of Sailor Irons.

"Look, it's not rocket science. Me, Clive, you …," Clive said as he buttoned up his shirt. He grabbed a pair of shorts and slipped them on, too.

"Owen, Si—r."

"Owen, nice to meet you. I admit, I'm more than a little confused as to why you are here right now." Clive put up a hand to stop Owen from speaking and continued. "Not that it matters. You're here on orders to take me somewhere. I, despite having my record cleaned of naval service, still, as it happens, work for the navy. So, I will follow you." Clive slipped on a pair of Crocs before opening the front door and gesturing for Owen to lead the way. "But I'll be damned if you're going to make this formal, so lighten up and look less like you just got out of basic training. Can you do that for me, Owen?"

"How did you know I just completed basic training?" Owen said, turning around to look at Clive as he walked down the hall.

"Call it a hunch," Clive said with a smile. "Also, we're swinging by Tims on the way. The least the government can do is get me a double double and an everything bagel with herb and garlic cream cheese." Clive slapped Owen on the shoulder. "You want anything, Owen?" Owen thought for a moment.

"Actually, I'm dying for an iced capp," he said as they reached the elevators to head down.

"That's the spirit."

Owen escorted Clive into the main building. Getting through security was easier than normal, given the fact that Clive had little on him other than his clothes and a large coffee. He gave the large security guard a wink as he strode through the metal detector.

He wasn't surprised when he saw Commander Hammond waiting for him inside.

"Commander, looking as rigid as ever."

"Master Sailor Davies, I see you're sinking into your role comfortably." He smiled as he eyed Clive up and down, landing on his footwear. "You own multiple pairs of Crocs?"

"You haven't lived till you've worn a pair," Clive said with a toothy grin. "Sailor 3rd Class, Irons, I'll take him from here, thank you," Hammond said to Owen, who was standing patiently off to the side.

"Thank you, Sir," Owen said, turning to walk away.

"Bye, Owen. And remember, don't say yes to everything," Clive said, giving him a small thumbs up as Owen smiled and walked away.

"Good kid, that Owen," Clive said ruefully.

"My god, I hope you weren't giving him advice," Hammond said drily.

"Only the useful stuff." Clive took a sip of his coffee. "So, you going to tell me why I'm here and not at home in bed?"

"Easy, Son, I'm still your commanding officer," Hammond said, a smile curling at the side of his mouth.

"Right, and I'm still hungover. So please come out with it."

Hammond stopped and turned to face Clive. His smile was making Clive uncomfortable.

"Remember how I said there wasn't a catch?" Hammond said, seeming to enjoy Clive's discomfort as he nodded warily in response. "I lied."

...

"This won't hurt a bit, Master Sailor Davies," said the tall, thin nurse, holding an injector pen with a wide tip the size of a dime.

"Call me Clive," he said, knowing full well she wouldn't. He attempted a cheeky smile, but had trouble masking the knowledge of the searing pain he was about to experience.

This was by no means Clive's first needle, as he'd had multiple inoculations for various tours around the world.

"I'll assume it's the swab that smells of alcohol," she said as she rubbed Clive's arm.

"If I had known, I wouldn't have …"

"Yes, you would've." She smiled.

"You're right. But a boy can pretend."

"First shot?" she asked when Clive flinched at the needle.

"No, I've been shot three times. Though I have to admit, none of those compared to the eleven days in bed when I had malaria. Cold sweats and fluids coming out from—"

"I meant needles, vaccinations," she said, laughing, as she cut him off. Commander Hammond stood off to the side, shaking his head.

"Right, no. I've had a few of those, too. I've just never had a fricken pencil stabbed into my arm." He said, nodding at the rather larger injector needle she was holding.

"Don't worry, I've got steady hands."

"Oh, I don't blame you for this. It's him I blame." Clive nodded at Commander Hammond, who was grinning from ear to ear. "What the hell is it, anyway?"

"After what happen to Corporal Keen," Hammond said, watching Clive grit his teeth, "we felt it was necessary for us to have some sort of monitoring system on you while you were there. For your protection."

"You're putting a tracker in me?"

"No. It's a universal SIM card, able to amplify any phone it's in. It will be linked to a number only I have, to relay messages back and forth." He chuckled as he watched Clive wince at the injection.

"You're enjoying this, aren't you, you sick bastard." Clive said before a quick yelp of pain as he felt the metal tag slide under his skin.

"Isn't this pointless?" Clive asked as the nurse placed a small piece of gauze around his arm. "Thank you," he said to her, forcing a smile. "From everything I've read about this facility, it is state of the art tech in there. Wouldn't they have no problem detecting something like this?"

"The card is encased in thick bio skin and only emits a frequency once it's been activated. So, it will be undetectable until you—" Hammond began.

"I have to remove this damned thing?!" Clive shouted as he swapped out the bloodied gauze for a fresh piece. "How in the hell am I going to do that?" Prepared for this question, the nurse handed him a little bag. He opened it up, revealing nail clippers, a file, tweezers, Polysporin, and various other useful items.

"Perfect, thank you," Clive said mockingly as he took the bag from the nurse. "Canadian government spends millions on research and development, and I have to, what? Remove this with a pair of tweezers?" Clive asked, looking at Hammond, who remained silent for a moment before giving Clive a shrug.

"Simple is always better."

"Obviously." Clive dropped the bag on his lap. "So, is this everything? Can I leave now?"

"That's everything, Clive. I just wanted to say." Hammond stopped, looking at the nurse expectantly. She got up and left the room, leaving the two of them alone. "I just wanted to say that I'm sorry for dragging you back into all this, and I appreciate you taking on this operation—" he began, turning away from Clive.

"What's with all the sentimental crap? You're basically paying for me to visit one of the world's most interesting places and keep tabs on a potentially sociopathic billionaire. This is going to be a piece of cake." Clive jumped up from the chair and gave his old friend a gentle slap on the arm.

"Right," Hammond said, pausing. Clive felt a sudden pang in his gut as he spotted a fleeting moment of hesitation from his old friend.

"Unless there's something you're not telling me?" Clive asked. Hammond waited a second before putting on a broad smile and returning to his normal self.

"No, you're right. This will be a piece of cake for you. Have fun, Son." Hammond gave Clive a slap on the shoulder.

"Look, I know there are areas of this operation you can't tell me about. That's part of the job. But don't worry, I'll be fine."

"Of course." Hammond turned to leave the little operating room with Clive following hesitantly behind him.

3

The Halo chopper was loud as it rushed over the Atlantic Ocean, heading due east somewhere off the coast of South Carolina. They hadn't been given clear instructions on the actual location of Atlantis, only that they would be traveling for about an hour.

Clive had never been great at math, but knew roughly how fast a helicopter was, so he calculated they were about one hundred and fifty kilometers off the coast. Where exactly that put them was a guess for someone a little brighter.

He had to admit, the modifications to the Halo were a nice surprise. Typically, he would be in the belly surrounded by metal walls. Instead, he sat on a plush chair next to tinted windows that allowed willing passengers to look out over the ocean.

Clive couldn't take his eyes off it; the vantage point from the Halo was spectacular. He was amazed at how similar the horizon was. Whether you were on a boat one hundred feet up, or in a Halo two thousand meters in the air, the horizon always seemed so endless. The sight of it, for Clive, always marked a new adventure, and this moment didn't seem to be any different.

The Halo shook suddenly, and Clive heard a gasp from the

man beside him, who was clutching his briefcase with all his life. His eyes were closed, and he looked as though he might pass out any minute.

"You okay?" Clive asked, keeping his voice calm. He knew the question was redundant—this man was clearly not okay—but it seemed the right thing to say.

At first, the man didn't bother to look up at Clive. He kept his head down and lied.

"Fine. Thank you," he said shakily.

Clive couldn't help himself. He began to laugh. This caused the man to open an eye and look oddly at him. He was well-dressed in brown khakis and a maroon button-up shirt. His deep-brown skin was highlighted by the bright yellow turban he had wrapped around his head.

"Sorry. I'm Clive." He put his hand out to greet the man. "And clearly, you're not fine."

The man took a deep breath and put an uneasy hand out. It was pale and sweaty from gripping his leather bag.

"Akmed," he said slowly, and let out a feeble laugh. "And no, I'm not fine. I'm not a huge fan of flying." He opened up the other eye to meet Clive's.

"Fair enough. A flight like this will rattle a few bones," Clive joked as he pointed out the other travelers inflicted by the same distress as Akmed.

"Not you, though?" Akmed asked tentatively. This caused Clive to laugh again.

"The way I see it is, we all have to go at some point. Sure, it would suck for it to be in a stupid fricken helicopter, but hey." He looked at Akmed. His words did nothing to ease his fears, so he quickly added, "Besides, we're traveling to a billionaire who is building a city in the middle of the ocean. I like to think that if she can do that, she can get us there safely."

It wasn't much, but Clive thought he saw Akmed's shoulders drop slightly, and he seemed able to keep his eyes open at least.

"What is it you do, Akmed?" Clive asked, turning his head away from the window to face his neighbour.

"I'm a botanist. I specialize in hydroponics. With a PhD in melittology." He was sounding a little more at ease now.

"Study of plants, yeah?" Clive said, getting a nod from Akmed. He was happy he could remember some things he'd learned about in the past. "But what's hydroponics?"

"Well, it's basically growing plants without the use of soil," Akmed said slowly. Seeing Clive's head nod absently, he continued. "We're going to a floating city in the middle of the Atlantic Ocean, where there is likely not any actual soil." He smiled.

"Fair point," Clive chuckled.

"So, what I do is create alternative methods of harvesting vegetation without the use of soil. My specialty is working with different varieties of fruit trees," he said proudly.

"Ah, so you'll be the reason I might get a strawberry out on this little island, then?" Clive mused.

"Strawberries, bananas, avocado, grapefruit, I'll make sure you have it all, my friend." Akmed said, amused.

"I appreciate that. So, what's a, uh, mellogist," Clive began, knowing he was butchering whatever word it had been. Luckily, Akmed wasn't offended. It only made the man laugh harder—obviously this wasn't the first time this had happened to him.

Clive was also happy to see his body fully relaxed now. Clive knew from experience that when someone was in distress, the best way to calm them down was to get them talking about something they loved. *The mind has a funny way of helping people cope with difficult situations.*

"Well, that's where my work gets interesting," Akmed said excitedly. "Melittology is the study of bees. Ms. Alice wanted me to try a pilot project to see if we could introduce bees onto Atlantis."

"Bees?" Clive asked skeptically. "On a ship."

Akmed laughed, then stopped when he saw how serious Clive's face looked. Clive had been on many ships before, once on the largest ship in the world. He couldn't image anyone letting bees onboard for any reason.

"Atlantis isn't a ship, Clive," Akmed said sounding serious. "How much have you heard about it?"

"To be honest, not much, just a few things here and there," Clive admitted. He'd done research on it, but there hadn't been a lot of information. Everything was hush-hush about the project. "I know it's big."

"It's big, alright." Akmed laughed.

"What do you know about it?" Clive asked. Akmed smile broadened at the question.

"I know it's unlike anything that has ever been built before. It is beyond the most sophisticated piece of technology that we have in this world. Ms. Alice has brought together the greatest minds in the world, scientifically, socially, creatively, and basically given them free rein to try, and create, and solve any problem they can imagine." Akmed seemed inspired by his own words.

"Doesn't that seem dangerous?" Clive asked, getting a skeptical look from Akmed. "Only the idea of someone having so much control." Clive tried to not let his words sound as worried as he felt.

"You have to understand. For us scientists, she is opening a pathway to truly change the way our society exists, and co-exists with our planet." Clive was less than convinced. "Think about what can be achieved when you remove money from the equation, when no technology can be bought up and tucked away because it threatens large corporations or challenges their dominance." He shook his head with distaste. "It's happening all too often, in our world. But here we can innovate, reimagine without fear that our work will get gobbled up and tossed under the rug. It's … refreshing," he said softly.

"You don't think it gives Grace Alice too much power?" Clive asked.

"Power is only as bad as the person wielding it," Akmed said calmly. "She has a plan, and in twenty-eight days she will announce what that plan is."

"Twenty-eight days?" Clive pretended not to know anything. "What's in twenty-eight days?" Saying it aloud made Clive aware of his probationary timeline.

"Grace Alice will share a gift with the world," Akmed said with a smile.

"What gift?" Clive asked suspiciously.

"I'm not sure. Some people guess it's when Atlantis will start to travel." Akmed shrugged. "I guess we will just have to wait and find out," he said with a laugh.

Clive couldn't share Akmed's blind fanaticism for Grace Alice. But the man was right about one thing: Power is only as bad as the person wielding it. *But what does anyone really know about the prodigal daughter?*

Clive also declined to point out that the flip side of that coin was that power corrupts those who have it. Regardless of what her intentions may have been when she began, who knows what will happen as her support grows larger and larger?

As for the twenty-eight-day countdown, the shock of it all finally began to kick in. In twenty-eight days, she was going to unveil something to the rest of the world, and Clive had a feeling that it wouldn't just be Atlantis sailing off into the sunset. *I've got to find out what the hell is going on in this place.*

"Sorry," Akmed said, giving Clive a polite waving gesture with his hand, "I never asked, what do you do, Clive? What made you want to join the team?"

"I'm a maritime engineer and deep-sea welder," Clive said casually, and when Akmed looked confused, he added, "I basically do plumbing for boats." Clive laughed. "It's far less exciting."

Akmed smiled but then his face took on a sudden look of awe as he stared wide-eyed out the window behind Clive.

"Well, I think you'll have your work cut out for you here, friend," Akmed said slowly as Clive turned to follow his gaze out the window. What he saw took his breath away.

Atlantis was not simply a ship, which was made obvious by the dazzling cityscape glittering on its surface. At first glance, Clive felt it looked like a generic description of a flying saucer, with its outer ring easily topping a thousand meters in width, jutting out from a glass-domed structure at its centre, which looked to be easily five hundred meters high and a kilometer wide.

The dome reminded Clive of half a snow globe as he noticed various objects moving about the inside.

What truly caught Clive's attention, however, was the outer rim. From the sky you got the sense that the ring wasn't a solid structure, and as he focused on the waves rolling in around Atlantis, he realized the rings were designed to roll with each wave.

Looking closer, he thought he saw people working along the surface with the help of what appeared to be large robots carrying cargo containers the size of a car. The various integrated structures made it look like a giant data chip, with all the bits and bobs coming together to form a connected web across the surface of the outer rim. The result was that the main structure stayed flat in the water. Each unit was independent, yet it was all connected.

"Hydrodynamics?" Clive said, more to himself than anything.

"What's that?" Akmed asked timidly.

"You see the outer tract there?" Clive said, pointing to the outer ring of buildings, each resting comfortably on top of the water. "You notice how the entire structure appears to be flat and stable despite the waves rolling in underneath it?" Clive said as a particularly large wave rippled through the ring. "The entire outer ring is a collection of smaller units, each able to rise and sink independently from one another." He was getting more and more excited by the idea.

"I don't understand," Akmed replied. Clive noticed his new friend was looking out the window curiously, unperturbed by the height of the flying. *It's amazing what a little distraction can do for a person.*

"Basically," Clive began, "when a wave hits the edge of the structure, that piece can lift independently from the others." He pointed to another wave, then to the corresponding structure. Akmed nodded politely. Clive laughed. "What it means, in theory, is that all of Atlantis is absorbing the kinetic energy from the waves, so it would be impossible for the entire structure to flip over."

"Fascinating." Akmed watched the structure ripple with a newfound respect for its design.

"I would wager the entire structure acts as some sort of power supply for Atlantis. Although it seems like loads of energy for something that size," Clive said, pointing the central glass dome.

It was Akmed's turn to laugh. "Only thing is, that," Akmed said, pointing to the glass dome, "is not Atlantis." He added, amused, "At least not all of it."

It was Clive's turn to be confused.

"I don't understand," Clive said, looking out the window as the Halo veered in towards what appeared to be a large landing zone. "What do you mean, not all of it?"

4

The Halo touched down on a large pad a few hundred yards away from the central dome. Clive hadn't been able to get anything else from Akmed, who had insisted that he would prefer Clive to *see for himself*. Since then, his new friend had forgotten all fears of flying and switched his attention to watching Clive with a quiet amusement. Clive wished he hadn't found himself in this little role reversal and he hated that his palms were sweaty, despite the cool breeze coming off the ocean.

However, the more he looked around the less able he was to hide the wonder on his face. Seeing the nautical design elements from the air did little to make the view any less impressive now that he was on the ground. It didn't take him long to confirm that each of the units was connected with a thick cord that appeared to be threaded throughout the surface of the outer rim, and that it was absolutely collecting the kinetic energy from the waves passing underneath the city. Although he'd been wrong about it being the only power-generated system, as witnessed by countless fields of solar panels scattered about the surface of the city. Every inch of the outer rim was being used for some form of energy creation or transportation.

Clive spotted a series of highspeed trains that glided atop the surface of the outer rim, crisscrossing their way with cool efficiency. It was a stark contrast to the slightly less efficient military transport he was used to. Despite having ample money to design, grow, and optimize their position, there would always be something that stood in the way of actually doing it. A general fear of change, as if adapting to new techniques might make someone's position obsolete. They were quick to adopt the old expression: If it ain't broke, don't fix it.

To Clive this was simply a desperate act for people whose only wish was to maintain control and power. If you were to ever let things get away from you, then you would no longer know what you're doing. And if that happened? Then what is your value? How many amazing breakthroughs like this had Clive watched be backlogged by military commanders and politicians because they didn't align with their vision.

Then again, how many brutal weapons programs had been dismantled for the safety of humanity? Just because we can do something doesn't mean we should. *What sort of weapons could exist in the world if people like Jakub Nowak had the ability to create whatever they wanted?*

Clive looked around the rim as people busied themselves on the various platforms each filled with an unusual contrast of maintenance workers and scientists all picking away at their respective projects—the wonderous sight of innovation and unbridled creation. Which filled Clive with both excitement and fear.

"My friend, you are in for a surprise," Akmed said, pulling Clive from his thoughts and back to reality. Clive forced a smile before answering.

"Well, if this isn't the main event, then I can hardly wait to see what comes next." He tried to keep his tone light.

Clive, Akmed, and the sixty or so other travelers were led off the Halo and into a large terminal that reminded Clive of the monorail terminal at Orlando International Airport. The domed glass walls curved up fifteen feet above his head, their clear panes allowing the sunshine and light to stream in and warm the holding area. Across from the entrance was plexiglass wall, with six sets of sliding doors equally spaced across it.

"Maglev?" Clive heard a short, older woman say behind him, her hand pointing past the plexiglass wall to the rail system behind it. She looked at the stout man beside her and continued. "A zero-friction magnetic rail system. It allows the train to levitate off the tracks, but I'm not sure what those are." She gestured to the long poles angled in around the tracks, which continued as far down the track as Clive could see.

"Magnetic thrusters," said another woman standing in the back of the entryway, loud enough for everyone to hear. There was no need for any introductions, as the entire room already recognized the casually dressed billionaire. She had a dark complexion and wore a high ponytail that opened up her face, highlighting her confident, white smile. "You're absolutely right, Dr. Tam," she said stepping further into a now-silent room. "This is a maglev. However, our team on Atlantis has been playing around with various alternative propulsion techniques to increase the speed and control of the train. Those thrusters have increased both speed and stability by fifty-six percent, and I believe with your help we can make it to seventy." Her smile, remarkably, grew even larger.

"I apologize, I was hoping to be the one who greeted you all off the Halo, but as I don't make it out to this sector nearly as often as I should, I took the opportunity to talk to Gavin." She turned, gesturing to a large man with salt and pepper hair and a scruffy beard, wearing a safety vest. He held a yellow helmet tucked under his arm, and gave the crowd a small nod that hinted he was not used to addressing groups of strangers.

"Gavin's our head engineer out here on the outer rim. He specializes in—" She paused and turned back to him before letting out a little laugh. "Well, everything power related, I suppose. He and his team are responsible for eighty-six percent of all the power generated for Atlantis. If you need to charge a computer or plug in a phone, it is all thanks to him and his team." She gave Gavin a warm smile. The gruff man said nothing, but Clive was sure he could see flash of red under his beard.

"Ah, the train," Grace said sweetly, as the mag train pulled in and all six doors opened smoothly into some very spacious carriages—big enough for many more than just the rather large group of people that came in with Clive on the Halo. "Gavin, I won't keep you any longer. Please let me know how it goes this afternoon with the new upgrades. I'm excited to see what happens." She spoke with an impressive amount of confidence and kindness as she stepped forward, the crowd parting like the red sea, making a small path for their own messiah to walk down.

"If you'll all follow me," she said, stepping through the central door and onto the train. Despite there being five other doors, Clive wasn't surprised when he watched everyone file into the central cabin behind Grace. Clive, who'd spent enough time with groups in tight spaces, caught which way Grace had turned in the train. Giving Akmed a light elbow in the side, he gestured for him to follow. Akmed frowned but didn't say anything as he followed close behind Clive, cautiously looking back at all his other colleagues funnelling in through the central door.

"Trust me," Clive said with a wink.

Akmed didn't put up any resistance, though he still looked unsure of Clive's plan as he moved around the group to the first door, to the right of where Grace had boarded. As they entered the carriage, Clive was pleased to see that his hunch was correct—the train was in fact one large, open space. Which meant that rather than being behind the horde of people following Grace in, they ended up right behind the space where Grace was now standing which was conveniently in the centre of the two doors. As everyone else wanted to be facing her, it meant that only Clive and Akmed stood behind her. This made Clive grin and Akmed shrink into himself.

"Last time I trust you," Akmed whispered to Clive.

Grace turned to see the two men behind her and smiled. Clive responded with a wink, which the billionaire either didn't see, or ignored, as she turned back to face the rest of the group.

"It will only be a few moments before we hit the landing bay. I can't thank you all enough for choosing to be a part of this great endeavour," Grace said to the crowd as the train moved fluidly along the track. Clive watched in amazement as the walls outside moved past him. Had it not been for those, he wouldn't have thought he was even moving.

"As you all know, in twenty-eight days we will give the world a gift, unlike anything that anyone has ever seen, and you will all be a part of it."

"What is this gift?" Clive interrupted. Grace turned to meet his eye again, only this time she was accompanied by a sea of scowling faces from people who clearly didn't want to hear from him.

"It is a surprise," she said coolly. "But one thing I can tell you is that, in due time, each of you will be given the opportunity, along with your families, to decide if you wish to stay on Atlantis with us, or leave." She paused, looking Clive up and down one last time before turning back to the hungry crowd before her. "Until then, each of you has been brought to Atlantis to provide us with your own unique perspective and be part of a team that I believe will shape the world for years to come." She smiled to the crowd, which showered her with applause. "Including you, Mr. Davies," she said, turning back to meet Clive's eye for a brief second before looking away.

"Atlantis is THE state of the art city, and like its namesake, it too is sunken beneath the seas." Clive could practically feel Akmed grinning behind him.

"Sunken city?" Clive whispered to Akmed, now able to see the man's smile broaden. As Clive looked around, he was delighted to see that the room was nearly split, with half of them equally if not more stunned than he was. The mag train glided effortlessly into the sky-high glass dome Clive had seen from the Halo. Only now he was looking inside, and what he saw he couldn't believe.

Through the windows of the mag train Clive saw an impressive indoor green space, with rivers and waterfalls winding their way through a vast network of plants, and various types of trees offering cool shaded areas, which people were utilizing for either work or leisure. There were also people running, biking, and swimming all around the makeshift floating plaza. And this was only what he could see right in front of him.

"The upper dome is a mile long, and fifty-two percent of that is green space for everyone in Atlantis to take full advantage of. Trails for walking and running, places to swim—anything you can think of, we have. And if we don't, we will design it," Grace said, gesturing to the mound of land in front of them that looked as though it would be part of a hill. "Another eighteen percent is used for water treatment and purification. This leaves the remaining thirty percent, which we call the drop-off, which, as you probably can't tell from where we are currently, drops to over eight hundred and fifty feet below the ocean's surface." Grace paused, and the space was filled with excited clapping and hushed conversations. "Don't worry," she said, raising her hands in a calming gesture. "You won't have to walk it all; we have an elaborate network of mag lifts, which can carry you to any location in the facility in only a few minutes." This received another heavy round of applause, though Clive was too stunned to join in.

Clive's mind raced as he tried to wrap his head around the logistics of the unbelievably massive suboceanic structure. He couldn't fathom how anyone would be able to live that deep, without getting sick.

"How do you compensate for the pressure?" he said, to no one in particular. It was unsurprising that it was Grace who began to laugh before she answered.

"Great question, Mr. Davies, and none too surprising given your background." She gave a gracious nod that Clive barely saw. "Well, since we built Atlantis from the surface down, there is no additional weight to add pressure, so we are only dealing with standard atmospheric pressure. Think of it like an open mine, only less damaging to the planet," she said proudly. "However, your particular work will still not be without its dangers. Mr. Davies will be working with our diving teams to ensure everything inside the wall moves smoothly." Grace gave him a smile before adding, "However, our team has managed to create some *unique* little devices that should help you quite a bit, Mr. Davies." She finished by giving him her own little wink, which Clive caught, before she turned back to face the group.

"How many personnel do you have on-site?" asked a broad woman with thick dark hair.

"We have nearly eighty-two thousand personnel and fifty-seven thousand of their family members," Grace replied patiently.

"And wadda the family members do?" asked a tall man with short red hair, a long matching beard, and an accent Clive guessed was from Newfoundland. Clive had heard it enough times, having visited the George Street Festival in St. John's more than once.

"As I said, this is a city, and like any city we have jobs that need to be done. We work with each and every one of the people who come onboard, and we find solutions that work for them. Our schools are state of the art learning facilities for kids, and again, if we find something isn't working, we adjust as needed," Grace said with more than a hint of pride.

The large red-headed man pulled in his wife and child, who must have come with him, and gave Grace a warm smile.

Clive, on the other hand, was barely listening. He was still shocked as he peered out the train window and watched as more and more of the city began to appear. With every turn of the train, he kept feeling like he hadn't even seen the actual city yet, even as they pulled into the main transfer depot as the train doors opened up and Grace and other passengers began to funnel out.

"Each of you has had a long day of travel. Your bags, should you be wondering about those, will be delivered by our team to your homes, so feel free to explore as much or as little as you want. With that, I'll take my leave for you to rest." She turned to leave but was stopped by a small woman, who whispered in her ear. "Oh! I almost forgot!" she said, as several more people from the city entered the landing bay each with a large briefcase.

Grace opened the first case as the other four were laid out and opened in front of everyone. She pulled out a cuff, about six inches long, that looked like a wrist coach a quarterback might ware—only this was metal and appeared to be a small computer. Grace turned it on.

"This is your Lightweight Utility Control Yield, or LUCY. You can use it to get into pretty much any room in the facility that you need access to—only rooms containing sensitive technology are off-limits. Each unit has been programmed to your living quarters and it will help guide you there. It is your very own built-in travel companion, so, should you find yourself lost, or if you have any questions about Atlantis, simply ask LUCY and it will assist you." Grace stepped forward and placed the bracelet on one of the young women in front of her. "Simply enter in your name and all details will come up."

"Mine says one million credits?" asked the young woman.

"That's right, all currency on Atlantis is digital, and each of you will be given one million credits to start, which should be enough for anything you want. Our true currency here is the ability to help each other and learn from one another, so I encourage you to open yourself up to new experiences and new people. Great things happen when we trust one another."

Maybe Clive was just being paranoid, but he couldn't help but feel like she'd said this last part to him. *Did she glance over at me?*

Brushing off the idea, he walked over to grab one of the metal arm bands with the word LUCY engraved on the belly. On the other side was a small digital screen. Thinking it made the most sense for the screen to be on top, he slipped the band around his left forearm accordingly. It was snug, but not too tight, and the LED screen lit up as he turned his wrist to look at it.

As per Grace's instructions, Clive followed the prompts on the screen. He entered his name and then it asked him for a thumbprint. Clive placed his right thumb in the little box provided on the screen. The box flashed green, and the screen lit up to what Clive guessed was some kind of home screen as a soft feminine-sounding voice spoke from the device. "Welcome to Atlantis, Clive Davies."

5

Getting to his room ended up being easier than Clive had suspected, at least directionally speaking, all he had to do was head down. But he was, on more than one occasion, sidetracked by the immensity of the city itself, and found himself talking with LUCY more then he'd imagined. The AI programming was incredible, and the real-time response was like having a person with him at all times, showing him around.

He'd stepped off the mag lift into a section of the city named Nu II.

"LUCY, what does Nu mean?" he asked, his words feeling a little stiff. He felt silly about lifting his arm up to speak into his wrist, especially now with people wandering around him. More than once he caught a couple of the kids and even some adults laughing or smiling over at him. *This must be the Atlantis version of a tourist. May as well have a sign on my back that says "new guy."*

"Nu is the thirteenth letter in the Greek alphabet and was used to represent the "N" sound in ancient and modern Greek. However, on Atlantis the Greek alphabet is used to distinguish the seventeen districts located here." LUCY spoke in a calming English accent. "The Roman numeral following represents one of the four quadrants; you are currently in the second quadrant of the Nu district." Clive likely could have figured that out on his own, given the affinity for Roman design seen in the buildings, but sometimes it's healthy to just be told you're not wrong.

"I thought there were twenty-four letters in the Greek alphabet. Why only seventeen districts?" Clive asked, impressed with himself for remembering anything about the Greek alphabet.

"Good observation. Atlantis currently has seventeen districts, housing one hundred and thirty-nine thousand two hundred and eighty-six people. The optimal number of people Atlantis can hold in its current design is one hundred and seventy thousand. However, Grace has designed Atlantis to have the ability to extend further down, adding another seven districts and increasing the optimal population to two hundred and forty thousand. But there are currently no plans in the works to do so," LUCY said promptly.

"Why not?" Clive asked.

"It's an inefficient use of people, time, resources, and money. The current capacity limit leaves room for thirty-three thousand seven hundred and fourteen people. With new growth from invited residents limited to approximately two hundred and fifty people per year, that leaves one hundred and thirty-four point eight-five-six years before we'd need to expand the current design," LUCY stated, very matter of fact. Clive couldn't be bothered to work out if the math was right. He suspected a supercomputer in a high-tech city was likely able to calculate this basic math correctly. But one thing did hit him.

"What about births?" he asked skeptically. If there was

one thing humans knew how to do, it was have sex, and he suspected that in such a tight community it would be rampant.

"Given the current population of Atlantis and the expectancy of natural growth and death, the numbers at this time are expected to counter one another for roughly fifty years before any real change occurs," LUCY said. Clive was shocked by its precise predictions about human behaviour. LUCY seemed perhaps a little more optimistic than Clive. "This also doesn't account for people who wish to leave Atlantis. We suspect over time that one percent will request to return to the mainland," LUCY added.

"So, people can leave if they want to?" Clive asked.

"Of course, no one is here on Atlantis against their will. People are free to request to leave at any time," LUCY said in their elegant voice.

"Has anyone ever left Atlantis?" Clive asked hesitantly, and for the first time LUCY did not respond immediately. It was only slight, but there was definitely a moment's pause before she responded.

"No one has left Atlantis yet."

Clive's mind turned to Sasha Keen. She'd been stationed here and had disappeared without a trace. Does this mean Sasha is alive somewhere on Atlantis? Or had Grace Alice and her team corrupted the data to leave out that one of the residents had been captured or killed? Clive wanted to ask LUCY about Sasha Keen directly, but he had no way of knowing just how LUCY's operating system was being monitored. And if he was to bring her up now, there was a chance it would blow his cover.

He ignored the urge to ask LUCY anything about Sasha as he continued down the hall, acutely aware he was lost again.

"LUCY, where am I?" Clive looked around, realizing that nothing would as yet look familiar.

"You seem to have made a wrong turn. Your apartment is behind you. Please follow the green line located on the wall."

Clive looked up to the ceiling, and for the first time noticed an intricate gathering of colourful lines, all leading down the path he was walking on before branching out into various corridors. He suspected each colour correlated with a different housing section. "You will reach Nu unit 1895 soon."

"How new is it?" Clive said, at laughing his own silly joke. Apparently, LUCY was less skilled at understanding good humour, as evident by the response—"The room was designed less than one,"—which caused Clive to laugh again.

"Never mind, LUCY. How come all of the lines seem to be leading that way?" Clive said, looking back towards the way he'd been heading.

Clive wondered if LUCY would understand the question given the fact it doesn't have eyes. *Or does it?*

"This way leads to Nu district observation deck and the main avenue. There you will find views of Atlantis, as well as shops, cafés, and other amenities for you to enjoy." LUCY's voice rose slightly higher than normal, as if attempting to portray a hint of excitement.

"Café, you say?" Clive said, thinking for a moment. He looked at his watch and figured it was a little late for a coffee, but maybe… "Is there a pub in the city?" Clive asked with a little more enthusiasm.

"Yes, there are currently eleven pubs, fifteen gastropubs, twelve fine dining, sixteen restaurants, thirteen diners, and four ready-to-order locations open in Atlantis, and the nearest pub is located just off Nu's Main Street. You can find it if you continue down the path you're on," LUCY said. Clive resisted the urge to ask what happened to the old Main Street and instead walked down the path toward the observation deck.

"LUCY, what's the ready-to-order thing you said?" Clive asked. He was skeptical that a place like this would offer fast food.

"They are locations where chefs prepare food for takeout. Each of the locations can be express delivered directly to your room. Think of it like a giant kitchen where chefs are able to work together to prepare basically anything you want."

"You mean to tell me there are catering chefs around whenever you want something?" Clive asked incredulously.

"Yes. Precisely," LUCY confirmed. This left Clive in a bit of shock while he wrapped his head around the whole thing.

"Well then, thank you LUCY for all of your help."

The paths were wide enough for five people to walk side by side and felt comfortable. Looking at the light fittings, Clive would have imagined that their output would be pretty stingy. Instead, they illuminated the halls as if sunlight was streaming in from some unknown source around the walls. The overall affect was almost comforting and warm. *Almost.*

As he reached the end of the hallway, he saw that it opened up into a marvellous space that, had Clive not been looking at it with his own eyes, he wouldn't have believed possible.

The Nu observation deck was a couple hundred feet across in a perfect circle. Stepping onto the deck itself, felt as if you were stepping out on a balcony of staggered terraced apartment made up of many ascending observation decks above him. Each one set back to allow sunlight to wash over the level below it.

Clive even felt a slight breeze, and he wondered if that was a trick of the city's air circulation or if they had actually discovered a way to send a natural breeze this far down. Given what he'd seen so far, he wasn't ready to rule out anything.

Walking out from the path, he stepped onto a carpet of grass that covered the entirety of the observation deck. Kneeling down, he pressed his hand against it, unsure if it was fake or not. It was most definitely real, and incredibly lush and thick. Even when he pressed his hand into it with force, it bounced back. The feeling of the grass under his hand was so nostalgic that he had a sudden urge to take off his shoes and run through it. Which he thought would be ridiculous until he saw a group of children running around barefoot, playing a rambunctious game of tag. The scene made him smile.

Looking around at the living floor, Clive couldn't help but think about the logistics of something like this. He tried to imagine the enormity of the network of pipes that must run underneath the grass. *But did that mean there was soil under here, too?*

He was about to check, thinking he couldn't do that much harm just by sticking a finger in the ground, but he was distracted by a nearby tree. For a minute he thought his eyes must be playing a trick on him, that the tree must be a fake, placed there to make it look like it was growing. But as he walked over to examine it, he realized it was just a tree. He placed a hand on its trunk and pushed it, as if he might be able to topple it and then someone would yell at him for ruining the illusion. But instead, the tree felt strong and sturdy, tightly hugging the ground underneath him. Clive began to laugh at the whole thing.

Moving past the tree, he stepped up to the edge of the railing and peered over, taking in the view. The entire city was built like an open pit mine, only this mine was filled with green trees, shops, bridges, and in a few areas Clive even spotted ziplines, with people racing along wires, screaming as they flew over the mouth of the city. *Is this a city or a playground?*

Looking up, Clive was amazed at how far he was from the surface and how fast he'd been able to travel the distance. Thinking it must have been over six-hundred feet to the green space at the surface of the city. From the top he counted twelve rings, each with its own observatory jutting out from the walls. Trees popped up from the ground and plants and flowers flowed down from level to level on a latticework support structure.

He saw a similar structure on his own observation deck; it was a gridwork of bamboo that arched over the walkway leading up to the floor above. The effect reminded Clive of a drawing he'd seen once of the hanging gardens of Babylon. The ancient city had always been depicted as a place that blurred the line between nature and man-made design.

Then, as if somehow his brain hadn't been unable to compute the sound, Clive began to hear chirping coming from somewhere around him. He assumed it was an audio recording, something to give the illusion of being on the mainland. But when he looked up, there was a bird nestled in the tree.

Clive was by no means a specialist on birds, but even he knew the distinct red coat of the cardinal. Looking around, he saw more of them soaring through the air; they were perched on the railings, trees, and vines of the many observation decks, chirping and hopping around. For the second time Clive found himself laughing out loud, like he'd just watched a daring feat of magic, uncaring of the people walking by.

"What is this place?" he said to himself as he spun around to take it all in again. "Now I think I definitely need a drink."

Clive looked back towards interior of the observation deck, where there were rows of shops and restaurants lining the path. He took note of the pathway with the green lines running along it.

Unsure of which way to go, and feeling content to wander, he decided not to ask LUCY for any assistance. He'd been in enough foreign cities to know that if you simply choose a path, eventually you will find somewhere you want to be.

Strolling along the grass, he continued to look around at the many varieties of plants hanging from the bamboo latticework above him. He couldn't believe how beautiful it all was. Moving out from under the observation deck above, instead of a sun, all he saw was a yellow hue creeping into the city's glass dome, confirming that it must be late in the day.

This was emphasized by the loud grumbling from his stomach, and Clive realized it had been ages since he'd had anything to eat. He spotted a sign in the distance for a place called the Snailbox. The name was funny enough, considering where they happened to be, and Clive was happy to find it was a gastropub. Not bothering to skim the menu, he made his way inside.

It was relatively full, with only a handful of open tables scattered throughout the restaurant. The Snailbox was designed to look like an authentic Irish pub, with Irish paraphernalia on the walls, accented by the Irish flag hanging on the back wall near a tiny stage that was, unfortunately, empty. Clive noticed a set of empty stools up at the bar and slipped his way through the tables to get to them.

On his way, Clive was surprised to recognize no less than three different languages being spoken. From his time at sea, he had heard many languages over the years, and he was fairly confidant he heard a young couple speaking Arabic, a family from Norway and four Finnish women howling at what must have been a funny joke at the table.

Saddling up to the bar, he was greeted by wiry-looking man with thin, dirty-blonde hair and a gaunt face. He approached Clive and spoke with a thick Irish dialect.

"Can'a get fur ya,' he said slapping his hand on the bar in front of Clive and greeting him with a wide smile.

"Hiya, can I get a menu please." The barman began to laugh.

"Aye, right. You must be new then."

"How did you guess?" Clive said, looking around, as if someone had put a sign on him or something.

"Well, first'ov all, the grub is up there on the board. If yea prefer to read from a menu of sorts, ya can'av LUCY scan dis, and she'll pull it up for yea." He pointed to a QR code laminated into the bar. "Name's Aiden. Welcome to the Snailbox, my little home away from home, away from home."

"Clive. Great to meet ya." Clive put his hand out, and Aiden gladly took it. "Is it so obvious that I'm new?"

"Aye, well ya don't seem to have the way of it all sorted, ya still walk like the entire place is made of glass. Which it is, mind ya. But she's yet to break in the year I've been here. Can I get ya started on a drink?" Aiden said with a smile. Clive took a moment to scan the taps. There were plenty of options, including a few he guessed were brewed on-site. But peering down the row of taps, he noticed one in particular he felt would be good for the occasion.

"I'll have a Guinness, please," Clive said, catching the smirk from Aiden as he said it.

"Beezer choice my friend, although mind ya it's not as good as it is back home," he said, shaking his head. "But it'll do the trick." He gave Clive a wink before turning around and grabbing a glass from the shelf.

"Anything else I should know about this place?" Clive asked. Aiden glanced back at him as he finished the first pour and set the pint on the counter to rest.

"Aye, and I don't think I know them all yet misself, to be honest," he said with a smile. "First thing ya should understand is the entire city is carbon zero, no waste, nuthin." He watched the pint, waiting for it to be ready for the second pour. "I know that doesn't sound strange, but trust me it's a bit of an eye opener when ya realize just how much stuff ya used every day that got thrown away," he said with disapproving shake of his head. "I take it ya know this is Nu Main Street— don't asked me what happened to the old one." He laughed, and Clive couldn't help but like the guy. "We call that area the atrium, for obvious reasons. Then ya have the pathway, which I assume ya must've taken one or two of them to get here from the landing bay?" Clive nodded as Aiden placed the pint in front of him. "Aye, listen to me talk at ya when you must be starven. Have ya decided what ya want?"

Clive scanned the chalkboard menu and decided on a classic.

"Chicken fingers and fries," Clive said with a smile. Aiden met him with his own.

"Right, good choice." He turned to leave, but Clive stopped him.

"Wait. It is chicken isn't it?" Clive asked, genuine curiosity on his face.

"Aye, I think you'll be very surprised by what this place can do." He laughed and walked away.

Clive took a deep drink of Guinness and smiled at how good it tasted and marvelling at how they managed to get all of these things onboard Atlantis.

If Clive had any fears about eating on a floating city in the middle of the ocean, they were immediately dispelled with the first bite of his chicken fingers. Despite what people believe, you can ruin chicken fingers. In fact, Clive considered chicken fingers to be the Margherita pizza of pub food—a marker of the quality of the establishment.

It also didn't hurt that Aiden was great company, and Clive was very interested in how a bar owner from Ireland had made his way to Atlantis.

"My partner Nick worked as a logistics coordinator fer one of the largest distribution facilities in Europe. He's bin tasked with setting up new facilities over the years, so we're used to moving from place to place," Aiden said while he poured some drinks for the laughing Finnish ladies.

"Sounds exciting," Clive replied around the fries he was shovelling into his mouth.

"Aye, it was. But everything has its limits. Hard to settle down when ya don't know where you're gonna be called to next," Aiden said with a shrug.

"So now you're here?"

"Aye, this place had a promise of at least two years, which meant I could have my dream of settin' up a pub like my dad. Save for a couple modifications." Aiden laughed as he gestured to the QR codes on the bar.

"So, you'd say it's not a bad place to live? Atlantis." Clive said.

"Aye, I think you'll be pleasantly surprised. I mean, you must've loved your room."

"I actually haven't been there yet."

"Smart man, finding the pub before the house." Aiden laughed and gave Clive a wink.

"Well, I have to say it was a pleasant first stop," Clive said, and Aiden gave him an exaggerated bow. "Which reminds me, how much do I owe you?"

"Twenty-four credits," Aiden said. "Tap your LUCY on here; she'll do the rest," he added when he saw the confused look on Clive's face.

Tapping LUCY on the small black scanner built into the bar, Clive watched as the screen lit up to display 999, 976 credits in his account. He had to laugh at the ridiculousness of it all. Aiden had also laughed when he saw his face.

"Aye, ya start to realize that money isn't important when everyone has it," he said with a warm smile. "Everyone here does what they are doing because they enjoy it, not because they have to."

"Good to know." Clive got up from his stool. "And thank you for the good food and conversation, Aiden."

"Aye, I hope ta see ya again, Clive."

"I'm sure I'll be back."

Letting out a big yawn, Clive left the pub feeling tired and much more wobbly than he would have imagined after only three pints. The atrium was now cast in darkness with only dim lights glowing like streetlamps all along the observation deck. The air was still warm, but cooling down, and when Clive looked up, he was amazed that he could see the stars so clearly through the dome, as if it wasn't there at all.

Taking in the night sky for a long moment, Clive was reminded of all the nights he had spent out on the ships doing the same thing. Only this was certainly different than a ship. For starters, the sheer size of it was ridiculous. *Just how big is this place?*

He figured that was a question better asked at his orientation in the morning.

"Take me home, LUCY," Clive said with a sigh as he stepped away from the edge of the observation deck.

"Certainly," she said immediately, leading him away from the Snailbox and back toward the green pathway.

Whether from the drinks, the dim lights, or the long couple of days, Clive felt incredibly tired as he groggily followed LUCY's directions through a maze of pathways. He felt like he'd never know where everything was, but knew from experience that those feelings would pass. He had felt the same way on his first ship. It was smaller, but Clive was young then; things have a funny way of seeming too big before time makes them small.

Clive somehow arrived at Nu II unit 1895 and, after being instructed by LUCY, he placed his wristband up to the door. He heard a soft click, pushed down on the handle and stumbled into his new home.

6

Clive woke the next morning to the comforting sound of birdsong as his room slowly came into focus. It was one of the more pleasant wake-up calls he'd experienced—until he startled himself awake, unsure of where he was.

It took him a moment to collect himself, reminding his terrified brain that he was on Atlantis, fully clothed, in one of the most comfortable beds he'd had the chance to sleep in for a long time. Between ship cots, random hotels, and plywood base beds, he couldn't remember the last time he'd slept so well.

Looking around the now-bright room, he admired how it was both minimalist and high-tech. One of the walls was some sort of low-light LED screen depicting the sun rising over the water off some coast somewhere; he guessed southeast Asia. The tranquility of it threatened to keep him in bed, but he forced himself to sit up. The only other furniture in the room was a dresser. There were two doors, one that Clive vaguely remembered coming in through the night before, and one he assumed led to the bathroom.

"Morning, Clive." LUCY's voice emerged smoothly from what he guessed were household speakers. Clive was surprised that the voice hadn't startled him. "I hope you don't mind, but I took the liberty of getting you up one hour and thirty minutes before you need to arrive at the dive bay for orientation. If you would like to change these settings to have more or less time, feel free to let me know," they said sweetly.

"No," Clive said, letting out a big yawn. "This is perfect, thank you, LUCY."

Looking down at his outfit, which was now on its second day, he wondered where his bag might have ended up.

"LUCY?" he said, as if there was a chance they'd somehow left him.

"Yes, Clive?"

"Where exactly are my clothes?" He was on his feet, checking the empty dresser drawers.

"Your bag would have been delivered through the Express Delivery Carrier Unit or EDCU for short, which is located just off the main entrance way, opposite your front hallway closet."

"Thank you, LUCY," Clive said, as he made his way into the main living area.

Stepping out into the space, now with all the lights on, Clive was finally able to take in all that the apartment had to offer. Which was a lot.

It felt a little like he had broken in and stolen someone else's life, someone who was far more organized, wealthier, and had incredible style. The open-concept living space gave the eye something to land on in every direction. Straight ahead of him was a U-shaped kitchen with clean white cabinets and a breakfast island with four comfortable-looking stools nestled under it. To the left of the kitchen were five columns, floor to ceiling, of long white tubes containing a living garden of fresh herbs, along with at least fifteen different varieties of vegetable, each labeled and organized alphabetically. When he looked into the white tubes, he saw only roots and water, which reminded him of his conversation with Akmed and his work with hydroponics. *I wonder if he does this, only on a massive scale?*

Reading through the list of vegetables, he noticed a few he recognized, including a large arugula plant sprouting up at the top of the wall. Reaching up, he carefully pulled off one of the leaves and ate it. His first impression was how fresh it was, flavourful and crisp, then he immediately chastised himself. *Of course it's fresh, you idiot, you literally just picked it off the plant!*

He wondered if that was what he was supposed to do and made a mental note to find Akmed and ask him. He supposed he could always ask LUCY, but something about waiting to ask someone in person felt right to him. Not to mention he didn't have any friends here, save for Aiden and Akmed, if you could call them friends. So, he would need to seek out conversations with people or else his only friend would be LUCY.

Across from the living garden was a fully stocked fridge, with essentials including soy milk, regular milk, and orange juice, all labeled and in heavy glass containers, along with eggs, bacon, jam, etc.

"LUCY? Why is everything in a glass container?" Clive asked, turning one of the glass containers around suspiciously.

"We are a zero-waste city. Anything you need can be purchased through me and expressed delivered in under ten minutes. When you're done with a container, simply put it in the EDCU, and I will have it delivered to the right location," LUCY said.

Clive found it hard to believe that the facility could be zero waste, but as he looked around the rest of the kitchen, he couldn't find a single trash or recycling bin. Instead, he found reusable cups, and various sized takeout containers.

Clive had half a mind to whip up some of the eggs and maybe some toast while he was at it, but there were still things to see. Standing at the sink in the island, Clive could see a large sofa and two chairs sat in the centre of the room, all facing what appeared to be a thin TV mounted on yet another very large LED screen. The entire thing rose up fifteen feet to the top of the room.

From the reflection in the screen, he saw a ladder that led up to a raised loft area just above the main entrance way. Clive walked around the island to peer up at the loft, which was an office, outfitted with a desk, chair, and lamp. Behind the desk were two wing back reading chairs, with an electric fire nestled in between them. The room screamed relaxation station. He had turned back round to figure out how to turn on the TV when something caught his eye. He stepped closer, unsure if what he was looking at was real or a display on the LED screen, but as he put his hand on the display, he flinched. It wasn't a screen. His hand was touching glass, and now he knew for certain that the fifteen-foot whale shark in front of him was very real, and so close he could reach out and touch it.

"LUCY, is this wall real? Is that really the ocean?" he asked, stepping back from the wall as if touching it would shatter the whole thing.

"Correct. You were provided with an exterior room. Unlike other residents, who might find it difficult to know they are under water, Grace thought, given your affinity with water, that you would appreciate the view."

"Is it safe?"

"Yes, the walls are made of a high-density polymer designed in Atlantis specifically for this purpose."

"It's incredible," Clive said, stepping up to place his hand on the glass again. "It's so dark, I could barely tell."

"If you lessen the light pollution in the room," they said as it dimmed the lights, so that only the foot lights around the room were shining, "you get a fuller picture."

Clive gave his eyes a moment to adjust to the new light, and as they did, he began to see not only the whale shark but also many other varieties of fish swimming around his room.

"Incredible." He laughed.

"Atlantis is built to retain its interior light so that we don't add any unnecessary light pollution to this depth of water. Light is only used on the exterior when workers like yourself are performing maintenance work outside," LUCY said, as if it knew what Clive was thinking.

One of the things that Clive had always disliked about the work he did in the water was that humans felt the urge to change the environment to suit their own needs, even at the expense of the environment itself.

He stepped back from the glass, took in the massive ocean view, and smiled.

"Thanks, LUCY, that's good to know," Clive said, as the lights in the room slowly began to come back up and the whale shark swam away.

Clive made his way to the front door and spotted what must have been the door LUCY mentioned. Grabbing the handle, he pulled the latch and slid the door across. Sure enough, resting on the platform was a large box containing his bag.

He pulled it out; it seemed so light, given the enormity of his new apartment. He'd packed as if he was about to board a warship for a month, not live in a giant aquarium.

He took his bag into his room and unloaded the contents into the dresser, barely occupying two of the six drawers. Pulling out his shaving kit, he spotted the gear provided to remove the chip in his arm. His other hand rubbed the injection site, despite there not being any real pain there.

He took the shaving kit into the bathroom and tossed it on one of the shelves on his left as he walked in. He traced his hand along the fine white sink that the shelf hung over. Beside the sink was a toilet and across from the sink was a large bathtub. Clive had never really taken to baths. They always seemed like something that just took up time, and he figured if he was going to spend an hour in the water, he wanted it to be on a dive, not in a tub. So he was pleased when he spotted the shower area tucked in the back corner of the bathroom. As he approached the glass door, he noticed tiles covering the entire shower including the floor, the ceiling, and a bench built into the wall.

There were two shower heads, one regular head on the wall and a waterfall tap in the ceiling. But what got Clive most excited was the metal nozzle at the base of the shower that appeared to operate a steam function. Clive had never been much of a religious man, but seeing this shower, he felt he needed to thank something.

Clive undressed with cool efficiency before swinging open the shower door and hopping inside. Turning on the waterfall setting, he perched himself up on the bench, letting the warm water fall over his body and watching the steam billow up the glass doorway. He closed his eyes and took a couple deep, slow breaths, letting the steam and heat fill his nostrils.

The feeling of relaxation the long shower produced was quickly replaced by panic when Clive realized he'd only given himself forty-five minutes to get to work. He started throwing on his clothes as he called out.

"LUCY? How long does it take to get to the dive bay?"

"The dive bay is located in Zeta III. The nearest transport terminal is five minutes from here." Clive was trying to do the math in his head when he realized he had no idea where Zeta III was in the Greek alphabet, so he waited for LUCY to continue. "Total time until arrival will be approximately fifteen minutes," LUCY said, and Clive sighed with relief.

A fifteen-minute commute to work didn't sound so bad, but as he'd already scared himself into being fully dressed, he no longer felt the desire to cook.

"LUCY, is there anywhere I can stop to grab a coffee and a bite to eat along the way?"

"Yes, there is a small café. What would you like to order? I can have them prepare it for you while you walk over."

"Really? Wow, okay, just a large black coffee, and do they have breakfast sandwiches?" Clive asked.

"Yes. Are you hoping for anything in particular?" Clive thought for a moment.

"Maybe a bagel BLT?" he asked, unsure where exactly the limits would be in terms of what he could order.

"Great, I'll put the request in. If you wouldn't mind picking which size of mug you would prefer from your cabinet and placing it in the EDCU, I'll have it sent over to be filled."

Clive remembered seeing the mugs in the cabinet and went to pick the largest one he could find. It was nice, made of glass with a curved handle. Its top had a lip like a sippy cup, and he couldn't help but smile as he placed it in the EDCU. The large box that had arrived holding his bag was still on top of the conveyor belt, and he figured it might be too big to use for one empty cup.

"Your luggage box can be folded up and placed in the holder located under the conveyor belt," LUCY said as if it was watching his confusion. "You will find various sizes of folded boxes which can be used at any time to send packages throughout the city. The boxes go from largest on the left to smallest on the right."

Clive folded up the box easily enough and slid it in the opening with the picture that best matched the box. He also slid the box top in the corresponding slot beside it marked "Tops".

He grabbed one of the smaller boxes along with its corresponding lid and began to construct the five sides he needed. He was pleasantly surprised when he placed the mug into the box and closed it up—it all fit perfectly. Clive stood for a moment staring at the box, waiting to see what would happen. Nothing did.

"Go," he said, whooshing his hand through the air and feeling silly. "Now what?" Clive asked LUCY.

"Simply close the door and you can head over to pick up your breakfast," LUCY said, like it was the most obvious thing in the world. *Perhaps it is?*

Clive shrugged and closed the door. He walked over to the door and slid on his shoes. Taking one last looked around at his apartment, and smiled as he turned the handle to leave.

It was eerie how precise LUCY was with the timing to the dive bay, even with Clive stopping to pick up his food, which had been waiting for him by the time he arrived at the café.

He even stopped briefly to have a nice encounter with the young woman working at the café. Her name was Kissa. He discovered, in that short time, that she had come from Egypt, after piecing together some broken English. Although he never did understand why she'd kept tapping the small device in her ear but managed to understand the part where she gestured at him and giggled.

"New?" She said smiling politely as she waved good-bye sending Clive away, wondering how everyone could tell he was new to this place. *Do I have a sign taped to my back?*

The bagel was delicious. It reminded him of a Montreal-style bagel, which he loved, and he was pleased that at least one thing from home would be easy to find. Not that he'd ever spent much time in Montreal, but everyone in Canada knew about those bagels. He made a point to grab a bag every time he had to drive through the city. And there was that knock off, almost-Montreal-bagel shop he'd discovered just over the bridge in Dartmouth, on his way out to the base in Shearwater.

Clive had never complained about the commute in Nova Scotia. It was simple and rarely took more than twenty minutes even on a bad day. But he could get used to the fact that he would be working so close to his apartment; fifteen minute walk was hardly stressful.

After leaving the café, LUCY had guided him down the observation deck towards a secondary pathway on his left, which led to the elaborate elevator system he'd used the night before to get down to Nu II.

Atlantis was already up, and alive with activity. People walked around enjoying the morning sun that warmed the dome. The temperature of the city did not seem to have changed at all from the night before; it was still comfortable. However, with the light pouring into the atrium, it had a different kind of warmth to it.

"LUCY, are these the only elevators on this level?" Clive asked as he approached the shiny metal doors.

"These are not elevators."

"They're not?"

"No. They are called the Thrusted Omnidirectional Transport System, or TOTS for short. And they are located every two hundred and fifty feet in the city, roughly."

"How does it work?"

"There are currently 1,234 TOTS in Atlantis, varying in sizes, each with the ability to travel in any direction along the pathway, carrying people and items anywhere in the city in minutes," LUCY explained.

Clive had his doubts about the speed of the transport, seeing as he was about to travel to Zeta III, which was practically the other side of the city. But when he arrived in under five minutes, he had to admit he was impressed.

Now ten minutes early, Clive took a few extra moments to finish his bagel as he looked out over the Zeta III observatory, trying to spot his own observation deck. This turned out to be more difficult than he'd imagined, as he found himself constantly being distracted by the view. It was no less impressive than the one on Nu II, and from here the bowl-shaped city was so clearly presented, with its cascading vines flowing over the edges of the deck like a waterfall of tangled gardens. He was so high above his own deck he even felt that the air was warmer.

"Your orientation begins in five minutes, Clive," LUCY said, its tone as unchanging as ever. Determining to sort out where he lived another day, he turned towards the pathway.

"Take me to the dive bay please, LUCY."

Two minutes later he arrived at a large double door. A couple of people, who clearly knew where they were going, strolled confidently past him and through the door. Clive followed them in and found himself standing on a large grate platform, big enough to hold twenty people, with stairs going down either side to a lower level.

His jaw dropped as he stared out over the massive hangar, which could have held four jumbo jets. The first thing Clive spotted, against the side of the left wall, were three submersible Human Occupied Vehicles (HOV) transport units, all differing in size. The largest among them looked as though it could hold five, maybe six people. Between the first two there was a gap, which he suspected held a fourth carrier that must have already been sent out. The three remaining dangled in a manicured line from the ceiling, each with a corresponding pool beneath, wide open and ready to receive them at any time.

The centre of the room was an open machine shop outfitted with a ten-ton factory crane, currently moving what appeared to be a new hood that Clive assumed was for one of the HOVs. Looking around at the various instruments in the room, including two 3-D printers, he guessed there wasn't much this place couldn't do.

Clive tried not to slip as he took his first step down the metal staircase. His hand gripped tightly to the railing as his brain was overwhelmed by the many distractions around him. When he finally managed to get to the bottom, he was met by an average-sized man with short dark hair neatly styled on the top, and thick, dark-rimmed glasses. He had an inviting smile and a trusting face despite being in the middle of what appeared to be a rather intense conversation with a slightly more mild-mannered Japanese woman. He stopped only briefly to say "Just a minute" in the universal language of putting up his index finger towards Clive.

What was even more impressive was the fact that they were speaking different languages: the man Portuguese and the woman Japanese, both languages Clive had heard during his time in the Navy and neither of which he understood. How they were managing to understand one another was a complete mystery to Clive. The conversation reached a conclusion as she reluctantly gave him a nod and was off with a new determination.

"Como você está?" the man asked Clive, who, trying to remember what little Portuguese he could, stared blankly at the man.

"Eu sou Clive," he replied shakily. For a moment the man just stared, and then broke out into laughter.

"Hello, Clive," he said in much better English than Clive's Portuguese. "I'm assuming you haven't been fitted with an interpreter yet," he added with a smile. "I'm Tiago Pereira, but you can call me Squints. I'll be your dive team leader here on Atlantis." He shoved his arm out for a handshake, which Clive took gratefully.

"Happy to be here, Sir," Clive said, realizing too late that his military formality had shown through. But if Squints noticed, he didn't let it show.

"Just Squints is fine," he said, turning and walking into the hangar bay, with Clive staying tight on his tail.

"What's an interpreter?" Clive asked as he caught up to Squints's side.

"This little beauty," he said, tapping his ear. Clive noticed a device, similar to a hearing aid, resting in it. "It provides real-time translations from all languages into your preferred language." He smiled again. "It's a beauty."

"Wait." Clive put his hands up and laughed. "So you don't speak Japanese." Squints shook his head.

"But real-time translation is impossible. Isn't it?" Clive was trying, and failing, not to sound shocked. Squints stopped and gave Clive a toothy grin.

"This is Atlantis, my friend," he said, putting a hand on Clive's shoulder. "I think it's time that you stop thinking anything is impossible." He continued on through the dive bay. "I'll set up a time for you to see the tech team tomorrow morning before your shift. You'll find it a lot easier to communicate with the team if you have it. Unless you speak …" He started counting on his fingers playfully. "Twelve languages, and remember I heard your Portuguese." He laughed.

Clive was finding it difficult to believe what Squints was saying, but he didn't have much time to dwell on it.

"Today is show and tell, and believe me, there is lots to show." Squints said, grinning like a child who just walked into a toy store. Clive began to wonder if he ever stopped smiling.

"Over here you have the babies." He gestured to the HOVs. "I'm not sure what your experience is in one, but they offer courses for people who want to learn. Research teams are always looking for extra hands and I won't lie, they are pretty awesome to drive," he said, staring up at the massive vehicles and letting out a deep sigh. He gestured to the pools underneath. "Each of these tunnels leads out to the ocean so we are able to take them out smoothly. It's a dream, Clive."

He turned to face the other side of the facility. "Here you have the machine bay. Be careful wandering through here. Best to keep your head on swivel and stick to the paths." Squints gestured to the HOV hood Clive had seen earlier and the yellow lines painted on the ground all around the machine bay.

They walked through the bay and came out the other side, where Squints pointed out four large locker units, though none of them appeared to be locked. Clive couldn't see what was in them, but each locker was labeled.

"Over here we have ocean research equipment, dive gear, maintenance supplies, and then the last one, and my personal favourite, development prototypes." He turned to look at Clive. "It's where they let us test the new equipment they are developing. They are generally working on something. But what you'll need most, you'll find in maintenance supplies and dive gear."

Clive pulled on the gate, touching the unused lock as he walked in. "The gates are more of a precaution, not really a lot of places to go and the whole facility is under surveillance. Not to mention, anything you want to use you can request permission for," Squints added with a shrug. "They really want people to grow and learn here." And Clive thought he sounded sincere. "I'll walk you through the tools you'll be using the most," Squints said confidently, "and if you ever think of something that could make things better, don't hesitate to speak up. The research team is constantly evolving the equipment to fit our needs. It's awesome!"

"How long have you been here?" Clive asked.

"Just over two and a half years. I was a lead on a dive crew for Gold Star Oil before this. That sort of work takes a lot out of you." Clive got the feeling it wasn't all sunshine and rainbows at his old place.

"And this doesn't?" Clive asked, and was surprised when Squints began to laugh.

"Not at all. The team here is great. We only work four days a week, so I actually get time with my family. Way better than six months away at a time," he said, shaking his head.

Clive had never had a family, but he'd toured with quite a few people who had them and understood how hard it had been for them to leave for so long.

"Absolutely," he replied with a sympathetic nod.

"I haven't even shown you the best part!" Squints turned to walk towards the section of the hanger furthest from where Clive had entered.

As they approached the wall it began to shift with the light, slowly unveiling a goliath version of the window in Clive's room, the entire wall of glass that easily stretched a hundred feet high, showing a view of the ocean outside.

"That's the observation deck, from there you can see the HOVs heading out and obviously all of the sea life." Squints pointed up to an observation deck that sat about halfway up the window. Clive could just barely make out some couches and chairs. A few people were already up there taking advantage of the view. "It's a good place for a beer at the end of the day." He winked at Clive.

"How did I not notice this when I walked in?" Clive asked, his eyes still not sure if he trusted the massive whale swimming by the heart of the window.

"It's a trick of the glass. They have various scientists and engineers coming down to assist on projects and not all of them love being reminded they are under water." Squints laughed. "This glass allows only people who come to the dive side to see it."

"The dive side?" Clive asked.

"Yeah, our own personal section of the city. I'll show you to our lockers," Squints said, pointing to a cluster of small units convenient marked "lockers".

Squints began leading Clive through the maze before reaching one with Clive's name on the front of it.

"This one's yours. It already has some gear in it based on the specs you gave us."

Clive didn't remember giving them any specs. Then he realized that Commander Hammond and his team would have filled all that out. Squints must have seen the look of confusion on his face, because he quickly added, "You can make adjustments to anything you have easily enough."

"I'm sure it will be fine," Clive said running his hands over his name tag.

Clive pulled the handle, and the door didn't budge.

"Hold LUCY up to it for it to unlock." Squints laughed again.

Clive placed LUCY up to the lock, and sure enough, the door clicked, and Clive opened it up to find a full set of dive gear in his locker.

"This is mine?" Clive repeated, as he slid his hand down the wet suit.

"Yep. You just have to maintain the gear and it will be available whenever you want it," Squints said, seeming to find a lot of joy in Clive's shocked expression.

"I can use it anytime I want?" Clive repeated before laughing. "Awesome."

"I'm glad you're excited, 'cause it's time to go," Squints said.

"Change rooms are on either side of the lockers. Suit up and I'll meet you back here in fifteen minutes." He turned away to leave.

"We're going out now?" Clive said with a grin.

"I told you, today is show and tell," Squints said, putting emphasis on the word *show* as he patted Clive on the shoulder and walked away.

Clive took a moment to look over the wet suit before eagerly snatching it off the rack.

7

"How's it fit?" Squints asked, as he walked up to meet Clive back at his locker.

"Perfectly," Clive said slapping his stomach to emphasize his excitement to get out in the water. "Where's the gear?" Clive looked around, realizing he hadn't seen a single oxygen tank on the tour.

Squints waved a mask in front of Clive. It looked like a hood with a full see-through face mask and ten weird flaps on either side where his ears would be.

"It's called a gill," Squints said, holding up his own mask and pointing at the flaps, "for obvious reasons. One of the little toys the R&D team whipped up. Yours should be in the top shelf of your locker." He pointed to a little cubby at the top of the locker and Clive opened it up.

"A gill?" Clive asked, holding the mask up skeptically.

"This little beauty allows us pull oxygen out from the water. Unlimited supply of oxygen and no need to lug around any damn tanks. Makes repairs a hell of a lot easier, too." Squints added with a grin.

"I've heard about this kind of thing but I didn't think it actually existed." Clive looked at it with awe.

"Well, it's still in the early days, and you need to monitor your unit. If you find any discrepancies, report it." Squints's voice hit a serious tone for the first time since Clive had met him. "But don't worry, there are numerous safety measures in place, including," he said, reaching into Clive's locker and pulling out a normal-looking fanny pack, "this. It will be mandatory for every dive. It has reserve air exchangers, goggles, AND we have direct oxygen lines hooked up every twenty feet or so to the city's perimeter. If all else fails, you can grab one of those and you'll be right as rain."

Clive was still handling the mask as if he didn't trust it was real. But he grabbed the fanny pack from Squints and opened it up to examine the contents. It held a standard scuba mask along with three handheld temporary breathing devices that he'd used on shallow dives in the past, so he knew each unit was good for up to fifteen minutes. He wrapped the pack around his waist, more excited than ever to get in the water.

"Ready?" Squints asked, slapping him on the back.

"You bet your ass I am," Clive said with a grin.

"Good, 'cause there is nothing quite like the first time with one of these," Squints said, holding the gill in the air as he laughed and waved his other arm for Clive to follow.

"You'll be working with me on the sublevel pumps. We've be finalizing some of the pipe work down there to help optimize air flow throughout Atlantis. It's not exactly riveting stuff, but it will be a good test to get introduced to the new equipment."

"New equipment? Is there more than just the dive gear?" Clive said, as one of his brows rose questionably.

"Oh, brother, you have no idea." Squints clapped Clive on the shoulder. "But no worries, I read your CV and I have no doubt you'll fit into your role nicely. The welding gear you'll be using has had a few modifications as well, but nothing they do makes things more difficult, trust me. After a couple days down there, you'll almost be bored." Squints led them to a set of elevators nestled under the observation deck. "This is a private TOTS unit for the dive team." The terminal doors opened to reveal a space big enough for six people and was outfitted with fold-down seats. Squints put his arm out to stop Clive from entering.

"One last thing," he said, his serious voice returning. "Do you have LUCY on under your wet suit?"

"Yeah, I didn't know—" Clive started as he pulled back his wet suit to reveal the metal cuff under it.

"Good," Squints said, tapping his one wrist. "LUCY can monitor your mask and give you access in and out of the facility. There are some overrides as well and all those can be accessed by any of the emergency bays. But trust me," he said with a light laugh, "it's a hell of a lot easier to have LUCY with you." He stepped into the transport terminal, and Clive filed in behind him. "LUCY, Sublevel II please," Squints said, folding down one of the chairs and taking a seat. Clive followed suit as the door closed and the transport sped away.

Clive was happy there were no windows in the transport terminal, 'cause he wasn't sure he wanted to know just how fast they were traveling. His stomach felt woozy by the time they finally stopped.

"That feeling goes away after a few times," Squints said, making Clive wonder if his face had lost a bit of colour on the trip.

Luckily, the doors opened into a decent-sized break room with various couches and its own bar fitted out with water, juice, and snacks. Clive was happy when Squints led him over to it and poured him a glass of water.

"This will help," he said, sliding the glass over to Clive and pouring one for himself.

"Thanks." Clive took a big gulp before looking around the room. There was a scattering of people in the room, some taking a break, and others over by a dive pool in the corner looking as though they were about to head out. On the opposite side there was a second dive pool, which Clive assumed was where people returning would come up. His assumption was confirmed when a yellow light flashed, and he saw two figures swimming up from under the glass floor.

"This is Sublevel II holding bay. It's not much, but if you need a break, food, drinks, you can come in here and grab it." Taking his glass, Squints walked over to the massive LED screen that took up one of the walls. The screen was filled with various tasks, a description of each, and a completion time frame. Each was colour-coded with green, yellow, or red. It reminded Clive of something, but he couldn't quite put his finger on it.

"This is the task list; each line corresponds to a task. Green is open, yellow is under progress, and red is completed. The yellow and red have teams attached to them—you can see there who has been working on it. Each team is required to complete at least twenty-four hours a week to fulfill their roles. You and I are a team," he said with a nudge, "in case you were wondering."

"I assumed as much," Clive said, taking another sip of water, happy that the wooziness was beginning to fade. "But I'm happy to hear it confirmed."

"We will start work tomorrow. Today I'm just showing you around, introducing you to how things work and maybe a couple of people. But since you don't have your interpreter yet," he said, tapping his ear, as Clive nodded in recognition, "you'll be limited to who you can chat with. But," Squints said, scanning the board, "looks like Hamish is out today. He's not Canadian like you, but he is Australian, so you won't be completely lost. Although I have to admit, sometimes I don't think he's speaking English." Squints laughed.

"I'm excited to meet him," Clive said earnestly. He'd always been a big fan of the people he'd met on the boats from Australia and had had a few great nights with a group of them when he was docked in Sydney.

"So, let me see if I have this right," Clive said, looking back up at the screen. "We pick a task to complete, no supervisor, nothing? We just pick it and go?" He sounded a little mystified.

"Basically. That's a standard completion time, but the onus is on us to complete it, as it's our names that will be attached to the work. Most people work about eight hours, taking a few breaks for food and rest, but it's on you to complete in your time."

"And when do we work?"

"Well, that's the beauty of it, we have a time commitment of twenty-four hours per week. When we do that work is up to us. For the first week I've set days for us to come in—I hope you don't mind, I just try to optimize time with my family. But after that you and I can plan out our schedule together."

"That's incredible," Clive said letting out a half laugh. "And for the record, I'm happy to work around you and your family. It's just me here and honestly I don't know anyone yet," Clive said with a shrug. "So I can't imagine I'll be doing much."

"You know me, partner! And tonight you're coming over to my house for dinner. My wife is making *bifanas* and *pastéis de nata.* You will feel like you've died and gone to heaven," Squints said, his eyes distant, resting a hand over his heart. "Sound good?"

"Sounds great," Clive said, leaving out the fact that he wasn't entirely sure what the food was. From the expression on Squints's face, he assumed he was in for a big treat.

"What do you say we get in the water and go for a little dive?" Squints said, finishing his drink and making his way back toward the bar. He set the used glass in a tray marked "dirty," then pulled the gill over his head and gave Clive a wink. Clive followed suit, feeling back to normal now.

His first thought as he pulled the hood over his head was that he couldn't breathe, and he was about to panic when he looked over at Squints, who was signaling him, his hands moving slowly up the front of his chest and back down, telling Clive to take deep, slow breaths. Clive centred himself, tried a controlled breath, and was relieved when the air kicked in and he was breathing normally again.

"The first breath is always a little strange." Squints's voice startled Clive in his mask. "Sorry, I linked our gills so we could chat, I hope you don't mind." Clive began to shake his head, but stopped.

"That's perfect," he said, his breath a little short. He forced himself to take another deep breath.

"It gets easier in the water." Squints gestured to the pool Clive saw when he first arrived. "Shall we?"

"Yes, please." Clive followed behind Squints as he went over to the pool. He sat down on the edge and hopped in. Clive followed him, letting his feet and shins dip in first, the cool feeling of water running up the leg of his wet suit. The water wasn't nearly as cold as it would have been without it on.

Smiling to himself, he hopped off the edge and submerged himself in the water. It felt great as the cooling sensation of the water covered his body, and as he sucked in his first deep breath, he was relieved to discover it was easier in the water than it had been above.

"Not bad, eh?" Clive said, taking in another deep breath.

"Not bad at all, my Canadian friend," Squints said, floating in front of him, giving a wink as Clive understood he'd recognized the country's famous slang. "Just don't start hitting me with a million, sorry," Squints added as he swam ahead.

The tunnel was about fifteen feet across, easily big enough for them to swim side by side, but Clive decided to stay an arm's length behind to give Squints some space. After about twenty feet, they reached a wall with a conveyor belt–like design holding small weights the size of hockey pucks.

"High density weights to help with your buoyancy," Squints said. "You have some pouches around your waistline." He gestured to his own waist and pulled out a bit of fabric. He then grabbed one of the pucks and slid it into the pouch. "With no oxygen tank, you shouldn't need a lot." Squints grabbed three more and placed them around his waist.

Clive swam up and grabbed one of the weights, which was heavier than he imagined it would be, and slid two of them into his front pockets and two just above his butt, matching the weight of his partner.

"After a couple dives you'll figure out what's comfortable," Squints said, moving forward toward the front window. Clive followed him, and when he caught up Squints gave him a nod.

"LUCY open Sublevel II exit bay, please" Squints said over the comms.

"Sublevel II exit bay opening now," LUCY said, and Clive was more surprised than he should have been when he heard its voice over his comms, too.

A door shut behind them, and in front of them the door opened up into the dark blue ocean.

Swimming out from the exit bay, Clive was surprised when he felt the pressure on his body. His first instinct was to tighten up, but instead he took a deep breath and waited a moment.

"The gill is slowly adjusting your body to the right pressure. It should only take a moment or two before you're good to go," Squints said, as if reading Clive's mind.

"Impressive," Clive said between swallow breaths. After a couple seconds he began to feel things return to normal. "These things are impressive, why don't they have them in the … you know, mainland." The hesitation in his voice made Squints laugh.

"You'd think so," he said, settling his breath again. "But think about it, how often do people on the mainland need tech like this? Not to mention the cost involved to develop and test it, legal issues. All for what? So divers have an easier time? What business is going to deal with all that when the tech they have works fine?" Squints said, a hint of bitterness in his voice.

"Alice Industries did," Clive said.

"Because they want to," Squints said, spinning around to face him. "Look where we are." He gestured to the water around them. In the distance, Clive could see a school of fish swimming past, thousands of them in tight formation. He could also make out various other species swimming lazily through the cold waters.

"We're over eight hundred feet from the surface, swimming without oxygen tanks, because someone in there," he said, gesturing to Atlantis, "thought it would be cool, and it would help. I don't know how many companies you've worked for, but even the ones with money never seem to think like that. Either they are too scared to try, or someone who's never been on a dive in their life decided it wasn't worth it." He dropped his arms. "I don't need to be reminded of what the mainland is like, I lived that life for thirty-four years and it was a struggle. Here I feel free and protected."

Squints's words settled into Clive and, despite him not wanting them to, they struck a chord for him. He'd been part of the military for fourteen years and he'd seen firsthand how indecision and fear had stifled progress. He'd often thought how the military machine had run for so long that the fear of it all collapsing often made change impossible.

"Don't get me wrong, it's not just some industries, it's most of them," Squints said as he turned and started swimming away from the exit bay. "Think about banks, industry leaders, heck, even governments. The cost of changing and failing is so devasting to them that they push forward like a steamroller, ignoring innovation and forgetting that the fear of evolution is death." He turned back to make sure Clive was still behind him.

Clive was afraid to comment, for fear of what he might say.

"I'm sorry. My wife tells me I blab on too much. You're here for a tour, not a rant," Squints said, waving his arm and giving Clive a big smile.

"I don't mind rants," Clive joked as he swam up beside Squints. "Let's see what we're working with."

It only took a few minutes of swimming to reach their

destination. Squints pointed out the emergency oxygen bays along the way for Clive to take note of, before they spotted a couple of other divers up ahead, working on what appeared to be a forty-foot-high pipe at least fifteen feet in diameter. Clive noticed four robots surrounding the pipe, attached evenly at the top and bottom.

"What are those?" Clive asked, pointing to the robots, which he could now see were several feet wide and looked like massive movie projectors with two arms poking out the sides.

"Assistance bots. They carry the pieces from the manufacturing floor to where they need to be assembled. Then they hold them in place while we work. Makes things a hell of a lot easier." Squints smiled, and Clive wondered if there were more bots he couldn't see on the other side of the pipe, helping to keep it in place.

"Very cool." Clive watched as the divers moved like snails around the edge of the massive pipe, sealing the gaps between them.

"Hamish, its Squints, I brought the new guy out to get a sense of what we'll be working on tomorrow." Squints was linking up his gill with Hamish's somehow. "Hamish, Clive. Clive, Hamish."

"G'day mate, welcome to the party," Hamish said in a thick New Zealand accent.

"I thought you said he was Australian, eh?" Clive said, hearing a little giggle through the comms coming from Squints.

"Good on ya, I like this one, Squints," Hamish said, shutting down the gadget in his hand and swimming over to meet them. "Sunny, get over here and meet the new guy." Hamish waved a hand to the person working on the other side of the pipe. They spotted the three of them and quickly shut down their gear and swam over to meet them.

"You should know better, Squints. New Zealanders and Canadians know what it's like to be in the shadow of a larger brother," Hamish said, giving Clive a knowing wink. Having often been labeled as an American when he'd been traveling, Clive knew exactly what he meant.

"Clive, this is Sun-Young. We call her Sunny," Hamish said, and somehow must have patched her through, as a soft, polite voice rang through his gill.

"Annyeong haseyo," Sunny said, and gave a polite bow, which, when Clive tried to replicate, was much harder in the water then she'd made it look.

"Annyeong haseyo," Clive said, realizing once again he'd burned through what little Korean he knew, which happened to be "hello". But it must have sounded pretty good, as Sunny continued.

"Mannaseo bangawoyo, Clive," she said, giving him a gracious smile. Not knowing what to say, Clive simply floated there for a moment until Squints swooped in to save him.

"Clive's only being nice, Sunny. He hasn't been fitted with a interpreter yet," Squints said, which caused Sunny to giggle. "But she said it was nice to meet you."

"It's nice to meet you, too," Clive said, attempting and somewhat achieving a bow.

"Right-o, so you wanted to bring him out to test the gear? Should be easy enough. I was thinking about taking a break," Hamish said as Sunny hit him in the arm. "I'm only joking, I wouldn't leave you, Sunny," he said, giving her a playful smile before turning back to Clive and Squints with a mock look of sympathy. "Poor thing wouldn't know what to do without me," he said with another wink. This time Sunny tried to smack his head; the effort was lost in the water, but the meaning was there for everyone as she began to giggle again.

"Ugh, meong-cheong-i" Sunny said, narrowing her eyes at Hamish.

"That's nice, Sunny. She said there has never been a better person to work with than me," Hamish said, trying hard to hold in a laugh.

"She said he was an idiot," Squints said to Clive as Hamish let out a good howl. "Got a spare melder on you?" he asked Sunny, who reached around for a satchel that crisscrossed her body. As she pulled down on one of the straps, the pack moved up her back and over her shoulder, stopping to rest on her chest. She opened the bag and pulled out a small black device that looked like a combination of an impact driver and a taser. She also pulled out a couple rods of hard wire and handed them over to Squints.

"Thanks, Sunny," he said, taking the tools before handing the melder over to Clive.

"We'll let you fellas get to it. And please don't bugger it up, it's got our delicate names on it." Hamish said as he laughed and began to swim away. Sunny swam after him, shaking her head.

"Hwa-i-ting," Sunny said, heading back to the section of pipe she'd been working on.

"She said good luck," Squints explained before leading the way over to the pipe connection as Clive followed.

"First things first," Squints said, taking the melder. "Your finger will get tired, so I highly suggest you lock it in." He pulled a cord with a little latch from the bottom of the gun and hooked it to a metal tab dangling under Clive's arm. "These things are a pain in the ass to get replaced and well … the ocean is pretty deep." He gestured down to the blueish black abyss that fell endlessly below their feet.

It was the first time Clive looked down, and he was struck by the openness of it all. It felt ominous and deathly silent, like all sound was eaten up by the sheer expanse of it all.

"First time open ocean diving?" Squints asked, likely noticing the shift in Clive's face.

"First time this deep," Clive said, looking up at the warmer blues that often come with the light and sunshine.

"You'll get used to it quickly, trust me," Squints said, looking down into the darkness himself. "Well, used to some of it at least," he added, letting out a slow breath. "This melder acts the same as your stinger but without the cords and wires. It's all built in, so that will be easy. LUCY, activate welding mode." Squints's face mask darkened and five sets of LED lights shone brightly from his gill. "Give it a try."

"LUCY, activate welding mode," Clive repeated, and just like that, the suit adjusted and everything seemed to get a lot darker. It took a moment for him to adjust to the new light. He couldn't be sure, but he felt as though it took less time than it did in normal gear.

"That's the other reason for the attachment," Squints said, tugging the cord attached to Clive's side. "The melder won't turn on if your shield's not up, which is helpful for not burning your eyes. Then you have your hard wire," Squints said, handing Clive one of the metal rods, "and that's basically it."

"Really?" Clive said, surprised. "What about electrode coating? Where's the power for the melder?" Squints held up his hand as he laughed.

"All great questions," Squints said, and Clive could practically see the man's smile without seeing his face, thinking that he was going to enjoy working with someone so positive. "The melder has enough power on its own. Don't you worry about that. And as for the electrodes, the team has managed to design new rods with something that can withstand the pressure at this depth better, so they don't need any electrode coating."

"So, I just go?" Clive asked, and Squints gave a nod. Sure enough, the process was much easier than Clive had been expecting, and after a couple minutes of playing around with melder positioning, he found a comfortable rhythm.

"You know, you likely could have shown me how to do this tomorrow on the job. I hadn't realized it was this easy," Clive said, continuing to work while Squints floated behind him.

"I know that," Squints said, "but then I wouldn't get the chance to show you the fun stuff."

"Fun stuff?" Clive repeated, as he stopped welding and turned to look at Squints, now just a floating dark mass in the water.

8

After thanking Hamish and Sunny for letting him borrow their tools, Clive left them to work on the massive pipe and began to catch up with Squints, who'd refused to give Clive any clue as to where they were heading. Even after they swam back inside and grabbed a bite to eat and a drink, Squints kept his secret closely guarded.

Squints led Clive back to the TOTS terminal and discreetly began typing instructions in, letting LUCY know where to go.

"Wow, you're really keeping this tight-knit, Squints," Clive said, not sure if he should be worried or excited.

"You only get your first time once, and I'm not going to ruin that by giving anything away," Squints said with wink.

The two of them sat in silence for a few minutes. Clive's nerves were clearly rising with Squints giddiness. Whatever it was, Clive assumed it must be good if Squints was so eager to take him there. They finally arrived at a deck Clive had never visited, which was, oddly, earmarked as the aquarium, given the fact that the entire city was, more or less, a working aquarium in the middle of the ocean.

The terminal they'd arrived in must have been one of the service bays, which was tucked a little further back from where most people were entering the room. There were three additional transport terminals along with five massive doorways all flowing with a steady stream of people, ranging from groups of children, to young adults, to people in lab coats, all moving throughout the spacious landing bay.

To the right of them was another observation deck like the one Clive had seen in the dive bay earlier that morning, only the water here seemed a much brighter shade of blue and there was a lot more marine life swimming around outside of the windows, even more than Clive would have guessed, given that they were in the ocean. He walked over to the edge of the observation deck and could see three more decks, one above him and two below, all looking out over one of the most beautiful views Clive had ever seen.

Just below the deck he was on was an expansive coral reef system, which stretched out for miles.

"Holy shit," Clive said, unable to stop himself from letting the curse slip out of his mouth.

"Easy friend, there are kids here," Squints said, stepping up behind him with a smile.

"What?! How?" Clive began, but the words didn't seem to come.

"It's magnificent, isn't it?" Squints paused, and since Clive's mouth appeared permanently agape, he continued. "The team here started to develop the idea when they first opened the facility. It was one of the original programs. It was supposed to be a test to see if it was possible to develop an ecosystem off the facility itself. And then, when it was, they wanted to see how big they could make it."

"And? How big is it?" Clive asked, sounding like one of the many children walking around with their parents or teachers.

"Right now, it's about seven kilometers out and surrounds the entire facility. But they're planning on expanding it to as far as fifteen kilometers," Squints added, not bothering to hide the joy he got from it all.

"It's incredible," Clive said, looking out at the expansive, colourful network of coral and underwater plant life that sprouted out from the observation deck in both directions.

"Come on," Squints said, pulling Clive off to the side. He wanted to stay and take in the view, but when he turned and saw the wide grin on Squints's face, he had a feeling there was more to see.

The two of them walked up to a set of doors labeled "Research Area: Restricted Access," and Clive wondered how they would get in. But Squints simply held LUCY up to the door and it clicked open.

"We have access to the research bay?" Clive asked, his mind shifting back to the entire reason he was on Atlantis in the first place. He'd left his USB key back in his room, thinking there was little chance he'd be getting access to anything important on his first day; he wondered now if he'd missed an opportunity. He made a mental note to start carrying it with him just in case.

"This is the coral development bay," Squints said. "As part of the dive team, we have access to any areas with dive access," he said with a knowing wink.

"You mean we get to dive out there?" Clive asked, his excitement building.

"Only if you want to," Squints said teasingly, with a nonchalant wave of his hand.

"Hell yeah I do," Clive said, a little louder than he'd intended, as he received one or two glances from the researchers in the room. One woman in particular met his eye and let it linger a little longer than Clive felt his remark warranted. He might have chalked it up to flirtation had she not remained so serious through the interaction. Clive began to wonder if she knew him somehow. If she did, she didn't stick around for a chat.

Squints led them through the lab until they reached another pool of water nestled into the corner of the facility. It was an identical design to the one they'd used in the sublevels, but the water here was significantly warmer. So much so that Clive would have wanted to ditch the wet suit.

"Water's nice," Clive said through the gills' internal communications, after they'd dunked into it and Squints led them down the tunnel.

"It's impressive, hey? They didn't know if the reef would survive out here, but as they started to expand it, it created a natural shelf that warmed the water, brought new life, and made it possible to keep expanding," Squints said, before requesting LUCY to close the exit gate. They swam out, floating about sixty feet above the reef.

From this view Clive could see metal arms protruding from the sides of Atlantis. They looked like the prongs of a forklift, only there were hundreds of them attached to a large, circular metal ring that curved elegantly around the city.

"It's a lift system," Squints said, when he saw Clive looking at the ring. "A temperature regulated hydronic lift system. It finds and monitors the temperature for the reef and adjusts the ring to the optimal depth to survive."

"You mean it moves?" Clive said, getting a barely readable nod from Squints in the wet suit.

"It's also like a waterfall system, so it drops in depth a little every thousand feet or so, to allow different species to thrive."

Clive was happy for Squints to continue spewing out information, as he still found himself in awe of it all and unable to speak. He'd of course been to the Great Barrier Reef before, and it was spectacular. But he'd never imagined a man-made reef could ever come close to it. Looking out over the reef, he caught sight of an abundance of beautifully coloured fish swimming around, hiding in the flora of the reef system.

Most of the fish he couldn't recognize; he'd never studied them as hard as some divers might, but he knew enough to recognize that they weren't the types of fish you found anywhere near the open ocean, which meant they must have implanted them into the ecosystem. Clive suspected that everything here must have been selected in some way to cultivate the natural ecosystem of places like the Great Barrier Reef. He even caught a glimpse of a few massive sea turtles in the distance, gliding above the towers of coral. And every so often Clive could see holes that opened up to the depths of the ocean.

"What are those for?" Clive asked Squints.

"Light channels to help send natural light down through Atlantis. Not that it seems to do much by the time you get down to there." Squints laughed. "But as you would have seen, the light coming in from the dome provides the majority of the internal natural light." Clive had seen just how much light traveled into the space, and it was impressive. But something about all the light coming down didn't make sense to him.

"Wait, I thought the outer rim up top was like a mile long? How is the light getting through? And come to think of it, how the hell did I miss this when we flew in?" Clive said, thinking back and wondering just how into the conversation he'd been with Akmed.

"All great questions. The upper deck is heat glass. It catches the heat from the sun and transfers that into energy we use on the ship. Like solar panels, only this allows light to shine through it. It's not the most effective way to get energy, but it does let the reef under it thrive which is why, I suspect, they use it instead. As for why you didn't see it? I'm not sure. On a bright day you'll get a great view on the way in, but if it's cloudy, it's harder. Not to mention the reef is fairly low right now, likely due to the storm that's coming. I suspect it will drop another twenty feet before tomorrow."

"There's a storm coming?" Clive asked, sounding a little too surprised. Of course, there were storms. They were in the middle of the ocean. But typically, a ship would run a course to avoid the worst of it. *I wonder what they do here?*

"Don't sound so worried, storms are great. The energy we collect from the waves alone is enough to run the whole facility for a week. Other than the occasional dip, you really don't feel it. I think a guy like you, who's spent so much time on a ship, will be very surprised," Squints said as he began to swim around the reef.

Clive likely could have spent another few hours out exploring, but after three hours of diving Squints looked like he was ready to head in, and Clive still wasn't confident enough to get back on his own and would feel a little foolish having LUCY talking to him out loud again. He was excited by the chance to get the interpreter, as he also suspected LUCY would be synced with the device so he wouldn't need to feel as silly asking for so much help.

Squints led them back to the research labs before they hopped on the transport back down to the dive bay, where they both undressed and jumped in the shower. Clive was excited to see both a sauna and steam room there as well, which he knew he'd be using often.

Rubbing his arm, he felt the spot on his shoulder where the contact chip had been placed. It acted as a reminder of the fact that, no matter how amazing the day had been and whatever interesting things they were doing on this facility, he was there for a reason. Somewhere beneath the man-made reef and cool gadgets there were people in this city with a history of death and destruction, and whatever they were doing here couldn't be as magical as everyone thought was. He would need to keep reminding himself of that before getting too sucked in.

Clive said good-bye to Squints who he'd thought was just being nice, but had insisted and re-insisted that he come over for dinner. He'd even made LUCY send over his housing details along with a time, so that Clive had little excuse not to come.

It wasn't that he didn't want to go; the way that Squints talked about his partner's cooking, you'd think he'd died and gone to heaven. By the end of his description, Clive could barely hide the fact that his mouth was watering.

But something about it made him feel wrong. He would be lying to Squints and his family about who he was and why he was here. He had no intention of staying past the end of the month, regardless of what he discovered. He had his life back on the mainland and he liked it. Or at least, he liked aspects of it. Regardless, he was committed to his duty as a soldier, and after everything they'd given him over the years, he couldn't simply turn his back on them and leave.

He told himself that it was only a dinner, and since he was

going to be here for the month, he should make the most of it, same as he would on any other assignment.

Clive decided to take a longer route home, giving himself the chance to get lost a little along the way under the veil of exploration. Really he was avoiding going home and the nagging thought of setting up the transmission back with Commander Hammond. He scratched subconsciously at the arm where the chip had been inserted.

Yesterday he'd been impressed with the technology behind the chip, but today his eyes had been opened to a world where technology had the training wheels removed and ideas were free to evolve and grow—and that was only what he'd witnessed while diving.

The people here seemed so carefree, it was hard to believe that under the surface there was a smaller group building some sort of weapon. *But people don't usually set out to hurt people when they are developing new technology. More often it is someone else who sees that potential. Does that mean that the issue is Grace Alice?*

From the brief interaction Clive had had with her, he hardly got the sense she was some sort of criminal mastermind. She certainly had the respect of both people onboard and the newcomers.

Clive had been so distracted by his thoughts, he hadn't realized he no longer had any idea of where he was.

"Take me home, LUCY, I have a dinner to get ready for," Clive said, talking to his wrist with the kind of confidence one can only have in a hallway by themselves.

Once again, LUCY managed to make quick work of getting Clive home, and he was thankful for her help, because somehow he still had no concept of where he was going.

In fact, he'd completely forgotten what room number was his. He stepped into the apartment, which still didn't feel like it was his, and went into the bathroom to prepare.

Grabbing his shower bag, he removed the tweezers, a pack of razor blades, and an alcohol swab. He then ran the hot water for a few moments, letting it heat up to the touch before he removed a face cloth and ran it under the water briefly before wringing out the extra water. Then he removed his shirt, opened the shower door, and took a seat on the tiled bench.

Taking the alcohol swab, he cleaned the blades and the tweezers, then rested the tweezers on the bench beside him. He slowly ran a finger over the entry wound, which had now lightly scabbed over. He hoped that the relatively fresh wound would be easier for cutting into. He didn't even want to think about how bad the alternative would be.

Taking the hot cloth, he held it over the incision. The heat from the cloth caused him to flinch a little. The hot water was uncomfortable, but he knew it would help to soften the scabbing around the wound. The hope was that he might be able to wipe the scabbing away rather than scrape it.

After a few minutes of letting the heat warm his skin, he removed the towel, revealing a patch of reddish skin, and rubbed the cloth over the scabs. It worked perfectly, the cloth taking away a majority of the previously dry and flaky skin. However, with the protective layer of new skin now removed, the cut began to bleed, and rivulets of blood seeped into the previously white cloth.

Picking up the razor blade, Clive delicately ran the sharp edge of the blade over the wound, wincing a little as he worked his way across the tiny incision. Blood began to pool out of the incision with each movement of the blade. He was thankful it wasn't very big, and after a few seconds of slicing, he managed to open up the wound enough to spot the edge of the chip.

Using the cloth to clear away the fresh blood snaking down his arm, he exchanged the razor for the tweezers and efficiently parted the skin enough to pinch the end of the tiny chip. Taking a deep breath, pulled with the tweezers, causing a tingling sensation as the metal chip slid smoothly from his arm.

With a sigh of relief, he looked over the chip, wiping it and his arm with the cloth before leaving the shower to cover the cut with a bandage.

He wondered, as he picked up his phone, which he only just realized had been in his bag all day, how much they really needed all the cloak and dagger stuff. As far as he could tell, they hadn't gone through any crazy security when they arrived. Though he supposed that didn't mean they didn't have some advanced screening systems in place that he couldn't see. Given all the new technology he'd seen already, it wouldn't surprise him. Come to think of it, he wasn't even sure if he'd seen a single security person on board Atlantis yet. Looking down at LUCY, he wondered if it somehow had more capabilities then he knew about.

"LUCY?" Clive said out loud, before he could give himself more time to overthink everything.

"Yes, Clive?" LUCY responded, giving no heed to the clear apprehension in his voice.

"Does Atlantis have security?" The question seemed strange even as it left his mouth, but he didn't really have any other ideas for how to probe for this sort of information.

"Of course. Atlantis has numerous safety protocols in place

for any number of situations that might occur," LUCY said with a carefree tone that likely put many at ease. It was a politician's answer, descriptive enough that it answered his concerns, but vague enough that if he wanted more information, he would need to get specific. But without knowing what LUCY's role was on Atlantis, he wasn't sure how safe it was to ask questions like these. Would LUCY see him as a possible threat? Or just an overly cautious resident?

"Are you part of the security network?" Clive asked.

"I act as a mediator between the people of Atlantis and the city itself. I offer security protocols for various hazardous situations, including injury, fire, and various other on-site situations. Atlantis as a city is in a unique position. There is always fear of threat, as we are in the middle of the ocean under international law. Therefore, precautions have been taken and equipment made to ensure the safety of the citizens of Atlantis."

And there it was—the first real proof that Atlantis was creating some sort of weapon or defence tactics to keep itself safe. LUCY had not even tried to hide the fact that they were developing ways to protect themselves. *But I wonder where the line in the sand is for the city of Atlantis? Or for Grace Alice? Is Five Eyes right to be suspicious of everything going on here? LUCY had also claimed that, as of yet, no one had ever left Atlantis, but what did that mean for Sasha Keen?*

Slipping the chip he'd pulled from his arm into his phone, and finding the lone number that he knew would be Commander Hammond's, he began writing a short message.

Arrived on Atlantis and cover has been set. Strong evidence of advanced tech onboard. Unsure of weapons. I will continue to search and will update at the end of the week.

He sent the message and removed the chip. Going back into the living room, he scanned the room for a place to hide it. He settled on a small bookcase filled with various books on marine life. Picking out a copy of *The World Beneath* by Richard Smith, he slipped the chip into the spine of the book and tucked the book back on the shelf.

Taking a mental note of where it was located, he turned to go to his room to find something suitable for a dinner with new people.

...

Squints's home was a whirlwind of excitement from the moment Clive was greeted at the door and pulled in by five-year-old Martim, who did not understand immediately that Clive didn't have an interpreter and or understand any of the Portuguese he'd been speaking. The confused expression on Clive's face must have given him away, as the young boy smacked his head with the palm of his hand before his speedy ramblings switched effortlessly to English.

Clive was then quickly introduced to Martim's older sisters—Ilyana, who Clive learned was seven, and Mia, who was ten. The two of them also spoke remarkable English but seemed a little more preoccupied with the game of Uno they were trying to play, the same one Martim kept running away from.

"Clive, welcome!" Squints called from the kitchen, where he was chopping up some green onions. He turned to his wife, who shared her husband's large, gracious smile and sense of joy. "This is my beautiful wife, Margarida," he said, giving her a big kiss.

"Stop that," Margarida said as she playfully swatted him with the dish towel resting over her shoulder. "I'm sorry about all of this," she said gesturing to the screaming children and Martim jumping from couch to couch. "I'd say they are not always like this, but I'd be lying." She laughed. "Martim! Stop jumping and finish playing cards with your sisters or else next time we won't put up a fight for you when they refuse to let you play because you … do this," she said in a stern yet playful tone. Martim recognized the threat, hunching over and taking a seat with his sisters, and the room quieted down a little.

"What can I do to help?" Clive offered, rubbing his hands together eagerly.

"You can help me out by drinking this," Squints said as he placed a beer on the counter in front of him.

"I can do that," Clive said happily, sitting down at the kitchen island.

Looking around the room, he was surprised by how similar their apartments looked. Like him, they had an ocean view, only theirs had handprints smudged all over the lower part of the window. And unlike his apartment, they had a full second floor with a network of rooms up top. Clive assumed this was the family accommodation.

"Beautiful place you have," Clive said honestly. He was still shocked by how impressive everything, everywhere, was.

"It works for us," Margarida said over her shoulder as she stirred something on the stove that smelled delicious. Clive leaned over to get a better look at the dish, which appeared to be some sort of meat simmering in a thick sauce. Off to the side was a stack of large rolls that were still warm.

"That smells incredible," Clive said, his mouth beginning to water. He supplemented it with a swig of cold beer. "Did you make all of this?" he asked, trying not to sound a shocked as he was.

"Margarida is a brilliant cook," Squints said lovingly as he chopped up more vegetables and tossed them into a salad bowl. "You won't find a better cook in all of Atlantis," he added with a wink to Clive. Margarida must have sensed her husband's play as she turned and kicked him.

"We are certainly blessed to live in a place where we can offer our kids such a variety of amazing foods. But there are some things I continue to make the way my mother taught me," Margarida said, spooning more sauce over the meat.

"And your mother taught you wonderfully, my love," Squints, said turning to give her a kiss, which elicited a series of groans from their kids. "You forget, my little ones, if it wasn't for our love, you wouldn't exist, so cease your moaning," he said, laughing at the larger groans that followed.

"I hope you don't mind me saying this, but you all speak English so well," Clive said. "Is that an Atlantis thing?" Squints shook his head as he popped a cherry tomato in his mouth.

"I worked for Gold Star Oil, so we spent a few years living in America. Not my favourite post, but it did give us all a little time to work on our English. Martim, on the other hand was forced to learn. He also speaks Italian, French, Spanish, and a little Mandarin. That I accredit to Atlantis," Squints said, with an approving nod to his son.

"How did he do that?" Clive asked, wondering what kind of trick they offer here that they don't have on mainland.

"The interpreters were adjusted so he can listen and learn languages as people speak. It's a helpful tool when you're young. Even the girls were able to learn a couple of extra languages, but neither of them enjoyed it as much as Martim." He added quickly, "But they have other passions they can indulge while they are here. Ilyana wants to study plants and tends to all the plants you see in the house, and Mia wants to be a marine biologist," he said, gesturing to the ocean view. "It is helpful to live here. She's even started her dive training."

"That's amazing," Clive said. "And do you all like living on Atlantis?" He turned to the kids and received three smiles and some heavy nods.

"This place changed our lives, Clive, as it has for so many others," Squints said somberly.

"What does that mean?" Clive said. He didn't want to drop the conversation, but Margarida had finished up and before he could get more out of Squints, she announced, "The food is ready! Clive, please start us off."

As much as Clive wanted to know more about Atlantis saving people, he wasn't about to delay the hungry kids behind him, or himself, from eating the delicious smelling food that was in front of him. Grabbing a plate, he listened as Martim graciously pointed out what he needed to know to fix up his bifana, which he learned was marinated pork on a bun.

The rest of dinner was a loud cacophony of voices, the likes of which Clive had only experienced in a ship's cafeteria. Having not grown up with a family of his own, he found every moment fascinating, especially when the three siblings began to bicker with one another over everything from Mia having too much food, to Martim attempting to steal some of Ilyana's food off her plate. It was entertaining and the entire ordeal could best be described in Clive's mind as controlled chaos.

He found the night coming to an end much quicker than he would have liked. Despite the occasional shouts and tears, he knew that this house was filled with love. *Could I ever have something like this?*

He did his best to ignore that thought as Margarida said, "I think it's time for the three of you to get off to bed." Mia had crawled onto her lap, her little hand trying to hide a yawn.

"But Clive—" the kids began.

"Is also needing to get to bed," Clive said, mimicking Mia's yawn.

"Either way, Clive isn't the one up past his bedtime," Squints said, giving Martim a gentle pat on the behind as he sluggishly rolled off the couch.

"I wouldn't say that," Clive mused as he made a show of looking at his LUCY. He stood up from the couch. "Thank you all for the most incredible night. I had a great time."

"I'm sorry the little ones are …" Margarida smiled and opened her arms wide as if to say, "all of this." Clive laughed.

"I can honestly say that was one of the best nights I've had in a long time," Clive said, as Margarida stood and embraced him. Even Mia, still in her mother's arms, wrapped her arms around his neck. It was even more unexpected when Martim and Ilyana did the same. Clive could feel their little arms around his waist.

"Nice to meet you," Ilyana said, trying to stifle a yawn.

"Come back soon. We can play cards again!" Martim said, trying to sound excited through a yawn of his own.

"Goodnight," Mia said shyly.

"I'll hopefully see you out on the reef soon enough," Clive said with a little wink, which caused Mia to smile and blush as she nodded her head in excitement. With that, Margarida took them all upstairs to their rooms, leaving Clive and Squints alone, making their way towards the door.

"You have an amazing family, Squints, thank you for sharing that with me," Clive said as Squints pulled him in for a hug, catching him off guard.

"Sorry, in this family, we are huggers," Squints said proudly.

"I'm beginning to realize that." Clive laughed as he awkwardly embraced his new friend.

"Thank you for coming tonight, I know it's likely not what you're used to," Squints said. And he was right, it wasn't at all what Clive was used to.

"I wasn't kidding when I said this was the best night I've had in a long time," Clive said, hoping his words sounded as sincere as he meant them to be. "Everything was incredible."

"Well, I'm glad you liked it, and obviously this is an open invitation whenever you want to come. I know how difficult it can be to be away from family and friends," Squints said, a smile masking the sadness behind his eyes.

Clive didn't have the courage to tell him he didn't have any family, not unless you counted the people he knew through the Navy. Even then, his work had been so independent the last few years, he'd hardly had time for any of them either. That made tonight all the more special. Clive was about to step out the door when his mind trickled back to something Squints had mentioned. He turned back to his new friend.

"You said earlier that this place changed your life, and that it did for a lot of people." Clive felt strange broaching such a personal topic as he was leaving, but now it was out there and all he could do was keep going. "What did you mean?"

Squints looked at him thoughtfully as he paused for a moment.

"Others' stories are not mine to tell, but as you get to know people here, you will learn that most people are happy to share. As for me, let's just say that people are not always kind to those not from their country, and it took a toll on me and my children. But on Atlantis, everyone is here for a reason. It gives people purpose beyond simply making money and trying to live. When the fear of not maintaining a minimum quality of living is gone, what you're left with are the things that matter." He looked up towards where his kids were being put to bed.

"I understand," Clive said after a long moment. He'd never had a family, but he'd worked months on and months off in the past, and it's not conducive to sharing a life with someone. Which made Squints and his life even more impressive. "I guess I'll have to wait to hear some more of those stories," he said, surprising himself when he gave his friend a hug before he turned to leave, knowing this would give him a lot to think about on the walk back to his apartment.

9

Clive woke in the morning to the sound of birds chirping and an imagined sunrise warming up his room. The effect was wonderful, but he wished he'd had the chance to sleep a little longer. And looking at the time, it was no wonder why.

"LUCY, why did you wake me up so early? I thought Squints and I didn't start until 9:00 a.m.?" he said, admonishing the android for the unnecessary 6:00 a.m. wake up while wiping the gunk from his eyes.

"That is correct. You and Mr. Pereira start work at nine this morning. However, Mr. Pereira took the liberty of booking you in with the Atlantis technology department to be fitted for a interpreter. That appointment is at 7:30 a.m.," LUCY said, giving Clive's mind the reminder it needed.

"Thank you, LUCY." Clive's head flopped back down on the pillow one last time before he forced himself up and made his way to the washroom for a hot shower.

"Not a problem. It's my job," LUCY said confidently.

"Well then, let's be thankful one of us can remember," he said, keenly aware he was carrying on an open dialogue with an android. Yet despite how weird he wanted to make it seem, he couldn't shake the oddly comforting feeling he was getting from it.

After a quick shower and a steam, which had the pleasant surprise of smelling of eucalyptus, he felt awake and ready to go.

Clive wasn't in the same hurry he had been the morning before, but he still had LUCY place a bagel and coffee order at the café. Sending the mug ahead, Clive did his best to make it to the café on his own, only getting turned around twice along the way.

It was Kissa, the same young girl behind the counter who had been there the day before. Clive, now understanding that she had been asking him about his interpreter, gave her a thankful smile before telling her, "I get my interpreter today," and was happy when she understood what he was saying. "Sorry for the confusion yesterday," he added.

"No problem," Kissa replied in very broken English.

"Have a great day," Clive said, somehow finding it easier to communicate now that he knew the other person could understand him. This also made him very excited by the prospect of getting fitted for a interpreter himself.

Kissa waved good-bye before turning to help another patron, and Clive made his way to the edge of the observation deck. He still had thirty minutes before he needed to be at the tech bay, and he assumed it wouldn't take long.

"The tech bay is only twelve minutes from here. It's located in Beta III and you can use the same TOTS system as yesterday," LUCY happily confirmed.

"Thank you," Clive said, as he spotted an empty bench on the observation deck. Breakfast in hand, he walked over and took a seat.

The bench was raised up on some sort of earthen rise, with a thick carpet of grass over it. A series of steps on either side led up to a levelled platform, which was just high enough to see comfortably over the edge of the observation deck, but far enough back that you didn't feel as though you might fall off the edge.

There was so much about this place that Clive didn't understand yet, and he doubted if twenty-eight days would be enough to truly discover everything Atlantis had to offer. He wondered if living in Atlantis would be like getting a new cellphone, sure it had all of these amazing capabilities, but would he ever figure out how to use them all?

That's when it hit Clive, realizing that this would be the first time he would get a glimpse of the tech bay, and since it was located on Beta level, he assumed it would have been one of the first areas they built and therefore most likely to house some of their weapons.

Clive hadn't seen any of the weapons that were mentioned in his brief yet, but figured they must have weapons somewhere onboard. It would be impossible to believe they could be this exposed in the ocean without some form of defence against pirates and any number of threats. They were under no jurisdiction and therefore had no protection from any nation. *How does a high-tech city ensure the safety of their people in the face of all that?*

Looking around, he saw vignettes of people going about their regular day. It was still early and the light from the dome had only just started to shine down on the lower levels, but it wouldn't be long until the entire city was bathed in the day's sunshine.

Looking out over the lower levels, Clive saw the swirling whirlpool of water that gathered at the belly of the city. The intricately designed series of waterfalls cascaded down into it, creating a pleasant, soothing thrum that echoed throughout the city.

It would have been easy to sit there and eat believing he was in something like the West Edmonton mall. That man-made structure housed many makeshift designs to emulate nature from inside. But there it had always felt like something was off; it never felt natural.

Here, in the atrium, the building truly felt alive, as if Atlantis had a pulse of its own. There was a sense that it was something worth protecting, and Clive wanted to understand more about how they planned on doing that.

Finishing up his food, Clive made his way to the TOTS and, as LUCY predicted, it only took twelve minutes to get to the tech bay.

Walking up to the large metal door, Clive scanned LUCY and the light flashed green as he pushed the swinging doors open and walked into a space that was straight out of a George Lucas film. The facility was roughly fifty feet high and three hundred feet long, with what had to be hundreds of see-through walled rooms lining the sides of the immense warehouse. At first glance, each unit housed a different project, ranging in size from tiny cubes, with only one or two people, to rooms the size of three stacked shipping containers, with twenty or so people running around in them.

On the main level, people walked about in varying styles of colourful coats that blended the imagination of Dr. Seuss and Willy Wonka, were they ever to team up and design a laboratory.

Robotic arms popped up from the ground like metal trees as they moved various materials over the heads of the people working below. Clive watched as a middle-aged woman finished soldering some wires together before closing up the tiny door and casually flipping a small device, which reminded Clive of a skateboard with no wheels, on the ground. She proceeded to tap the board with her shoe, and it lifted about seven inches off the ground. She studied it a moment, circling the device before casually stepping on top of it. Clive watched as the board shifted slightly but held the woman in the air effortlessly.

Clive was still staring, waiting to see what the woman would do next on what he now assumed was a hoverboard, so he didn't notice when an older Chinese woman with cropped black hair stepped up beside him.

"You must be Clive Davies," she said, reading a hologram chart that shone from her LUCY. Clive jumped a little at her sudden proximity to him. She was small, only reaching as high as his shoulder, but her voice had the authority of someone who was used to being heard.

"Yes," Clive said, trying to regain his composure, "and that is amazing." He pointed at the hologram. "Can mine do that?" he asked, fighting the sudden urge to start pressing all the buttons he could see on LUCY. The woman laughed.

"Soon. But this is a prototype. We like to test all new upgrades in here for a while with our team before we introduce them to the general public. Although, I have to agree, it is very cool," she said, her voice somehow managing to remain confident and playful at the same time. Clive was impressed by her English as well, with only a few words giving away that English was not her first language.

"I'm Dr. Xu Chen," she said, her eyes running over the screen. "You can call me Dr. Xu," she added with a thin smile. Clive noted the "shoo" sound of the name in his mind for use later.

"Yes, I'm here for an interpreter," Clive said with smile of his own. Dr. Xu nodded as she re-examined the hologram in front of her.

"We can certainly get that fitted for you today. If you'll please follow me." She began walking into the chaos of the room. "Stay close and try to stay inside the yellow lines, unless you want to lose an arm," she said, turning to give him a wink. Although seeing some of the gadgets moving around, Clive hardly felt like it was an empty threat.

"Do you always take people this way?" he said, looking around and seeing if there was a slightly less dangerous route.

"No, but you seem responsible, and this way is much faster," she said, walking comfortably through the yellow-lined pathways. "Besides, this way is so much more exciting, isn't it?" She looked back at him with a childish grin.

Clive noticed some people working off to the side, his eye catching sight of a small team standing around two people, one of whom wore a thin set of black gloves and was using American sign language.

"What are they doing?" Clive asked, pointing over to the small group of scientists.

"That's rather interesting. Those gloves they're wearing sync with the interpreters to incorporate ASL users into its translation abilities. And those glasses," Dr. Xu said, gesturing to another member of the group, who was sporting a rather thick pair of glasses, "are testing alternative ways of translating various languages into ASL for people with compromised hearing." She gave them a nod of approval and received some enthusiastic smiles in return. "The prototypes have already been released in the city and I suspect we will have real-time translations any day now. The uniqueness of the language and the variants in user preference can only be assessed once we have enough documentation of the language. Do you sign?" Dr. Xu asked.

"No more than to say, 'How are you?'" Clive said as he pressed the backs of his fingers together against his chest, with his thumbs pointing away from him, as his hands made a sort of W shape before he broke them apart and pointed his right index finger towards Dr. Xu.

"Not bad," Dr. Xu mused. "Well, with any luck we will have it as fluid as me speaking to you now!" she said, pressing forward through the maze of machinery, until they were roughly a quarter of the way down the main level. Turning left, she walked to a small platform with railing around the edges. She led Clive up onto the platform and closed the gate, making sure to securely lock the bar in place.

"Hold on," Dr. Xu said, although she herself stood comfortably in the centre. Clive wished he could have followed her lead, but he faltered when the lift started to move as if on invisible strings. His feet wobbled at the movement and he stumbled back, bracing himself on the rails. That's when Clive caught sight of Dr. Xu giggling to herself.

The lift was fast, rising quickly up to the second level of clear cubes, and then sliding further down the warehouse till they reached where Clive guessed was about halfway, before it finally stopped. As it did, a clear set of doors slid open into the cube and Dr. Xu lifted the safety bar on the lift and signaled for Clive to step off.

Clive walked into the clear room with Dr. Xu close behind. He watched as she resecured the safety bar before the clear doors slid closed again and the lift disappeared, likely off to pick up its next rider.

"Welcome to my office," Dr. Xu said, turning around and showing off a simple room. It had three chairs off to the side with a matching white desk in the centre. The only thing Clive couldn't recognize was some sort of giant metal box, about the size of a vending machine laid out on its side.

Looking out the entrance way, Clive realized they must be over twenty-five feet in the air and because the clear walls dropped right to the concrete floor it gave the added illusion of the floor disappearing in front of him.

"It's a little freaky the first time you come in one of the pods, but I assure you it is very safe," Dr. Xu said, as if she'd been reading Clive's mind as he inched closer to the edge. Building up his courage, he stepped close enough to the edge to be able to peer down and get a glimpse of the workers below, admiring the organized chaos of the main level now with a bird's-eye view.

"A little freaky seems to be a common theme here," Clive mused as he turned back around to face Dr. Xu, who was tapping away at yet another hologram, only this one was shining up from her desk.

"You have no idea," Dr. Xu said, giving the chair near the desk a pat to let Clive know he should have a seat.

"Does everything get made in here?" Clive asked, striding across the room and taking a seat in the chair closest to the desk.

"Made? No." Dr. Xu reached into her desk and pulled out a leather-bound bundle. She placed it on the top of the desk, untied the strap, and rolled out the carrier, which was filled with various tools Clive didn't recognize. He thought some reminded him of mini screw drivers. From another drawer, she pulled out a tiny device no bigger than a cashew before glancing over and visually examining Clive's ear.

"But most things are invented here, unless they are chemical or living. Those developments are done in separate labs, for obvious reasons. Tilt your head for me please." Clive tilted his head away for a moment and she made an approving sound. "Would you prefer your right ear?" she asked.

"I haven't actually thought about it, to be honest. I only just learned what these things were yesterday."

"Impressive piece of technology if you ask me, and I'm not just saying that because I helped invent them." Dr. Xu chuckled to herself. "They take real-time translations and match the tonal output of the speaker to give a smooth translation in any language."

"Impressive," Clive said, and Dr. Xu laughed.

"I hope so. It was my life's work," she said, tossing out the comment as if it wasn't a huge deal. She picked up the cashew-sized earpiece and a tiny spray bottle she'd pulled out of her bundle. She casually misted the earpiece and wiped it down with a cloth before placing it in Clive's ear.

"Why didn't you develop it on the mainland?" Clive asked her, and she responded with an irritated look.

"I did. But my work got purchased and buried in a pile of litigation and patent infringements, because the original design was too similar to the hearing aid. I'll admit it offers many of the same benefits. Only mine is so much cooler," she said with a wink.

"Let me guess, Grace Alice picked you up and said you could build it here on Atlantis without infringement?" Clive said, trying not to sound cynical.

"Not quite," Dr. Xu said with a smile. "I found her. I'd heard she was planning some sort of international project on the ocean. International usually means multiple languages, so it wasn't too difficult to convince her my tech might be of value for her project. She gave me a year and I've been here ever since." Dr. Xu said, as she twisted something in his ear and the nut thing snuggled into place. "Now, does that feel comfortable?"

"Yeah, a little weird but not bad," Clive said, fighting the urge to rub his hand over his ear.

"Well, that's all I need from you right now," Dr. Xu said, standing up and clapping her hands together. "You're welcome to stick around if you have the time. It will be about an hour. Or I can have it delivered to your room this evening?" Dr. Xu said with a courteous smile.

Looking at the time, Clive realized that not only did he have the time, he was curious to learn more about Atlantis from someone who had lived here for so long.

"Happy to stay," Clive said with a wide grin.

"Wonderful, you can just stay right here then," Dr. Xu said, removing his earpiece and walking over to the large machine in the corner. She slid open one of the glass panels on top and placed the earpiece into a tiny holder. Clive stood to get a better look.

"It's a 3D printer. It's scanning the template I've made, which luckily fit you very well." She pressed a button on the side of the machine and a red light started scanning the earpiece. "It will take the dimensions of the unit and simultaneously add in the different electrical elements as it prints it out."

"So, it will print out a interpreter?" Clive asked, amazed. He looked at the machine and noticed three other windows, two of which were also being used. Clive guessed he wasn't the only one this morning in need of an interpreter.

"Printing I've never felt gives the machine enough credit. It is taking a pre-existing design and building that design into a new shell for you to wear. It's like a tiny elf. Every time it still feels like magic," Dr. Xu said, leaning in to watch as the machine started up and the first stroke was made. Clive had to admit it was hard to believe this machine was about to make the same thing he could see in Dr. Xu's ear now.

"So, you've been on Atlantis since the beginning then?" Clive asked, trying to creep his way into more of the information he needed.

"Yes, although the facility has changed drastically since then. For instance, it's no longer a facility, is it?" Dr. Xu mused as she took a seat at the desk, leaving the machine to fabricate the nuances of the device.

"I guess not. What do you mean by change?" Clive asked.

"I take it you don't know much about Atlantis, Mr. Davies," Dr. Xu asked, her eyes narrowing slightly.

"Please, you can call me Clive, Dr. Xu," Clive said, trying to sound casual as he returned to his seat. "And I confess, I don't know much other than it looked like it could be a good job for a while." Clive shrugged. Dr. Xu began to laugh.

"For a while, you say. You certainly don't sound like many of the recruits that come through here." She grinned. "Would you like some tea?" she asked as she slid up a panel from her desk, revealing a Chinese tea set.

"Sure, that would be great."

Dr. Xu pulled out two cups and a tea pot. Lifting off the top of the pot, she pressed a button on the side of the panel. A little spout under the button began to fill the pot with hot water. Then, picking up a pouch from her desk, she sprinkled in some loose tea leaves. "I hope you like green tea. It's all I have." She smiled.

"Perfect," Clive said. "What do you mean, I don't sound like most recruits?"

"Well, sure, we've had a few who come on for a project here and there, but a majority of the people who come onboard typically have their own reasons for wanting to be *here* specifically. And with the 1—" she began, but stopped herself with a smile. "I mean, being so close to the big day, I'm surprised." Dr. Xu put the lid back on the tea and let it rest a moment.

Clive knew she was referring to the countdown but wondered if she had possibly been about to let something else slip out, something that she shouldn't have. As much as he might have wanted to, Clive knew better then to press the point further. It was unlike most people to slip up twice.

"I'm here to help finish the sublevel pipelines, and I suppose it's because it needs to be finished before ..." He paused. "The big day."

"You would be right," Dr. Xu said with a smile. "But you won't stick around after?"

The thought hadn't really crossed Clive's mind. Since he was told about the operation, he'd always seen it as a twenty-eight day in and out, after which he could get on with his life. But he supposed that he could stay on board for a little longer, especially if he was to discover they weren't hiding anything. *Why couldn't I stay? The Navy? Was that the only reason for leaving? The obligation I feel towards the institution that raised me?*

"I'm not sure, to be honest. I have things back home that I

never really sorted out," Clive said, hoping it was enough to leave it there. Dr. Xu smiled but didn't say anything. Instead, she poured him a cup of tea and handed it to him with a slight bow of her head, which Clive reciprocated.

"Did you spend time in China, Mr. Davies?" Dr. Xu asked, her voice lacking any suspicion.

"I have. I spent a lot of time on boats traveling around the world, keeping them afloat," Clive said, finding it easy to tell a version of his own truth.

"Must have been exciting," she said, taking a sip of her tea.

Clive did the same and the warmth of the green tea sank into his body. He hadn't had anything like this since he'd last been to China, over five years ago. He could still remember taking a trip into mainland China when they had been docked. He'd found himself in a temple somewhere tucked into the countryside, where he had been greeted with a similar cup of tea. The tea now reminded him so much of that experience, it was like he'd been taken right back.

"Do you enjoy the tea?" Dr. Xu asked politely.

"I do, thank you." Clive said, letting the warmth from the tea linger in his body a moment longer. "You mentioned before there were other labs. What do they do?"

"Yes, chemical and living labs. Chemical labs here aren't like other chemical labs you might think of. Here they use only chemicals they can derive from the materials grown on Atlantis, in order to create various bio plastics, containers, nutrients for plants, vitamins, enzymes for fighting of infections, basically everything we need to help keep Atlantis clean and safe. The living labs, obviously, create life. The oldest one is on Zeta level and has been working on the various plants and animals for the coral reef. I'm assuming you've seen it?"

Dr. Xu said excitedly.

Clive guessed that the living lab was what he'd gone through in order to get into the water yesterday.

"I've seen it and it was incredible," Clive said, smiling at the memory.

"Most of our divers like to take people there first. It's a particularly enticing sweet spot for young people like you." Dr. Xu chuckled affectionately.

"How'd you know I was a diver?" Clive asked, wishing it didn't sound as suspicious as he thought. It had been, it didn't faze Dr. Xu in the slightest as she tapped her LUCY.

"Your file. How else would I know your interpreter needs to be extra water resistant?" Dr. Xu said, her eyebrows shooting up playfully.

"Are there any other labs?" Clive asked, trying to turn the conversation back around to Atlantis.

"Yes, a few of different sizes. But my favourite is the atrium," she said with a wide smile.

"Wait, the atrium is a lab?" Clive asked, now genuinely confused. Dr. Xu's smile widened.

"The atrium is the largest living lab in the world," Dr. Xu said, her excitement seeming to build, and when Clive couldn't think of anything to say, she continued. "Next time you're in there, really look around. Each floor is connected through an intricate design of fungi, which help regulate the temperature and plant growth through all the levels."

"Fungis?" Clive blurted out, unable to stop himself.

"Fungi is one of the most interesting natural phenomena in the world. There is a team here in Atlantis that only studies the atrium for that reason. Not to mention the water systems that feed all of the plant life in the building. I'm not a biologist by any means, but even I have to admit that when you're in there, you can feel it." Dr. Xu seemed to be almost rejoicing over the space.

Clive thought back to earlier that morning, when he'd been in the atrium and felt as though the room had a pulse, like it was alive. *Was that just a feeling? Or was the room actually alive?*

"I swear this place continues to challenge my mind every year with new discoveries, and new fascinating people," Dr. Xu said, gesturing towards Clive.

"I'm not all that fascinating," Clive said humbly. "Look what you created. All I do is weld pipes." Dr. Xu tossed her hand aside like the interpreter wasn't a big deal.

"We are like a giant organism here. It wasn't only me that made this work possible," she said, turning her head and gesturing to the small device in her ear, "but a massive team, each one of us laying out a different piece of the puzzle. Without the work you're doing on the sublevel pipeline, our facility won't be able to pump all the water we need to keep things operational. No pipes, no atrium. Don't sell yourself short, Clive, if you are here it is because you need to be here. Everyone has a place." Dr. Xu spoke without any hint of irony, and for a moment Clive almost felt important. But the warmth in his stomach quickly turned sour as he remembered why he was there in the first place.

Although he hadn't seen anything up to this point that would make him believe something nefarious was going on, and there was always the chance that whatever information he was sent here to retrieve didn't actually exist. That their intel was inaccurate.

"There's so much tech on board, I'm surprised no one has

tried to steal it," Clive said, his voice thin.

"Why do you think that?" Dr. Xu asked, her eyes not hiding her surprise.

"It's just, I've spent a lot of time on boats and have been boarded more than once." It wasn't a lie; they had been boarded by an enemy pirate ship while he was undercover with a crew of potential arms dealers. It had been one of the more terrifying experiences of Clive's life, but that wasn't why he'd been asking. "I know what happens to people when they are unprepared."

Dr. Xu sat back and examined Clive for a long moment while she appeared to be formulating her thoughts.

"I'm sorry that happened to you, Clive," she said earnestly. "But you have nothing to fear here. Although we don't showcase our defences, I assure you Atlantis is one of the most protected cities in the world. You have nothing to worry about." Her voice was thoughtful as she spoke.

"So, Atlantis doesn't make weapons?" Clive asked, and to his surprise Dr. Xu began to laugh.

"I never said that. In fact, some here would argue Atlantis is a weapon," she said, her voice growing serious. "We, like everyone else in the world, do what we have to do in order to protect ourselves."

Dr. Xu had somehow managed to give him both a lot of information, and no information, leaving Clive confused by the entire conversation. *Did she just admit that Atlantis has been building weapons?*

"I suppose that's true," Clive said, trying to hide the various threads of doubt now tying his mind up in knots.

The rest of Clive's time in the lab was spent on miscella-neous rounds of small talk ranging from life in Canada to

Dr. Xu's time in China and how she inevitably ended up here in Atlantis. Clive had to admit, her story was far more interesting than his own, though he did have to leave out some key elements.

The time chatting with Dr. Xu was fascinating and happened to be very much the distraction he needed. So much so that they both nearly missed the small ding that rang out from the 3D printer.

"Finished!" Dr. Xu said with excitement, and she carefully opened up the machine and pulled out the interpreter. "Can you please turn your head?" Clive did, turning so that his right ear now faced her. From his seated position, his head was only slightly lower than the now-standing Dr. Xu, who gently placed the tiny device into Clive's ear. She fiddled a moment with the implant before finally flicking what Clive guessed was some sort of switch as a long beep signaled in his ear.

After the beep, it seemed nothing had actually changed—that was, until Dr. Xu began to speak Mandarin and his brain quickly felt very overwhelmed. His left ear was still recognizing that she was speaking Mandarin, but his right ear was on an almost imperceptible delay converting the foreign language to English. It was one of the stranger sensations Clive had ever felt.

"It will take a few days for your brain to adjust to the new audio feed, but when it does, you'll find it a lot easier to understand everything," Dr. Xu said. Her rhythmic Mandarin to casual English was throwing audio curve balls at him while he sat in stunned silence. Up until this point, he hadn't actually believed that what was happening could really happen, and after a short moment he burst into uncontrollable laughter. It was like he was a child again, and in a moment the impossible had been shattered. All the beliefs he carried as someone who'd spent the majority of his adult life traveling the world were now fundamentally changed.

"I take it, it's working." Dr. Xu said, mimicking his joy.

"You sound like you. I mean, it's just, how?" Clive couldn't put his words together.

"Like I said, it matches the tonal sounds of the speaker and equates that to their voice in the language you want to hear. It's distracting now, but you'll soon discover how useful it is in a room full of people." Dr. Xu laughed.

"Thank you," Clive said, his body still thrumming from the excitement, then looked at the time and realized he only had thirty minutes to get to the dive bay. "I'm sorry to run, but I should be heading to work."

"Absolutely, I've sequestered your time for long enough. Right this way," Dr. Xu said, and to Clive's surprise, she led him to the opposite wall from where they entered.

"We're not taking the lift?" Clive asked, looking at the blank white wall with confusion. Dr. Xu gave him a wide smile before pressing a hidden button in the wall that opened up an even more impressively hidden square panel, revealing an opening which housed a metal tube about six feet in diameter.

"We could, but this way is much more fun!" Dr. Xu said with a mischievous smile as she pointed at the darkened tube. "After you, Clive." She gestured for him to get into the hole.

He approached it nervously, although he wasn't entirely sure what he had to be nervous about, other than the unknown of it all. He brushed the feeling aside and with a deep breath placed his hands on two handles jutting out from the top of the tube, which he guessed were handholds to help people get in. Pulling himself up, he hopped in the tube, wondering what was about to happen, when he felt a set of small hands on his back give him a push.

"Have fun," Dr. Xu said as she began to chuckle.

Clive couldn't help but let out a little yelp as he began sliding down the dimly lit hole. It was a slide! All of the fears he'd had when he first entered the tube washed away as once again he started to laugh at the sudden and unexpected wave of joy washing over him.

It didn't take nearly as long as Clive would have liked before the slide began to slow and he could see the light at the end of the tunnel. The final section of the slide was completely open to the room. In front of him was a flashing sign, which read, "Please exit the slide area as quickly as possible. Thank you and have a nice day."

Clive hopped off the lip of the slide and spotted a yellow square with the words "Caution: Slide Exit Zone" surrounding the area beneath his feet. As he looked up he saw the entrance bay of the lab directly in front of him. Stepping out past the yellow line, Clive didn't have long to wait before Dr. Xu came sliding out of the chute, her hands covering her mouth as she laughed.

"I'm sorry, but you seemed to need a push," she said between bouts of laughter.

"You could have told me what it was!" Clive said, aware she was speaking Mandarin to him still. The awe of it still hadn't faded; he wondered if it ever really would, though he was surprised how quickly his brain was adjusting to the new speech patterns.

"Where is the fun in that?" Dr. Xu shrugged. "Besides joy is found in the moments we least expect it." She stuck her hand out as, if to ask for help getting off the slide. Clive stepped in and offered his hand, which she happily took.

"Fair enough. But you realize now I'm going to have to come back and visit," Clive said with a broad smile.

"You are welcome anytime; I have tea and a slide!" Dr. Xu said playfully.

Clive finished saying his good-byes quickly and left the lab the way same way he'd entered. It had only been an hour since he'd last been there, but once again he had no idea where he was.

"LUCY," Clive called and was momentarily shocked when he heard LUCY's voice in his interpreter.

"Yes, Clive?"

"How did you link up to my interpreter so quickly?" Clive wondered.

"Your interpreter is linked to your ID and once it was activated, I had immediate access to its system."

"Wait, so you have access to everyone's interpreters, rooms, everything?" Clive said, suddenly worried about the android presence around him.

"Not exactly. I'm coded to handle your information and no one else's. Think of me like your private server. All LUCY's are linked into a mainframe where information is stored, and we are able to share new and relevant information with each other, but we are unable to share personal data we collect. Does this make sense?"

Clive didn't know if he'd understood it entirely, and he certainly had more questions, but he had to admit that what he took away from it did seem to make him feel mildly better.

"Sure, but how—wait no," he said, catching himself and the time, "I was actually wondering if you could guide me to the dive bay," Clive asked politely.

"Sure, Clive. Continue down the hall you're in now," LUCY said, and Clive followed.

It didn't take long for LUCY to get Clive to the dive bay. He was happy with the walk, and being able to mindlessly follow LUCY's directions, as it gave him ample time to consider all of the information he'd learned that morning from his chat with Dr. Xu. *Had she really implied that Atlantis itself was a weapon? And if it was, then what exactly did that mean for everyone onboard? If it was a weapon, did that mean that Five Eyes was planning on destroying the entire city? But what did that mean for the citizens of Atlantis?*

Dr. Xu and Squints both made it seem that, unlike himself, they weren't in a position to, or rather they wouldn't want to, leave. Would that change if they were going to be destroyed? One fact remained: Clive still didn't have any proof of what was actually happening. He needed to wait, keep his head down, and hope that something would reveal itself soon.

10

The next few days flew by as Clive began to settle into a routine on Atlantis. There hadn't been too much in the way of discovery, at least not with regards to any potential weapons they may have on board.

At first Clive had been diligent about always carrying the USB key, in case an opportunity came up for him to use it. But he quickly realized that it was highly unlikely he was going to randomly walk into the Atlantis server rooms and be able to place the key inside. So, he figured it was better to keep it safe in his room rather than risk having it fall out of his pocket and losing it.

He needed to think outside of the box, so Clive decided to change things up. Since he had a day off, he thought it would be worthwhile to spend the morning walking around the topside of the city, which everyone referred to as sky side. He hadn't been back up there since he'd arrived at the city on the Halo. He'd spent a majority of his time exploring the sublevels of the city, and he figured now would be as good a time as any to discover what else was out there.

As it happened, there wasn't much to be found, at least not at first glance—nothing other than a few non-lethal defence weapons, which were standard on any vessel that had the potential for incursions at sea. He'd even spotted a few less-standard military grade anti-air and subsonic defence weapons. But there hadn't been anything Clive would have deemed out of the ordinary.

One of the more interesting defence tools he spotted was a high-accuracy EMP rifle, the first he'd ever seen in person. He was told by one of the maintenance workers that it had the ability to disrupt control frequencies from up to six kilometers away. In theory, this meant they could wipe out all weapons' capabilities in an aircraft without damaging the engines, meaning whoever was there to attack them would still be able to fly back to where they came from. It was one of the more polite weapons Clive had seen.

The entire trip might have been uneventful, had it not been for the fact he was happy for the chance to explore more of the city, and the people who worked sky side. They lived completely different lives from everyone on the sublevels.

Because they spent a majority of their days up on deck, they found alternative ways of having fun, which were more in tune with the life Clive was used to from his days living on the boats in the Navy.

One of the things that caught Clive's eye was the construction of various makeshift pools using steel rods and a fishing net to act as a barrier between them and the marine life. Given it was such a hot day, there had been multiple ones set up all around the edge of the city.

Clive had been invited to go for a swim in one by a maintenance guy named Oli, who had planned on taking a break before completing his work on the various solar panels he was tasked with for the day.

Oli, Clive learned, was originally from Nevada, single, and

absolutely loved living on Atlantis. He was all too happy to talk to Clive about anything he wanted.

"What are they doing?" Clive asked Oli when he spotted some guys in white coveralls with large packs on their backs spraying the ship with some sort of clear liquid.

"Not totally sure," Oli said as he kicked his feet in the water and looked where Clive was pointing. "They've been doing that for the past couple of days, some sort of new polymer they are testing out. Likely has something in it to protect the outer rim from all the salt water? But I don't know." Oli shrugged.

"Must be important if they are in those damned suits in this heat." Clive laughed and continued to watch them spraying for a little while longer. "What was I saying? Right, so you wouldn't leave?"

"It's too good of a position to ever give up," said Oli. He was lounging in an innertube wearing a navy-blue bucket hat and white Oakleys, thick zinc cream covering his nose. They all popped against his dark-tanned skin. "Not to mention the people here seem to actually be trying to modify the solar industry. I don't think you'd be surprised if I told you the measures taken on the mainland tend to be a one foot in, one foot out kind of deal. It's become so political that nothing will ever really get done." He picked up a beer from his innertube's cupholder and took a swig.

"So, you think the tech here is better?" Clive asked, his own body sprawled out on a floating mattress. Oli laughed.

"Better doesn't begin to describe it. Look, I'm not a specialist by any means, but the shit these people are using, just on the outer ring alone, makes the mainland stuff look like a toy from a Kinder Surprise." He took a quick drink before diving back into his point. "They are constantly applying new tech, looking at reflective capability, anti-reflective panels. Some of them have been set up to store energy to test the max load each can have," Oli said excitedly.

"What does any of that mean, Oli?" Clive said, laughing.

"It means they can store energy in a device and use it later. There is a network of them all across the top of the city, and all they do is store energy, waiting for it to be used for something."

"Wait, so you're saying there are power stations on the ship that don't send power anywhere?" Clive was confused.

"Well, not nowhere. Just nowhere right now. They all seem to be wired into the same connection feed, but right now all they're doing is trying to build up their reserves. My guess is they are trying to achieve one hundred percent efficiency, or at least as close to that as they can get," Oli said with a shrug.

"Why would they need that?" Clive asked. Oli shrugged again.

"Well, in theory, if they were hooked up to a device that had a similar output to the design loop of the panels storage, they would recharge at the same rate or faster than the device that would be using the power."

"Dumb it down for me, Oli."

"Right, sorry, basically the device could run indefinitely. At least in theory. No one has ever been able to achieve anything greater than eighty-six-point-six percent, and no one has ever been crazy enough to store the energy in the unit itself." Oli laughed. "Then again, no one has spent that much time on it."

"Why not?" Clive asked, warning bells going off in his head.

Oli was very descriptive as he placed his hands together and in a smooth motion erupted them towards the sky with a hushed, "Boom." Clive nodded his understanding.

"How bad would it be, if the power was used all at once?"

"What do you mean?"

"Like what if they decided to channel that much energy into something, like, say, a weapon?"

"A weapon?"

"Hypothetically." Clive shrugged. He could tell the question made Oli uneasy.

"Honestly, I don't know that much about weapons. But if it's storing one hundred percent power and it erupted here … the city, the reef, not to mention millions of gallons of water would likely be vaporized."

"Holy shit. Aren't you concerned?" Clive asked.

"I think I would be, if they hadn't explained the multiple layers of fail-safes in place to release the energy if anything seems amiss. Look, I know they do some crazy things in this city, I mean we're floating over a man-made reef for Christ's sake. But, from what I know, they have always been open about answering the concerns we have. In fact, Carrie, one of my leads, had a similar concern and they performed the fail-safe for her to demonstrate what would happen. It was only at sixty-two percent at the time, but the flush of energy was enough to run the general operation of the ship for a week. It was wild. And it worked," Oli said, kicking his toes in the water.

"So what could the city need that much consistent power for?"

"Who knows, but my money is on whatever they plan to announce in twenty-two days."

"Why would you say that?"

"Grace Alice and a couple of scientists I hadn't seen before have been up this way a lot since they made the announcement. Especially to look at the storage bays. My guess is that's the team working on whatever it is the power will be used for."

"But you have no idea what that could be?"

"I'm not sure my imagination is big enough to guess what they're planning. I'm still trying to wrap my head around the underground gardens of Babylon and being able to talk to Chinese people," Oli said, shaking his head. But whatever it is, I'm sure it will be cool as shit!" Oli laughed. *So, the city is looking for a way to have a continuous source of power. But what on earth needs that much power?*

Oli rolled off the inner tube and into the water, leaving Clive alone with his thoughts on his little floating bed. He couldn't help but wonder who the scientists were working on the project with Grace Alice. He suspected he knew one of the faces would be that of Dr. Nowak. Meaning whatever the power supply was would most likely be used for project Blue Crest.

Given Dr. Nowak's history of attempting to weaponize thermal energy for the US military, Clive guessed whatever they were planning would act as a golden arrow for the city of Atlantis—something to suggest the rest of the world either plays nice or pays. This was the first real proof that Atlantis was planning something big and potentially dangerous.

But was this enough information for Clive to forward to Commander Hammond? No doubt he would reply back with "Get the key into their system," which had become a common mantra after each transmission. As if Clive hadn't been trying to find a way to plug the key into the main server. It wasn't enough to just use the general access point in his room or the research bay, which he'd tried with both. The key would only be useful if it was directly linked into the primary servers, and Clive still had no idea where they were located.

It wasn't as if there had been signs put up to say *Primary servers this way!* And even if there had been, there was the simple matter of getting into them. Clive highly doubted they let just anyone in.

In the end, Clive opted to leave out the information about the power supply until he managed to find more facts. *Was it the right call? Who cares? I'm the one on the ship, and it's my call.*

That was enough to put his mind at ease.

Which was good, because as it turned out, the rest of the week had been nice and simple. No more mention of anything about weapons or solar panels. He woke early each morning and had fallen into the routine of picking up breakfast from Kissa. Now that he could actually communicate with her, he'd learned she was eighteen and her dream was to practice medicine on Atlantis. Kissa had started to work at the café when she arrived two years earlier, in the mornings before she went to class.

Clive, who had never been much of a school person himself, was eager to learn what the school system was like on Atlantis. Given that nothing ran as he'd anticipated so far, he imagined school would be no different.

Once he'd enjoyed his morning chat with Kissa, he'd head out to explore and wander through various parts of the atrium. After what Dr. Xu had told him about it being alive, he couldn't unsee the magic of it all. When he was finished with his exploration, and his breakfast, he would head off to work.

Squints had never stopped being the same exciting and chatty person Clive had met on day one, and the fact that he could now chat to Clive in Portuguese had somehow managed to turn him into even more of a talker.

Dr. Xu had been right, it had only taken a couple days to get used to the interpreter in his ear. Clive might have gotten used to it sooner, but he'd been trying to keep a low profile, and Squints hadn't been exaggerating when he told him how little they worked. So, between Squints and Kissa, Clive still hadn't met a ton of people to practice the new device with. Not that he was complaining about the work, it was a regimented yet very relaxing work schedule. Each day they would take on a project to complete, which would usually take about six or seven hours. And Squints tried to work about four days a week, breaking it up as he liked to spend more time at home. It was hardly the months on, months off kind of work Clive had been used to. He found the days flew by and the work was actually fun.

The biggest surprise had come after his first shift, when two hundred and fifty credits were deposited into his account.

"The hell is this?" Clive had asked. When he showed Squints his LUCY, all he did was laugh.

"We are paid per day here. The credits will be added after each shift automatically," Squints said before giving him a comforting "It's okay" pat on the back.

Seeing as Clive had estimated that he'd spent roughly sixty credits on food before his first paycheck, he figured he would never spend anything remotely close to the million credits they gave him when he arrived.

"What about rent?" Clive had asked, trying to figure out just where his credits were supposed to go.

"All housing is free on Atlantis," Squints said with a grin.

"So how the hell am I supposed to spend all of these credits?" Clive said, only partially sarcastic.

10

"I think the point is, you can't. They explained to me, nothing in your life should be about the money. You should do it because you want to do it."

"That seems too good to be true." Clive tried and failed to hide his mistrust.

"Maybe, but what's the point of making all of these advancements in the world, creating things that should help make life easier, if all we're doing is leaving the people they replace in the dust? What happens when people in the world no longer serve a purpose?" Squints said with a shrug. "I've had too many friends who've lost jobs because of so-called "technological advancements." Something that was pitched to them as making it easier, that really existed to make someone else more money. What good is that if people can't afford to buy anything? Maybe it's about time that we moved into a little too good to be true."

Squint's words had made an impact on Clive, and each day he watched his bank account grow, despite continuing to eat and do whatever it was he wanted in the city. Even after a couple weeks of living in the city and seeing everyone in the same boat as him, he didn't know if he was ready to believe in such a socialist idea. Sure, it worked now, and the theory sounded good in practice, but surely it would eventually crumble. Once humanity sunk its teeth into it, someone would find a way to exploit it.

Or maybe Clive was simply just cynical, having watched as changes made with good intentions popped up, only to be manipulated by people with the power to do so. Politicians claiming one thing, then hiding behind a party line while they do another, humanitarian aid being funded by the various industries who helped destabilize the situation in the first place, green products being sold in plastic containers. Maybe that was why, no matter how much good Clive saw on Atlantis, he couldn't shake the feeling that he was simply waiting for the other shoe to drop. *When will the wizard pop out and ruin the illusion?*

11

Clive arrived at the diving bay and, for the first time since arriving in Atlantis, he'd beaten Squints there. From what Clive knew about Squints, he was rarely late for anything. So when he walked into the locker room, Clive got the distinct impression something was off.

Squints's button-down shirt had been tucked in, but only barely, and his short, cropped hair was sticking up on the sides as if he had only just fallen out of bed and stumbled his way here.

"Jesus, Squints, you look terrible," Clive said, not bothering to hide the surprise in his voice. As if his body was trying to confirm Clive's estimations, Squints let out a massive yawn that he tried and failed to cover up before he answered.

"Tell me what you really think," he said in stifled Portuguese, and even the interpreter was able to pick up the nuance in his words, as they came out slower, and included the tail end of a yawn.

Clive couldn't tell when exactly it had happened, but over the last few days he'd hit the point where he no longer noticed the interpreter was working, and was able now to have a full conversation with anyone, in any language, in real time. Even if the person he was talking with wasn't their normal self. *Or maybe that was just with Squints?*

"What is going on? You okay to go out today?" Clive asked him.

"Yep. No, don't worry about me, I was just up late helping Ilyana with her history assignment. It ended up taking longer than I thought, and I didn't get that much sleep. But I'll be fine once I hit the water." He let out another tight-lipped yawn.

"We can push till later, or tomorrow?" Clive suggested.

"No, I promised Mia I would take her diving tomorrow. I'll be fine. I've done more work on less sleep before," Squints said as he grabbed his gear and made his way into the change room.

After a few minutes, just as Clive was wondering if he should go check on Squints and make sure he hadn't fallen asleep on the change room bench, he finally walked out, fully dressed and looking at least half prepared for the day.

"Let's hit the road! There's a final weld on a pipe I thought would be cool today. You'll get to see the testing process, which you haven't seen yet. Should be fun." Squints visibly hid a yawn as he tried to smile, his eyes tightening up in the process.

"You sure we don't want to just do a simple attachment? We can just take it easy today," Clive said.

"Don't be silly, this is going to be fun!" Squints said, this time sounding more like his regular self.

They hopped in the TOTS shuttle and traveled down to the sublevel dive bay, where Squints selected the task he'd had in mind, then the two of them jumped in the water to head out.

The unit they would be welding was already in place by the time they arrived, with the robots bracing the missive pipe in place. Someone had already done one half of the pipe before they got there. This left the final connection of the pipe back into the internal plumbing system of Atlantis.

"What does this pipe do exactly?" Clive asked, trying to trace the pipes up and down the exterior of the city. It had only just occurred to him he'd never really asked about what any of the various pipes they'd been working on did. It took Squints a second to respond as he too studied the exterior pipe.

"It's a cooling line. It will take water from the lower parts of the ocean and run that water through various sections of the city to help regulate the core temperature of the entire place," Squints said.

"What needs to be cooled down in the city?" Clive asked.

"The server room, the power room, the engine room. Those are just a few off the top of my head."

"Engine room? Why would the city need an engine room?" Clive asked skeptically.

"What's the point in living on the ocean if you're stuck in one place?" Squints said with a shrug.

"Wait. You mean to tell me the city can move?" Clive asked, trying to not sound shocked.

"Not yet, but that's the plan," Squints said, turning to face Clive. "You didn't think they would just sit in one place forever, did you?" He laughed.

Clive didn't know what he thought, but he hadn't imagined the city could move. He tried to understand what that would mean for the rest of the world, to have a city that could travel freely throughout the ocean.

"I guess I just never expected it. What else can it do?" Clive asked, as he settled into a good starting place and began welding around the pipe. Clive and Squints had begun to fall into a good rhythm, starting on opposite sides of the space and working their way around to finish off where the other had started.

"Tons," Squints said yawning through his comms and Clive was not sure if he was up for this type of conversation today. But they had six hours to kill and it was probably best to keep Squints chatting. "Well, you know how it started off as a research vessel?"

"Yeah." Clive remembered he'd been told this on his first day.

"Well, they designed the entire thing to be one massive research facility, constantly monitoring the water for temperature changes." Squints's usual excitement started to build as he spoke. "They fitted the outside of Atlantis with thousands of thermometers to read the temperature, as well as additional air pressure sensors topside. This means they can predict weather surges more accurately than anywhere else in the world."

"So that storm when I first arrived? They knew it was coming?" Clive asked.

"Not just knew, but knew when it would start, when it would end, and the severity of the storm," Squints said. "That one happened to be a category one hurricane."

"I barely felt that storm!" Clive laughed. "How is that possible?"

"The city is built to withstand the natural flow of the ocean, so no matter how big any of the waves get, we maintain an element of normalcy. Don't get me wrong. If you're on Alpha, Beta, or Gamma, you'll feel woozy. But that's why those are mostly offices and research labs. Pretty much all of the living quarters are on the lower levels." Squints was sounding almost normal at this point.

"I guess that makes sense." Clive had never manned a submarine before. The idea of being trapped in a small space for so long never seemed that appealing. *Ironic.* Most of his work had been topside on various cruisers and a few battleships. He remembered hitting a few storms that were impossible not to feel, the waves crashing into the ship as the water rolled across the top. Getting stuck in a storm was not for the faint of heart, and not something Clive would wish on someone's first outing. But he knew submarines didn't have the same issues; they could travel under the most turbulent waters and no one onboard would even bat an eye. It still wasn't enough for him to want to try it out. But something didn't add up.

"Wait, even if we're under water, the top of the city is still rising and falling like forty feet on the waves. Wouldn't that mean that we would still feel the shift even in the sublevels?" Clive asked, imagining an iceberg going over a wave.

"Smart." Squints laughed. "I wondered if you would catch that. Atlantis is a closed network, so anything and everything can be adjusted."

"Including the air pressure," Clive said, catching on to his train of thought. "You don't see the motion and your ears don't feel the motion, so you don't get motion sickness."

"Correct, my friend," Squints said, and Clive could almost hear the smile on his face. *Maybe he was right, all he needed was to get into the water.*

"Any other fun facts I haven't learned about?" Clive asked as he muddled his way through a particularly stubborn section.

"Well, you know how I said they want Atlantis to move?" Squints said after taking a few moments to think about the question.

"Yep." Clive replied as he bonded a new piece of the pipe to the ship.

"Well, there is a section in Delta III that acts as an internal waste management facility. No, I'm not talking about our poop, that is a different section of the city and you'll be either relieved or concerned to hear that it's used for soil generation." Squints laughed when he heard the groan from Clive. "Waste not, want not. So why have this waste facility? And before you make the obvious point, we don't use anything on this ship that isn't either reusable or compostable. So why would we need it?" Squints said, pausing as if to give Clive a moment to think. But despite his best efforts, Clive had no idea why that would be of importance.

"I give up. Why would Atlantis have a recycling plant?" Clive said, his voice inflecting upwards at the end as if he were walking into a knock-knock joke.

"Each level of the city is outfitted with a through line that is designed to pull plastics and waste from the ocean. They are sent to the waste management facility to be sorted and repurposed on the ship or—and here is the cool part—they have a bacteria that can eat and break down plastics. So they are able to compost pretty much everything they bring in and are unable to use. How cool is that?"

At this point Clive shouldn't have been surprised to learn that the facility in the ocean was also designed to help clean the ocean. I guess if your plan is to live out here, you might as well keep it clean. Not that it's been a huge mandate on the mainland, though Clive suspected that was one of the reasons for the condition of the oceans.

"That is very cool, Squints. How did you learn about that?"

Clive asked.

"Would you be surprised if I told you Mia was the one who found out about the facility and requested a tour of it almost immediately after she heard?" Squints laughed.

The couple of times that Clive had met Mia, she had shown an incredible love for the ocean. Clive could tell it made Squints happy when she decided she want to learn how to dive, because obviously it was something that meant a lot to him as well.

"No, it wouldn't." Clive laughed, knowing Mia was unafraid to ask for what she wanted, especially when it was something that she cared about. "I bet she'd practically forced you to agree to take her out into the water tomorrow."

"Come on, Clive, you know I will never have to be forced out into the water," Squints said with a laugh. "But yes, she didn't really give me much of a choice on the matter."

The day passed steadily, and despite his pace being a little slower than normal, Squints was thankfully as prepared as always. Likely years of practice being overworked gives a guy the ability to dig through the sleepiness.

At about the three-hour mark, Clive and Squints agreed to take a break and with a little help from LUCY they ordered in some lunch, which they hoped would arrive shortly after they got back inside. Clive wasn't surprised when Squints only managed a couple of bites of his pizza before he laid down on one of the hanging chairs in the lounge that overlooked the water and dozed off for the remainder of the break.

Clive decided it wouldn't do either of them any harm to let Squints sleep a half hour longer. It meant he was able to relax a little longer and enjoy another coffee and the particularly tasty sandwich he'd had sent down. By the time Clive finished his coffee and his food, Squints was waking up from his nap and seemed grateful for the extra time.

"Let's go finish this bad boy up," Squints said as the two geared up and hopped back in the water.

The rest of the day carried on without any hiccups. The pair talked endlessly about everything from various dives they'd been on to different meals they'd had. Other than the occasional yawn, Squints managed things alright, and Clive was relieved that despite taking a little longer, they finished up the pipe in good time.

"Looks like we're good for a test run, I think," Squints said excitedly as Clive swam over to meet up with his friend.

"Why are you getting so pumped for this test?" Clive asked, his own excitement building despite himself.

"So much of what we do is task work. I rarely get to see what the project looks like when it's finished," Squints said with a little shrug. "I guess it's just nice to see that when we finish something, it eventually gets put to good use. A kind of reminder of why we do it." Squints let the words sink in as he examined the rim of the pipe. "LUCY, prepare for testing of sublevel cooling pipe A4, please."

"Test of sublevel cooling pipe A4, commencing now."

There was a short rumble as the pipe fired up. Clive suspected it was more about the idea of it working and not the visual, as it seemed hard to imagine they would see anything happening.

Squints swam up to the pipe after a couple of seconds, placed his hands on it, and shut his eyes. For a long moment Clive just watched, until he became too curious not to try it.

He placed his hands on the pipe and as he did, he could feel the rushing of the water through his palms, the slight rumbling of the pipe as it forced thousands of tons of water through its system.

"Tell me again how the salt water doesn't shred the inside of the pipe?" Clive asked, his eyes still closed as he considered the nuances of floating in water as he felt that same water rushing past his hands.

"The lab created some sort of anti-corrosive liner that they use to coat the inside of the pipes," Squints said, but he seemed distracted, and when Clive opened his eyes his friend wasn't beside him anymore. He was over by the final section they had patched up. "Hey Clive, take a look at this," he said, sounding cautious.

Clive swam over to get closer to what Squints was examining and by the time he realized what it was doing, it was too late.

"Squints, move!" Clive shouted through the intercom, but he wasn't fast enough. The seal between the two pipes was weak and the bond on the welding metal had cracked. The pressure of the water inside of the pipe shot out, along with bits of debris, which hit an unsuspecting Squints. A couple of the smaller pieces sliced through his wet suit and already Clive could see spools of blood drifting out from various gashes around his body.

Clive noticed a particularly large piece had ricocheted off Squints's gill. The force of the blow had caused Squints's body to go limp.

"LUCY, shut down the test," Clive shouted as he swam over to grab his friend. At first glance none of the cuts seemed to have penetrated the skin very deeply, but that didn't mean the blood from the various wounds didn't look bad as it slowly turned the water around Squints a murky copper colour.

What bothered Clive the most was the crack that had formed in Squint's gill. The pressure from being so deep in the ocean was causing the original tiny crack to expand rapidly across the mask face. which was already beginning to take on water. It was only a matter of time before the entire thing shattered and flooded Squints's gill.

Clive thought for a moment about pulling Squints's gill off and replacing it with one of his temporary breathers from his pack but then didn't know if those worked while the user was unconscious or not, and this didn't really seem like the time to test it out. He made a mental note to ask someone later.

Squints must have been hit hard, as his body was still limp from the blow. As Clive started to examine his head, he noticed a large gash just above Squints's right ear. Clive could already see a rather large bump beginning to form around the wound, despite the cold temperatures of the water.

Clive had found himself in much worse situations in the past, and thought how lucky Squints had been that none of the metal shards had lodged in his body. Once Clive had to drag a friend two kilometers through the water to reach an extraction point. His friend had been shot twice and around the one-kilometer mark had passed out from the shock.

"LUCY, how far to the nearest oxygen station?" Clive asked, trying desperately to remember but finding it difficult while he held onto Squints.

"The nearest oxygen station is fifteen meters down. I've activated the emergency lights to help guide you to it. I've also contacted the med bay and they have been sent the vitals and initial injury assessment of Mr. Pereira. They will be waiting on standby in the dive bay to take him in." The calm in LUCY's voice was just what Clive needed to hear. He was beginning to feel like the situation was under control.

That was, until he saw the fifteen-foot great white shark swim out from the shadows less than a hundred feet from where Squints and he were floating.

12

Normally, Clive would have been excited to see a great white shark, even out in open water. Despite being so large, they preferred to eat things that were a little smaller than Clive.

However, something wounded would be right up their alley, so holding an unconscious Squints, who was bleeding all over the place, wasn't the most ideal scenario to be caught in with a shark.

Make that two sharks, Clive realized, as he caught a glimpse of another, slightly smaller, great white drifting a little further above them. This unfortunately meant they were likely some sort of hunting party, and Clive and Squints were welcome guests.

"LUCY, you wouldn't happen to have any defence against predatory animals, say, like a shark or something," Clive said as he slowly began swimming backwards, dragging Squints along with him. He tried to keep as close an eye as he could on the two sharks while making sure there wasn't a third lingering underneath where he was now swimming. Luckily, from what he could tell, it was just the two sharks. Regrettably, those two sharks stalked closer despite Clive's efforts to get away.

Clive knew it was only a matter of time before one of them

attempted to nip at them, to get a sense of how much effort a kill like this would be. The way they were swarming them now left Clive with little doubt that they were here to feed if they could.

"There is a cage outfitted at the oxygen station. I can activate it now so that it's prepped for when you arrive." LUCY was so calm, it was agonizing to listen to as Clive's heart thrummed in his ears.

"That would be great, thank you, LUCY," Clive said with more than a hint of sarcasm.

"Squints, wake up, man!" Clive shouted over the comms. He began to shake his friend, causing fresh red rivers of blood to leak out from his wet suit and his head. It was no use, Squints was out cold and, to make matters worse, the crack in his gill had gotten larger. It was only a matter of time before the entire thing filled with water and he began to choke.

Clive ignored the heavy feeling in his gut and continued to slowly propel his body downward, turning only briefly to make sure he was still in line with the flashing yellow light. It was now about seven meters away; he only needed to survive a short while longer.

As if knowing their prey was about to get away, the larger of the two sharks moved in tighter, closing the gap to a little less than two of its massive body lengths. Thinking they were coming for them, Clive did his best to cross Squints's arms across his chest as he hugged him as tightly as he could with one hand. With his other hand, Clive managed to crisscross Squints's ankles and quickly pulled his thighs up to his chest. He wrapped his own legs around Squints's body until the two of them were tucked into as tight of a ball as Clive was able to make. This meant the only dangling piece of meat the shark could go for was the arm Clive was now using to slowly propel them towards safety.

It didn't give him much comfort, though, as the shark approached and opened its gaping mouth, revealing long, jagged teeth. But the size of their human ball was too big and the shark turned away as its nearly one-ton body of pure muscle slammed into Clive, pushing him off course and slamming him into one of the metal walls of Atlantis. A searing pain shot down Clive's shoulder as he collided with the city, causing him to lose the grip he'd had on Squints. The two of them began to drift slowly apart.

The force of the blow must have fractured what little structure remained in Squints's gill, as it was now filling rapidly with the surrounding ocean. It wouldn't be long before he began breathing in salt water.

Looking up, Clive barely had time to react as the second shark barreled down towards them, veering toward Squints as his limp body starfished out, giving the shark an appetizing view of his displayed appendages.

Before he had time to think, Clive launched himself off the wall of the city towards his friend, embracing Squints's flailing arms and pulling them and his body as tight to Clive's own body as possible. Clive wrapped his legs around Squints, but not before the shark barreled past them, its sharp teeth grazing the side of Clive's right leg as it passed, its huge body nudging them further out to sea.

Clive ignored the new and painful sensation and the fresh rivulets of blood surrounding them. He also tried to suppress the strong desire to scream out in agony. He'd got lucky, all things considered, and it was only a matter of time before their luck would run out.

Squints's own luck, whether he was aware of it or not, was quickly dissipating as his mask has nearly completely filled with water. Clive wished he had more time to think, but now was the time for instincts, not thinking, and his instincts were screaming at him to *get to the damned cage right now!*

Clive began to pump his legs as fast as they were able. He hadn't taken the time to examine how bad the cut had been on his leg because it didn't matter, the only thing that mattered was making sure he and Squints made it to the cage before the sharks decided to make another run at them.

Clive stopped bothering to look for the sharks, well aware that he and Squints were in their territory and their only option at this point would be to somehow make themselves a less appealing target, or get a few lucky attacks in by poking at an eye or kicking their gills. But to do so meant being in front of them, and their teeth, and since Squints was currently unconscious and Clive only had one good leg, it was unlikely he would win in a standoff.

The cage was less than four meters away. All Clive needed to do was fight through the pain. Taking a cautionary look behind him, he caught a glimpse of one of the sharks coming back round. It was currently about a hundred feet away, which did little to invoke confidence in Clive, as he knew the prehistoric creature could easily close that gap.

"LUCY, prep the cage to close!" Clive shouted the words, as if there was some chance that LUCY wouldn't hear him. LUCY's calm voice did nothing to make him feel better. The nagging thought that LUCY would go on existing no matter what the outcome would be made his blood boil. That's when an idea struck him.

"LUCY, can you override one of the spare oxygen masks

to release a bunch of oxygen into the water?" Clive said frantically, turning his head to see the shark had already covered more than half the distance. If he was going to do something, it needed to be now.

"Yes—" LUCY started to say.

"DO IT! Release as much as you can!" Clive shouted. He saw one of the oxygen masks disconnect from the wall. For a what felt like an eternity, Clive watched as the shark rushed forward, its meter-wide maw opening up wide to reveal layers of sharp, jagged teeth sticking out from fleshy pink gums.

Clive's breath caught in his throat as a sudden rush of bubbles shot out over his head towards the shark's mouth, the sudden shock of the explosion causing the shark to pull away and dart off in another direction. Clive let out a long, slow breath as he pulled Squints into the cage, unable to distinguish between the rush of air around him and the thumping of his pulse. Looking down to celebrate with his friend, he was immediately reminded as to why he needed to get to the wall in the first place, as he took in the murky red water around them.

"LUCY, shut down the oxygen and close the door," Clive said, sounding a little bit more level-headed now that he was in the safety of a steel cage.

The cage door closed in front of them as the bubbles from the oxygen stopped. Clive finally let out a long breath he hadn't known was caught in his body and silently congratulated himself on a strategy he'd had no idea would work.

Acting quickly, he pulled off Squints's gill and placed a new mask over his head. As the bubbles began to dissipate around them, Clive felt a crash as the second shark made an attempt to reach them. Clive ignored the shark, knowing the pair would eventually give up now that their prey was no longer accessible. He needed to focus on getting Squints breathing again.

"LUCY, can you start the air flow into his mask." Clive's biggest concern was that he didn't know just how long Squints had been without oxygen, though he surmised the whole ordeal couldn't have been more than four minutes. This meant Clive only had another minute or two to get Squints breathing again before he'd run the risk of permanent brain damage. He also needed to clear his airway of any water he might have ingested.

The air flowing into the mask had already started to flush out the excess water in the mask, and after a few seconds the mask was emptied, but Squints still hadn't started to breathe. Clive hoped he hadn't miscalculated how long Squints had been out; he hadn't exactly been counting while he was swimming away from the sharks.

Clive turned Squints's body away from him and wrapped his arms around him, then, locking his wrists together, he squeezed tightly in and up against his belly. Behind him, one of the sharks banged its body up against the cage. The two were now swimming closer to the cage, hovering around, waiting for another opportunity to attack. Clive reminded himself they were safe in the cage, and now was the time to focus on getting Squints breathing again.

With a firm grip, he heaved his hands into Squints's gut, trying to force up any water and air he had left in his lungs to clear them out. After a four good pulls, Squints finally gagged and vomited up a good amount of water into his mask. A second cough splatted more bile-looking vomit against the inside of his mask. Clive watched as all Squints's bodily fluids were slowly pushed out and released into the water.

"Squints!" Clive turned his friend around and began to examine him. His eyes were red and puffy, no doubt burning from a combination of salt water and vomiting, but at least they were looking back at him. Clive was relieved when Squints's shaky voice rang out.

"Clive? What the hell happened?" his voice was strained, but the important thing was, he was speaking. He began flailing his arms around in confusion and Clive was afraid he might rip off his mask.

"You were in an accident. You're still in the water. You need to keep the mask on. You stopped breathing for a bit there, buddy, do you understand?" Clive said, trying to calm his friend down as he gave his shoulders a light squeeze.

"Yes," came the slow reply. Squints had been a diver for years, and somewhere in his mind he was computing what was happening around him, even if he didn't fully know what was going on.

Just as Squints was calming down, one of the sharks bumped the cage with its tail, causing Squints to jolt upright, which likely caused fiery pain to flare up across his many cuts and wounds. He looked shocked as he backed away, watching the fifteen-foot dinosaur swim impatiently past their cage.

"Is that a… great white shark?!" he said, his sudden burst of terror bringing him back to reality.

"Yes," Clive said simply, as he turned to face it. From inside the cage, and with the threat of being bitten by one of them no longer on the table, Clive took in the beauty of the two sharks swimming around them. "Technically, two sharks," he added, gesturing to the second shark swimming nearby.

"They're impressive," Squints said, with the interest only

someone who spends a lot of time in the water can express. "We're in a cage? How did we get here? And I'm bleeding? So are you!" He pointed down at the large gash across Clive's thigh that was still oozing blood. "What the hell happened, Clive?" Squints said, rubbing his head and wincing as he felt the sharp pain along with lump that had formed there.

"I will catch you up on that later. First, I think be both need to get inside," Clive said, patting his friend on the shoulder.

"LUCY," Squints said calmly as he felt around his body for his various wounds, "take the cage to the entrance bay."

"Of course," LUCY said over the comms as the cage began to move along the side of the building, the sharks circling by one last time before swimming off into the darkness.

"I didn't know it could do that," Clive said, a little shocked and happy at the same time that he wouldn't need to swim again. His fatigue was beginning to kick in.

"You should really get a once-over of some of the capabilities of the city, especially the stuff out here. I think you'll be surprised," Squints said, his eyes shutting as he leaned back against the cage.

Clive followed suit and let the cage carry them through the water. When they finally reached the entrance bay, the adrenaline from the situation had worn off and replaced with the brutal pain he could now feel across his body. All that was left was for them to swim the short distance down the tunnel, and they would be in the city.

Clive and Squints assisted each other as they slowly swam through the tunnel, and when they reached the inside of the dive bay, they were greeted by a round of applause. The room was filled with various dive team members and medical staff all waiting to help them as best they could.

Looking up at the main screen, Clive spotted a camera feed showing where they'd just been working and realized they all must have seen what just happened. A few of the other divers lifted them out of the water and Clive happily removed his mask, dropping it to the ground as he took a deep breath.

Sun-Young and a medical officer Clive didn't know helped him onto one of the hovering medical tables that had been set up close to the pool.

"Looks like we may need you to go clean up our mess, Sunny," Clive said, his words coming out slow and weak. Sunny began to giggle.

"Don't worry, Clive, I will happily fix your mess," she said playfully. Her soft Korean voice lightened the mood, and a few people around him started to laugh. "We're just happy you're both safe." She nodded and Clive thought he saw a tear forming in her eye.

"Was it a good show at least?" Clive asked, looking at her, then around at the other divers. Some of them looked as though they'd been crying too, but they were now laughing with Clive as he laid down on the bed. The moment his head touched the pillow, he couldn't help himself from letting his eyelids fall from exhaustion.

But before he would let them close, he turned and saw Squints lying in his own bed. The two friends' eyes met for a brief moment and Clive knew Squints would be okay. He looked up towards the bright lights of the ceiling and let the soft pillow cradle his head as he drifted off to sleep.

13

Clive awoke to a gentle breeze and the rhythmic sound of beeping from the heart rate monitor he now found himself attached to. He tried to remain calm as he slowly began to remember where he was and what had happened. A stout man wearing small glasses, with a crescent moon hairline complete with a shiny bald top, stepped to the side of his bed. The older man couldn't have been more than a foot and a half higher than the bed, and Clive imagined if he could find the strength to sit up, he'd almost be looking down on the man.

"Mr. Davies," the man said in what Clive assumed was Hindi, noting the interpreter must still be in his ear. Clive's mind didn't seem to be as prepared for the language conversion, and he found it difficult to follow. "You had quite the adventure now, didn't you," he continued with a little chortle. "I'm Dr. Kashyap. I've been the one treating your wounds. You'll be happy to know that nothing was seriously damaged during your little rendezvous with the sharks. May I also add how very impressed I was with the way you saved your friends' life," Dr. Kashyap said as he placed a hand on Clive's shoulder. "Stupid. But very impressive," he mused.

"Couldn't exactly leave him," Clive said, as he slowly tried to sit up. Dr. Kashyap pressed a button and Clive was relieved when the back of the bed began to lift. He eased himself comfortably into the cushioned back rest, happy to let the bed do the work for him.

"I suppose not. But you did manage to get a fairly nasty cut on your leg, which caused more blood loss than we initially thought. I imagine most of that was after you left the water," he said as he lifted up the sheet to examine the leg. "But the good news is, we managed to get you some extra blood and the wound is healing nicely, though you will have a bit of a scar when all is said and done." He looked up at Clive. "I suspect one more scar is hardly going to make a difference," he added with a wink.

Clive hadn't imagined he'd be in a position where he would need to try and explain his numerous scars, especially to a doctor, who likely knew what each one was actually from, rather than the stories Clive told his friends.

Clive had been running special operations for the better part of six years and, needless to say, he'd had his fair share of deadly run-ins, having had to dodge a few bullets in his past, both figuratively and literally. And occasionally he hadn't been so successful at the dodging part. Clive wondered if he should be concerned about any of his secrets getting out, but the warm smile on Dr. Kashyap's face said it all.

"Doctor–patient privacy is something I take very seriously. However, I confess I wouldn't mind hearing a tale or two sometime," he said, letting out another friendly chortle.

"I promise you, they're not all that exciting," Clive lied. Some of them he imagined the good doctor wouldn't believe, and others Clive wouldn't be too eager to share with anyone. He hadn't always been proud of the work he'd needed to do.

Dr. Kashyap recognized something in Clive, but if he

wanted to follow up, he didn't press it. Instead, he got to work running through a series of tests, starting with flashing a light in Clive's eyes and touching areas around his leg to see how much pain he was in, which wasn't as severe as Clive would have imagined. Sure, it hurt like hell, and he'd likely needed crutches to help him move around for a few days, but the pain wasn't excruciating.

Considering he'd evaded being shark food, he was happy with this little reminder of how wild the ocean could be. Many people who found themselves up against a great white shark weren't so lucky to come out with just a cut.

"How's Squints?" Clive asked, silently berating himself for not asking sooner.

"Your friend is fine. He has a mild concussion from the accident, along with some cuts, but he'll make a full recovery. He'll likely be on his feet before you, given how deep your leg laceration was. Any deeper and we might have been having a very different conversation," Dr. Kashyap said as he pressed around the wounded area.

"Doesn't feel too bad," Clive said as he watched the doctor poke around his leg. Dr. Kashyap let out a short laugh.

"Right, well, let's see how you feel when the freezing wears off." Clive became aware that he couldn't feel any of the poking the doctor was doing, only that the pressure of each touch was there. He groaned at the reality of what was to come. "Don't you worry too much. I promise I have some very effective treatments for you that a couple of my team and I have been developing for times just like these. You'll be the first to get to try it," Dr. Kashyap said with a broad smile.

Somehow the idea of being the doctor's guinea pig didn't give Clive the warm feeling he'd hoped for inside.

"You've been developing treatments for shark bites?" Clive asked.

"Well yes, and no." Dr. Kashyap smiled. "For deep lacerations that are typically sutured and left to heal over time. We think we have solved the time problem, and the suture problem," he said with a wink. "I can see the concern on your face Mr. Davies! But I promise you this treatment will be the difference between a couple of days and a couple of weeks of recovery. We've mostly used it on injured animals before releasing them back into the ocean, but you're the first human with a serious wound like this that we've had the chance to try it on." Dr. Kashyap sounded every bit as excited as Clive felt nervous. *But what am I supposed to do? Turn down the opportunity to heal faster?*

"Sounds good," Clive said, before he could give himself the time to overthink it. "Can I go and see Squints?" he asked, and Dr. Kashyap gave him a solid looking over, tilting his head side to side while he thought over his response.

"I suppose we can get you in the chair, but you have to promise me you will stay put and not try and get up for any reason," Dr. Kashyap said, pointing an authoritative finger at Clive.

"You got yourself a deal. Now where is this chair?" Clive started looking around the room, before he landed on the grinning face of Dr. Kashyap.

"Hold on!" he said with a playful smile.

Clive didn't know what he should hold on to, but Dr. Kashyap walked over to the wall and picked up a little remote about the size of a large cell phone. He pressed one of its buttons and Clive began to feel the bed he was on adjust. He stopped himself from letting out a frightened gasp as his body began to lower and his legs bent down until they were at a ninety-five-degree angle with his hips. His head lifted slightly, and in a matter of seconds Clive was in a seated position on what had just been his bed. Looking around, he realized the chair, bed, thing he'd been laying in was floating off the ground with some sort of propulsion.

"Pretty cool, isn't it?" Dr. Kashyap said with an exaggerated nod. "One of the tech team invented it. It uses magnets to lift itself off the ground, which is convenient 'cause there is metal layered throughout the floor of the entire city, so we can take them anywhere." Dr. Kashyap handed Clive the little remote. "They call it a levi-bed."

"I think they used one to bring me up here," Clive said weakly.

"Most likely yes. Very handy, these things."

"I think I saw someone replace their wheelchair when I arrived, too."

"Oh yes. As it turns out, a modified levi-bed is far more reliable than the traditional wheelchair. Especially here in Atlantis. Though I'm told they're still working out the kinks for use on land. But before I get too carried away, these are your controls to move it. But take it slow, it can be a little tricky to get started." As Clive pressed the button, he jolted forward, then stopped abruptly. "Like I said, tricky. Just take your time and follow me."

Dr. Kashyap began to leave the room and Clive gave himself some space before he attempted the floating chair one more time. Clive eased into the movements as he slowly made his way out the door and into the hallway, managing to only bump the side of the door once on his way through. Dr. Kashyap must have heard the bang, as he began to chuckle to himself.

By the time Clive got into the hallway he was more confi-dent, and the extra room in the hall gave him a little more freedom to test how the chair moved and reacted to his touch. When he finally reached the room at the end of the hall where Dr. Kashyap had stopped, he felt confident he could manage the next door.

Dr. Kashyap knocked on the door and opened it slowly, and Clive could see that Squints wasn't alone. Margarida, along with Mia, Ilyana, and Martim, were all crowded around him. They must have been crying at some point, as their eyes all seemed puffy and red, and Clive began to wonder if now was the best time.

"I brought someone who wanted to see you," Dr. Kashyap said as he stepped inside and away from the door.

When they turned to face Dr. Kashyap, they spotted Clive sitting in the chair just outside the door. Margarida, who'd been holding Squints's hand, was the first to see him, and a fresh set of tears began to stream down her face as Clive entered the room. She got up and without a word embraced Clive as tightly as she could. The scene made Dr. Kashyap wince, the action likely causing more movement than he would have preferred.

"Thank you," Margarida said softly in his ear, and Clive began to feel his eyes tear up as the kids filed in and embraced him as well. "We saw what you did for him, you saved his life," she said forcing the words out through her emotion.

"He would have done the same for me," Clive said, trying to hold back his own emotions.

"I'm not sure I could have done what you did," Squints said, wiping away a few tears of his own.

"You saw what happened?" Clive asked, looking around the

room, as everyone began to nod. But it was Dr. Kashyap who spoke first.

"I'm not sure there is a person in Atlantis who wouldn't have seen it by now." He chortled to himself. "You're famous."

Clive didn't know what to make of that statement, or how he felt about everyone in the city knowing who he was. It would certainly make being under the radar a lot more difficult than it had been before.

"How did you know the bubbles would scare the shark?" Mia asked, her gentle voice carrying through the silence.

Clive looked around as the various faces in the room all began to look at him expectantly and his insides began to churn, as he felt the bile rise up in his throat.

"I didn't," he said slowly as he looked down at his lap, and the room remained silent as if they were waiting for more. "Honestly, it was just a hope." He smiled sadly.

"Bubbles," Squints said slowly, and Clive was forced to look up at his friend as he broke out into a fit of laughter, immediately dissipating the tension from the room. "I for one am happy you thought of it," he said, wiping away an entirely new set of tears.

"Me too," Clive said, as he let out a little laugh of his own.

"I'm going to leave you all to it, but I would like to keep both Mr. Davies and Mr. Pereira overnight to monitor their systems. I'll be sure to have Mr. Pereira home in time for lunch tomorrow. Mr. Davies, you may be here until dinner, but that will all depend on how our treatment goes." Dr. Kashyap grinned at Clive before turning to leave. He stopped at the door, briefly adding, "I'll be down the hall if anyone needs anything." With that, he was off, leaving the six of them in the room together.

"So." Clive was beginning to feel as if he was intruding on Squints's family time. "I should give you all some space," he said, turning the chair to leave, when Margarida put a hand on the chair to stop him.

"Stay. You're family," she said softly.

"Besides, the kids have so many questions, and seeing as I was passed out for most of it, I can hardly answer them," Squints said with a rueful smile.

"We will not be discussing that today!" Margarida said sternly and before the kids jumped in to argue, she shot a finger at them. "That's final."

The kids seemed a little disappointed, especially Mia, who Clive guessed would have had plenty of questions for him about the sharks.

Clive, who had found himself in a number of precarious situations in the past, didn't think he would have any trouble reliving the experience. He'd lived through it, after all, so what else could he ask for? He also managed to get Squints out with only minor injuries, so in his book it was a win.

However, he knew that not everyone shared his ability to compartmentalize difficult situations and not let it affect them. Despite the brave face Squints was putting on for his family, Clive could tell there was still fear and sadness behind his eyes, especially when he looked at his kids and his wife. He likely hadn't known how close he'd come to dying, and if Clive had his way, he never would. But he'd seen the video of the events already and there was nothing he could do to take that back.

"I'll just say this," Clive said slowly, catching a narrow eye from Margarida. "There was a moment when we had finally gotten into the cage and your dad was awake beside me. We were safe," he added quickly for Margarida, "when one of the sharks, which was easily fifteen feet long, swam in front of us and bumped the cage. And despite everything that had happened, it was still one of the most beautiful things I've witnessed in the ocean." Clive's mind was back in the water as the one-ton creature, made of pure muscle, glided past them, it's entire existence a testament to the power it has in the ocean. He looked up and he could see Squints looking at him, nodding in agreement.

"Awesome," Mia said under her breath as she received a cautionary glance from her mother.

"Today was just a reminder that we will always be visitors in the water. So, it is our job to leave it better than when we found it," Squints said, taking a moment to look at each of his children, who gave him a nod.

The six of them chatted a little longer, the kids finding it harder to not talk about the attack. But Margarida was steadfast in her determination not to speak of it. Eventually Margarida took the kids home because it was getting late, which seemed odd to Clive, until he discovered he'd been asleep for well over six hours.

Clive could feel the pain in his leg begin to tingle and winced as he gently rubbed it.

"How you feeling?" Squints asked, not bothering to hide that he'd seen him do it.

"Good, but I think the pain meds they gave me are starting to wear off a little," he said, giving the area around the top of the wound a tight squeeze. "But it's not bad, I swear," he added quickly, noting the look on Squints's face.

"If you want to get back to your room, that's fine, we both likely need a little rest," Squints said, sitting up to touch the button for the doctor.

"No," Clive said, lifting his arm, the gesture coming out a little more aggressive than he intended. "Honestly, I really don't mind being here. It's been nice. Beats being in the room by myself for the next few hours, twiddling my thumbs while I try and sleep." Clive laughed.

"I guess I kind of forget what it's like to not have people around," Squints said, as if he'd been reading a part of Clive's mind he wanted to keep hidden. But hearing the words out loud softened them for Clive, who nodded slowly.

"It was usually just me growing up, probably one of the reasons I … joined the ships." He caught himself before bringing up his work in the Navy. "They always had people on them, and it was nice to get to know people so well."

"I know what you're saying. Before Atlantis, it was so hard to leave the girls for weeks on end. When they were that young, three months is a long time to be away, let alone six. You always feel like you're missing so much, and the reality was, I had. But you do what you need to do, I guess, to give your family what they need," Squints said, the not-too-happy memories seeming to sink into his mind. "But one of the saving graces was a couple of the people I worked with. They made it a little easier to be away, some of them were going through similar adjustments with their own family. Misery loves company, as they say." Squints laughed sadly.

"That must have been difficult, to leave them," Clive said, seeing the sadness darken Squints's features. But he shook it off as quickly as it had come, and forced a smile back to his face.

"What about you, any family?" Squints asked.

This was a complicated question for Clive, who had never

really had much of a family. What little family he'd had came from his time in the navy, and even then, the work he'd done forced him to distance himself from them over the years. Not that he was prepared to talk about any of that with Squints right now.

"I was in the foster system in Toronto for most of my childhood. Never really knew my parents and bounced around from home to home until I was eighteen. There's really only one person, I guess, who I would call family. My foster sister, we were in the same home for seven years together. She was the only reason I might have stayed around. But she told me to go," Clive said, finding it somehow easier to share this memory, which he didn't share with many people, with Squints.

"What happened to her?" Squints said after a few moments.

"She stayed in the home for another four years. We stayed in touch and still do a little, usually a birthday card. I used to send her money when she was younger, so she could get some supplies. She's an unbelievable artist. I still do send her money sometimes, but now it's different. She still paints and lives in Toronto. But she runs an organization that helps underprivileged kids have art programs, so I donate some money to help each year." Clive felt guilty that he hadn't thought about her in so long.

"She sounds like an amazing person," Squints said and Clive responded with a small nod of agreement. "What's her name?" Squints asked after a beat.

"Hazel Davies," Clive said softly, smiling at the reminder of their connection.

"Well, she sounds great," Squints said gently. Clive tried to shrug off the emotions he was feeling.

"It's not as big as the football team you're trying to fill, but it's something," Clive said jokingly, and Squints must have realized the turn in mood, as he didn't try to bring up Hazel again.

"Well, I think they would agree that you would make a great addition to the team, especially after what you did this morning." Squints's words were light but each one fell heavy on Clive, though it felt more like a comforting blanket being tucked around his whole body.

"That's nice of you to say, Squints," Clive said, trying to keep his tone light.

"I'm serious. I know my family was happy to see you were okay." Squints tapped the side of the bed nervously. "I know I was. What you did for me … you …" The words tripped on his tongue.

"It's okay, you would have done the same for me," Clive said, pretending to look at his leg. His hands floated aimlessly over the wound.

"I wasn't joking when I said I probably couldn't have done what you did, Clive. You saved me, and I will never be able to thank you enough for that." When Clive finally looked up to meet his friend's eyes, he saw Squints was crying.

"It was nothing," Clive said, trying to tuck his own emotions back inside.

"It was not nothing," Squints said, half crying and half laughing. "What you did for me was most certainly something." He continued wiping the tears away with another laugh. "Because of you, my kids still have a father, and Margarida …" he said, the choking on the words. "Well, it was not nothing, so thank you, Clive." He blurted out this last bit while he still could and forced himself to keep looking at Clive, who had to turn away before the tears in Squints's eyes broke him.

"Anytime," Clive said, half to the floor and half to Squints. After a couple seconds, Clive looked up just in time to catch Squints trying to stifle a long yawn, his eyes closing with the effort.

Clive should have realized that Squints needed sleep. He was no spring chicken when it came to injuries and knew that what Squints needed most was rest, and here he had been trying to keep him up because he didn't want to be alone.

"Oh man! I'm tired," Clive said, forcing out a long, hard yawn, which came out a little easier than he thought it would have. "I think I should get back and get some sleep, before they try whatever it is they are going to do on me tomorrow." He grabbed his controller to turn the chair round towards the door. He knew Squints would never ask him to leave.

"You sure?" Squints said as Clive turned his head back to look at him.

"Yeah, we've had … a long day," he said with a little amusement in his voice, and the two of them laughed as Clive left the room and headed down the hall back to his room. Before he left, he took a moment to look back at Squints, who'd already fallen asleep.

14

"How are we feeling this morning, Mr. Davies?" asked a cheery-eyed Dr. Kashyap as he stepped into Clive's hospital room the next day.

"I had a surprisingly restful sleep, thank you," Clive said, still wiping the sleep away from his eyes. Given the day he'd had, he'd hardly felt like he'd be able to fall asleep—until he was given a pain pill by Dr. Kashyap when he got back to his room. He'd barely managed to convert his chair back into a bed before he was out cold.

"Well, that's what we like to hear!" Dr. Kashyap said as he scanned Clive's leg with a little device that looked like a bar code reader. After a few seconds, he pulled up several images on the screen in front of Clive. One looked like an X-ray and the others were some combination of thermal and digital imaging. Dr. Kashyap examined each for a long moment before he turned back and smiled at Clive.

"Great news! Everything looks good on our end for the procedure, and if everything goes to plan, we could have you up and walking around, possibly with a leg brace, by the end of the day," he said, his voice full of excitement.

Clive wasn't sure how any of that could be possible, as the tingling feeling was starting to return to his leg, and from what he could tell from the image, the cut had been pretty deep. *But then again, what do I know?*

"I mean, that would be amazing," was all Clive could think to say. There was a soft knock at the door and both Clive and Dr. Kashyap turned to see who it was.

"I hope I'm not interrupting anything," Grace Alice said from the doorway. She had a confidence about her. Her hair was tied back in a tight ponytail that draped over her shoulder, and she wore a beige mid-sleeve blouse, showing off a rather impressive looking LUCY on her left wrist. The other wrist was covered with a series of elegant gold bands that Clive noticed as she pulled her hand from the pocket of her well-fitted dress pants.

Clive's second impression was how gorgeous she looked, and immediately his next thought was how shabby he must look, having not showered for the better part of thirty-six hours and being wrapped in bandages. In spite of himself, he could feel his cheeks begin to redden.

"Ms. Alice! Thank you for coming," Dr. Kashyap said pleasantly, not at all thrown off by her intimidating presence. "Clive, I hope you don't mind but I've asked Grace to join us for the procedure today, to show off its capabilities. Would you mind if she accompanies my team into the surgery room?" he asked, his eyes pleading a little with the question.

"The more the merrier, Doc," Clive said with forced enthusiasm.

"Perfect! I'll prep the surgery and we should have you in there in under an hour." He skipped out of the room, but not before turning to look at Grace. "You will not be disappointed."

"I'm sure I won't be, Doctor Kashyap," Grace said with a

genuine care in her voice before the Doctor hopped off to another room, leaving Clive and Grace alone together.

"For the record, you are allowed to say no, if you would prefer to not have me in the room," Grace said, as if she had been reading his mind. "We will be videotaping the procedure for research so I can always watch that if you'd prefer. Dr. Kashyap is just … excitable," she said, turning her head to look where the doctor had just run off.

"Thank you, but honestly I don't mind," Clive said, and in the moment, he'd meant it. "It's not like I have much more to hide." He gestured to himself in the bed in his hospital gown.

"I'm so sorry, I shouldn't have just barged in," she said, flustered, and turned to leave.

"Wait! No, sorry, that's not what I meant." Clive put his hand up to stop her from leaving. He'd been trying to get the chance to talk to her since he'd arrived and here he was alone with her, and he was ruining it.

"You don't have to go. I was just kidding," he said, and when she didn't look convinced, he added, "I swear."

It must have been convincing enough, because she turned around and stayed. Glancing at the images of his leg on the screen, she began to walk over to examine them. With her back turned, Clive took the chance to make sure he was properly covered up and took a whiff of himself, though he regretted that immediately.

"Sorry, I smell," he said, wincing at the terrible topic of conversation. But he was rewarded with a pleasant laugh.

"It's okay. Given what you went through, I think I can forgive a little smell." She turned to face him and he was disarmed by her smile.

"You saw that?" Clive asked, feeling somewhat embarrassed

by the attention.

"I think you would be hard pressed to find someone who hasn't," she said with a caring smile, though the words made him feel even more embarrassed. "What you did was heroic," she added softly.

"It was nothing." He shrugged and she began to laugh again.

"I'm not sure what kind of things you've done in your past that makes you think evading sharks and saving a man's life is nothing." Clive wondered if she had somehow known more about him then she was letting on. But her words hadn't been invasive in any way, so maybe she was just being kind.

"Maybe you can tell me what is going on with this procedure?" Clive asked, wanting to change the topic.

"Doctor Kashyap is a brilliant man, but he is not the best at explaining things, is he?" Grace mused as she took a step closer to Clive. She stopped and pointed to the screen. "I brought Dr. Kashyap and his team onboard because they had been developing a biological compound that, when combined with the precise heat and proteins from a source material," she said, pointing at Clive, "are able to—" She paused while she tried to think of the right words. "Knit the muscle and skin tissue together. The result is an almost immediate healing of the cell tissue."

"That's … awesome," Clive said, his vocabulary failing him. All he could think about was all the times something like this would have been useful. "Why have I never heard of it?"

"That's one of the problems with the mainland. There are hoops people need to jump through to get particular medicines and techniques approved for use on people. Often the cost associated with the procedure is too high and no one wants to invest the money and resources into creating it.

Especially when there are far cheaper ways of dealing with the same issue. Things like this are not a priority." Her voice sounded almost sad.

"Is it safe?" Clive asked slowly. Grace laughed.

"Of course. We wouldn't do anything to you that hasn't gone through the appropriate level of testing. Everything created on Atlantis needs to be peer reviewed, tested, then approved by an anonymous panel before we grant permission for general use or use on individuals. I promise you, nothing we do here is bad," she said with a warm smile, and Clive couldn't help but wonder if that included safety and weapons. *Do they have the same provisions for those things?*

"Are you okay?" Grace asked him.

"Fine." Clive coughed. "Sorry, I'm fine, it all just seems too good to be true," he added quickly.

"Dr. Kashyap is just excited because we haven't had any reason to perform the surgery on an injury this severe before. It's a real opportunity to see what results it can have on deep muscle abrasions. If it goes well … well, you can understand what that could mean." She gave him a warm smile. "But I'll let you get ready for the procedure, and I'll see you after," she said, turning to leave the room.

Clive wanted desperately to tell her to stay, but he couldn't find the words to do it, so instead he watched as she made her way down the hall to where Dr. Kashyap and his team were getting things ready. He hoped that he'd not just blown his one chance to talk to the person who could give him more information on Atlantis.

"Mr. Shark Attack!" announced a young man with wide, toothy smile. "I'm Akima." He stepped into the room with a giddy bounce in his step, his dark skin and colourful garb both popping next to the white lab coat he wore. Clive took a second but wasn't able to recognize the language he was speaking; the interpreter, however, had no issues with it at all.

"I'm Clive." He stuck his hand out to greet the young man. "You seem excited."

The young man took Clive's hand and then cupped it with his other and, creating a cocoon around Clive's hand as he shook.

"I'm sorry, it's just an exciting day for all of us here. We have been waiting so long to have someone to test our treatment on, and as you can see," he said, gesturing to the space around them, "we don't get many visitors."

"Well, I'm glad I can help," Clive said with a little laugh, and the young man's face darkened.

"I'm sorry, that's not what I meant. Obviously, we are happy things here run so smoothly, and we will make sure that you are one hundred percent when you leave," Akima said, his voice very serious.

"I'm only messing with you. I'm grateful for the chance to see what you can do here and if it helps speed my recovery, then I'm all for it. I appreciate how great you've all been," Clive said, trying to ease the sudden tension he felt in Akima's hands.

"We are happy to help," Akima said humbly. "I only get excited about these things because of the work I used to do back home. I'm originally from Rwanda but my work took me throughout different parts of Africa. Treatment like this would have changed so much of what I was able to do, and a seventy-two-hour recovery would be incredible. So much of the damage comes from one's inability to go back to work.

I'm sure you can understand the dangerous paths that leads to," Akima said softly.

Clive could imagine but he certainly couldn't relate. He'd been privileged enough to live in a place that provided him with both the treatment and a place to recover, not to mention the government helping out with the compensation needed to keep his life in order. But even there, a seventy-two-hour turnaround would be a dream.

"Well, I'm excited to see what you guys can pull off!" Clive said, trying his best to turn the mood back around to a more positive vibe. It wasn't too hard with Akima, who bounced back quickly.

"You'll be running around the city soon enough, Mr. Shark Attack!" he said with a wide smile. "Come, follow me!" He turned to leave the room.

Clive fiddled with the remote for a second before he managed to get it moving. With a few jolty movements he found a rhythm, and soon he was right behind Akima.

"So, Akima, I don't recognize the language you're speaking. What is it?" Clive asked, trying to make small talk as he glided down the hallway toward the surgery rooms.

"Kinyarwanda." Akima turned to face Clive with a proud smile. "I'm grateful that here I won't lose it. I may have left my home but a part of me will always be with my people," he said, his toothy grin shining brightly.

"Do you think you will ever go home?" Clive asked, regretting how the words came out. "I'm sorry," he added quickly, "I'm just nervous and I chat when I'm nervous."

"Don't worry, firstly there is nothing to be nervous about, it will all be over in an hour or so. I've seen the images of the wound and I'm confident it will be an easy fix," Akima said, his directness doing a lot to help calm Clive down. "As for staying in Atlantis or going home, I struggle with that each day. On one hand, I came here for this treatment, which we have completed, but who knows how the mainland will adopt the procedure, or if they will at all? Whereas here I can continue my work and be a part of a group of people who truly want to see change. It is a real struggle." Akima raised his hands, pretending to weigh something in them.

"So, you think the work you're doing here is good?" Clive asked honestly.

"Last time I checked, you don't speak Kinyarwanda and I don't speak English. Yet here we are having a conversation on the way to provide you with a new treatment that will reconnect your muscle and skin tissue in a matter of hours. If that isn't proof enough the work here is good, I'm not sure what is," Akima said, letting out a little laugh.

"You make a good point." Clive followed Akima into a large surgery room, where a handful of people inside were all clapping excitedly.

At the front, arms opened wide to greet him, was Dr. Kashyap, and Grace Alice, who had donned a white lab coat for the occasion.

"Clive, are you ready for the treatment?" Dr. Kashyap said, moving in towards Clive like he might embrace him, had he not be seated in a floating chair. "I hope you don't mind. We have a few of the key members of our team here. They wanted to be here for the treatment and we were hoping you might—"

"I don't mind at all. From what Akima has told me, your team has been waiting for an opportunity to see their work in practical use, and who am I to deny them the opportunity?" Clive said, giving the four silent doctors behind Dr. Kashyap a wave. The joy in their faces said it all. "However, I have one request of my own, assuming it's possible," Clive added, as Dr. Kashyap's brows shot up in surprise.

"What is that?" he asked nervously.

"I want to see what you do. Can I be awake while you perform the operation?" Clive asked. He had to admit he was now curious to see first-hand what all the excitement was about.

The group of doctors in the back whispered to themselves as Dr. Kashyap and Akima joined them. After a little deliberation, they came a consensus and Dr. Kashyap turned back to Clive.

"How is your stomach?" he asked with more seriousness than Clive thought the question deserved.

"I can handle it, if that's what you're asking," Clive said confidently. He'd performed various procedures during combat on both himself and others, so he wasn't too worried about the gore of it all. Clive watched the doctors deliberate once again before Dr. Kashyap returned with a smile.

"Well, it is an odd request and definitely not standard procedure, but it's certainly doable. We will, however, need to restrain your leg and you will be temporarily paralyzed from the waist down." He watched Clive for signs of uneasiness, but he remained steadfast.

"You do what you need to do," Clive said casually. Dr. Kashyap and his team all nodded in agreement. The final look was given to Grace Alice, who had remained silent throughout the entire exchange as if she wasn't even there. But she had been there, and Dr. Kashyap recognized that it might be his operating room, but it was her city. When he finally glanced over to her, she gave a light shrug, letting him know the decision was his.

"Well, isn't this exciting?" he said, clapping his hands. "Let's get to it."

The next little bit went slowly as Dr. Kashyap's team moved efficiently around the room performing different tasks. A very tall man with short blonde hair and round glasses wordlessly hooked Clive up to an IV and adjusted Clive's chair so that it was partially reclined, allowing Clive to see the work to be done on his thigh while leaning back comfortably.

"You can watch from here. However, if you get tired of looking down there are monitors above you. They will be displaying and recording the treatment for future use. You can watch those as well," said a small woman with thick dark hair pulled back in a bun. Clive recognized the Arabic speech and wondered where she might be from.

To his surprise, it was Grace Alice who approached him. She stood a moment, looking him over before settling on his eyes and meeting his gaze with an intense one of her own.

"Why would you want to watch?" she asked, her tone even.

"My guess?" Clive said with a shrug. "Same reason you want to."

He didn't know if this was what she'd been expecting or not, but she took another moment to look at him before giving a curt nod and walking away.

"Alright everyone, I think we're ready," Dr. Kashyap said, holding a long needle. "This is likely to hurt," he said to Clive as he moved behind the chair, and Clive felt something open up behind him. Then he winced and sucked in a deep breath as the needle was jabbed into his lower back. The pain subsided quickly and Akima tapped Clive on his uninjured thigh.

"Anything?" he asked.

"Nothing." Clive said.

"Let's get to healing," Dr. Kashyap said to the team.

The procedure began with the bandages being cut from Clive's leg, revealing a deep wound about nine inches long up the outer edge of his thigh. For the first time since the accident, Clive realized just how lucky he'd been to not have cut his artery.

The wound itself was clean, likely due to the salt water and the work the team had done beforehand. But it was fresh and deep, and Clive's mind began to wonder if Akima was right when he said it didn't look too bad.

Where Clive sat, he could see that the thick gash had not only exposed but also separated a few of the muscle tissues. The team took a moment to clean around the wound, but if any of them had been surprised by what they saw, they didn't show it.

One of the attendings entered wearing plastic gloves and holding a sealed jar of thick, dark pink goop that reminded Clive of a mixture of cornstarch and water, like the stuff he and his sister would play with as kids. They open the glass jar and placed it on a table beside Dr. Kashyap.

Then, in a particularly undramatic fashion, he used his gloved left hand to reach into the mixture and remove some of the thick goop, then pressed it firmly down into the wound, making sure he filled it with as much of the pink stuff as it would allow. The remaining goo was sealed back up and taken away by the same attending.

Then a small attending with her hair in a bun re-entered pushing a new device that had a large metal arm and looked a lot like something that would be used in a Bond film to shoot a laser at someone.

To Clive's surprise, it was in fact a laser, and Dr. Kashyap positioned it so that it was pointed directly at Clive's leg. Once Dr. Kashyap was happy with its positioning, he pressed a large red button on the back of the machine. As he did, many tiny green lights began scanning his leg. Once this finished, Clive watched as a thin red light shot out from the tip of the arm as it began tracing its way up and down his incision, edging its way around the wound like an artist shading in a tree with a pencil.

Dr. Kashyap and the team all stepped back and watched the machine work.

"So then, what do we do now?" Clive asked, watching as the laser continued to trace the wound, then repeat the process.

"Now we wait," Dr. Kashyap said, taking off his gloves. "The machine and the proteins are working together to fill in the missing gaps in your muscle tissue. It will take an hour, maybe two, for the wound to fully close up," he said confidently.

"I just thought there would be more to it," Clive said, caught off guard as the people in the room all stepped back to wait and watch.

"The best things in life are often the most simple," said Akima, which gathered nods from the rest of the room.

Clive, on the other hand, was still confused. But seeing as he couldn't move, he just lay back in his chair, getting comfortable while the other doctors watched intensely as the laser moved swiftly along.

After thirty minutes, the goop in the wound began to ooze a combination of pink juices, blood and a white creamy mixture.

The doctors made "Eww" and "Aww" sounds, and by the forty-five-minute mark there was now a steady flow of fluid, which regrettably upset Clive's stomach more then he would have admitted. He wondered if he should be concerned about the excretion of the fluids, but everyone was still watching and not one of them appeared at all concerned about the by-product.

"The oozing white stuff is infected dead tissue that has been broken down and replaced," Grace Alice said as she stepped up beside Clive. "Your wound is the largest we've treated, so the run-off is more … substantial. But that was to be expected," she said evenly.

"Well, nothing like a little dead run-off in the morning to start the day," Clive said jokingly. Grace allowed a little laugh and Clive turned to meet her eye.

"You're an interesting person, Clive Davies." Grace said, looking at him with a calm intensity Clive hadn't seen before.

"I feel like I'm talking to the queen of interesting," he said, trying to match her gaze.

"Hardly," she said, turning away. "I'm just someone who wants things to change. I also happen to have the means to do so," she said, throwing his compliment aside.

"There are a lot of people with money. None of them have done what you've done," Clive said, glancing down at his leg. "I've got pink goop apparently knitting my muscles together," he said playfully. Clive looked around the room, wondering if their intimate conversation seemed odd in this place, but none of the doctors seemed concerned with what either of them were saying, as they huddled amongst themselves, talking and taking notes.

"That is Dr. Kashyap and his team. Everything here is because of someone else," she said mildly.

"Don't sell yourself short," Clive said.

"I would like to thank you. For saving Squints's life," she said quietly. "He's been with us for so long, I couldn't imagine …" she began to say, and a sad smile formed on her lips. "Well, I don't have to, thanks to you," she added, gifting Clive with a warm smile.

"It's—" Clive began, but she stopped him.

"Join me for dinner tomorrow night. I'd like to treat you for everything you've done," she said quickly.

"You've already treated me to one million credits," Clive mused. "Shouldn't I be thanking you?" he said, laughing.

"I'm serious. I would like to do that for you." She was looking into his eyes, and Clive would have thought it was romantic if his leg hadn't been squirting out ooze while it was happening. "Please," she added innocently.

"Sure. Yeah. That would be nice." Clive tried to convince himself he was doing it because of the operation. But something about the way she was looking at him made him forget about the entire reason he was there, if only for a brief moment. "Assuming this all works," he said, gesturing to his leg.

"I have no doubt you'll be on your feet in no time." Grace smiled. "I'll send the details to your LUCY later this after-noon," she said politely, then she turned and walked away.

Clive wanted to stop her but was quickly reminded he couldn't move, and when he looked down at his leg to curse it, he saw a particularly large piece of puss shoot out of the pinky soup, which got the doctors all excited again.

It was another forty-five minutes before the oozing began to simmer down and stop. His leg looked like someone had vomited a bottle of Pepto-Bismol all over it. Clive sat patiently, waiting for someone to tell him they were ready to wipe it away. There was a particular odour in the room, though Clive had to admit the stench wasn't nearly as bad as he would assume, given total amount of bodily fluids that had been expelled. Or perhaps it was just that Clive had been sitting in it for so long it no longer bothered him, not that he wasn't relieved at that. His stomach could handle blood and gore—though this adventure was a new one for him—but smells always hit him harder. *Give me a bullet wound over spoiled milk any day.*

He hadn't told the doctors that beforehand, worried they would have insisted on sedating him—and had they done that, he wouldn't have a date, or a meeting rather, with Grace Alice.

Dr. Kashyap was giddy after he and his team agreed that the work was done, and he walked over to Clive, wearing a very large smile.

"Are you ready to see it?" he said, looking as though he was trying not to jump with all the excitement.

"Sure, let's see it, Doc."

Dr. Kashyap took a white cloth, dipped it in warm water, and began wiping it across the top of Clive's leg. After he'd wiped away the pink goop and puss, all that remained was a thin white scar that trailed down Clive's leg.

"Holy sh—!" he said. "Sorry," he added quickly, looking around the room at the other attendants. "I'm sorry, it's just, this is incredible," he said, his own amazement filling him with joy as he began to laugh incredulously. Even Grace Alice stepped in and looked a little shocked by the results.

"Congratulations to you all. Incredible work. This is … it's everything," she said, as tears fell from her eyes, and she greeted them each with hugs.

The room was bustling as they all started embracing one

another and chatting about what had happened.

"How do you feel?" asked Akima.

"Great," Clive said. "Though I think I'm still frozen from the waist down, so it's hard to give you any real insight on my leg."

"Of course!" Akima laughed. "That should wear off in a couple of hours."

"Good to know." Clive grinned, still unable to lift his eyes from the freshly formed scar on his leg.

"It looks like it healed up well," Dr. Kashyap said as he wiped joyful tears from his eyes. "I'd say there is a good chance you'll walk out of here on your own. Though I suspect you'll want some crutches. Your leg will be weak until you rebuild your muscles."

A few hours later, Clive was alone in his room. All of the doctors had left to go over their notes and findings, and Clive was left staring at the miracle that was his leg. Even as the anesthetic began to wear off, he was surprised by the lack of pain in the area as he prodded the fresh skin surrounding the old wound.

"How do you feel, Mr. Shark Attack?" Akima said as he stepped into the room. "You have any feeling yet in your legs?"

"You mean these little bad boys?" Clive said, as he began wiggling his toes to show Akima he was back up to full feeling.

"Excellent!" Why don't we try and get you on your feet?" he said, stepping to the side of Clive's bed. He reached for the remote and started fiddling with the controls to get Clive into a more seated position.

"You think I'm ready to walk? Really?" Clive asked suspiciously.

"No time like the present." Akima smiled. "Come on, I will

help you." He placed a hand on Clive's arm and used his other hand to give Clive something to steady himself on.

At first Clive felt wobbly, and he wasn't sure if it was from the anesthetic or the injury. But after a couple of short steps, he felt as though he could handle it on his own.

He began to laugh uncontrollably as he realized it had only been a little more than a day since a shark had sliced his leg open, and he was walking, albeit uneasily, on his own. As he looked down at his bare legs popping out from under a hospital gown, he could hardly believe any of it was real. *But if all of this is real, that means my dinner with Grace Alice is too.*

15

After another night to rest his leg and some light rehab work with a specialist both the day before and the next morning, Clive was amazed that, besides some tenderness in his upper thigh, he could walk around almost as normal. He was even able to walk back to his apartment, where he was grateful for a hot shower.

He kept running his fingers over the light pink skin that formed the newly acquired scar running up the side of his thigh, feeling nothing but pure astonishment each time he felt it. How many times would something like this have come in handy after some of his ops? Forty-eight hours ago, Clive figured his operation on Atlantis was finished and that he would be spending his remaining days in the hospital wing doing nothing—that was, if they even allowed him to stay in the city. Now he was having a shower without so much as a bandage on his leg, and he hadn't even missed a shift with Squints, although Dr. Kashyap had suggested they both take at least a couple more days to rest.

Still, what had happened the day before was some form of miracle treatment, something that came straight out of a *Doctor Who* episode. *Yet here is the proof*, he thought, rubbing his leg.

One thing was for certain: Clive had no idea how he was going to bring any of this up with Commander Hammond, and so, as any good agent would do, he decided to leave it out of his update for now. Since the procedure wasn't necessarily "mission critical," he figured this would be one of those experiences that would be best shared over a beer when he got home.

What really mattered right now was getting closer to Grace Alice, and with any luck he might be able to find some way of accessing the central servers. Once he had that he could finally have some insight into all the weapons they were carrying on board, if there were any. Clive pieced together a short message for Commander Hammond and was surprised when he finally managed to send it off that it wasn't the normal pride in his work he was feeling but something else, something a little emptier.

Save for the mysterious project that Dr. Nowak had been working on, where the consensus had been, from the people Clive had asked about it, that it was not a weapon of any kind, but some sort of alternative power generator, no one hinted at all about any sort of weapons being created in the city. They all believed that it would go against the original intentions of the city.

But none of the people Clive had spoken with had a military background. They hadn't seen what happens when fear and hubris collide. *People do stupid things.*

"Shit," Clive said aloud as he walked into his bedroom. *Speaking of stupid things.*

When Clive was preparing for this operation, he wasn't entirely sure what he was getting himself caught up in. So he prepared for this operation the same way he always would have, packing light and simple clothes. Certainly not something that would be deemed socially acceptable for going out for dinner with a billionaire. Not unless Grace Alice was one of those worn-out Hawaiian shirt–wearing billionaires. Which Clive doubted very much was the case. It wouldn't be so bad if she wanted to go to someplace like the Snailbox, but based on the information Clive had received about the restaurant, this was nothing like the Snailbox.

"LUCY," Clive asked, now entirely habituated to talking with the automated helper.

"Yes, Clive?" LUCY replied evenly.

"There wouldn't happen to be a place in the city where I could get a nice set of clothes, would there?"

"Of course, there are eighteen locations on Atlantis that offer various unisex clothing options. What exactly are you looking for?" LUCY asked calmly. Clive didn't know what to expect, but eighteen seemed like a lot of places for clothes. Although with over one hundred and twenty thousand people living here, maybe it wasn't so wild to think they might need a few places to shop.

"I'm looking for a nice dress shirt and pants … and I guess maybe a pair of shoes?" he added, looking at his Crocs and runners sitting by the door.

"Perfect. Let's see." Clive guessed the casualness in LUCY's voice was purposely designed to make people feel more comfortable talking with the helper. No doubt LUCY could process every answer to Clive's question before he could even finish asking it. "Well, there are two locations that seem to offer a selection of the items you're looking for, and the nearest is on Iota IV. Estimated travel time is thirteen minutes."

Clive looked at his watch and realized he still had a few hours before he was supposed to meet Grace at the address she'd sent him.

"Alright LUCY, let's go shopping," Clive said with a sigh. He was never a huge fan of shopping, but maybe it would somehow be different on Atlantis.

As it turned out, the shopping was no different at all. There were no technological advancements that had been made to make Clive not feel like a twit. The people were nice and friendly and very helpful. But it was still just shopping for clothes, and Clive did his best to get what he needed quickly and get out. He would have preferred to silently walk in, get his things, and leave, but Rita, the overly chatty Norwegian saleswoman with long blond hair and high cheek bones, enjoyed small talk more than Clive would have liked.

"Let me show you around. All of our clothes are made in the city from recycled plastics we pull from the ocean, old clothes, and plant fibers," she said with massive smile on her face. Clive would have assumed it was fake anywhere else, but given her obvious pride in the way she discussed these facts, he thought it was genuine.

Clive managed to get out of the store in under thirty minutes. His first selection was a pair of black faux leather shoes with a squared toe, and black socks with a small shark stitched on the ankle, which he found very amusing.

"Those have been quite popular since the attack a few days ago," Rita said with a frown. "Personally, I think it is insensitive. The poor man must be bedridden and terrified of sharks now. I doubt he'll ever go back in the water again. I wouldn't."

Clive had to force himself not to laugh. He'd been worried

that people might recognize him and was happy to see that, although people had seen the footage, his face had been covered, which meant he could still skate by unseen. But he couldn't help himself from saying, "I'm sure you'd be surprised how quickly people bounce back."

If Rita was confused, she didn't let it show for long as she continued grabbing various items off the rack. In the end, Clive settled on brown dress pants with a black belt, and a light tan, long-sleeved button-down shirt, which he promptly rolled up his forearms. The overall look made him feel stuffy, but even he had to admit he looked good, which Rita was kind enough to say multiple times.

Clive walked out of the store with a fresh new outfit, which set him back 237 credits, but he figured, *What the hell, I just got attacked by a shark. The least I deserve is a new outfit.*

He had a little over an hour to get ready to meet Grace, which was plenty of time, as it didn't take much for him to "get ready," especially considering all his clothes were new and freshly pressed. So he decided to take his time getting back to the apartment.

He stopped by his usual café and was greeted by a very surprised Kissa.

"You're here?" Kissa asked, her eyes widening at the sight of him as she handed him his coffee, although now it was Clive's turn to be surprised. Kissa looked around her conspiratorially.

"You were the one from the video. Who got attacked by the shark?" she said in a whisper. Clive laughed.

"Yes," he said, glancing around, matching her conspiratorial vibe. "But you would be impressed with what they can do in this city," he said, tapping his leg as he added, "Managed to fix me up quickly."

Kissa smiled at him and handed him her e-reader, using her thumb to unlock the screen.

"Not as surprised as you might think," she said with a smile as he saw her copy of *Medicine and Its Future* by Dr. A. R. Kashyap. Clive laughed as Kissa turned the e-book back around.

"Well, so far you're the only one who's recognized me," Clive said looking around, still speaking in hushed tones. "Maybe it's best to keep it that way?" he added with a wink.

"Secret's safe with me." She placed a thin finger against her lips.

Clive smiled and, taking his coffee, he made his way over to his regular bench, which overlooked the main belly of the atrium. He was happy to see it unoccupied.

Resting his new clothes on the bench, he took a seat beside them and took in the view. Until now he hadn't really had a chance to be alone and process the last couple of days. He was lucky to get himself and Squints out of the shark encounter with such minimal injury. There had been the real possibility that the sharks could have taken at least one limb from either of them, and that would have still been considered a positive outcome.

Given that most people die of the blood loss suffered by a shark attack, they had been lucky to be in the depths of the ocean, where it was much colder and the pressure was higher, rather than in the warmer surface levels.

"The moments behind us do not determine the moments in front of us," Clive said quietly as he closed his eyes.

"I like that," said a withered voice. Clive opened his eyes to see an old woman standing beside him. Her arms arched back around a cane which propped up her back as if it were helping to keep her upright. Her sudden presence startled Clive.

"I'm sorry," she said in a soft voice. "I didn't mean to sneak up on you," she added with a warm smile.

"It's fine. Here, let me move over," Clive said, hanging his new clothes off the back of the bench as he slid over.

"Thank you," she said, as she slowly stepped up on the raised seating area. Clive put his arm out to help brace her, and she happily took it. She was a tiny woman, no more than five foot two if she was upright. Her dark skin was heavily creased by deep wrinkles across her face. She was, without a doubt, the oldest person Clive had seen since he had arrived in Atlantis.

"Your language, I recognize it. Where is it from?" Clive said, helping her down onto the bench.

"Inuktitut," she said proudly, and Clive dropped his head, thinking for a moment before the answer came to him.

"Nunavut?" Clive asked sheepishly, and was rewarded by a big smile from the old woman.

"Just outside Iqaluit," she said, patting her hand on his as if congratulating him. "Not many people guess that," she added with a laugh. "Are you from Canada, too?"

"I came from Halifax, but I've moved around a bit," he said, finding it satisfying to be talking with another Canadian. Nunavut was one of the northern territories that stretched all the way up to the Canadian arctic. Clive had only ever passed by on his way through the Hudson Strait, but from what he'd managed to see from the ship's deck, he understood that it was a place he'd definitely want to visit.

"Very nice," she said, turning to look out at the view. "A little bit different here, isn't it?" Her eyes scanned the atrium. It certainly was very different from the cold climate of northern Canada.

"You can say that again," Clive said with a laugh. "I'm Clive, by the way."

"Sinnatomak, but you can call me Sinni. It's nice to meet you, Clive." She tapped her hand on his again.

"Nice to meet you, too."

"What you said before, what does it mean?" Sinni asked.

"Oh, that." Clive waved it away. "It's nothing. Just some stupid thing I tell myself sometimes."

"I liked it. There was comfort in it."

"Yeah," Clive said shyly, and for a long moment neither said anything. "I guess it just helps me recentre myself, gives me permission to move forward," he said, realizing he'd never actually shared that with anyone. But there was something calming about having Sinni sitting beside him, and he felt open to admit it to her.

"It's beautiful, would you mind if I also used it?" she asked, giving him an even stare.

"Of course. If you find it helpful," Clive said with a shrug.

"The moments behind us do not determine the moments in front of us," she said softly, not to Clive but to herself. After a few deep breaths, she turned to him. "I think many people would benefit from those words." Her smile faltered.

"My daughter came here to do research on the ocean. She asked me to leave my home and come to this place that I'm not connected to. She told me it would be better, and maybe in some ways it is. But it isn't home." Sinni's words were sad and distant. She turned to face Clive. "I haven't told anyone that," she said, her smile a little brighter, as if an invisible weight had been lifted off her shoulders. "My daughter says the work here will change the world, do more then she could ever have imagined. But I'm afraid that when people lose sight of where they come from, it is easy to lose sight of why you are doing it. Does that make sense?"

"Yes," Clive said solemnly. "Do you think that is happening to your daughter?"

"I'm not sure," Sinni said thoughtfully, "but I believe real change has to come from within. Or else aren't we just being afraid?" Sinni gave him a wary smile.

The alarm on Clive's phone began to go off, and he realized he only had twenty minutes before he needed to meet Grace. He stood with a start, before catching the slow gaze of Sinni following him.

"I'm so sorry, but I have to go. I've enjoyed talking with you," he said, meaning every word. Sinni looked up at him and gave him a broad smile.

"I've enjoyed our time as well. Thank you for your wisdom," she said, and had it not come from this woman, Clive would have assumed she was joking. But her words came so honestly that Clive trusted them.

"Thank you for yours," he said as he grabbed his clothes from the bench. "Until next time." He smiled before racing off to his apartment.

Clive hurried in through the door, quickly pulling off the clothes he'd been wearing and tossing them on the ground. Not bothering to pick them up, he began putting on his new clothes.

He found it strange watching his reflection in the ocean window. His hands grazed the newly formed scar on his leg, which caused him to flinch as he pulled up his pants. The sight of it was still so new that he had trouble believing it was real, that any of what happened wasn't just some sort of dream. The fact that he was even moving right now was disarming.

"And yet I'll still show up late for dinner!" Clive said as he began sliding the black belt through the loops of his pants.

"How much time do I have, LUCY?" Clive said as he buckled his belt and zipped up the fly of his pants. *Can't forget that!*

"If you leave in the next three minutes, you should be right on time," LUCY said in a painfully positive voice.

Clive reached down and pulled on one of the new shark socks before slipping on a black leather shoe, and repeated. *All I need to do is have a quick shave, try and style my hair, and put on a shirt,*Clive thought as he tied up the laces. *I can do that in three minutes.*

He was feeling mildly optimistic as he rushed into the bathroom and pulled out a razor and some cream. Looking in the mirror, he noticed just how much he'd let his hair go since arriving at Atlantis. His normally tidy, cropped hair had some length to it, as did his beard.

It was too late to do much with his hair, but he tried to style it as best he could. He then pulled out his beard trimmer and began buzzing away at it. Setting the length to low, he ran it over his face, watching as small tuffs of hair fell away, leaving behind a light stubble. He quickly lathered some cream, which had a pleasant lavender smell to it, over his face, calmly ignoring how poorly he was doing it.

"One minute," LUCY, said as if reading his mind. Though Clive was beginning to feel like the countdown was making this feel more like heist movie than a casual dinner date.

"You know, when you read my mind it starts to get creepy." Clive laughed as he began running his razor down his face, trying his best not to cut himself in the process. LUCY, however, didn't respond. *Maybe that's for the best.*

After running some warm water over his face and wiping it down, Clive was satisfied with the overall outcome, despite it not having his usual military precision. He rummaged through his bathroom kit until he found a small bottle of old cologne. He only used it for special occasions and so shouldn't have been surprised when he checked its contents that the bottle was nearly full.

He spritzed some in the air and walked through it, unsure if that was even what you were supposed to do, before adding a little more to his wrist and rubbing some around his neck. *That's what they do in the movies, isn't it?*

He was about to walk out of the apartment when he caught another glimpse in the mirror and realized he didn't have a shirt on. Smacking his palm against his forehead, he scanned the room till he saw the shirt folded over the edge of the couch. He ran over and, as quickly as he could manage, he began unbuttoning it, getting about halfway down before giving up and pulling it over his head like a T-shirt. He began buttoning it up, taking one final look in the mirror.

"You should hurry, Clive, if you want to make your appointment on time," LUCY said, pulling Clive out of his self-assessment to race off towards the TOTS, leaving the final few buttons to finish on his way.

Clive traveled up to Beta I, where Grace had made a reservation at a place called Amore. Clive learned along the way that it was a rather nice restaurant in the city. But once he arrived, he found the word nice didn't seem to be the appropriate term for where he was.

He also learned that Grace, unsurprisingly, had already

arrived and been seated. He silently berated himself for not showing up earlier, but it was too late now. The hostess did a double take when Clive told her who he was there to meet. At first, he thought maybe she had recognized him from the video. But when she giggled and gestured at his shirt, he realized that in his haste that he'd mixed up the buttons and the shirt looked a little lopsided.

She gestured to a little alcove where he was able to run and adjust it before she led him over to the table.

The hostess walked much faster than Clive would have liked, as it didn't give him nearly enough time to take in the grandeur of the restaurant, which was set close to the surface on the outside rim. Its sides were made up of rounded glass windows revealing spectacular views of the ocean all around them. At various points, Clive could see tiny pods popping out from the glass walls, with tables in them, giving diners what Clive guessed was the feeling of being surrounded by water.

To Clive's surprise, the hostess led him over to one of the little pods, which he thought seemed a little more romantic than just a thank you dinner. Grace Alice stood up to greet him, and he was immediately struck by the shimmering black and green gown she wore that floated off her body until it finally met the ground. Her hair wasn't in its usual ponytail, but instead dropped neatly around her face, framing her angular cheek bones.

"You look incredible," Clive said, feeling very much out of his league, even in the fresh clothes he'd just bought. As the hostess moved aside to let him pass, Grace moved out from the table to meet him. She reached out to take his hand and Clive couldn't help but feel the warmth in her touch as she did. He became aware of how flushed he must look.

"You don't look too bad yourself," she said with a grin.

"Compared to you, I look like yesterday's peach," Clive said, which earned him a giggle from the hostess. He'd never really known what the expression meant, but he'd once heard a general from Georgia say it to his wife and it had stuck with him for some reason.

"Well, thank you. I think," Grace said, leading him to the booth. "I hope you don't mind, but I thought I would bring you here because it is truly one of the best places in the city and the view is wonderful. But I realized too late that it might be too much, what with everything you've been through. ... I can have us moved if you like." She sounded flustered and embarrassed.

"Absolutely not! This is incredible. And trust me, it's going to take a more than a little run around with a shark to stop me from getting in the water," Clive said, this last bit getting another double take from the hostess as she walked away. But Grace didn't look convinced. Clive pulled up his pant leg to show her his new socks, the little shark nipping at his ankles.

Grace caught a glimpse of the socks and laughed.

"I promise you, it's fine," Clive said reassuringly, and Grace relaxed, her shoulders dropping from a position Clive hadn't even noticed she was holding.

"Well, I guess I should be relieved you have a sense of humour about it all," Grace said as she took a seat across from Clive, who had stood waiting to sit until after Grace had, another trick from the Georgian general.

"Is there any other sense worth having?" Clive said thoughtfully, as he turned to watch a school of fish swim by. His gaze followed the fish down beneath his feet, to the vast reaching reef system that sprawled out as far as he could see in the dimming evening light.

"I suppose not," Grace said as she followed his eyes downward. "It's pretty incredible, isn't it."

"I can't believe you did all this," Clive said softly.

"Not me," Grace said, brushing off the compliment. "I couldn't do half the things we do in Atlantis."

"But you're the one who made it all possible. You gave Dr. Kashyap and his team the resources they needed to do what they did. Without you, and them, I would likely be in a bed for weeks. Not here in a fishbowl with you," Clive said, gesturing around the room.

"It's kinda like a fishbowl. Though not really. More like a reverse fishbowl, where it's the fish's turn to get to look in on us," Grace said.

"A humanbowl," Clive offered.

"Something like that." Grace laughed, and Clive couldn't help himself from laughing along with her. An awkward moment fell between the two of them, as neither really knew where to go from here.

"What's good here?" Clive finally asked, and Grace thought something about the question was funny.

"Sorry, I guess I didn't tell you, the menu here is fixed. So, there will be fifteen dishes, and all of them are delicious. You don't have any allergies, do you? I didn't see anything in your file, but I should have double checked." Her brow creased a little at the thought.

"Nope, any food and every food at least once," Clive said with a wink. "And I have to admit, this is my first time with one of these fancy meals. You may need to be my guide so I don't mess anything up. I wouldn't want to accidentally eat a napkin or something."

"I'll make sure to keep a watchful eye," Grace said, amused, as she waved over the waiter. "Bottle of—" She looked to Clive, who would have been more at ease with a beer, but got the impression this was a wine sort of place.

"Red wine would be great. But I'll leave the final decision in your capable hands," Clive said forcing himself to stop leaning on the table. He hadn't realized how much work dinner could be.

"Bring us what the chef has paired with the meal, please," Grace said elegantly.

"So, Grace Alice," Clive said as the waiter walked away. "Are you, like, the mayor of Atlantis, then? Am I having dinner with the mayor?" Clive rubbed his hands together in a mock show of excitement.

"Hardly," Grace said as she brushed her hair back behind her shoulders, revealing a pair of emerald-green earrings embedded in her earlobes. They matched an equally simple but elegant necklace that hung in the centre of her chest. Clive forced himself to look away as he realized he was staring at it. "The city is updated and maintained digitally, with different teams of people working together to make sure it remains functional. Actually, I don't do much with the city, each department is in charge of hiring and enlisting new talent, and LUCY," she said, gesturing to her wrist, "basically handles everything else. LUCY is the backbone of the city."

"LUCY does seem to be capable of almost anything," Clive said with a laugh.

"You have no idea. LUCY is the most advanced AI on the planet," Grace said, and Clive's eyebrows must have pinched together because she tilted her head and looked at him inquisitively. "Don't tell me you're one of those people afraid of AI?" she said with a grin. "The man who took on a shark?"

"Sharks are tangible creatures with strengths and weaknesses that can be exploited. AI seems … well, a lot smarter than me." Clive tried to hide his obvious discomfort in a laugh.

"LUCY has weaknesses and strengths. One of those strengths is the ability to run an entire city while simultaneously storing and handling all the private information of everyone in Atlantis. LUCY allows our teams to have up-to-date information on everyone when they need it, while making sure no single person goes overlooked."

Was that was happened to Sasha Keen? Clive thought with a frown, and Grace must have seen it but misunderstood it's meaning, as she continued.

"LUCY is the pinnacle of a completely unbiased society. The moment you step on this ship you are treated exactly the same as anyone else, as long as you respect the rules of the city," she said, her voice becoming a little more commanding at the end.

"I don't mean to upset you. LUCY is amazing. Even I have grown to rely on that assistance here in the city. I'm certainly not saying LUCY isn't impressive." Clive put his hands up in a pleading gesture.

"But?" Grace said, folding her arms. Clive cursed himself for somehow managing to piss off the only person in the city he needed to befriend. He let out a deep sigh and pressed on, in spite of himself.

"But. Isn't there a fear in relying too much on one device?" Clive said calmly. Grace thought about this for a moment as she leaned in against the table.

"Let me ask you this. Do you believe in democracy?" she said simply.

"Yes. Of course I do. It's the worst form of government—"

"Except for all the others," Grace finished for him. "Winston Churchill," she said, slowly nodding. "I believe in fair and equal treatment for everyone. We have tried over the years to succeed in that regard, but we always fall short. Why?" She looked at Clive for an answer.

"I don't know, trust?" Clive proposed.

"Maybe, I think that has something to do with it. But also fear of innovation in a system we believe is so fragile that if we mess with it, it will shatter. But what good have we found at any point in history when people remained rigid in the face of innovation? Look around this room," Grace said, gesturing out over the two hundred or so people in the restaurant. "Every single person here has the freedom to decide what they want to do. They can stay or leave, but they choose to stay because here their voices are heard. Atlantis has the power to change the world," she said excitedly.

"You say all of these people have a choice," Clive replied skeptically. "Has anyone chosen to leave?" Looking into her eyes, he saw her flinch at the question, but she hid it well.

"One person. She refused to see what we were really trying to do here, and despite my pleas for her to stop, her actions threatened everyone in the city. We had to let her go," Grace's voice seemed to drift off along with her thoughts.

Let her go? Clive thought.

"She was sent back to the mainland. I'm not sure what happened to her," Grace said, but her eyes told a different story all together. There was sadness behind them, and possibly something else. *Anger?*

Two waiters appeared. One had a bottle of red wine, which Grace was kind enough to sample, as Clive didn't know what to even taste for. He imagined it would taste something like red wine. And the second held a tiny plate with a thin slice of tuna and some sauce on it. At least that was what Clive heard when the waiter told him what it was. He looked over at Grace as the waiters left and she was smiling. She held up a glass.

"No more chat about politics, we're here to celebrate you being alive! Cheers," she said, and Clive picked up his glass and clinked it with hers.

"Fair enough," he said taking a sip of wine, which he had to admit tasted a lot better than the wines he'd had in the past. "But I'm not sure I'll be able to talk between such large portions of food," he added, gesturing to the tiny plate and tuna. Grace nearly spat out the wine she had in her mouth, which Clive thought would have been hilarious, but she managed to compose herself nicely.

"I'll make you a bet. If you're not full by the end of the meal, I will take you out another night for a meal of your choice. On me," she said boldly.

"And if I'm full?" Clive asked with a smirk.

"You have to take me out, my request, on you," she added with a wink, which made Clive laugh.

"Deal, although I should remind you, they are your credits," Clive said, tapping his LUCY.

"Wrong. Those are yours. But we've talked enough about the city! Eat your nibble of fish and tell me about yourself."

Clive smiled, spearing the tuna with his fork and plopping the piece of fish into his mouth in one go. His eyes lit up at the sudden explosion of flavour. It felt as though his taste buds were doing cartwheels, as he no longer understood what it was he was eating. It had a sweet quality to it, with a hint of what Clive guessed was wasabi, although he'd never actually seen any on the plate.

"Oh my god," he said happily. "This is incredible. What's the sauce? I won't lie, I ignored all aspects of the description once I saw the plate, but wow. That's good." Grace laughed.

"It's a balsamic reduction with cracked peppercorn, chives, shallots, a hint of wasabi, and a light dusting of Maldon salt over a thinly sliced ahi tuna," Grace said. Clearly this hadn't been her first time.

After the first plate, the waiters began to appear at predetermined intervals based on the size of the dish, which never looked like enough, surprising Clive and amusing Grace.

The conversation got easier as well. Clive didn't find it difficult to open up to Grace, especially after she'd done the same for him. He'd read the details about her in his briefing, but briefings never tell you about the memories and emotions behind the events in someone's life. In Grace's case, the time surrounding her father's death and how she vowed she would make him proud with what she'd built.

"Do you think he would be proud of Atlantis?" Clive asked, giving Grace time to think.

"I think he would find it threatening. But ultimately, he would see its value," Grace said confidently.

"Threatening?"

"My father built his success on power. He was a product of his generation, and it served him well. But once you have power, you tend to reject and ignore anything that threatens that power. Most people would do anything to keep it. And my father was no different," Grace said calmly.

"What about your parents?" Grace asked, putting a stopper on that conversation.

"I'm not sure. I was a foster kid, bounced around, got into diving, then boats never really stayed in one place long enough to have meaningful "parents," so to speak," he said, brushing over his tragic childhood story with a gulp of wine. He leaned back in his chair and rubbed his belly. "How many rounds is that?" he said confidently.

"That was ten, so five more, Mr. Davies. Think you can handle it?" Grace said coolly.

"I know I can," Clive said, trying to ignore the tightness in his belly.

As if sensing his pain, the waiter appeared to drop off another bottle of wine and another round of tiny dishes.

"Just what I was hoping for, more thin meat," Clive said, once again ignoring the elaborate description from the waiter. He'd decided after round four that he couldn't understand what made them taste good, so he would just be happy eating them.

"I have a question for you," Grace said, leaning into the table and pouring Clive and herself another glass of wine.

"Ask away," Clive said, putting a tiny leaf in his mouth and chewing it. He assumed everything was meant to be eaten, or else why was it there?

"Why did you go back for Squints? You had to have known that the chances of you both getting out of there alive were slim, and yet you risked your limbs, and your life, to try and protect him. Why?"

Clive took a sip of wine and thought about it for a long time. There were plenty of reasons he had done it. Squints was a friend, he had a family, it was the right thing to do. All of which would have been truthful answers, and yet none of them really were the truth. At least not his truth. Grace didn't press him on it while he thought, she simply gave him the space to answer as he felt best. She waited so long, the waiters had returned to remove their plates and prep for the next round before Clive finally gave her an answer.

"Truthfully," Clive said at last, and Grace moved in closer, "I would rather die knowing I tried to do something, than live knowing I didn't." He shrugged. It had felt like a long build up for nothing, but if Grace had been disappointed with the answer she didn't show it in any way.

The waiters returned with another plate of food and neither of them touched it as he walked away.

"You're different, Clive," Grace said after a few moments. "The people in this city, they want to be here for one reason or another. They lost something, or it was taken away, whatever it is. But not you. I think you're here for a different reason," she said, her eyes narrowing in on him. Clive's stomach began to tighten up in knots, and not just because of the food. He wondered if he'd given away too much information, or if she knew why he'd been sent here. *Did I say too much about the disappearance of Sasha?*

Clive desperately ran through the conversation in his mind, wondering where he went wrong. But when he looked at Grace, her eyes had softened. They were no longer giving him a harsh, piercing stare but a warm, welcoming invitation.

"I think you're here because you need to be here. You're meant to be here," Grace said, reaching across the table and gripping his hand. "Do you believe in destiny?"

"I'm not sure I believe in much," Clive said honestly.

"You believe in people," Grace replied softly.

"Sure, but who doesn't?"

Grace laughed. "It's not as common as you might think," she said lightly.

"But you do?" Clive asked.

Grace looked at him and with a tight squeeze of his hand she stood up.

"Come with me," she said, plopping her napkin on the table.

"Now? We haven't finished our food. What about the bet?" Clive asked.

"You win another meal on me of your choosing," Grace said with a wide smile. The waiter approached the table and looked at Grace. "Thank Alessia for me, but we won't be staying for the final plate. Everything was delicious," she added coolly as she ran her LUCY over the scanner on the table.

Clive quickly plopped the last tiny bit of food in his mouth. He was sad to be missing the final dish. It was like skipping the end of a movie. But he was eager to learn what had come over Grace, as she seemed excited to show him something. He smiled at the waiter as Grace practically pulled him away from the table.

Without another word, Grace began to lead him through the tunnels with no help from LUCY at all. She stopped at a set of TOTS. The doors opened and the two of them stepped in silently, Clive pleasantly aware she was still gripping his hand. As the doors closed, she turned to him eye him sheepishly.

"How do you feel about heights?"

16

After being dropped off on Alpha I by the TOTS, Grace began leading Clive through a maze of hallways. She still hadn't told him what they were doing, but she maintained an excited expression each time she looked back to make sure he was still following.

"Where are we going?" Clive asked, for the fifth or sixth time.

"Stop asking me that! We're almost there and I promise you, it will be worth it," Grace said, heading down a particularly narrow hallway until she got to a large double door. After Grace put her LUCY up to the monitor beside the door, then entered a six digit code into her LUCY. Clive watched as both sets of doors opened in on themselves, revealing a large, and currently empty, room. But Clive could see as he stepped inside that there were a handful of monitors and various pieces of lab equipment scattered around. However, compared to some of the other research departments Clive had seen in the city, he had to admit this one seemed almost modest.

"This is the old server room," Grace said. Clive's ears perked up before his excitement deflated at the word "old."

"So, there are no servers in here anymore?" Clive asked as

Grace turned to glance at him. Clive tried his best to not look nervous. Luckily, Grace laughed.

"You haven't seen too many server rooms, have you?" she said, gesturing to the space. "This was our first room when we built the city prototype. My team keeps a couple in the back room for internal projects," Grace added, pointing to a closed door with a glass window, through which Clive could see fifteen, or maybe twenty, large servers. "The new server room is substantially bigger than this one," she explained, "and we placed it lower in the city to optimize the natural cooling provided by the ocean water. As you would expect, it gets pretty hot when you have that many servers. Those in there are only for pet projects." All Clive could think about was whether or not the USB he carried on him would work in one of these servers. After all, they likely held the unregistered projects that Grace wouldn't want everyone to know about.

"Dr. Nowak, I didn't expect to see you here this late, though I should have guessed," Grace said, and Clive turned away from the servers to see a balding man in a white lab coat walk out from one of the back rooms. His name was clearly tagged to the front of his jacket.

"Ms. Alice, I'm sorry to interrupt you," Dr. Nowak said in his native Polish as he shot Clive a wary look. "I was just going over some of the numbers for project Blue Crest, looking into some of the adjustments you suggested. It's not perfect, but I think we are moving in the right direction," he said, his eyes narrowing as they landed back on Clive. "Who is your friend?"

"Right, my apologies. Dr. Nowak, this is Clive Davies. Clive is the man from the shark attack." Dr. Nowak pursed his lips as he looked at Clive from top to bottom. "Dr. Nowak is a brilliant scientist helping me on one of those pet projects I told you about. It's with his help we will change the world," Grace said with a wide smile.

"I assume by the fact that you're up and walking around that Dr. Kashyap and his team's theories seemed to work well?" he said, expertly ignoring the praise he'd just been given.

"Yes, it was pretty impressive. I have to go in tomorrow for a check-up, but I feel great," Clive forced himself to say after he noticed both Nowak and Grace were looking at him.

"Very good! Well, it is time for me to sleep. These old eyes are not what they used to be," Dr. Nowak said as he skirted past the pair of them, his eyes landing on Clive's one last time. "Nice to meet you, Clive."

"Nice to meet you too, Dr. Nowak." Clive heard himself say as he watched the scientist leaving the lab. Clive couldn't believe his luck; not only had he found the location of an access point to the servers, but also he finally found out where Dr. Nowak and Grace had been working on Blue Crest. He unconsciously patted his pocket, panicked momentarily when he couldn't feel it, and then mentally kicked himself, as he remembered he stopped carrying the USB around with him some time ago.

"Are you okay?" Grace asked. Clive must not have hidden his disappointment well.

"Fine. Just curious if there would happen to be a bathroom nearby?" he asked, as he moved his hands so they hovered over his stomach.

"Of course, just up through those doors," Grace said, pointing to a set of doors at the end of the hall. "I'll wait for you here. Don't worry, this boring lab isn't what I wanted to show you."

"I'll just be a minute." Clive forced himself to smile before he moved off towards the bathroom.

How could he have been so stupid? His first real opportunity to do his job and he forgot the USB key. He could've smacked himself, if he didn't need his brain to come up with an idea of how to get back here. Once in the washroom, he moved into one of the stalls that lined one side of the room. He sat on the toilet, ran his fingers through his hair, and sighed heavily. Whatever he was going to do, he would need to do it fast, and there was only one thing he could think of. But he didn't know if it was insanely stupid.

"LUCY," Clive said softly.

"Yes, Clive?" LUCY responded back into his interpreter, which Clive was thankful for.

"Is there any way you can pin our location so that I can find it later?" he said, wincing at the idea. He imagined alarms going off and Grace storming in, wondering why he would need to know where a private lab was. But the reality was much less intense.

"Of course. How would you like to label the area? Alpha I lab bathroom?" LUCY suggested.

"Yeah, that would be great," Clive said, not caring what it was called, just happy that no one immediately came running in to take him away.

Clive got up and exited the stall, feeling somewhat relieved that it all might not be a big waste of time. That it didn't matter, as it would have been too hard to get the USB in with Grace next to him the entire time. *No, it's better to come back another time.*

Clive returned to Grace, who was tapping away on one of the computers in the room. His smile felt much less forced now that he'd pumped himself up a little.

"I'm sorry, it's hard to be in here and not do work." She laughed as she finished up what she was doing. "I practically live in here."

"Well, I'd say you got shafted, because my view might be better," Clive said with a wink.

"Good! You like your room. I have room just down the hall. It's nothing flashy, but it's an easy commute." She rested her hand on Clive's shoulder, and he wondered if her bringing up that her room was so close was an accident. "Feeling better?" she asked, giving his shoulder a gentle squeeze.

"Loads, thank you," Clive said, finding it difficult not to meet her intense gaze. He tried to shake away his thoughts about her. *She's just being nice.*

"Follow me," she said, making her way down the long hallway at the back of the lab, past the bathrooms, until she reached an older designed TOTS door, which opened as she touched her LUCY to it. "I think you'll find the view here to be better." She motioned for him to enter the little elevator. Clive stepped in and Grace followed. It was a dark inside, despite the fact that the walls were made of some sort of heavy glass, with a steel frame connecting them. As soon as the doors shut, the elevator began to move with calm efficiency.

"This was one of the first lifts I had installed in Atlantis. Before all the TOTS and logistics elevators. It's never been updated, I wanted it to be a reminder for myself for how much we've accomplished here," Grace continued as the lift popped out from what had felt like a dark cave into the upper edges of the enormous exterior dome that protected the city from the elements outside.

Clive, who felt like the ground had fallen away from him,

reached out, grabbing hold of the nearest thing to him, which happened to be Grace's arm. Although he'd never been "afraid" of heights, he wasn't totally in love with them, either. Especially when he was looking down through a glass panel below his feet as he moved further and further away from what he considered to be the ground.

"You okay?" Grace asked as she grabbed firmly onto his arms. Clive doubled down, reaching with his other arm to embrace Grace's free hand, and squeezing it tighter than he would have liked.

"Peachy," Clive said, trying to play it cool but unable to let go of Grace's hand, although he did manage to stop squeezing so tightly. "Sorry," he added, as his cheeks flushed red.

"Maybe I should have warned you," she said with a little laugh. "Then again, I have to admit you look kinda cute when you're uncomfortable," she said, her eyes meeting his.

Clive was immediately absorbed by her gaze, and for a moment he forgot where he was and what he was doing. He wasn't imagining this, was she really looking at him this way. Clive found his body began to relax a little, and he felt his legs stop wobbling as a calm washed over him. Before he knew it, the elevator stopped and the glass door opposite from where they'd entered slid open. Grace led Clive off the elevator, still holding his hand, and into a smaller room that had a few couches and chairs scattered throughout. Besides the couches and chairs, the first thing Clive noticed was the other three lifts sitting over other points of the city.

"Each zone has its own elevator. When we first built the outer rim of the city, and the dome itself, it was the fastest way to get from one side to the other. It's not the quickest way around anymore, so it's primarily just used as a meeting-slash-observation area," Grace said, spreading her arms out towards space as if to show it all off. In the centre of the room was a large glass floor, and Clive found himself creeping over to it, as if he might fall through. Grace, on the other hand, walked confidently into its centre and plopped down on the ground, sitting cross-legged as she removed her black high-heeled shoes and tossed them aside. She put her hand out for Clive to join her.

"Are we sure it can handle my weight?" Clive asked, tiptoeing to the edge of the glass.

"Positive," she said, curling her finger to call him over. The gesture was cute, but it did little to ease Clive's mind. When he didn't move, she hopped up on her feet and walked across to him. Putting her two palms up in front of her chest, she stood, waiting until he moved in and clasped her hands.

"Close your eyes," she said softly. Clive hesitated, but closed them. He could feel her slowly pulling him forward and, despite not seeing where he was going, he still found it difficult to let her lead him. "Trust me." He let her words pull him forward. It felt like he'd only taken a couple steps when he felt Grace pull him down to the ground until he was firmly planted on the floor.

"You can open your eyes," she said and Clive could have sworn her lips were right beside his ear as she said it. His eyes fluttered open, and it was no surprise that he was seated in the centre of the glass floor. When he looked down between his legs, he was looking in the dead centre of the city. Below him, Clive knew, was the water basin where the numerous waterfalls surrounding the city all cascaded down from its seventeen levels. Knowing this did little to ease the nauseating feeling in his gut as he stared downward, trying to fight the strong desire to shut his eyes again.

"Just watch," Grace said, giving Clive's hand a gentle squeeze. "LUCY, activate nighttime viewing lights." The lights in the room began to dim and the glass around them absorbed the remaining light. "We call it anti-light, it helps reduce light pollution so you can see more clearly," she said, looking down.

Clive hesitated but eventually followed her eyes back down to the now very visible city below, where he was able to make out the different rings as they cascaded down from the upper rim. Each level flowed into another through various plants, trees, and other vegetation growing between them. Clive could even make out lights in the depths of the city still shining, as microscopic people wandered around the pathways.

"This is where I come to remind myself of what we are doing here," Grace said softly.

"What is that?" Clive asked, still marvelling at the world below him.

"Trying to create harmony."

"I don't get it." Clive looked up at Grace. Her eyes had drifted upwards. For the first time, Clive noticed the clear night sky above them. He managed to pick out some of the constellations, which could've told him a little more about where he was, if he hadn't known already. He picked out Ursa Major and Minor, Draco, and Cepheus all shining brightly in the sky.

"Humanity has lost its harmony. For millennia, indigenous communities survived in harmony with the earth, using only what they needed. Now all we do is exploit everything to meet our ends. We exploit the earth, its resources, even each other. Our system is broken," Grace said passionately.

"And you want to fix it? How?" Clive asked, wondering if she was about to share her secrets with him.

"How do you fix a system that is fundamentally flawed?" Graced replied.

"Destroy it," Clive said, wondering if he was giving too much of his hand away. But Grace didn't seem bothered.

"Sure, you could do that. But destruction never benefits the people who need to be changed. Too much power and control for anyone leaves them fearful of losing it. If we maintain power by systematically oppressing those without it, the fear of losing that power comes from the risk of being oppressed yourself. You start to believe that everyone will do to you what you've done to them. All that really means is that you know what you are doing is wrong, but you can't change it because your fear is that if you relinquish some of your power, one day you will be on the other end of that status quo." Grace pointed down at the city. "We have trialled a society that exists on the premise that everyone is equal, that you have value and you add value. We've removed the need to make money, which allows people to work as they want and contribute to society in a way they see fit."

"Your society is hand-selected, you have no homelessness, no mental illness, it can't be replicated in an existing city with existing problems," Clive said, not caring that it sounded harsh.

"Atlantis is a hub of innovation. We have created methods with real-world uses that are cost effective and built for sustainability. We are generating systems that even the poorest countries could thrive in, with limited intervention. As for hand-selecting our citizens, you are right, we have. And part of that selection process was integrating people with criminal pasts, mental disorders, and unhoused people into our society, and giving them proper treatment and access to the assistance they need. We've introduced over ten thousand people from these various backgrounds, and by eliminating the pressure of money, food, and shelter, they are all living completely normal lives and contributing to the Atlantis society. For the record, that is more than the unhoused population of San Francisco." Grace spoke with absolute confidence.

"So, you're saying everyone here is happier? They are safe?" Clive prodded.

"Everyone here has a voice. Our society is a true democracy. When our city needs to make changes or adjustments, it is called to a vote and everyone in the city votes through their LUCY." Clive opened his month to speak, but Grace stopped him. "And before you ask, we have a ninety-five percent average voter turnout on every issue proposed. We have LUCY, but that is no different from a cell phone. Roughly ninety-two percent of the population of eligible voters in Canada owns a cell phone. Yet we still insist that we pay someone, who was voted in by a small percentage of the population, to vote on behalf of everyone. In 1799, the system was adjusted to represent as many people as it could, and it worked. But it's archaic now, and worse, it's exploited by some for their own selfish gains. The by-product is an unfair system where the primary purpose seems to be to sow distrust and anger in the general population, to distract them from the follies of those allegedly representing them."

"What you're describing is communism," Clive said harshly.

"What I'm describing is fair and equal representation for all humans. One that removes the power from a handful and puts it in the hands of the many," Grace shot back.

"Okay, well, if you have all of these innovations, why are they not in the world now? Why horde them here?" Clive said, refusing to back down.

"We can't share them, not yet. We're not prepared for that yet." Grace's tone was suddenly more guarded. Clive pressed on.

"Are you saying you're preparing for something? Is that this big countdown?" Clive's words were coming on in a flurry.

"I can't share that with you," Grace snapped.

"You can't, or you won't?" Clive asked, his eyes laying into her.

"Both," she said sternly.

"What are you so afraid of?" Clive stood up, no longer bothering about the glass floor beneath him.

"That!" Grace shouted, standing up to meet him as she pointed down towards the city. "I have over one hundred and thirty-six thousand people down there relying on me to keep them safe, and I can't promise them I will be able to do that yet."

"How are you going to keep them safe?" Clive demanded.

"We have a small army in this city ready to fight if that is what we need to do. We have anti-air and water defences to hinder anyone trying to attack us. But soon we will have what we need to make sure everyone here is safe."

And there it was—Clive's proof that they were indeed up to something.

"An insurance plan," he said simply.

"Sure," Grace said coldly, her eyes burning holes in Clive. "Maybe you're not who I thought you were." But her voice was no longer angry; it was sad.

"And who did you think I was?" Clive shot back, not ready to drop his own anger and frustration.

"Someone who cared about people," Grace said softly. Clive was fuming. *What does she know about me? I've given my entire life to the service of people. Who is she to tell me I don't care?*

"Not all of us were born with a silver spoon, Grace," Clive said coldly.

"You're right, I had advantages not many people have. But at least I'm fighting to give others those same advantages. You seem content with being used by a system designed to keep you under its thumb." All of the fight in her had drained away and she looked at Clive with pity and sadness, which only served to fuel his own anger. But still there was a part of him that let the words sink in a moment, and he began to wonder what she meant by it. *Does she know I was sent here? Is that what she just admitted?*

"You don't know anything about me," Clive said after a long moment, and Grace let out a deep sigh.

"Apparently not." She turned towards the elevator. "I think it's time we go," she said, picking her shoes up off the floor, not bothering to put them back on. She looked deflated as she pressed LUCY to the scanner and the elevator doors swung open. The two of them rode in silence until they got off the elevator and left the small lab. Clive was about to walk away when Grace called after him.

"Look around the city, Clive, I mean really look. Maybe then you'll understand what I'm fighting for here," Grace said as she walked down the hall. Clive made his way in the opposite direction, unsure if he was going the right way but just wanting to get as far away as possible. A part of him wished he could turn around, get the USB drive, and leave on the next flight out. But he didn't have access to that server room without Grace, and Grace was unlikely to want to talk to him again.

Why would she think for a moment that I would buy into her little act? Everyone has ulterior motives, even I have reasons for being here that I can't tell her. She's likely no different. She can't tell me what they are doing at the launch. For all I know, they're planning to display a nuclear weapon that they could use to threaten the world while they float comfortably in their little ocean oasis. What did she mean by "look around"? Since living here, all I've done is look. What could she possibly think I'm missing?

17

Clive woke the next morning after a terrible night's sleep. It had taken him forever to fall asleep, and when he finally did, he kept having the same agonizing dream about shooting Grace and seeing her body fall into the ocean.

He wasn't one to dwell on dreams, but he had to admit he was a little shaken by how real the entire thing felt. *Will I have to kill Grace? Is that why I'm here?*

He lay in bed a little longer before he finally got up and reached for the phone he kept in the drawer with his socks. Then he went to the living room to grab the SIM card, which he kept hidden in one of the books on his shelf, *The World Beneath.* He hadn't bothered to dress, as he planned on going straight back to bed. He slipped the SIM card into the phone and waited for it to turn on. Once it had, he found a single message from Commander Hammond.

Clive, we don't have much time left. Five Eyes need to get those documents before the launch at the end of the month. Or else it may be too late. Can I still count on you, Son?

Clive read and re-read the message, trying not to be as hurt as he felt by the lack of confidence from his mentor. Clive had never let him down, and he still had eleven days before the launch.

Despite his frustration with Grace and the argument they'd had the night before, Clive thought she might have radical views, but she hardly seemed dangerous.

"Clive, just reminding you that your check-up with Dr. Kashyap is in forty-five minutes," LUCY said, filling the room with its gentle voice.

"Thank you, LUCY." Clive said, as he jumped back into bed and did a big stretch before sending a brief message to Commander Hammond: *On it, Sir.*

He tossed the phone to the foot of the bed and lay starfished on top of his sheets. He wanted more than anything to just go back to sleep, but instead he forced himself up and headed for the shower.

He was a little stiff as he bent over to remove his boxers, much more than he had been the day before, and he wondered if he'd overdone it. *Surely I'll have to build my muscle tissue back up?* He made a mental note to ask Dr. Kashyap about it when he saw him.

"LUCY, put in a coffee and bagel request at the café, please," Clive said with a yawn before he hopped in the shower, hearing only the muffled sound of LUCY's response.

It wasn't long before Clive was dressed, out the door, and making his way to the atrium. He was unable to resist peeking up at the lookout point. He couldn't see it from where he was, but he knew it was there, hanging above the city. Clive also couldn't help but wonder if Grace was up there now. *Why should I care? She expected me to buy into her little free world speech and not question her at all. How can I blindly follow someone without knowing their intentions?*

Her ideas may have seemed noble, but Clive knew from experience that everyone wanted something, and he didn't think Grace Alice was any different. Sooner or later, he would discover what that was and she would be exposed for the person she really is.

He shook his head, wishing he could stop himself from thinking about her. He needed to stay focused, and something told him that after last night, his chances with Grace had disappeared. But that didn't seem to stop his mind from drifting back to the way she looked at him as she turned to walk away. *Stop it!*

"Morning, Clive," said the pleasant voice of Kissa from behind him. Clive turned and was greeted with a warm smile, a coffee, and a bagel.

"Morning, Kissa," Clive said, shoving his feelings and thoughts about Grace somewhere deeper down in his body. "Thank you for this." He was about to turn away when a thought occurred to him. "Kissa? Why do you read all those medical books?"

"I'm hoping next year to get into one of the medical intern programs they offer in the city," Kissa said with a smile. "It's what I've wanted since we came to Atlantis."

"I was thinking," he said, before he had a chance to stop himself, "could you take some time off for a couple of hours this morning?"

"I'm sure it wouldn't be a problem. Why?" Kissa said nervously.

"I have someone I want you to meet."

Kissa still looked a little nervous, but not enough to stop her from running off to talk to one of the people in the café. After a brief conversation she hung up her apron and walked out to meet Clive.

"So? Where we going?" Kissa asked curiously, and Clive

gave her a mysterious smile.

"Follow me. I promise you won't regret it," he said, waving a hand as he walked off towards the TOTS.

Kissa stayed quiet for most of the walk, which was fine with Clive, as it gave him a moment to finish his bagel. It wasn't until the TOTS finally stopped and they'd hopped off that Clive noticed Kissa begin to look around with excitement.

They were in the med bay, and Clive could see Kissa's smile widen as she spotted various instruments and tools being used in each room, pointing out things to Clive that he had no idea about. She was obviously a very smart girl.

He led her into a small room with glass walls and took a seat in the hovering chair in the centre of the room. Kissa, who spotted the images of Clive's leg that were still up from the day before, began examining them in a way Clive never would.

"Clive! My most successful patient. How are you feeling this morning?" asked an excited Dr. Kashyap as he entered the room. He turned and was startled to see someone else there. "And you brought a friend?" he said, looking sideways at Clive.

Kissa's mouth dropped open when she saw the man in front of her. Obviously Clive's suspicions had been right; she hadn't met him before.

"Dr. Kashyap, this is my friend Kissa, she works in Nu II, but she is studying to be a doctor," Clive began, but Kissa stepped in.

"I've read all of your books on muscle regeneration and your thoughts on future adaptations of accelerated cellular growth and its impact on bacterial infections," she said quickly.

"You have?" Dr. Kashyap said, his brows raised. "But they

were so boring!" he added playfully.

"I think you are a genius," Kissa said, sounding a little flabbergasted.

"I'm hardly a genius, I just have a great team," he said, although Clive noticed his cheeks begin to flush a little.

"Kissa wants to join the intern program in Atlantis, and I thought you might be able to share some insights with her."

"That is an excellent idea! I for one am thrilled we will be offering those types of programs to future doctors. Perhaps we can share contact details and I would be happy to answer any questions," he said with a very wide smile. Kissa looked as though she might pass out as the blood drained from her face. "In the meantime, would you be interested in seeing the results of our updated protein solution?" He pointed up at the screen. Kissa nodded. "Clive, do you mind if I discuss this with her?" he added, looking over to Clive.

"Not at all, Doc," Clive said with a grin, and Kissa clapped excitedly.

"Clive here suffered a large incision to the left lateral rectus femoris approximately one inch in depth," Dr. Kashyap said, pointing to the incision in the image. "Stop me if I'm talking too quickly," he added, looking to Kissa. Clive, whose leg it was, had already gotten lost, but Kissa seemed in her element.

"Not at all! You were lucky, Clive," she said, turning to face him as she ran her finger along one of the images. "Another quarter inch or so and you would have severed the femoral artery. I'm assuming from the water depth and temperature that a majority of the blood loss would have occurred once he re-entered the city? Although the salt must have kept the wound relatively clean, no?" Kissa added, and Dr. Kashyap looked impressed.

"You're absolutely bang on, my dear. What else do you think?" he asked, giving Kissa a moment to think. If she still felt nervous, it certainly didn't seem that way to Clive.

"Well, I would guess, and this is just off of some of your more recent work, that you would have cleaned and sanitized the wound, then extracted a tissue sample to use as the base protein for the tissue regeneration. Then you would have given the tissue sufficient time to develop, maybe six to twelve hours, before adding it to the wound?" Kissa said hesitantly.

"More or less exactly right," Dr. Kashyap said with a laugh. "We gave the tissue more time in the development stage due to the size of the injury. Closer to fourteen hours. We wanted to make sure it would be enough to close the wound completely. It was also our first time, and we wanted to be sure we did it right. Our initial calculation called for eleven hours, but we added an additional three to be sure. But everything else was spot on. You are a bright young person, Kissa."

"I just like to read," she replied sheepishly.

"Well you are a most excellent reader," Dr. Kashyap said to an almost glowing Kissa. "And now, would you like to see the outcome?" Kissa nodded.

"Clive, if you will." Dr. Kashyap turned to Clive now, who had worn shorts for this very reason. He rolled up the edge of his shorts, revealing a long, light pink and white scar running up almost the entire length of his thigh.

"Wow!" Kissa exclaimed, covering her mouth at the outburst. Both Clive and Dr. Kashyap laughed. "That's incredible. This happened to you three days ago?" she asked, looking at Clive.

"More like two," Clive said proudly. "Dr. Kashyap and his team definitely undersell their genius." He caught another blush from the doctor.

"I'm just happy it worked. Can you imagine, seven years of work, only to fail when we needed it? Needless to say, we are thrilled with the results, so much so in fact that Grace has allowed our team to start working on a balm that can be used on minor wounds as a take-home remedy. Imagine cutting yourself with a knife and simply rubbing on a cream. Then poof! It's gone." He laughed.

"That would change everything," Kissa said, amazed.

"Indeed," Dr. Kashyap said distantly. "But let's not forget our patient who is right here. Clive, have you been experiencing any pain, soreness, anything at all?"

"It was stiff this morning when I woke up, and it seems to be weaker than the other leg. Is there anything I should be doing?" Clive asked.

"All of that is to be expected. Your new tissue will not be as strong and will be tighter than the old tissue. But given time, along with stretching and some light training, I see no reason why you shouldn't be back to normal in a week or so. My best advice is to listen to your body, and don't push it," Dr. Kashyap said, smiling. "Now, how does it feel? May I?" He put his hand over the scar, and Clive nodded. The doctor then began running his fingers down the wound and on either side of the cut. "Any areas that seem tender?" Clive flinched when he got to the middle of the wound.

"There," he said, adding quickly, "but it doesn't hurt much, just feels weird."

"Not surprising, it's where the wound was deepest and I suspect that some of the nerves will take more time to repair. I should warn you that some of them may never fully heal," Dr. Kashyap said, removing his hands from Clive's leg.

"I can live with that," Clive said with a grin.

"But other than that, there is nothing else?"

"Not really, honestly, everything seems amazing, all things considered," Clive said confidently.

"Well then, I think my work is done. Clive, you've been a wonderful patient, and Kissa, it was a pleasure to meet you," he said, tapping on his LUCY before glancing up at Kissa. "Ms. Salah, I just sent you my internal contact. Please don't hesitate to reach out. Who knows, I may even have a spot for you on my team," he said, adding a wink at the end.

"Thank you, Dr. Kashyap, that would be amazing," Kissa replied, trying not to stumble over her words.

Clive was enjoying watching their interaction, but was caught by movement from out in the hall and, although he couldn't be sure, he thought he'd seen Grace looking into the room for a moment.

"Thank you, Clive, for bringing me," Kissa said, bringing him back into the little observation room.

"No worries," he said, pleased to see how happy she was. "And Dr. Kashyap, I can't thank you enough for what you and your team have done for me."

"We were just happy we could help," he said with a with a small wave as he made his way out of the room.

"Was it worth it?" Clive asked Kissa.

"Are you kidding me? That was incredible! I don't know how I can thank you," she said, beaming.

"It was nothing. I'm glad you enjoyed it."

"Wait, come over to our house for dinner tonight. I'll make ful medames and ta'ameya! Please, it is the least I can do," Kissa said, clasping her hands to plead with him.

"Sure, why not? That sounds great," Clive said as he got up

from the chair. "But you're sure your mom will be okay with me coming over?"

"Of course! When I tell her what you did for me, I'm sure she would kill me if I hadn't." Kissa said, laughing.

By the time they got back to the café, Kissa had calmed down enough from the excitement from having met Dr. Kashyap to send Clive the details of where to go for dinner that night.

"I wouldn't miss it," Clive said, after the third time Kissa brought it up. It wasn't until he finally left the café that it dawned on him that he didn't have anything to do for the rest of the day. He wasn't expected back at work for another two days, so he decided he would explore the city a little and maybe try to figure out just where this other server room was.

Clive hadn't completely given up on the possibility of getting into the private server room in Grace's lab, but given the very real possibility that he was on her "I hate you" list, it would was unlikely he would be invited in. A part of him also wondered if his LUCY would even be allowed access to the server room. He was a diver and a welder, and it would hardly be in the job description to be anywhere near the servers. *One problem at a time.*

One thing that had been troubling him about last night's conversation was Grace's comment that he needed to look around to understand what she was fighting for. Clive didn't believe they were fighting. They were living here cut off from the problems of the outside world, not fighting for it. Clive had fought for it. He had fought to protect the freedoms of Canadians, put his life on the line, and he was doing it again now.

Clive wandered around aimlessly as he scoured his mind for any semblance of an answer. He hadn't landed on any by the time he found himself outside the Snailbox, and even though it was early, he wondered if Aiden would be around.

Clive stepped into the dimly lit bar as a voice he recognized as Aiden's called out from somewhere inside.

"We're opening up in a few hours," Aiden said, and Clive saw him pop out from behind a doorway carrying a couple of boxes that looked heavy. He placed the boxes down on the bar and peeked out from behind them. A bead of sweat fell from his forehead as he spotted Clive in the doorway. "Right, Clive, fine are yea?"

"Hey Aiden, didn't mean to bug you, just wandering around and thought I'd swing by," Clive said, hands in his pockets. "You need any help?"

"No. Not to worry. These were the last of 'em," he said wiping the moisture from his forehead. "Have'a seat, and what can I get fur yea."

"It's too early," Clive said.

"Nonsense. My bar, my rules. Guinness?" Aiden said with a wink.

"I shouldn't," Clive said, but not nearly as convincingly as he wanted to sound.

"I spend most of my day pouring pints, I tink I can recognize when a man needs it," Aiden said, slapping the bar in front of him. "Aye, saddle up here and tell me what seems to be da problem."

Clive walked slowly over to the bar and climbed onto a stool, watching as Aiden began to pour him a Guinness.

"Do you like living here, Aiden?" Clive asked as the barman looked back at him, his brows shooting up. He turned all the way around to study Clive, and was clearly giving some thought to the matter before he answered.

"If the question is, do I miss Ireland? Aye, every day of my life," he said, taking a moment to look up at the large flag he had hung at the back of the bar. "Unfortunately, Ireland had a wee bit of trouble loving me," he said sadly. "As a boy, it was because of the whole being a gay thing. Boys can be mean, but you don't have to be gay to know that boys are mean. Eventually you grow up and you realize that's all rubbish anyway, and you meet people like Nick," Aiden said, his voice distant.

"So why did you come here? I mean, you and Nick could have lived anywhere. I assume logistics coordinators can find jobs wherever they want." Aiden placed a beer in front of Clive and another in front of himself.

"Aye, that's true. We never had a problem finding work." Aiden smiled as he took a swing of the frothy black beer.

"Then why here?" Clive needed to understand why people were so loyal to Atlantis.

"You mean to tell me, you don't feel it?" Aiden smiled when he saw the confused look on Clive's face. "Aye, well, if you haven't, you will. I promise you that."

"I don't understand," Clive said, still very much confused.

"Aye, well for Nick and me, it was the fact that no matter how hard we worked, we always felt one step behind. A weight, so to speak, that never lifted. I don't feel that here. I'm here, lifting these bloody boxes because I want to be here, not because I have to be here. Understand?" Aiden said, taking another big gulp, his beer nearly empty now. "Everyone who stays seems to find a similar path. Think about it. What brought you here?"

I was sent to find out if Grace Alice is building a weapon that could threaten the world outside this floating metropolis, Clive thought as he took a long drink of his own beer.

"I'm not sure anymore," he said finally.

"Well maybe you'll feel it, or maybe you won't, but even you have to admit, Atlantis is unlike any place in the world," Aiden said, finishing his pint. "Speaking of, I got some work to do. You gonna be alright?" he asked as Clive drained the rest of his pint and stood.

"Yeah, I'll be fine," Clive said with a shrug as he turned to leave, before stopping and looking back. "Thanks, Aiden."

"Anytime." He began pulling out bottles of liquor and lining them up along the bar.

Clive stepped outside, walking over to the railing overlooking the atrium. *What the hell am I doing here?*

"Master Sailor Davies," came a female voice from behind him. The sudden use of his more formal military rank caused him to stiffen as a woman with thick, wavy, dark hair stepped up beside him. Her dark green eyes turned towards Clive and stared him down intensely. Clive got the impression he'd seen this person somewhere before, but for the life of him he couldn't remember where. "I figured it was about time we met."

18

"Don't look so nervous, Clive, we're on the same team," the stranger said calmly. She laughed and patted him on the back as if they were long-lost friends. "At least I think we are," she added suspiciously. "Imagine my surprise when I caught that video of you in the water. Don't worry, I didn't tell people I recognized you, that would be too hard to explain. But by the time I managed to track you down, it seemed you had gotten fairly close with a certain founder. I thought maybe your skills had blown your cover or something. I suppose not though." She gave Clive a thin smile.

Clive stared wordlessly for a long moment until he was finally able to compose himself enough to speak.

"I seem to be at a disadvantage then, because I have no idea who you are," he said taking up the defence.

"Special Agent Danika Spencer, US intelligence," she said, Clive looking around to make sure no one was around listening to them. "But you can call me Danika." She put out a hand to Clive but he ignored it, not ready trust anything she was saying.

"What are you doing here?" Clive said, rising up to his full height, which was a full head above Danika. If she found it intimidating, she didn't let it show.

"Officially?" she said with a shrug. "I work in the marine bio lab studying bioluminescence and its potential alternative uses," she said flatly, and Clive was reminded of the woman he thought was staring at him when Squints had given him the tour on his first day. "Unofficially, I'm here for this," she said, pulling out a black USB identical to the one Clive was currently carrying around with him. He reached into his pocket; it felt heavy in his palm. "You didn't really think you would be the only one, did you?"

"I thought the US military wasn't sending anyone else after—" Clive began, but Danika cut him off.

"Sasha. They weren't. I requested this position specifically," Danika said.

"Why?" Clive pressed, and Danika's face darkened for a moment before she turned it around.

"Because I like the ocean, Clive. And because I want to take down the bitch who killed Sasha."

"Who would that be?" Clive asked, but he knew before she said it.

"Grace Alice." Danika spat out the name in disgust.

"Do you know she killed her?" Clive asked. He tried his best to remain as neutral as possible, but his shifting feet betrayed him.

"While you were off smooching the enemy, Mr. Davies, I was doing my job. The server rooms are nearly impossible to get into without being granted direct access. But I did manage to pull up this clip from the security system before it was conveniently deleted." Danika pulled out a phone and pressed play on a video.

"Blue Crest can't leave the facility. You don't understand how

dangerous it can be," said a tearful Grace Alice as she pointed a gun at Sasha Keen, who face was bloodied as she crawled back along the ground. "The world needs Atlantis to launch, and you would be killing everyone if I let you do what you came here to do. I need to protect the people here. Why did you have to do this?" Grace's hand began to shake as she held the gun.

"You're a terrorist," Sasha said. She crawled back along the ground and Grace began to cry in earnest.

Then the screen went black.

"It's all I could manage to get before I was booted from the system, and by the time I managed to get back in, everything was gone," Danika said quietly, looking at the phone. "But I think it shows enough of what that monster is willing to do."

"I'm sorry. Did you know her? Sasha?" Clive asked sincerely.

"It doesn't matter. I'm here to do a job and I'm going to do it. Only now the damned server rooms are locked up tighter than Fort Knox." Danika put the phone back in her pocket. "I was wondering if you'd had any luck with them since you've been here?"

"No," Clive said, ashamed that he didn't even know where the actual server rooms were located yet. "To be honest, I haven't found the main server room."

"What exactly have you been doing?" Danika said, dropping her chin to her chest and letting out a long, angry sigh.

"Getting attacked by sharks," Clive said with a grin, but Danika didn't seem impressed.

"I'll admit I'm surprised you're up and walking around after that, but from some of the research I've seen in the labs, maybe

I should be less surprised." She looked down at Clive's newly healed leg, the sliver of a pink scar running out the bottom of his shorts. "But you've been here for nearly three weeks, and you haven't found anything?"

Clive thought about it for a moment. *That isn't entirely true.*

"Well actually, there is a second, smaller server room that Grace and her team keep in a private lab in the Alpha I. I've pinned the location so I can find it again, although I'm not sure how much good that will do me, my guess is only Grace and her team, including Dr. Nowak, would have access." Danika's face lit up.

"You saw Dr. Nowak? I've been here a month and he rarely seems to show his face," she said, rubbing her hands together.

"Most of his work seems to take place up on the sky side." Clive was happy to have a little information Danika didn't.

"Maybe we can work with that. Dr. Nowak is the key to her plan. If we can kill him—" Danika started to say, but Clive cut her off.

"Kill him? We can't just kill him, we don't even know what he's building."

"We know her plan can only work if he is alive to help. We have to stop this countdown, Clive," Danika snapped back.

"I'm not here to stop anything, and so far I've seen nothing in this city that gives me the impression that anything nefarious is going on. I'm here to collect data and send it back for analysis."

"Nothing nefarious? I just showed you a video of Grace killing a US citizen in cold blood to hide her secrets," Danika said, straining to keep her voice low.

"You showed me a partial video of a wounded US operative on assignment in international waters. For all we know, she's alive and a captive. But either way, it's not enough to justify blindly killing anyone," Clive said unbending on his own principals, though Danika seemed ready to burst at the seams, her face boiling red.

"What good is analysis if we are running out of time? Didn't you hear what she said?" Danika hissed. "I just showed you the type of person you are getting close to. Don't be fooled by this place, Clive. There is more going on here than it seems, and we're running out of time before it launches."

"Before what launches?"

"That's what we need to find out! And we have eleven days, eight hours, and thirty-three minutes to do it in." She pointed to one of the clocks counting down to the announcement of the big surprise. "Remember what you came here for," she said, and turned to leave.

"Wait," Clive said, reaching out and placing a hand on her shoulder. She turned around to face him. "This place, Atlantis. What do you see when you look at it?" he asked, and was surprised by her snap response.

"I see a city filled with naïve dreamers who are unable to see things for what they really are."

"You don't see any good here?"

"How can a place be good when it's built on something so bad?" Danika said, her eyes almost pleading with him.

"It just seems hypocritical, considering the institutions we're here representing. You and I should understand that more than anyone."

"What exactly are you trying to say, Clive?" Danika asked harshly.

"Nothing, I'm just trying to understand why," Clive said slowly. "Don't you want to know why?"

"It's not our job to ask why," she replied, turning to leave.

"Shouldn't we?" Clive asked, shaking his head. Danika's head dropped and when she looked back up she was holding back tears.

"You do what you have to do, but I will not let Sasha's death be for nothing," she said, slamming her finger into Clive's chest and storming away before he had the chance to say another word.

Clive watched as she walked along the atrium before ducking into the nearest hallway and out of sight. *How could Hammond not have told me that I wasn't alone in the city? What else is being kept from me?*

Clive gripped the railing that surrounded the atrium wall so tightly his knuckles turned white. *Did Danika really expect me to just start killing people? Would she kill Grace if she managed to get near her?*

This last thought sat heavily with him. Grace was many things, but he couldn't imagine her as a killer. *But has that video shown me otherwise? At the very least, it was enough to know she might be capable of it.*

Clive didn't know how long he'd stood like a statue by the railing, playing over everything in his mind, before he felt a vibration in his wrist and LUCY's voice played in his ear.

"Message from Kissa. Does five work for tonight?" As Clive looked down at the face of his LUCY, Kissa's message scrolled across the screen, first in Egyptian, then in English. The time in the corner read 3:30 p.m., and Clive felt like he had wasted an entire day standing around.

"Five is great," he said, and LUCY picked up and sent the response for him. Clive took his time heading back to the apartment, still unsure of what he was going to do about any of this.

By the time he'd finally arrived at Kissa's home, he'd made no progress on what he wanted to do. He felt terrible, distracted, and not even the promise of delicious food brought him out of it. He wished he had, cancelled but it was too late. Clive reluctantly knocked on the door.

Kissa was hard at work, cooking something that promised to have at least a little spice in it, based on the aroma that wafted its way across the room.

Clive had managed to recoup enough of his senses to remember to bring a gift over to their house, something he had forgotten to do with Squints and his family and Clive had wanted to kick himself for it. Years of being at sea and being invited into strangers' homes had bedded in this tradition for Clive. And now, since he actually knew where things were in the city, he should have no excuse. He'd decided on a small box of chocolates, which he presented to Kissa and her mother when he arrived.

Clive stood in what he knew now was a standard layout for an Atlantis home, with Kissa and her mom, who was introduced to Clive as Bahiti. He was immediately captured by the works of art that tastefully decorated the walls of the main living area, and was happy to distract himself by admiring them, as he felt very self-conscious about being there.

"Do you like art, Clive?" Bahiti asked, her Egyptian words translated smoothly into his ear as she gestured towards the walls. Clive smiled.

"I like your art," Clive said, and Bahiti laughed.

"Thank you. Kissa told me what you did for her today. I wanted to thank you for giving my daughter that opportunity."

"Mom, you promised you wouldn't be weird," Kissa said, stirring a large pot as she sprinkled salt in the dish.

"Is a mother not allowed to thank the man who gave her daughter an incredible, once-in-a-lifetime opportunity? I didn't realize that was embarrassing," Bahiti said, turning back towards her daughter before giving Clive a smile.

"Don't mind her, Clive, she doesn't socialize much," Kissa said playfully.

"I do too! I just also work hard, and I expect you to do the same," Bahiti said in the nagging tone of a parent tired of her child talking back. "Do you have any children, Clive?" she added before Kissa could interrupt again.

"No, I don't, ma'am," Clive said, as Bahiti leaned over and began pouring a cup of black tea.

"Lucky you," she said, handing him a cup, as she shot her daughter a teasing look.

"She'd be lost without me," Kissa said, turning away to trim some herbs Clive didn't recognize that were growing in their hanging garden.

"I would, but don't tell her that," Bahiti said sweetly. "Is everything okay, Mr. Davies?"

Clive hadn't noticed but he must have drifted away in his mind for a moment, going back over the video he'd seen of Grace Alice potentially killing someone. He shook his head, half to rid himself of the memory, half to answer the question.

"Yes, I'm fine, sorry. I'm just a little distracted lately," Clive said, giving her a thin smile.

"Fair enough. Kissa told me about what happened to you. I suppose that would have given anyone reason to pause," Bahiti said, taking a sip of tea. Clive mimicked the act, feeling the warmth of the minty tea fill his body.

"It's not that entirely," Clive began, trying to decide if he even wanted to talk about any of this. But the words started to come out before he could stop them. "I'm only contracted till the end of the month, but I could stay, if I wanted to. But I can't decide if this place is—" He paused, trying to find the right word to capture what he was thinking.

"Real," Bahiti said softly after a moment's pause, and Clive nodded. "I can understand those feelings. Atlantis seems at times too good to be true and I often find myself waiting for the other shoe to drop, as it has everywhere else."

"Exactly!" Clive said, happy to feel vindicated, if only a little, in his thoughts. "Don't get me wrong, the work and advancements Atlantis seems to be providing are extraordinary. But can it really be as perfect as it seems?"

"Ask yourself this: Does it need to be?" Bahiti said slowly. Clive thought about it, letting the words linger in his mind.

"I don't understand," he said finally.

"Perfection will always be in the eye of the beholder," Kissa said from across the room. Clearly she'd still been listening in. "Some people will always look to find where things are broken, because they are afraid."

"Are you saying I'm afraid, Kissa?" Clive said with a smile. She shrugged. "Are you?"

"Kissa!" Bahiti chastised her daughter.

"It's okay. She's not wrong. Do you mind if I ask why you stayed?" Clive looked between Bahiti and Kissa. Bahiti set down her mug and poured some more tea into it before offering it to Clive, who accepted happily. He was beginning to think they weren't going to answer.

"Kissa's father was a journalist in Egypt. He was a brilliant man. He cared about freedom, the people, and about truth. He was less then beloved by our leaders, who he chastised often with his writing. He called out their hypocrisy, asking them to answer for their actions. He was brave." Bahiti paused, holding the hot tea close to her chest. "One day, we'd got word that he was taken by the police, and that they would be coming for Kissa and me next. She was only ten at the time. I'd been working at the university, doing research. Egypt had been our home, and in an instant, it was all taken from us." Tears welled up in her eyes.

"I'm sorry, I shouldn't have brought this up," Clive said, but Bahiti raised her hand to stop him.

"It's fine. It's important to remember our past, Clive," she said. She took a long sip of her tea before letting out a deep breath and continuing. "For the next five years, Kissa and I bounced around from country to country, trying to find one that would offer us permanent refugee status. Eventually, we ended up in Canada."

"Where abouts? I'm from Canada," Clive said, feeling a bit of pride in his voice.

"Regina. It was incredibly cold," Bahiti said with a laugh, "but we had a home and I was told that eventually Kissa could start back at school, which I was happy about, as home schooling was proving difficult with her being much smarter than me." She gave her daughter a warm smile.

"So how did you end up here?" Clive asked cautiously.

"Well, Canada was wonderful in so many ways, but fell short in others." She looked at him with sad eyes. "Most people were kind, like you." Her eyes told a different story as they filled with sadness. "But your country would never recognize my degree or allow me to continue my work in chemical engineering , not unless I went back to school, and since we had no money, I had to take work where I could get it. Because of my lack of English, all I could find was work at a local convenience store, which was owned by another family who'd immigrated there years before. They understood what we were going through and offered to help. Without them, we would have been lost. But two years ago, I applied to work here. They had no restrictions, and I could finally do what I was trained to do, what I love to do." She looked up at Clive. "When we first arrived, Kissa used to joke that this was the island of misfits."

Clive looked over to Kissa, who was wiping a tear away.

"I think it's time for some food," Kissa said, seeming all too happy to change the topic.

"Thank you for sharing that with me," Clive said, as Bahiti placed a comforting hand on his forearm.

"Dinner looks great," Bahiti said as she walked over to embrace her daughter, who didn't try to fight off the intimate hug.

"This is the Egyptian equivalent of breakfast for dinner, and I promise you, it is amazing," Kissa said proudly.

"Kissa makes a wonderful ful medames and ta'ameya." Bahiti kissed the side of Kissa's head, and this time Kissa did push her mother away playfully.

"It looks incredible," Clive said, looking over a pot of thick soup and a plate of what looked like falafel. On a separate plate he saw something he definitely recognized. He picked two up and set them on his plate. "I love grape leaves!" he said enthusiastically as he poured some of the soup into a bowl; its aroma was intoxicating. He added a few of the ta'ameya before taking a seat at the small table they'd set up beside the kitchen. As Clive waited for Kissa and Bahiti to fill up their plates, he noticed a picture on a side table, of the two of them with a smiling, happy man who must have been Kissa's father. He thought about Bahiti's story and how her husband never came home.

The rest of the meal was filled with laughter, despite the nagging thoughts Clive was having about Grace. The breakfast, as Kissa kept calling it, was incredible, and after a few hours, which passed with surprising ease, Clive left, thankful for the distraction and unexpected joy of the night, filled to the brim and then some.

It wasn't until he was back home in bed that the worry and dread washed over him like a flood, making it difficult to fall asleep. Clive wished he'd never seen the video of Grace and Sasha. The possibility that Grace was willing to kill someone to protect the city seemed so at odds with the woman he'd had dinner with. Her views seemed radical, but not homicidal.

In a completely useless attempt to distract himself from Grace and the video, Clive found himself thinking about Bahiti and the fact that Atlantis was the only place that would allow her to work as an engineer. Even Canada had made that nearly impossible. But here she had a purpose. Here her daughter would have the opportunity to work with some of the most brilliant people in the world. *Does that justify killing someone? Then again, I've killed people under the veil of the greater good. Is it hypocritical of me to believe that what I've done is right and what Grace may have done is wrong?*

Clive's mind unleashed a whirlwind of memories he would rather have forgotten, of the people he'd been sent to kill, or simply dispatched under the guise of collateral damage. *Was it always for a good reason? How many times have I blindly followed orders that resulted in someone losing their life?*

Clive began to sweat, despite the cool room. He ripped the duvet off his body so that only the sheet covered him. His arm rested atop his forehead as he stared unblinking up at the ceiling until his eyes burned so much, he was forced to nourish them one blink at a time. But this tiny torture did little to rid his mind of the stresses that plagued him.

19

At some point Clive must have dozed off, but that didn't prevent him from waking up feeling unrested and tired. In spite of feeling weak and sleep deprived, his body, now that he was awake, seemed unwilling to go back to sleep. He forced himself out of bed and made his way into the bathroom, where he primed the steam room, hoping a nice sweat and a cold shower would do him some good.

He sat on the tiles and let the aroma of eucalyptus seep into his body as he breathed deeply, the steam and sharp, fiery scent calming him. He tried to ignore the numerous questions burning in his mind, and all the answers he still needed.

He knew he must be tired when one of the riskier thoughts rattled loose in his mind. He'd spent so much time thinking he had to sneak around. *What if I simply asked about Blue Crest? What if I ignored all protocol and simply told her why I'm here and what I am after? Would she let me into her database to prove she has nothing to hide? Let me scan what I need then leave Atlantis? If my information is correct, all I would need is a few minutes with the servers and my program key would do the rest. What would Grace have to lose, unless she was really trying to hide something?*

Even though his mind had been playing hopscotch, he felt

his eyes begin to droop a little and decided he'd been in the steam long enough. Releasing the steam, he turned on the shower, the cold water falling over his body giving him the much-need shock he was looking for.

Clive hopped out of the shower feeling refreshed and was excited to see that he had a message on his LUCY from Squints. He felt guilty that he hadn't reached out at all the day before to check on his friend. He told himself Squints would want time with his family, but really Clive had just been so distracted by everything since his dinner with Grace that he simply forgot.

LUCY read the message out as Clive dried off with a towel. "Want to come for a dive with me and Mia this morning, around nine? She's been nagging me to take her out to the reef, but I think she's just afraid I won't want to get back in the water. Anyways, let me know, it will be fun."

He'd been meaning to go back to the reef. He'd only managed to go out on his own once after Squints had taken him that first day. He looked at his time. It was 8:15.

"LUCY reply, Would love to. I'll meet you there at nine," Clive said, as he slipped on a pair of swim trunks, a Hawaiian shirt, and sandals. Ordering a coffee and a bagel from the café for pick up, he planned to head to the dive bay before meeting Squints, to grab his gill.

Kissa wasn't at the café when he'd arrived. Instead, Clive received his order from a fresh-faced boy with thick, curly red hair. Clive wasn't surprised when he called out his name in a thick Scottish accent.

Clive wondered if he would need to go through the marine lab in order to get to the to the reef dive exit. *There must be other exits in the city I could use?*

The idea of running into Danika made Clive nervous. She

didn't exactly seem neutral about Atlantis, and Grace Alice in particular. Something in the way she spoke gave Clive the impression that somehow all of this was far more personal for her then it was for him. He wondered if she must have served with Sasha Keen at some point.

He made good time to the dive bay and realized he hadn't been back since the incident. So he was surprised and a little embarrassed when, as he made his way down the staircase towards the main level, one of the passersby gave him a clap on the arm.

"Good to see you back, Clive," said a tall German man with long, shaggy hair and large hands that thudded against Clive's back.

A few more people called out from around the main level and eventually someone, who Clive wanted to maim, began to clap. Soon everyone around him began to join in. Clive felt his face turn bright red as he finished chewing a particularly large bite of his bagel that he regretted shoving into his mouth.

He tried to gesture to everyone to stop but with his mouth full, and one hand still holding a coffee, the gesture looked a little more like a bird trying to flap a broken wing. He finally managed to swallow the bagel.

"Thank you," he choked out. "Thank you, I, ummm …" He didn't really know what to say and was overwhelmed by the whole affair. Luckily, Hamish and Sunny swooped in to save him.

"Easy, people! All the man did was risk his life to safe Squints and fight off a couple fifteen-foot sharks. It's not like he's a hero or anything," Hamish said, slapping Clive on the back.

"He seems more shaken from the attention than the shark

bite he got," Sunny said as she began to giggle. "Speaking of, I would have expected at least a small limp," she added, looking down at his healed leg.

Thanks to Hamish and Sunny's intervention, the clapping faded and all the attention on Clive stopped. He could have hugged both of them for the real rescue. Sunny had been right; Clive hated the attention.

"Dr. Kashyap and his team used some miracle goop and it seemed to heal it right up!" Clive said, lifting his swim trunks up to show off the red and pink scar that traced up the outside of his thigh.

"Impressive." Sunny looked more closely at the wound. "I would have said that was impossible, but I guess this is Atlantis, after all." That fact she'd been speaking to him in Korean, and he understood every word, only emphasized her point.

"You two heading out today?" Clive asked, desperately trying to change the subject, pointing to the dive gear they were both carrying.

"You betcha mate, Sunny and I got to pick up the slack from you and that lazy partner of yours," Hamish said, adding a little wink at the end.

"We will be back out there in a few days, I think. Doctor's orders and all that," Clive said, laughing.

"So what are you doing here now?" Sunny asked, tilting her head and looking him up and down.

"Squints promised Mia he'd take her to the reef. I'm guessing he thought it would be good for me to get back in the water again before we head back to work."

"You'd be right," said a booming voice from behind Clive. Clive turned, knowing it would be Squints. He looked casual in his swim trunks and a tank top that had two sea turtles high-fiving as they rode a wave. He had his arm around Mia, who was already in her wet suit and carrying a kid's-size gill under her arm.

"Squints! Good to see ya mate, you really had us on edge there last week," Hamish said, trying to hide the concern in his voice. All three of them eyed him up. They couldn't see any signs of damage on Squints's body, but they all knew the real damage was in the mind.

"Mia, good thinking getting your dad out in the water today!" Sunny said, having to bend over only slightly, her small frame nearly matched by an already tall Mia.

"Don't be fooled, Sunny, this little adventure is one hundred percent for Mia. She's been tormenting me to take her since before our little adventure," Squints said with a laugh. But Clive caught a little exchange of a wink from Mia and a knowing smile from Sunny.

"Well, either way, the waters are tranquil this morning, so you should all have a good time. Hamish and I should get to work," Sunny said, giving Hamish an elbow to the side.

"Easy there. This one's always pushing me around, it's like she thinks she's my boss or something," Hamish said, turning to go.

"It's funny to think I'm not his boss," Sunny said with a little giggle. "Have a good dive." She left to follow Hamish to the change rooms.

"What's the deal with them?" Clive asked, watching the two of them head off.

"What do you mean?" Squints asked.

"Like, are they … together?" Clive felt weird about asking, and to make it even more awkward, Squints began to laugh.

"I think Ji-hyun would have something to say about it,"

Squints said, still laughing. "Sunny's wife," he added when Clive still looked a little confused.

"Ohhh! Gotcha," Clive said, returning Squints's laugh.

"They've been partners for almost two years now. They've both been asked to be mentors, like me for you. But they trust each other, and having that trust is important." Squints gave Clive a knowing smile.

"Can we please get moving? You guys are taking forever," Mia said as she began to walk towards the TOTS. Squints laughed and Clive clapped a hand to his shoulder.

"Thank you for inviting me," Clive said appreciatively.

"You're welcome, but this is all Mia. She thinks if we don't go back in soon, we may never go back in." Clive could see the look of dread in his eyes, and he wondered if Mia hadn't been right to get him in the water quickly. Clive, who had had his fair share of danger in the water, had to admit there was something different about this one, although it would take more than a couple of sharks to keep him out of the water.

"We will always be visitors in the ocean, and sometimes she needs to remind us of that," he said, using Squints own words back on him as he tightening his grip on Squints's shoulder.

"Will you both hurry up! I'm not getting any younger," Mia said impatiently, breaking the moment between the two friends. She stood wide legged, with a youthful determination Clive hadn't seen in her before.

"Sorry, Mia," he said, as they broke into laughter and hurried off to meet her.

It took some time to get his gear in order. He'd forgotten that both he and Squints had lost their wet suits in the attack, which meant they needed to get new ones. It was easy enough to put the request in, although Clive had half a mind to skip the wet suit altogether. The cold water might not have been as cold as the look of impatience Mia had given them the entire time. It was nearly nine thirty by the time they reached the dive doors in the Alpha II labs, and Clive was very happy he didn't run into Danika at any point. It would be hard enough to try and explain how he knew her, but he also wanted nothing to do with her for the moment.

Clive still hadn't figured out what he was going to do about his encounter with her, and the worry must have shown on his face because Squints gave him a reassuring slap on the back, no doubt thinking it was the water that was filling him with dread.

Clive would gladly take on another shark compared to dealing with his current situation. It was his mission after all and the entire reason he was on this ship and in less than ten days he would be heading home. *Or would I? Could I just stay on Atlantis not go back to the mainland?*

Danika, Commander Hammond, and all of the people at Five Eyes thought there was something dangerous on Atlantis, so dangerous they needed to make sure it was destroyed. Or else why send so many agents to try to figure it out? *Why would Grace kill someone if she wasn't hiding something? Could Sasha still be alive and held captive somewhere in the city? The video never showed her death, though I'm not sure that fact will do much to deter Danika from trying to bring down Grace. But would Danika really do anything to stop her?*

Clive hopped in the cool water, letting the refreshing sensation wash over him and carry away his problems. He was grateful to be getting back in the water. Even in the short few days away from it, he missed it. He closed his eyes, feeling the water prickle his skin as he took a few long, deep breaths, trying to forget all his worries.

When he opened his eyes, he saw Squints and Mia swimming ahead of him towards the exit bay and he started kicking, eager to catch up and get into the open waters again.

It must have been sunny outside, because the water was bright, a crisp blue-green, and it felt warm.

"Has the reef risen since you brought me out last?" Clive asked skeptically.

"Yeah, about ten meters, the weather is cooling so the reef adjusts to meet the optimal temperatures," Squints said.

"Cool!" Mia shouted in the comms, as she raced ahead to a school of saddleback butterflyfish circling around one of the reefs.

"Stay close," Squints said, trying not to sound too much like an overbearing parent.

"I will," Mia said, turning to give him a reassuring wave.

"How you holding up, Clive?" Squints asked, and Clive wondered if he had made it so they could talk to one another privately.

"Good. You?" Clive said calmly.

"Good. Feels a little weird to be back out here. But honestly, not as bad as I thought. I think it might have had something to do with being blacked out for most of the hard stuff," he said with a forced laugh.

"You don't have to worry about me. One thing I've always understood is that if the ocean really wants me, she will take me," Clive said lightly.

"Sounds ominous." Squints chuckled.

"Maybe, but for some reason I find it comforting. Don't worry, I'll be good for tomorrow. I'll admit I'm happy you invited me out here though, I needed a good dive. Something to clear my head," Clive said, wishing he didn't sound so vague, that he could talk openly to Squints about what was going on.

"What's on your mind?" Squints said supportively as they swam down to get closer to Mia. "I know Mia. It is cool. It's a clown triggerfish," Squints said, and Clive assumed he'd kept his comms open to Mia as well. "Sorry, trying to keep it educational." He shrugged, though the gesture seemed slower in the water.

"I had dinner with Grace Alice the other night. She wanted to thank me for, well I'm not sure." Clive laughed. "Maybe not dying, I guess."

"Ohh la la. Having a date with the boss. Very classy," Squints said, the words trilling in his mouth. Even in his native Portuguese Clive could hear the sarcasm.

"I wouldn't say that," Clive said, although he wasn't entirely sure it hadn't been something like that. She certainly had an ulterior motive, or so it felt at the beginning of the night. "And if it was a date, I would hardly say it ended well."

"How did you manage to mess it up?" Squints laughed.

"What makes you think I messed it up?" Clive protested, and Squints turned to face him. Even through his mask, his face held a challenge.

"Okay," Clive continued, "I may have … I don't know. Thinking about it now makes me feel silly."

"Happens to the best of us. When I first met Margarida, I tried to impress her and we went for a late-night swim, where I proceeded to get stung by a jellyfish. Needless to say, after that I never thought I would hear from her again. But some things aren't always as bad as they seem."

"Honestly, I think I would have taken the jellyfish." Clive laughed. "How much do you know about Grace?"

"Just what she's done and what she vows to do for the city in the future. All of which I respect. But her as a person? I don't know much about her. She seems kind, I can see that," Squints said, as the image of Grace holding the gun to Sasha flashed through Clive's mind.

"But you believe her? You trust that she is doing good?" Clive pressed.

"I trust what I see. And here I see people from all walks of life being given a chance to be treated like equals. So far, Grace has delivered on everything she promised. I believe that has to earn her a certain level of trust. Until that trust is broken, I have no reason to believe otherwise."

Squints's words lingered in his mind for the rest of the dive, and by the time he got out of the water, he realized what he needed to do.

It had been a week since the attack and Clive was nearly back to normal. His leg was still weak, but improving. Being back in the water helped a lot. It wasn't too much strain on his muscles, and he was finally back into a rhythm with Squints. But something was still off. At least he could take comfort in knowing that if Squints thought there was anything up with Clive, he would chalk it up to being back in the open water.

Which, of course, couldn't have been further from the truth. In fact, being in the water was his only saving grace. It kept him busy and had allowed him at least a little time to really think about how he wanted to move forward with confronting Grace.

Clive figured everything he needed could be accessed by Grace's private lab, and thanks to the pin he had dropped, he knew how to find it again. This left finding a way to access the server room, and getting in and out without being caught.

He'd been trying to remember the details from what little time he'd spent in the lab, and the biggest problem he'd run into was figuring out how to get past the access panel for the server room. He believed he'd need not only a personalized LUCY from one of the few people in the city with access to the lab, but also an access code to go along with it. This posed a lot of questions, the most daunting of which was, was there one access code for the room, or did each person have their own code?

He'd hardly call the plan he'd managed to come up with a *master plan*, but it was something, and he still had one advantage. He wasn't alone anymore. He had Danika, which meant the odds of success would be marginally improved. All they would need is a little luck. *Okay, a lot of luck.*

Commander Hammond was also becoming more impatient with Clive with each passing day. Clive tried to understand and not take it personally, especially considering it was only six days before the launch of Blue Crest and he still didn't have any real insight into what it was or how it worked.

Clive had felt a pang of anger when he discovered Commander Hammond had known about other operatives on board and had chosen not to tell him, despite Clive being adamant that maybe things could have moved a lot faster if he'd known, not that his time with Danika thus far had been overly productive. Hammond seemed unwavering in the notion that it was best he hadn't.

The only good part of the exchange with his old mentor was that he'd revealed more of his cards. Clive had purposefully left out how many operatives he'd met, which meant there were more. If that were true, and they were all still on the mission, it meant none of them were having any more success than he was. *Which is a small victory, I suppose.*

"LUCY, message Danika Spencer," Clive said. He'd finished work and had just got home for a shower. Squints had requested the next day off to help Martim with a project, and Clive was more than happy to have the next forty-eight hours to himself.

He felt a little guilty when Squints had invited him over for dinner and Clive had to turn him down. Squints had been cagey since they'd gone back to work, and Clive suspected he wanted to know if Clive would be staying on after his trial run. As Squints was the one who got primary sign off on his appointment, Clive was confident that if he wanted to stay, he could. But he wasn't ready to discuss any of that, not before he finished what he'd come here to do.

But still, the look on his friend's face was difficult to ignore, and Clive couldn't help but feel like Squints had taken his distance personally.

"What would you like to say?" LUCY said with steady confidence.

"Wanna grab a coffee in the Atrium? Say Iota III, thirty minutes," he said calmly.

LUCY sent the message and Clive waited patiently for a response. It was lucky that LUCY had access to all of the people in the city as long as you knew their first and last name.

A message returned a minute later. "I'll be there." Clive tossed on a sweater and headed out the door.

He arrived early and was able to find another café, where he ordered himself a coffee. He ordered Danika one as well. He'd made it a black coffee, since she seemed like a no-nonsense kind of person.

Clive was right. She was also hyper-suspicious, and a tad paranoid, which was obvious when she wouldn't even sit beside him when she arrived. Instead, she chose to stand against the railing and not ever look at him.

"Are you an idiot? Why the hell would you contact me on a LUCY? For all we know, they monitor them and could be watching us right now," she hissed, refusing to look at him.

"All the more reason to stop acting like some sort of spy and just come sit beside me," he said, patting the empty bench beside him before picking up the coffee he'd set on the ground. "I got you a coffee," he said politely. She finally turned to look at him.

"Black?" she said, eyeing the mug in his hand. He nodded, holding it up for her to take. "How'd you guess?" She reluctantly took the coffee, but stayed leaning on the railing instead of sitting next to him.

"Call it a hunch." He laughed.

"I still think you're an idiot for contacting me like that," she said sternly.

"I think you're an idiot for not contacting me sooner. We could have formulated a plan or something." He watched as her brows shot up.

"A plan? What makes you think I wanted help?"

"You found me," he said simply. "I didn't even know there were other operatives onboard."

"Contacting you was a mistake, one I regret immensely by the way," Danika said smugly.

"A little late to be worrying about that don't you think?" Clive said shaking his head annoyed.

"You still haven't answered my question. Why did you contact me now?" Danika said, taking a sip of her coffee.

"We have six days before the launch and I'm not sure about you, but I'm not any closer to figuring out what project Blue Crest is." he said catching a concerned expression on Danika's face.

"The main server room is under heavy surveillance, and you need special access to even get through the first barrier.

I could modify my LUCY to mimic someone's signal easily enough. But then beyond that, additional access codes, I'm assuming biometrics, and God knows what else they have hidden in there," Danika said, rolling her eyes.

"Basically, you can't get in." Clive said with laugh.

"I don't think anyone could, unless they were granted access," she said, sounding defeated.

"What if there was another way?" Clive said calmly. Danika looked skeptical.

"What do you mean?"

"Grace Alice has a private lab on Alpha I," he said, pointing up to the main level atrium, where he could just make out the elevator to the glass crow's nest he'd been in only days before.

"And what were you doing in these private labs?" Danika said, narrowing her eyes at Clive, a hint of playfulness behind them. Clive ignored her and continued.

"Her team is small, so only a few people have access, and from what I can tell we only need the right LUCY to access it and a key code to get in. I'm not sure if it is connected to the main server room, or if it is even possible to get what we need from those servers, but we should at least get a handle on some of the secret projects they are working on up there."

"Sounds easier, but it's not the mission."

"That's assuming there isn't a direct link to the main servers. But at the very least, wouldn't you want to leave here with something?" Clive said, letting the idea percolate in Danika's mind.

"Fair enough. But how do you propose we get the code?" Danika said, now sounding more than a little intrigued.

"I'm going to try to get it tonight." Clive said. He tried to hide his embarrassment. It was the part of the plan he was least looking forward to discussing.

"Tonight, eh, Mr. Bond? What are you going to do, seduce her into revealing all her secrets to you?" Danika said, laughing.

"She technically owes me a dinner. That is, if she doesn't hate me too much after the other night."

"What'd you do? Shit on her precious city?" Danika nearly spat out her coffee when she saw the look of guilt on Clive's face. "You didn't! Why would you do that?"

"It was her vision for Atlantis. It got to me," Clive said regretfully.

"Well, good for you for not drinking the Kool-Aid," Danika said not bothering to hide her contempt.

Clive didn't have the courage to tell her which part of the city he took issue with. Or that he had made up his mind, at least he thought he had, that no matter what happened next, if he was allowed to stay on Atlantis, he would. He owed a debt to the Navy for everything they'd done for him over the years, but Clive figured he'd paid that debt, and after this operation he would have given more than enough to retire.

"Right. So, what do you think?" Clive asked, taking another sip of his coffee.

"If you can get the access code for the server room, I can get in and plant the drive," Danika said confidently.

"But whatever information you pull, I need a copy to send to my government. Or none of this," Clive said, pointing between them, "is going to happen. I know what your government's idea of teamwork looks like, and you can bet your ass that if I'm going through all of this, I'm sending in the information to my commanding officer." Danika mulled it over, and Clive had no idea if she was debating whether she should do it, or if she was simply trying to think of creative ways to screw him over. But at this point, next to flat out asking Grace for the information, he was out of options.

"Deal," she said after a moment. "Grace Alice needs to be shut down." She stuck out a hand for him to shake. Clive narrowed his eyes, waiting for her to say it. She shook her head. "If you can get the access code, I'll share the information I pull." Satisfied, he took her hand.

"How are you going to do it?" she asked, amused.

"No idea." Clive laughed. "But I got six days to figure it out." It wasn't exactly a lie. He did have a plan, but he wasn't ready to share that with Danika. She seemed hell bent on getting the information and destroying Grace Alice, which made asking this next bit more difficult. "How did you end up here? You don't exactly seem to enjoy being here."

"And you do?" Danika asked contentiously. Clive shrugged.

"I was told it would be easy," he replied casually. "Dive every day, get some information, in and out. I didn't realize what Atlantis was before coming."

"And what is that?" Danika replied as her jaw clenched.

"It's like an isle of misfits and outcasts, only it's filled with people who seem like they want make the world better ." Danika let out a harsh laugh.

"Ha. That's what they want you to believe, Clive. Atlantis will destroy everything we've fought for. They've already shown what they are willing to do to keep their secrets." Her voice was cold and distant.

"Are you talking about Atlantis, or Grace?" Clive asked, not bothering to hide the concern in his voice.

"Is there a difference?" Danika shot back.

"I don't know, but blindly believing there isn't is a dangerous path."

"Easy to say when it's not one of yours who was killed."

"You don't know that. The video only showed—"

"I know what it looks like before someone pulls the trigger," Danika said, slapping the railing in front of her before regaining her composure. "Grace Alice wanted Sasha dead, and she killed her to hide whatever secrets she'd discovered. When are you going to get this through your thick skull? We are here to bring them down, and to make Grace Alice answer for her crimes." Danika hissed the words, trying hard not to draw attention to either of them, and before Clive could respond she turned and left. Calling back over her shoulder, she added, "Find me when you know the key code."

Like that, she was gone, and Clive was left sitting in the atrium, wondering if he'd made the right choice of partner. After a moment, he got up and made his way over to the TOTS, headed towards Alpha I and Grace's lab.

He got lost a couple times, coming at the lab from a different way. Although the pin was accurate, he still got muddled up in the bland-looking hallways. He finally reached a door he recognized, and he tried his LUCY on it. The sensor flashed red.

"It's not going to work," said a deep voice from behind him, and Clive turned to find Dr. Nowak standing there holding a wrapped sandwich. "Besides, she's not in there," he added, unwrapping the sandwich and taking a bite.

"Sorry, I wasn't—" Clive stammered, but Dr. Nowak put a hand up to stop him.

"Pardon me. I tend get distracted by my work and never remember to eat. My wife used to joke I would forget to breathe if my body didn't do it on its own." He laughed quietly.

He walked over to the door and pressed his LUCY up to the sensor, tapped in a code on at his wrist, and watched as the door flashed green. He gestured into the room and showed Clive in.

"Should I be allowed in here?" Clive asked.

"Unless you can sight read advanced physics, in which case I would say you should absolutely be allowed in, then I doubt you will see anything Ms. Alice would deem secret," Dr. Nowak said with a smile. "She should be back any minute if you want to have a seat." He pointed to one of the empty swivel chairs at an unused desk.

"Thank you," Clive said, getting a nod from Dr. Nowak. "What are you working on in here?" Clive asked, trying his best to sound casual. He couldn't believe his luck—not only did he get access to the lab, he was talking with Dr. Nowak himself. *Could this be the advantage I'm looking for?*

"The work I do here is very hush-hush," he said with a smile.

"I'm guessing it will all be revealed soon," Clive said, nodding to a countdown clock on the wall and was genuinely shocked when Dr. Nowak began to laugh.

"Clever man, Mr. Davies," he said, shoving the last bit of his sandwich in his mouth and taking a moment to swallow it. "What I'm working on may or may not be part of the presentation at the end of the month," he said with a wink. "Although I suspect it will only be one of the surprises that day."

"Careful, what you say to this one, Doctor," Grace said, stepping into the room with a small tablet pressed up against her chest. She glared at Clive. "I don't suspect he shares the same vision for the world as you and me," Grace added coldly.

"May I remind you that most people share our vision. It's

rather the method of how we get there, people tend to take issues with." Dr. Nowak said, as Grace turned to give him an uncharacteristically stern look.

"I'm not sure what you said to her, my boy, but I for one do not want to stick around to find out what it was," Dr. Nowak said, turning to look sympathetically at Clive before leaving for a back room, adding absently, "I'll get started on those tests."

"I'm not entirely sure why you are here, Clive, but despite what you might think, I have work to do," Grace said, reading the tablet in her hand, her fingers scrolling carefully on it.

"I wanted to apologize," Clive said, noticing a slight hitch in her scrolling before he continued. "I was out of bounds the other night, and I think I'm starting to understand what you are doing here." Grace stopped and looked up at him, her eyes focusing in as if studying him.

"Somehow, I doubt that," she said finally before continuing to scroll.

"Look, I've gone my entire life believing that one way of life is superior to everything else. But that doesn't mean something can't be better. Now, I don't know if this is better, but it certainly seems to work here and that should count for something." Clive hoped she could understand what he meant. "I can't help it, my first reaction is always to be defensive," he added softly.

Clive waited for her to speak and eventually he saw her shoulders drop as she finally turned to face him.

"Progress and innovation should never be stopped because of complacency," she said quietly.

"Who said that?" Clive asked.

"My father," Grace said softly. "What's with the sudden

change of heart?"

"It was more a who than a what, and let's just say they helped me see what Atlantis is all about."

"And what would that be?" Grace asked, her high ponytail falling gently over her shoulder as her head tilted suspiciously at him.

"That Atlantis is a home for misfits. Somewhere they are free to be exactly who they were meant to be, away from the prejudices of the outside world."

Grace's lip puckered up a little. She paused briefly before giving him a smile.

"I suppose it is." She let the words linger for a moment before pacing across the floor, heading towards a desk and a computer. "So, what are you doing here?" she asked again, glancing up at him disinterestedly.

"Well, unless I'm mistaken, you still owe me a dinner, and I've come to collect," Clive said with a toothy smile. Grace shook her head and laughed.

"True enough. Where are we going?" she said, eyes scanning Clive from head to toe.

"The Snailbox." It was the first place that came to mind. He hadn't thought any of this would actually work, and yet Grace was mulling it over. She glanced down at her LUCY.

"Okay, I just need to upload these files and then we can go. That work?"

"Really? I mean, yeah, it totally works for me," he said, wishing his face didn't feel so flushed. It had all happened so quickly, Clive hadn't even realized she said she needed to upload something until Grace walked over to the entrance door for the server room. He stood watching, hit with a feeling of uncertainty. From where he was standing, he could just make out the top of her LUCY and the keypad that was now displayed on its face. *Is this what I want to do?*

Before he could talk himself out of it, he watched intently as her fingers keyed in the first three digits of the code before her body shifted, blocking his view of the final three digits. He heard the slight hiss from the door as it opened and Grace stepped inside. A wave of guilt washed over him as she turned back, giving him a warm smile. He tried to match her warmth, but it still felt cold.

047, 047, Clive repeated in his mind before he had time to forget it. He had half of what he needed to send to Danika. But the idea felt like a betrayal as he watched Grace through the thick glass plugging her tablet into a central computer. *Would Grace ever forgive me for this?*

He didn't give himself time to think about it. He quickly fired off a message to Danika before he could convince himself otherwise. He needed her to know he was prepared to follow through on the mission. It was, after all, the reason he was in Atlantis.

The thought ate away at him as Grace stepped back into the lab.

"Ready?" she asked eagerly, the words carrying more meaning for Clive than she could possibly know.

"I think so," he said, but quickly corrected himself when he saw the confused expression on her face. "I mean yes, definitely."

"Are you okay? You seem distracted," she said, taking a step towards him. "If you're having second thoughts about the dinner, we don't have to go."

"No, sorry," Clive said, straightening up a little. "It's not that. I'm excited for dinner. I was just thinking about some work stuff," he added hesitantly. "But I'm good to go!"

"Where we going?" Grace asked.

"Back down to Nu II atrium, the TOTS should bring us out right by it," Clive said, gesturing grandly towards the door and giving her an exaggerated bow.

"I was thinking we could get to the restaurant a little differently," Grace said, giving Clive a playful smile. "How are you with heights again?" she asked, putting her finger on her chin as she walked out with a confused Clive on her tail.

All thoughts of betrayal were absent from Clive's mind as he felt the straps around his waist tighten. He white-knuckled the handle in front of him and he wasn't even moving yet. He vaguely heard the voice of the baby-faced teacher pulling at various straps around his body.

Ignoring all advice to not look down, he seemed perpetually unable to do anything but. He stood on a platform that jutted out over the edge of the atrium, from which he could see all the levels below with their cascade of blooming vegetation. It looked horrifically beautiful.

He'd watched people do this before, but he'd personally never wanted to try it. Why anyone would feel the urge to dangle from a thin cord as they flew over a vast empty space, that would most certainly kill them if they fell, was beyond him.

The zipline system stretched out across the mouth of the atrium, each line connecting to a different floor. Clive had already done the math and realized he would need to do this stupid thing at least four times before they got down to Nu. Given the joy on Grace's face as she hooked herself in—clearly this was not her first time—Clive found it difficult to believe that there was any hope of him not having to do this the entire way down.

"That's everything," Casey said, their name tag shining like a beacon on their chest. Clive needed to remember the name of the person sending him to his death. Casey held the line in front of Clive, their body completely relaxed—the anthesis of Clive's own body. "Any questions?" they asked.

Clive had many questions, the biggest of which was, *Why the hell would anyone in their right mind ever do this?* But he couldn't manage to say that out loud so, presumably taking his silence as a misguided sign of approval, they left Clive alone at the end of the platform. *Come on, Clive, you've jumped from higher things before. This is child's play! All you need to do is close your eyes and jump.*

Clive stood there for a long moment, wishing he had the motivation of someone trying to shoot him, or being attached to a troop of men all about to do something stupid, like jump out of a plane. Things were always easier when it was life and death, because then Clive never had to actually think about it.

He opened his eyes and tried to focus on Grace, who had already completed the first stage and was standing on the other side of the atrium a few levels below, waving. He was strapped in, it was too late to back out now, so he did the only thing he could.

Taking a deep breath, he stepped off the platform, letting out what could best be described as a whimper as the line slackened and dropped. For a moment Clive wondered if he was actually attached to anything. A second later, he was gliding smoothly down the wire. The feeling of wanting to poop himself lingered the entire time he was in the air, but after the initial shock of falling Clive managed to open his eyes, and he began to see the city from a different perspective.

He felt like someone had suspended him in the centre of a snow globe, but instead of snow it was lush plants and people walking around. Another cry came out of him, only this one had a little more excitement behind it.

He watched in the distance as Grace began to laugh, clapping as she watched Clive raise his arms in the air. As he did, his body started to turn in the seat, no longer stabilized by the handle. The action startled him and he reached for the handle again, breathing a deep sigh of relief at the comfort it offered.

He glided onto the landing where Grace was standing, his face flushed red from the excitement.

"I had my doubts you would make it off the ledge without a push," Grace teased.

"That makes two of us." Clive laughed as she moved in to help unhook him from the line. Clive was surprised at how efficient she was at it. She must have caught the surprise in his face.

"When I was eighteen, I worked for a year in Costa Rica for a tree trekking company. Ziplining was one of the best experiences my father ever did with me when I was a kid. So, when we were building Atlantis, I thought it would be fun to have that experience here."

"You worked for a tree trekking company?" was all Clive could think to say. They both laughed.

"How was your first time? Ready for your second, or should we hit the TOTS?" Grace asked, her eyebrows shooting up curiously.

Clive looked at her, then began playing with the cords and harnesses around his waist.

"We're already geared up," he said, giving Grace a playful

smile. "It would be a shame not to keep going." He felt her hands absently tightening up the straps around his waist.

She was so close to him now that he could smell the floral shampoo she must have used in her hair, hints of lavender and eucalyptus. As she looked up at him, their eyes met. Despite being a couple inches shorter than he was, she seemed tall and confident.

"I agree," Grace said softly, and Clive could feel her breath on his neck. She finished with a final strap and their eyes lingered for a moment longer before she turned away to go to the next platform. "Keep up, Clive!" she said, not bothering to look back and see if he was following.

By the fourth trip across the atrium, Clive was over his fear of the zipline and was able to enjoy the views as he glided from one side of Atlantis to the other. It didn't hurt that after each run Grace would move in close to readjust his straps, and a part of him wondered if she was doing it because she needed to or because she wanted to.

Either way, he was happy for the attention, and when they finally landed on Nu II, Clive wished they were back at the top, if only to share more of those moments with her.

"Thank you for making me do that," he said as he slipped the harness off from around his waist.

"Thank you for doing it," Grace said, placing her own harness in a box that would likely be sent back up to the top level. "Would you do it again?" she asked excitedly.

"I would do it with you again," he replied, before he had a chance to consider his words. He handed Grace his harness, and she turned away from him abruptly, taking the harness and placing it in the box. But Clive thought he caught the flash of redness in her cheeks before she did.

"Where is the Snailbox?" she asked, glancing at him from over her shoulder.

"You don't know everything in your city?" Clive said jokingly.

"I told you, Atlantis isn't *my* city. The people here can do whatever they want. I can hardly keep track of everything everyone wants to do personally." She closed up the box and slipped it into a transport terminal.

"So, you've never been to the Snailbox?" Clive asked, trying not to sound surprised.

"No. I have not had the privilege of visiting every store and restaurant in the city," Grace said, laughing. "That would take … a long time."

"Well, maybe we will have to try it."

"Hard to do in six days," she shot back. Clive probably shouldn't have been surprised that she knew when he was scheduled to leave, but he still found himself a little shocked.

"You've been keeping tabs on me?" he asked. Grace gave him a calculated stare.

"I was curious about you," she said after a moment. "Have you decided if you want to stay?"

"I think I want to," Clive said cautiously.

"But?" Grace chimed in, and Clive laughed awkwardly.

"Well, it's complicated."

"Life is always complicated, Clive," she said softly.

"What do you think I should do?"

She shrugged. "I think you should take me to dinner. I'm starving," she said, resting her hand on her stomach playfully.

"Fair enough," Clive said, hopping off the platform before turning to give Grace a hand. She took it and hopped off the ledge.

Even though it was longer than taking the TOTS, the walk together was nice. Their conversation seemed to come easier now as they joked around. Clive left himself open for jabs about his earlier fears on the zipline, happy that she wasn't there when he whimpered on the first jump.

The Snailbox was busy, but Clive managed to spot a smiling Aiden as he whisked around from table to table taking orders.

"This is where you want to eat?" Grace said, surprised.

"I love pies," Clive confessed with a shrug of his shoulder. "And Nigel in the kitchen makes a mean one," he said, sliding his hands together eagerly.

"Fair enough." Grace laughed, her eyes scanning the room.

"You seem nervous." Clive laughed. "What's the matter? Pubs not your thing?" Clive said, giving Aiden a wave.

Catching Clive from the corner of his eye, Aiden finished with a table and hopped over.

"Alright then?" Aiden said in his thick Irish accent. "Usual seat at the bar, or—" He paused, taking in Grace who had moved out from behind Clive. "Aye, not the bar then," he said with a wink to Clive. "I can set yea down at that table in the corner, away from the noise. I'm Aiden by the way," he added, sticking out his hand, before doing a double take. "Wait, you're not … why in all the world would ya be out with this oaf, Ms. Alice?"

"Would you believe I lost a bet?" Grace joked, as she took Aiden's hand and shook it. "And please, call me Grace."

"Aye, well Grace, a lost bet is about all I'd believe. I appreciate yea coming all the way down here. I'll try not to disappoint," he said, tapping the top of her hand with his.

"You seem busy tonight," Clive said.

"Aye, the bloody dinner rush, I had to bring out Nick to

help. Mind you, I told him he'd get a free meal and a couple of pints when it was over, so he didn't complain too much, bless him," Aiden said, looking lovingly over at his partner. "Why don't I stop chatt'n your ear off and get you a couple pints to start. A Guinness for you?" he asked, pointing at Clive. "And for you, Grace?"

"I'll have the same," she said politely, and both Clive and Aiden tried to hide their surprise.

"Aye, perfect. I'll bring them over in a minute." Aiden said as he ran off to another table.

Clive walked over to their table and pulled out the chair for Grace.

"Have you ever had a Guinness?" he asked, smirking.

"No, but I've heard it's good," Grace replied as she set her purse down on the table and took the seat. "I figured, what the hell, when in Rome." And Clive couldn't help but laugh.

"You're certainly full of surprises today," he said, taking the seat across from her. "Ziplining in Costa Rica and never having a Guinness. Which is a tragedy by the way."

"Well, one I'm happy to rectify with you tonight," Grace said coolly.

A few minutes later, Aiden swung in with two pints and set them on the table.

"That was quick," Clive said.

"Aye, well it's not every day that the famous Grace Alice decides to have a pint in your pub now, is it," Aiden replied, laughing.

"It's actually her first Guinness ever." Clive smiled.

"Your first pint of the black in my pub! Incredible."

Grace looked at the pint in front of her, turning the black pint glass around in her hand and examining the four-leaf clover that had been delicately designed in the thick white top. Aiden didn't bother pretending to have a reason to stay, he simply stood by eagerly.

"He's not leaving until you try it," Clive said.

"Right, of course." Grace carefully picked up the glass, as if unsure what she was supposed to do.

"You just sip it, like a regular drink," Clive teased, and Grace shot him a look.

"Ignore him, the first time is special, love." Aiden smiled.

"Cheers!" Grace said, holding her glass up to Aiden, then took a tentative sip, which turned into a full drink. "That's delicious!" she said, sounding pleasantly shocked.

"Aye, isn't it grand," Aiden said, slapping the table. "Grace Alice likes the black! Wonderful!" He was beaming. "I'll be back in a minute to get your orders. Enjoy," he said to Grace before he ran off.

"He's excited," Grace said, laughing.

"The Irish really love Guinness," Clive joked as he took a sip of his own delicious beer. "So, you don't go to pubs often?"

"I never used to get out much," she said with a shrug. "Besides that little adventure in Costa Rica I never really had the chance to. My life has always been too hectic."

"So what? You just worked?"

"And studied."

"How exciting."

"Well, my dad got sick the year I got home from Costa Rica. I'd planned on going to Cambridge to finish my master's, but he needed help running things at Alice Corp. So I never had a choice," Grace said, spinning her glass around on the table.

"I'm sorry." Clive felt guilty for bringing up what seemed like a difficult topic. "Did you at least like working at Alice

Corp?" he asked.

"I'd always planned on taking it over. I grew up there and my father had a vision—designing things that would help people," Grace said passionately, but her face grew darker. "But when I got there, it didn't seem like the company I remembered. Too much of what they were doing there was designed to simply make money."

"You didn't want to make money?" Clive laughed. "Seems like a tough way to run a business," he said. Grace laughed, too, and he couldn't help thinking how beautiful she looked when she was laughing.

"Sure, making money is good, but it shouldn't be everything. Everything comes at a cost. If your focus is on making money, then the cost is the people who work for you. At least that's what I found," she said, sipping her beer.

"So what'd you do?" Clive asked. Grace looked at him, confused, before opening her arms as if to say, *Look around.* "Fair enough. But how did you do it?"

"I slowly bought back control of the company, then I severed the company in two, and created Alice Industries. Which is technically what Atlantis is, although with some weird nuances to it. Like the fact that it is a working city that exists outside of the control of any nation," she said casually.

"What, so you don't pay taxes, kinda thing?" Clive said dimly.

"Sure, that's one aspect of it. But it also means that we are free to govern as we want. We are a self-sufficient ecosystem that can generate ninety percent of its own resources."

"Not this Guinness," Clive said.

"Sure. There are some things we want that are outside of what we can create here—mined metals, Guinness." She laughed. "For that, we have a carefully secured Swiss trust, which provides the city with more than enough currency to get what it needs. And thankfully, people's greed for money will always be greater than their distrust for what we are doing on Atlantis." The words came out offhandedly, but Clive felt the weight of them. "But … but!" Grace said eagerly. "Our team is trying to develop new ways to recycle all the products we have, so that eventually we won't be nearly as, or ideally at all, reliant on the outside world. Even this Guinness will eventually be brewed in Atlantis."

"Wait, what?" Clive said, confused.

"It's amazing what you can build with enough money." Grace shrugged, taking a sip of beer. Clive examined his beer and took a long sip before he laughed.

"I guess so." He set his beer back on the table. "You said people distrust you?" Clive asked, hoping it came off as casual. Grace began spinning her glass around again on the table, and for a moment Clive wondered if she would answer the question.

"Not me, I guess. At least I try not to take it personally. But some people are afraid of what we are doing on Atlantis," Grace said, her eyes fixed on the table between them. "Like I told you, change is often feared by anyone with something to lose."

"What could people possibly lose by Atlantis existing?" Clive asked, attempting to laugh ofs the severity of her words. Grace pursed her lips together in thought, but Clive couldn't tell if she was thinking about what to say, or what she should say to him.

"Control," she said.

"Right then, what can I get yea?" Aiden said, stepping up to the table and looking between the two of them. He realized he'd just walked into the middle of something. "Or I can always come back in a minute," he added, noticing the look Clive was giving him.

"No, I think we should be good to go!" Grace said politely.

"Aye, well then what can I get for yea."

"What would you recommend?" Grace said, clasping her hands on the table and looking very proper.

"Aye, well Nige makes a cracken steak and Guinness pie." Aiden said, "Or if you're—"

"Perfect, I'll have that," Grace said firmly.

"A Guinness and a pie, a lady after my own heart," Aiden said pleasantly. "And you, big man?"

"Same."

"Wonderful. I'll put those in and bring them out when they're good to go. Anything else?" Aiden said, already halfway to another table.

"Another round," Grace jumped in, getting another warm smile from Aiden.

"Aye, coming right up."

"I'm paying, remember?" Grace said, giving Clive a mischievous smile.

After that the conversation turned back to old stories, which Clive was quick to reformat so as to not give away his time in the Navy. But he was more than happy to listen to Grace tell him about her childhood, which seemed like a dream compared to Clive's own unfortunate youth.

She talked about skiing in the Alps with her mother when she was ten and falling and breaking her wrist, whereas Clive had never been to the Alps, but he had broken his wrist in a fight in the sixth grade when someone was picking on his foster sister.

The stories continued, along with the pints, as the two of them opened up more and more. Which meant Clive never got the chance to bring up Grace's concerns about control again.

He kept wondering what exactly she meant by it all, and he desperately wanted to bring it up again. But given how well it went the last time they talked about Atlantis, Clive was hesitant to ruin such a good night.

After their meal they stayed at their table, chatting. The restaurant quieted down enough for both Aiden and Nick to join them for a drink. Both men were eager to meet Grace, the person who invited them to the city.

"Do you ever think Atlantis will be open to the public?" Nick asked, his own Dublin dialect booming at their little table. Nick was a large man with short salt and pepper hair. Clive still had no doubt that the man, despite being in his mid-forties, could easily destroy him in an arm wrestle.

"That depends on what happens next," Grace said, a little more forthcoming after several rounds of beer. "The launch this week will likely change a lot of people's perspectives about what we're doing here. I suppose, like everything in the world, half of the people will believe it'll threaten them and the other half will believe it'll protect them."

"Ominous," Nick said, laughing, as he took a large drink from his pint glass.

"Sorry, it's still hush-hush, so I'm not supposed to talk about it," Grace said, squinting her eyes at the three men while she tapped the rim of her glass thoughtfully. "I promise you it will be exciting, though," she added playfully.

"To something exciting," Aiden said, raising his glass.

If anyone else was still thinking about the launch, they didn't show it, but the conversation had left Clive with a little pit in his stomach that stuck around for the rest of the night.

An hour later and both Aiden and Nick seemed ready to close the pub. They refused to let Clive and Grace stay and help, leaving the two of them once again alone in the atrium.

Night had fallen and the atrium was dimly lit, but from this low in the city you couldn't really make out any of the night sky. But it was still so peaceful that for a few awkward moments they simply stood at the railing looking out over the city. Clive stole glances at Grace every now and then, transfixed by how beautiful she looked with her hair falling down over her shoulder.

A part of him wanted to ask about the launch, but a bigger part of him didn't want to ruin the great night they just had. *I have five more days after tonight to figure out what I need, why can't I just enjoy tonight?*

Clive turned to Grace and sucked in a deep breath, unsure of what he was going to say, but he was taken aback when Grace launched herself at him and kissed him. The act was awkward, since she was so much shorter than him, and their lips pushed together hard before she pulled herself away.

"I'm sorry," she said, shaking her head and brushing her hair back behind her shoulder.

"Don't be," Clive said. He reached up to brush a loose strand of hair behind her ear as he moved in slowly. He noticed the faint smell of flowers again as he pulled her body tight in towards him. He hovered close for a moment, his mind attempting to decide if this was something he should do before his body took control and he kissed her again.

He felt her arms grip him tightly around the waist, their

bodies entangling as they wrapped around each other. Clive could feel her body give way as he held her firmly. He slowly lowered her down to the ground, unsure of when he'd picked her up, but as he did they pulled away only enough for Grace to lay her head on his chest. Clive became overly aware of the steady pounding of his heart.

"You live around here, don't you?" Grace said softly, and Clive felt like his heart was going to explode through his chest. *Why do I feel like this is the first time I've ever been with someone?*

"Yes," he replied, the word getting stuck in his throat. He tried to clear it before he added, "Do you want to come over?" Grace ran her finger down his chest, the pressure causing a tingling along the path she'd drawn.

"Do you want me to come over?" she asked playfully.

Clive didn't say anything else, simply wrapped his arms around her waist, lifted her up to meet him at his full height, and kissed her. Moments later, back in the apartment, Grace tore away at his shirt and ran her hands down the muscles of his sculpted chest before the door to his apartment had even closed.

She paused, running her index finger along some of the old scars strung across Clive's chest and arms. If she wanted to ask him about them, she didn't. She just began to kiss each one as she saw them. It was so tender that Clive felt weak in her arms.

Clive began to slowly unbutton Grace's blouse while he kissed the crook of her neck, getting halfway down before he pulled the top away, tossing it heedlessly to the ground.

His hands free again, he reached around Grace's body and cupped under her butt, lifting her up and pressing her firmly against him. He felt Grace's legs wrap around him as he carried her into the bedroom.

<h1 style="text-align:center">21</h1>

Clive had forgotten how nice it was to share a bed with someone. Grace's legs tangled with his own as she pressed herself against his bare skin. She'd looked so peaceful and comfortable beside him that when Clive had woken up, he didn't move for fear that he would disturb her. *Maybe she'll regret what she's done? Maybe she will when she finds out who I really am?*

It was still the middle of the night, and Clive realized he couldn't have had more than an hour of sleep. But his mind raced, unable to sweep the feeling of guilt under the proverbial rug. He didn't like having to lie to Grace, especially after what had just happened. Their relationship had certainly been unexpected. *Maybe she would understand why I needed to keep this a secret?*

No matter how Clive played the situation over in his mind, he couldn't avoid the fact that he was deeply in the wrong.

To make matters worse, he could see a flashing green light from his LUCY, which he knew would be a message from Danika, likely wondering what he had to do to get the code.

A moment later he felt Grace's hand slide across his chest and rest over his throbbing heart.

"Feels like it's trying to escape," she said as her eyes cracked open and she looked up to meet his eyes.

"Sorry, just thinking," Clive said wishing he could just tell her everything.

"About?" Grace asked, looking worried. "If it's about what happened tonight—"

"No," Clive interrupted, "it's not about tonight, tonight was great. It's just me, I, umm." He stopped, unable to find the words he wanted to use. It seemed wrong to do it now. *Then again, is there a good time to tell someone you've been lying about who you are and how you've been sent to steal information from her?*

"I think I know what this is about," Grace said, pulling the covers up around her chest as she sat up in the bed.

"You do?" Clive asked skeptically.

"You're worried about the launch. You haven't decided if you want to stay in Atlantis yet or go home? And that's okay," she said softly. "I understand—"

"That's not it, Grace." Clive said, unable to stop what he felt was about to come out. He took a deep breath. "I'm not who you think I am."

Grace stared at Clive for a long moment before their eyes drifted to the end of the bed.

"You mean how you work for the Canadian government? JTF 2 right?" Grace said slowly.

"You knew?" Clive asked incredulously.

"I suspected the Canadians would send someone, everyone else has. Then, after the shark attack, I saw your training in the water, and your scars. Clearly you don't just work for an oil and gas company," Grace said, letting out a laugh.

"Wait? So all this was you just trying to get close to me? Figure out why I'm here? What do you mean everyone else has? Grace, what the hell is going on?" Clive shouted, and Grace put a finger up to his lips to stop him from yelling.

"First of all, I'm not trying to get close to you to learn anything, I know why you're here and I suspect I know more about what you're carrying than you do."

"What does that mean?"

"You're being set up, Clive."

...

Grace had left him alone on the bed, unsure of what he needed to do next. His body was shaking and he was in a cold sweat. He had the desire to vomit but managed to keep that at bay, for now.

She'd just opened Pandora's box and left him to wade through the information, trying to figure out how much he should believe. *She is lying, trying to manipulate me into doing something stupid, ignoring everything that is right in front of me.*

Yet, there had been some truth in what she'd said—just enough to make him wonder. He hurried out of bed, reached into the dresser, and pulled out the phone he used to contact Commander Hammond. He clicked on the one contact listed inside. He needed to hear his voice. He needed to hear him say Grace was wrong about everything.

The phone rang a few times before someone on the other end picked up. Their breath was steady but no one spoke.

"Commander Hammond, it's Clive."

"Clive? Why the hell are you reaching out like this? You know this is against protocol. Have you gotten any closer to accessing the servers?"

"How do you know I haven't accessed them yet?" Clive said cautiously. There was a beat before Hammond spoke again, almost imperceptible.

"Have you?" Hammond asked.

"What happens to me when I access the servers?"

"You come home, Son. What has gotten into you? Is everything alright?"

"Come home to testify?" Clive said, ignoring the question.

"I'm not sure what you're—"

"The incursion in Iran last summer, your hearing is coming up soon, isn't it?"

"I don't see why that's important right now."

"I'm the only link between you and Iran, the only thread of evidence to what really happened."

"What happened in Iran was an accident, Son. I told you I would handle it, and I am. You have nothing to worry about. No one blames you for what happened."

"I do," Clive said, hopping off the bed and starting to pace around the room. "I blame me for what happened. But that's not what you're worried about, is it. I was following orders, your orders."

"I'm not sure what the hell has gotten into you, Clive, but I suggest you complete your operation and get the hell home. I don't like what this place is doing to you."

"What does the key do, Sir?"

"I told you, it copies all relevant data and sends it back to us to go over."

"Then what? I come home and testify about Iran? If I tell them what really happened, they'll realize that assignment wasn't exactly by the book."

"Why are you thinking about that now, Son? Once you get home we can find a way to sort out Iran, I promise." Hammond's voice was calm as he spoke. Clive felt his throat tighten at each word.

"Except, I won't be coming home, will I?" Clive said slowly. "That wasn't part of your plan."

The line was silent for a long moment and when Hammond finally spoke, the reality of Clive's situation dawned on him.

"Clive listen, Grace Alice needs to be stopped, Atlantis needs to be shut down—"

"If you lay one hand on her, I swear to God." Clive shouted into the phone.

"It's too late, Son. The orders have already been sent," Hammond said dispassionately.

"What the hell are you talking about?"

"One way or another, this little project of hers needs to end. I'm sorry—" but Clive was done listening, gripping the phone tightly in his hand before hurling it at the wall in front of him. He cried out in anger as the phone shattered, sending pieces scattering across the room.

His blood felt like it was beginning to boil over and all he wanted to do was hit something, but the prime candidate was thousands of miles away.

Clive paced the room, each one of his breaths coming out as a gasp as he tried to calm himself down. He needed to understand more about what was going on. He needed to see Grace.

Grabbing a pair of brown shorts and his Hawaiian T-shirt from the ground, he raced out the door, only barely remembering to put on a pair of sandals as he left. He looked like he was prepared for the beach and not for whatever this was. If Clive understood correctly, he'd just been told that if they couldn't bring down the city, they were prepared to cut off the head of the snake. *Which would be Grace.*

Since Danika was by no means a fan of Grace Alice, Clive suspected she would be more enthusiastic about this news than Clive had been.

He ran down the hall and hopped on the TOTS. He hoped Grace had gone straight home after leaving his apartment, but there was no way to know for sure. *Or was there?*

"LUCY, can you call Grace Alice? It's an emergency," Clive said as he stood waiting for the TOTS doors to close.

"Of course," LUCY said, sounding unacceptably calm, given the circumstances. Then again, LUCY wasn't programmed to express fear or urgency, and Clive suspected it wouldn't be helpful if it was. "There was no answer," LUCY said finally.

"Shit!" Clive shouted. "Can you track where she is?"

"I'm not programmed to share tracking information with anyone in Atlantis. It is an impossibility," LUCY said, sounding like mainland politician.

"Well, that's not exactly helpful right now," Clive said as the TOTS began to move steadily through the city. *Where the hell did she say her room was?*

Knocking on doors wasn't the greatest strategy, but at this point he would have to settle for it.

For the first time since Clive had been in Atlantis, he felt as if the TOTS were slow. He finally hopped off at Alpha I and raced around the corner trying his best to not get lost in the maze of hallways. In the end it proved fortuitous that he'd been there earlier that day and managed to find the lab in good time. He began banging his fist against the heavy metal door.

"Anyone in there? Grace?" Clive called, trying his LUCY on the door and watching miserably as it flashed red. "Grace, are you in there?" *Even if she was, would she be alone? Could she even let him in if she wanted to?*

Clive tried to ignore the sudden rush of blood pounding in his head as he attempted to think through the problem. He had no way of knowing where she was or what was happening. He also had no way of knowing if she was already in danger. In fact, there was very little at this point he did know. What he needed to do was think, but with each moment it was becoming increasingly difficult. *Breathe.*

Clive shut his eyes and rested his head against the door. The metal sent a calming coolness through his body. He tried to let his training take over, taking long, slow breaths to slow his heart rate down. *What can I do?*

"Shit!" he said, as he felt the corner of the Lab 1 sign press into his forehead. He ran his fingers over the sign and a thought occurred to him. *How could I be so stupid?!*

He raced down the hall, stopping at the end, looking both ways to see which way might lead to the living quarters. On the floor, green lines led to the left. Clive took a guess and ran down the green hallway until he hit the first door, marked 001.

He took a deep breath and knocked calmly on the door. The last thing he needed to do was wake up a stranger and have them asking a bunch of questions.

For a long moment there was nothing, but then Clive heard some rustling on the other side of the door, and it opened. It was Grace.

"Clive?" she said, looking surprised. "What are you doing here?"

"We need to talk. Can I come in?" He took a step towards the door but Grace didn't move.

"Now's not the best time." Her voice was calm, but she

seemed off. *Is she alone?*

"I know it's late, but I think we need to talk," Clive said as he watched Grace closely. That's when he saw it—her index finger, which had been wrapped around the door, was pointing to her left. Her eyes also seemed restless, as if they were trying really hard not to look anywhere but at him. Clive pointed at the door as he mouthed the words, "Is someone there?"

"Yes. But I think we should do it later. Please leave," she said as she removed her hands from the door. Clive seized the opportunity to thrust his body into the door, which crashed into someone on the other side who hit the ground with a heavy thud.

Without seeing who it was, Clive grabbed Grace and they took off down the hallway.

"You have no idea how happy I am to see you," she said, her hand gripping his tightly. How did you find me?"

"I took a guess you would be room number one. It was more luck than I deserve."

"You mean, I deserve," Grace countered. "I think they were going to kill me."

"They were," Clive said, not bothering to try and soften the blow. "I asked about Iran, and the USB, and you were right. But I guess Five Eyes and whoever else is onboard have decided that if they can't destroy Atlantis, they can put an end to you."

"That's ridiculous. They can't believe at this point that if I die, Atlantis won't survive." Grace let out a cold laugh.

"They are desperate to stop whatever it is you're planning," Clive said, and Grace stopped in her tracks.

"Don't even get me started on the naivety, no, their stupidity of what they *think* we're doing?" Grace said angrily.

"Maybe the hall isn't the best place to discuss this. Can we get to your lab, or someplace with a gun perhaps?"

"We only have non-lethal weapons in Atlantis," Grace said incredulously.

"What? You have no weapons in the city?" Clive asked, more than a little concerned.

"Why on earth would we need to kill anyone?"

"What about Sasha Keen? Didn't you kill her because she threatened to destroy Blue Crest?" Clive asked. His mind flashed back to the video, to Grace standing over Sasha.

"I didn't kill Sasha Keen."

"But she was bleeding from the mouth."

"I'm not sure how you know all of this, but obviously you only have half the picture. I did shoot Sasha Keen, with a rubber bullet. But I'm a terrible shot and it ricocheted off the wall and I hit her in the face. She was injured, but fine." Grace sounded confused.

"Sasha is alive?" said a voice Clive recognized immediately from behind them.

"Danika! Stop," Clive yelled as he turned to face her. She looked dishevelled. Her hair was loose and she had blood around her nose. *I guess I know who was behind the door.*

Clive's arms began to rise instinctively when he saw her odd-looking, shiny, stout gun.

"You know her?" Grace asked.

"She US Intelligence. She's a friend of Sasha's," Clive said, as he slowly moved to put his body between Danika and Grace.

"Sasha wasn't my friend. She's my fiancé. Where is she?" Danika said through gritted teeth, "Or I swear to God, I will end you right now. This," she said, waving the gun at them, "may be plastic, but it is very much lethal." Clive took second glance at the gun. It was 3-D printed, lightweight, and could fire off a single round. A facility like this would have hundreds of 3D printers, which Danika would have access to.

"She's safe and healthy here in the city, I promise," Grace said, taking a step towards Danika, but Clive stuck out his arm to prevent her from passing him.

"Why should I believe you?" Danika shouted.

"I'm not trying to hurt anyone. That is not what this city was designed for," Grace said. "But Sasha refused to see reason and she would have killed us all."

"Sasha wouldn't have killed innocent people."

"It's not Sasha. It's your government. They want this place destroyed," Grace said, pushing Clive's arm away. When he wouldn't move, she glared at him, but he refused to lower his arm, not while Danika still had a gun pointed at her.

"The American government wants to know about Blue Crest and any other weapons you may have that could threaten us," Danika said, though her voice wasn't as firm as it had been.

"Blue Crest isn't a weapon," Grace said. Her tone was defensive. "Blue Crest is our reassurance that our city will remain safe after the launch. I can show you what Blue Crest really is. I can explain to you why we can't have you or any of the other agents in the city use that data key you're holding," Grace said, pointing to the key gripped in Danika's hand.

"She's right about the key, Danika. We were lied to," Clive said evenly.

"For all I know, you're both lying to me," Danika shouted. Grace stepped towards her and put up her arms.

"You can kill me now if you don't believe me, or I can explain everything to you. Your choice." Grace dropped her hands.

Danika stood for a moment, staring at the two of them, before she lowered the gun. Clive began to relax.

Then, in a flash, her gun was up, and before Clive had a chance to react, Danika fired. The shot echoed loudly through the halls.

The sound was deafening; Clive was forced to cover his ears. When he uncovered them, he heard cries of agony.

It wasn't coming from Grace, who was still beside him, hunched over with her hands pressed to her ears. She was equally surprised to find she wasn't injured in anyway.

Clive turned to face the cries, which were coming from a tall man with short-cropped blonde hair lying on the ground behind them. Blood oozed from his shoulder, pooling on the ground beneath him. Next to him was a large kitchen knife, which Clive promptly kicked away.

"I'm not the only one who was given the kill order. I suggest we move quickly. Take me to Sasha," Danika said sternly.

Grace seemed distracted by the man bleeding on the floor, unable to take her eyes off him. He'd only been a few feet from her when Danika shot him.

"Grace, we need to move," Clive said. When she didn't respond, he reached for her cheek and turned her gently towards him, forcing her to look him in the eyes.

"Take a deep breath," he said, slowing his own breathing and indicating for her to copy him.

Danika tossed the now useless gun aside. But if Clive thought she was no longer armed, he was wrong. He watched her pull a rather large steak knife out from behind her back. His eyes moved to the knife he'd just kicked away.

"Leave it," Danika said, catching Clive's eye.

"We might be attacked again. You could use the help," Clive said, but his reasoning was weak.

"I can handle it. Now, unless you want to get attacked again, I recommend we get out of here." Danika swivelled her head around, surveying the area.

"My lab, it's around the corner," Grace said. Her voice seemed distant, and Clive could see the look in her eye that said, *We need to help this man.*

"He will be fine," Clive said. "But Danika is right. We need to leave." He pulled Grace along as he moved around the body on the ground. He'd seen wounds like this before and knew the man would be okay as long as he got help in the next few hours.

Clive stopped. "Give me your scarf," he said to Grace, pointing to the decorative silk scarf she still had on from dinner.

"What are you doing?" Danika said sharply. "He just tried to kill you!"

"He was doing his job. Like the rest of us seem to be doing, he was just blindly following orders."

Grace handed him the scarf. He tore it in half and bundled one of the pieces in a ball, jamming it into the wound.

The man cried out in pain and gripped Clive's wrist as he let out a series of German curses Clive could easily make out, even if he hadn't been wearing his interpreter.

With the remaining piece, he rolled the man on his side and wrapped it tightly under his arm and around the opposite side of his neck, so that it covered the wound on his chest.

"Deep breaths," Clive said. The man's eyes widened as Clive tightened the scarf and pressed down heavily on the wound before tying it off. It wasn't perfect, but it would give him a few extra hours to get help. The man's grip on Clive's wrist tightened.

"Thank you," he said, with a nod to Clive.

"Great. He's bandaged up now. Can we please get the hell out of the hallway?" Danika said, pointing her knife at Clive.

Clive told himself the guy would be fine as they hurried down the hallway towards Grace's lab. Reaching the enforced doors, Grace held her LUCY up to the sensor and typed in her six digit code. It flashed green and she quickly stepped inside, followed by Clive and Danika.

They were standing in the open room, which was empty. As it was the middle of the night, everyone else was likely at home sleeping.

"Where is she?" Danika said, her eyes scanning the room, stopping briefly on the door to the servers. "Where is Sasha?"

"We have her in one of the old apartments. I will take you to her," Grace said, walking hesitantly through a corridor leading off the back of the room.

"Is this where Blue Crest is?" Clive asked, trying to distract her a little with work when he saw her hands trembling.

"Blue Crest is on the sky side of the city. But the control booth is secured in that room up there," she said, pointing to a nondescript door off to the side of the lab.

"That's the room that houses the weapon we're all supposed to be afraid of? I would have thought it would be behind some vault door or something," Clive joked.

"Despite what you think, I'm not a Bond villain."

"She says, as she leads us to a prison cell she's kept Sasha in for months," Danika said, brandishing her knife maliciously at Grace.

"I'd hardly say it's a prison cell," Grace said, rolling her eyes.

"Can she leave?" Danika pressed.

"No. But this is my original apartment in the city. She has a small gym, access to entertainment, and any food she wants can be delivered directly to her suite," Grace said defensively. "I'd hardly think your government would be easier on someone who was trying to destroy them."

"We're not here to destroy Atlantis," Danika said sharply. "We are here to discover what it is you're building in the city."

Grace scoffed. "Don't tell me you're that naïve," she said, stopping to face Danika. "Why didn't either of you try asking me what it is we were doing?" She turned to look at Clive.

"You would just lie to us," Danika shot back. "How could we trust anything you say?"

"You've been working in Atlantis for months! Has anything about this place seemed like we are hiding information?"

"You keep your servers pretty secure!"

"Because the outside world sent people like you to corrupt our systems and destroy the city, killing everyone in it. We needed to protect our people."

"You're lying. We are here to recover information, that's all," Danika said, though her words seemed less cocksure than before.

Grace laughed and continued down the hall. She reached a bare door, identical to all the other apartment doors in the city. She raised her LUCY to the sensor and it flashed green.

Inside at the end of the hallway was a thick glass wall with a door in the middle. On the other side was a neat-looking apartment, and sitting on a couch reading a book with a glass of wine was dark-haired woman in pajamas.

"Sasha?" Danika said slowly. Sasha looked up.

"Danika?" She set the glass of wine on the table as she slowly got to her feet.

Grace walked over to the door, unlocked it with her LUCY, and stepped inside. Once she was in, she let Danika and Clive enter after her.

The two women stared at each other in disbelief for a long moment before they finally embraced, tears streaming down their faces.

"I thought you were dead," Danika said slowly, her hands touching Sasha's face as if it might suddenly stop being real. Everyone watched as the two embraced again, and then without warning Danika slapped Sasha across the face. "I thought you were dead," she said again, only this time with a little more venom.

"Well, I'm not, clearly," Sasha said, rubbing her face where Danika's hand had connected.

"But you made me think you were!" Danika shouted. She pulled her hand back for another whack, but this time it was caught by Sasha.

"But I'm not," she said softly, as Danika's hand relaxed again and the two kissed passionately.

"I should kill you after what you did."

"It was the only way," Sasha said. "I didn't think …"

"You're right. You didn't," Danika said, though her words were less harsh now as she embraced Sasha once again.

"Sasha was always going to go home, as soon as we launched," Grace said, watching the two women reunite. "That is, assuming no one destroyed the city first."

"That's not why—" Danika said, turning on Grace, frustrated. But Sasha's voice stopped her.

"Yes, it is."

"What?" Danika said, looking at Sasha. "What kind of lies have you been filling her head with?!" Danika hissed, as she turned to glare at Grace, brandishing the knife she still held in her hands. Sasha placed a calming hand on Danika's shoulder.

"She's not keeping me here against my will," Sasha said calmly. "At least, not anymore."

"I don't understand." Danika reached for Sasha's hand and gripped it tightly. "Why would you stay here?"

"Grace and her team showed me what was on the key, and it took me some time to understand what that meant for me," Sasha said, the anger in her eyes beginning to flare up.

"Why would the government send you to die?" Danika asked incredulously.

"One life, to protect millions. At least I imagine that was the logic," Sasha said coldly.

"But why stay in here?" Danika said gesturing around the room.

"We decided it would be too risky to send me home, and living in the city would be dangerous, too. So, we agreed I would stay here until the launch, and then I would go home to you," Sasha said, her voice full of hope. But Danika pulled her hands away.

"We all thought you were dead. I thought you were dead! Do have any idea how hard it's been for me to be here, thinking you'd been killed? That she'd killed you?!" Danika shouted, pointing her knife toward Grace.

"If I knew they had sent you, I would have found you. I didn't know who they would send, and it was too risky." Sasha began to plead. "You have to understand, this was the only cover that would allow me to come home to you, the only way to hide the fact that I learned what their key really did!"

"What about the video—" Danika began, but Grace jumped in.

"The video was designed to sell her story. You think it's a coincidence your team was able to find that little nugget?" Danika didn't seem impressed. "You don't get it, do you?" Grace said sadly. "Neither of you do." She looked at Clive. "None of this," she said, gesturing at Sasha and the room around them, "matters. You were sent here to find weapons and I'm telling you that we don't have anything that could be used to create physical damage to any country."

"Ideas are free to grow," Clive said, more to himself than anyone. Danika shot him a harsh look.

"What the hell does that mean?" she snapped.

"Atlantis has never had any weapons; Atlantis *is* the weapon," Clive said, as the realization dawned on him.

"What do you mean, Atlantis is a weapon?" Danika finally asked.

"Follow me," Grace said, leaving the room without bothering to see if any of them were actually following her.

Clive looked towards the two women, who were unable to let go of one another. Danika's anger had begun to wash away at the sight of Sasha, and Sasha appeared remarkably calm.

It was at this point Clive realized they'd let Grace lead them into the only prison cell in the entire facility. If she wanted, she could have locked them away until the launch. He turned abruptly to see her standing in the main doorway, her arms at her side, calmly waiting for them.

"Thought I would trap you in my evil lair?" Grace said, as Clive stepped back out into the hallway.

"The thought never crossed my mind," he said with a smile.

"Sure." They all headed to the Blue Crest control room. Grace held her LUCY up to the sensor beside the door and led them inside.

The room was filled with monitors displaying various images of the sky side of Atlantis. A large half-moon desk with dials everywhere lay in front of them. Its surface reminded Clive of a sound board.

"What exactly are we looking at?" Clive said, fighting the urge to randomly press the buttons in front of him.

"Blue Crest isn't a weapon. It's a high-density particle refractor," Grace said, rolling her eyes at the confused look on everyone else's face. "It's a cloaking device. It's designed to keep us hidden in the ocean, completely invisible to drones, satellites, radar, and any other method of discovery."

"What about Dr. Nowak?" Clive asked. "His work was used to develop weapons."

"No," Grace said sharply. "His work was exploited by others to create weapons. The only way he could get the funding for his research was through military contracts. But his work is so much more. He developed a method of refracting light—"

"The film covering everything on the sky side?" Clive asked, remembering the weird spray he'd seen them using when he was swimming with Oli.

"Yes, the city has multiple conductors throughout its surface that generate large amounts of power, which is then distributed through the film to give it the power to refract the sunlight, hiding the city in plain sight," Grace said eagerly.

"Which means you'll be invisible?" Sasha asked.

"More or less," Grace said, pursing her lips.

"Let me guess, the energy required to make it work is some

form of thermal fusion?" Danika asked, starting to piece it all together.

"Dr. Nowak's original idea was energy production?" Clive asked skeptically.

"Yes, he's found a way of isolating sun phonons and using them to generate energy. All he needed was the resources to develop a better conductor for the process. Think about it, the ability to coat entire roadways, and more, in a film that could be used to generate enough energy to supply all the electrical needs of a city for free." Grace sounded genuinely excited talking about it.

"Or, say, enough energy to power an unmanned drone, or satellite, indefinitely," Sasha said slowly.

"Unfortunately, that as well." Grace sighed. "And once the military digs its claws into work like this, it rarely sees the light of day."

"Okay, so say I believe you," Danika said, "and Dr. Nowak is a good man who just wanted to help the world, blah blah blah. Why in hell would you need to make Atlantis invisible?"

"To protect us from the outside world trying to destroy us," Grace said simply.

"You keep saying that, but why on earth would any country care about your small little island?"

"You lived here, you saw what we can do, how society can function when it's even more free of burdens," Grace explained, as she moved away so she could face them all. "You all had a chance to live here. Was it hard? Danika? Even in all your anger towards me, could you actually find fault in the city itself?"

All eyes turned to Danika. Her face remained stony, even as she gave the question some thought.

"I guess not," she said after a moment, before adding, "No, I couldn't."

"We have brought people from around the world, with different backgrounds, to live in a city where all they need to do is respect each other and contribute in a way that makes them feel good. No pressure to make money, buy houses, afford healthy food. All of that provided. You remove those three obligations, for anyone, and the only thing left is to find a purpose. That's all anyone really wants," Grace said softly.

"So why destroy you?" Clive asked. "If what you're doing is so good?"

"Good for who?" Grace countered.

"Good for the people," Clive said quickly. "The technology you have here is decades ahead of what we have."

"The technology we have here is what happens when you give people the ability to work freely. Sure, there are tests, peer reviews, everything you would expect. But it all costs money. Money we don't expect to make back. Everything you have here was given to you. The LUCY, your gill, the interpreters—"

"Lousy name by the way," Sasha jumped in, and everyone looked at her. "I'm just saying, I think you missed the ball on coming up with a cooler name. Like, you have the LUCY, why couldn't you call it ROSIE?"

"What?" Danika asked, shaking her head.

"Rosie, after the Rosetta stone. I mean, just off the top of my head." Sasha shrugged, and everyone looked blankly at her before they all laughed. "Sorry, I've not had many people to talk with lately." Which caused another round of laughter.

"My point is," Grace said, "we do it because we want to. We want to provide people with the necessary tools to grow as a species. But, what's the point of growth and innovation if only some of the world can access it?" She shrugged. "I mean, what we've done isn't insane. What's to stop any country from having its own digital currency that it gives its citizens? Let them decide how it's used and valued in their country. Start everyone off on equal footing?"

"What you want is communism," Danika said sharply.

"What I want is for the power to be in the hands of the people, not in the hands of organizations or even governments. Votes could happen on phones, real-time analytics letting leaders know exactly what the people think. It's not communism, it's democracy 2.0. Hasn't democracy always been about putting the power in the hands of the people? When it was formed, it was revolutionary. It changed the course of humanity. And hundreds of years later that system stopped evolving because people don't enjoy giving up power. And that is exactly what they would be doing," Grace continued and Clive began to understand what it was she was saying.

"That's why killing you would do nothing," Clive said after a moment. "Even if you were to die, the idea of Atlantis would remain. It's a self-propagating system."

Grace nodded. "It's already too late to stop. Ideas can't be put back in the box."

"Unless you burn the box to the ground," Danika said darkly.

"That's why you are all here. Your governments can tell they are losing this fight, and they can't just destroy us on their own. There would be too many unanswered questions," Grace said. "Not to mention hidden data trails that the city has saved in case something like this happens."

"You're like folk heroes on the mainland. Destroying you

would only cause a revolt. But if it looks like you destroyed yourselves, then you're simply another Icarus," Danika said, a look of understanding finally dawning on her face.

Clive's own understanding was sinking in as well. When Grace explained it like that, of course Atlantis would be a threat. What she was describing was a new form of government that put the power directly in the hands of the people, and here she was holding the case study on how it all worked.

"But you say you have backup data?" Danika asked.

"Not if there happened to be a certain data key that was designed to wipe out all stored data in their system," Sasha added grimly.

"Right. Well, what do we do now?" Clive asked, turning to Danika and Sasha beside him before looking back at Grace, who appeared disappointed by the question.

"Whatever you want," she said, her smile quirking to the side and her brow raising as she looked at Clive.

But before anyone had a chance to respond, a sound like a computer being smashed, followed by a loud struggle, came from the main lab. A moment later, a man cried out in pain.

"That was Dr. Nowak," Grace said as she leapt towards the door. Clive only just managed to grab her arm before she hastily ran out of the room.

"Wait!" Clive said, trying to ignore the pleading look in her eyes. "We need to be smart here. It's you they're after."

"If they wanted me, I'm sure they would have had ample time to get me. This is about the servers. They still want to plant the key into the system. The kill order has simply given whoever it is free range to do it by any means necessary," Grace said sharply as she pulled her wrist out from Clive's hand and rushed out the door.

"Shit!" Clive chased after her, with Danika and Sasha close on his tail. Grace had been quick getting down the hall and was the first in the room. Dr. Nowak was on the ground, struggling to get to his knees. Even from across the room Clive could make out the large gash across his forehead that was spilling red blood down his face.

"Dr. Nowak!" Grace hurried off his side, placing a protective arm around her friend.

"My dear! You have to get out of here—" Dr. Nowak began, but he was cut off by the tall, dark-haired woman standing by the server room door.

"Good, you're here. This will make things a lot easier," she said in a soft but intense Hebrew that Clive's interpreter translated for him. "First, I will get the plans for your city, then I will kill you. Stay put." She blew Grace a mocking kiss and began to type in the code for the server room. When she finished, the light flashed green and she turned to smile at Grace and Dr. Nowak. "Thank you, Doctor."

"Wait!" Clive said, running into the room, trying to quickly assess the situation, which didn't look good. "You can't put in that key!" he said, his hands in a pleading gesture.

"And why is that? Because the US wants them first?" she said in a mocking tone as she pursed her lips.

"First of all, I'm Canadian," Clive said, rolling his eyes. "And second, no, it's because that data key isn't just designed to take the data from the computer." He was creeping towards the door but stopped when the stranger stared at him.

"Oh, really? Then what does it do?" she said as her hand began to turn the handle of the door. Clive was too far away to rush her. He needed to get closer.

"He's right, it's encrypted with a virus that will shut down our regulatory system and cause an internal power surge big enough to overload the main power generator," Grace said, still kneeling beside a now unconscious Dr. Nowak.

"Hebrew, please?" the woman said as the door to the server room cracked open.

"It will cause the entire city to explode!" Clive said, taking a step closer. "Please, if you do this, we are all going to die."

She paused at that, her fingers gripping the door handle as she contemplated her options, her eyes moving between the server, Clive, and Grace on the floor.

"What's your name?" he asked, seeing the nervous look on her face. But she didn't reply. "I'm Master Sailor Clive Davies, JTF 2 with the Canadian Navy."

"Such a long name," she said with a smile.

"Call me Clive," he replied, risking another small step forward. He stopped when he saw her waver.

"Talia Vaknin, Mossad," she said, her eyes narrowing on Clive.

"Talia, I know why you're here. I was sent for the same reason. But I'm telling you, we were lied to."

"Why would I ever trust you?" she said, and Clive watched her knuckles tighten around the handle. *She's going to make a run for it.*

"Go!" called Danika, who must have been hiding in the hall behind him with Sasha. Hearing her voice, Clive leaped forward, sprinting as fast as he could towards the server door.

Talia shouldered her way through the door. There was no chance Clive would make it to the door before she had the chance to close it. He watched as she rounded on the door and waved at him.

Just as she was about to slam the door into his face, Clive saw something shiny whiz past, just beside his head. The blade of the knife Danika had been carrying was now lodged between the door and the frame, blocking it from being shut and giving Clive the time he needed.

Dropping his shoulder, he barged through the door with as much strength as he could muster. His shoulder exploded with pain as he hit the heavy metal, which flew back with the full momentum of a two-hundred-and-twenty-pound body, smacking into an unprepared Talia. Her own body flew back and collided with one of the large server panels.

Clive fell into the room, rolling across the ground as the steal door swung back again, closing them both inside. Talia, still on her feet, was the first to recover. She rushed him, her knee up as she prepared to ram it into Clive's face. He only barely managed to cross his arms in time to shield himself from the knee, and the power behind the strike sent him flying back to the ground.

Talia, who was impressively quick, hopped on top of him while at the same time driving her fist into his face. Clive's body, which was still reeling from colliding with the heavy door, was now back on the floor of the server room as Talia still on top of him, drove her knee into his sternum and knocked the air from his lungs. Luckily, Clive was able to kick his feet off the ground and drive his hips into her, bucking her over his head, as he wrapped his arms around her waist.

Gripping onto her pants, he yanked her back towards him, using her new momentum to drive her spine and head into the concrete floor between his now spread legs. Clive tried to take advantage of his new situation by climbing on top of Talia, but she was faster and unsurprisingly agile as she wrapped her legs around his neck, breaking the hold Clive had on her. He attempted to regain some sort of upper hand by climbing to his feet, but the vice grip Talia had around his neck didn't weaken.

Clive needed to break her hold or he would soon be at risk of passing out, and of no use to anyone. Once again he tried to slam her body into the ground, but as he lifted her up she used the momentum to shift her position and wrap her arms around his neck, occupying the position her legs had been in and contorting herself so that she was encasing him like some sort of human backpack, choking him.

Clive's face began to redden as he saw Danika through the window, pounding on the door trying to get him to open it. Clive needed to dislodge Talia if he had any chance of winning this fight. Luckily, there was one advantage he'd noticed to being hunched over and strangled, which was that he could now see that the knife Danika had thrown at the door had also ended up inside in the server room.

It was an empty victory as he was still struggling, her legs wrapped tightly around him, locking in one of his arms. His other arm was desperately trying to pry her fingers loose from around his neck. To make matters worse, her wrist was driving deep into his trachea, which felt as though it was going to be crushed any minute.

With his free arm, he began elbowing her rib cage, and each blow felt empty, but on the third strike her grip loosened enough for him to suck in a much-needed breath.

With some fresh oxygen in his lungs, Clive ran backwards as fast as he could manage, until Talia's body hit something solid. He took a step forward before smashing her body back a second time. This time her grip loosened enough for him to rip her arms from around his neck and he flipped over, landing hard on top of her. Her legs broke free from around his waist and Clive managed to roll out of her grip, scrambling over to grab the knife he'd seen by the door.

He reached the knife, picked it up off the ground, and turned just in time to see Talia smash a stool into the electric operating panel for the door.

"I think this party is better with two," she said, spitting blood onto the floor.

"It doesn't seem fair, me with this knife, you without it," Clive said as he eased the grip on the knife, trying to relax his already tight body.

"I'd say it finally seems like a fair fight." Talia laughed.

"We don't have to do this. We can talk," Clive said, using the time to recentre his breath.

"I don't need to hear your lies," she said, taking a couple of quick steps towards him. Clive responded with a slash of the knife.

"I don't want to hurt you."

"Well then," Talia said, pulling out a small key from her pocket and moving towards the central console. "I'll just take what I need."

Clive thrashed the knife again in her direction. "I can't let you do that," he said, his breath beginning to settle, if only a little.

"Then it seems we are at a standstill," she said, putting the key back in her pocket.

"If you put that key in the console, we all die," Clive said, shaking his head. "Not just the people in this room, but everyone in the city." He thought about all the people who would be lost. Squints and his family, Aiden and Nick, Hamish and Sunny, Oli, Dr. Kashyap, all the faces of the people he'd gotten to know during his time here. He let out a heavy sigh. "You're following orders, so was I. But you have to trust me when I tell you that you're wrong."

"Trust the man pointing a knife at me?" Talia laughed, her eyes unwavering from the knife.

"You're right." Clive could see Danika still banging on the door to get in. He was never going to get Talia to believe him while he held a knife to her. Like him and Danika, she needed trust. "Here," he said, as he tossed the knife at Talia's feet. She looked at it for a second, trying to spot where the trick was, but Clive stood with his hands raised.

From the corner of his eye, he could see Danika's face flush red with anger as she yelled silently from the other side of the door.

"What is this?" Talia said as she crouched slowly, lowering herself down towards the knife at her feet.

"I'm not trying to trick you, and I'm tired of killing good people."

"What makes you think you could kill me?" Talia said with a smile.

"Maybe I could or maybe I couldn't. Either way, you die. That key," Clive said, pointing to her pocket, "will destroy this city and everyone in it."

Talia picked up the knife, letting her fingers roll across its hilt, before she turned and moved towards him threateningly.

"More tricks," she said as she swung the blade at him. Clive heard the banging of Danika and Sasha on the door, unable to get in with the now smashed keypad.

"No tricks," Clive said calmly. His voice was distant as he prepared himself for what would come next. Taking a deep breath, he stepped in as Talia lunged the knife at his chest. Clive caught her hands, but not before the tip of the blade pierced his chest, and blood began drip from under it.

"Fight back!" Talia shouted as she heaved her body into the knife. Clive's arms fought to keep it still.

"I'm done fighting," Clive said.

"Why are you doing this?!" Talia cried out, her hand beginning to shake as she continued to strain against the knife.

Grace's face flashed in Clive's mind, her vision of the world, the same vision that gave hope to people like Kissa and her mother. Clive smiled at the images.

"I would rather die knowing I tried to do something, than live knowing I didn't." Clive released his hands from Talia's and watched as her weight drove the knife deep into his chest.

All at once a searing pain rushed through his body and he cried out. Talia, in shock from the maneuver, dropped her hold on the knife. Her strength was all that had been holding him up and Clive's knees buckled beneath him as he dropped to the concrete floor. The hilt of the blade stuck out of his chest. Talia's hands covered her mouth as she fell to her knees next to him.

"Why did you do that?" she said softly. "Why would you do that?!"

"It's the only way you would have lived," Clive said, falling down on his side, his head smacking the floor beside him. He could feel warm blood spilling out from the wound in his chest as each breath sent a searing pain from his chest throughout his entire body. Talia stood over him, her hands covered in his blood, as she reached in her pocket and pulled out the data key.

Clive's vision began to blur as the shock and pain became too much. The last thing he saw was Talia wiping away a tear. His own vision dimmed as he watched her focus shift between him and the data key.

23

Clive heard the beeps long before he was able to open his eyes and take in the blurry white room around him. He was alive, which was made even more apparent by the excruciating pain he felt in his chest as he attempted to move.

"Shit!" Clive cursed as he sank back into his bed. He felt a hand on his shoulder as someone placed an interpreter carefully in his ear.

"Probably best to not move, Mr. Davies," said a calming voice from beside Clive. Dr. Kashyap's hand rested gently on Clive's shoulder. "Your wounds are going to need some time to heal. Unfortunately, we need to run some tests since this is, now, the deepest wound we've ever had to fix."

"I was stabbed," Clive said, groggily.

"Yes. And it appears your trachea was also damaged somehow, which might make it difficult to speak," Dr. Kashyap said, as the memories of his fight with Talia came flooding back into his mind, including the part where she tried to choke him to death.

"And between you, Dr. Nowak, and our first gunshot victim, it's been a busy twenty-four hours for our team." Dr. Kashyap sighed as he pinched the bridge of his nose.

"Twenty-four hours?"

"Some of your wounds were difficult. We thought it would be easier to sedate you. But things look good now," Dr. Kashyap said with an exaggerated double thumbs up.

"Dr. Nowak is, okay?" Clive asked eagerly. Though it felt as if someone was rubbing sandpaper in his throat.

"He's fine. He suffered a slight head injury and has a minor concussion, but he will be fine in a few days. Jan Wager will also make a full recovery, though he lost quite a bit of blood. I suspect he will be tender for a few days as well," Dr. Kashyap said.

Clive hadn't known the name of the man who'd tried to attack them, and despite the fact that he had tried to kill Grace, he was relieved that he would be fine, too.

"And I speak for myself and my colleagues when I say we think it's wonderful that you give us such challenging cases, but we would also prefer it if you stopped." Dr. Kashyap chuckled to himself. "This one came pretty close to being fatal, but lucky for you the knife managed to miss any major arteries."

"So, I'm not dead?" Clive said with a grin.

"Not yet, Mr. Davies. No."

"And neither is anyone else?" Clive said, sounding a little pleased with himself, causing Dr. Kashyap to stop and give him a curious look.

"We have not been told what happened in there, just that our assistance was needed for some urgent care. Perhaps—" Dr. Kashyap began, but was cut off when Grace entered the room.

"It's best, Doctor, if we keep what happened on a need-to-know basis. The important thing is that we got it all sorted out." Grace stepped elegantly into the room, looking nothing like the woman he'd last seen crying over Dr. Nowak while assassins tried to kill her. She was back to her seemingly carefree self.

"All?" Clive asked skeptically. She replied with a subtle nod.

"Dr. Kashyap, would you mind if I spoke with Clive in private?" Grace said, turning her attention back to Dr. Kashyap.

"Certainly, I should run a few more test anyways. Mr. Davies, please don't move too much, not least because we should be able to repair the damaged tissues, assuming nothing happens to make them worse. But also, I suspect any movement will cause you extreme and excruciating pain." He gave Clive a little wink before leaving the room.

As soon as he was gone, Clive tried to sit up to get a better look at Grace, but the doctor had been right—a surge of fire-hot pain flared through him, spreading out from his chest and gripping his entire body.

"Son of a—!" Clive hissed as he sucked in air and tried to relax back into the bed. "He wasn't kidding."

"He rarely kids about medical advice," Grace said, rushing over to his side to help him get comfortable. "I think it's best if you listen to him and just try not to move." Her hand rested atop of his own and she gave it a light squeeze.

"What happened?" Clive asked, trying and failing to ignore the intimate gesture as he weakly gripped her hand back.

"Well, for a moment I thought Danika was going to murder Talia on the spot, when she saw what she did to you. Especially when she hovered over your body afterwards. Then it was touch and go on what she was planning to do. She sat staring at you and the key for what felt like an eternity. We didn't know what she would do. But whatever you said to her worked because she activated the manual unlock in the room and surrendered immediately." Grace looked at Clive suspiciously. "What did you say to her?"

Clive thought for a long moment, trying to recall exactly what had happened. His mind was a little fuzzy with the details but eventually it came back to him.

"I gave her a reason to trust me," Clive said in a whisper. Inexplicably, Grace began to laugh, and Clive was almost certain he could spot tears welling up in her eyes.

"That's what she said," Grace said slowly, her eyes burrowing into him. "You couldn't think of a better way than letting her stab you in the chest? You should have died," she said, wiping her eyes with her free hand.

"That was the point." Clive tried to laugh but his throat was too sore. "Water?" he said softly. Grace filled a small glass with water and held it up to his lips. Clive felt her hand brush up against his face and was comforted by its warmth. The cold water felt good, soothing his throat as it traveled down. Clive couldn't remember the last time he'd felt this thirsty.

"Well, I still think you were an idiot," Grace said, taking the glass from his lips and setting the water back on the table beside him.

"Only if it didn't work," Clive said with a devilish grin. "And did it?"

"I think so," Grace said, and Clive was grateful when her hand returned to grip his. "After we managed to get inside, we called the medical team to come pick you up, and Dr. Nowak, and also sent someone to check on Jan. Then Danika, Sasha, and I met with Talia and after we showed her the encrypted virus built into her data key, she was much less hostile with all of us. I was particularly impressed with Danika's restraint to not punch her in the face, though I suspect Sasha had something to do with that."

"You bet your ass she did," Danika said. Clive looked up to see her leaning in the doorway, Sasha behind her, with an arm wrapped over her shoulder. "You all right, shit for brains?"

"I'll live," Clive said as his eyes perked up a little. "You?"

"Seems you managed all of the excitement. Not much damage to us spectators," Danika said, amused.

"Glad to see you're awake Clive," Sasha said, stepping around Danika to get a better view. "You took a serious risk in there."

"A stupid risk," Danika jumped in. "I believe is what she meant to say."

"Well, we're all here talking about it, so ..." Clive said, letting the words fill the air. A moment later Danika began to laugh along with everyone else.

"Sure. I guess we can call that a win," Danika said after the room quieted down.

"What about the other agents? No way—" Clive began, but Grace tapped his hand.

"Everyone is accounted for and has had the situation explained to them," she stated simply.

"As it turns out, Grace had knowledge on everyone in Atlantis who was sent by their government," Sasha added.

"We are a state of the art research facility, and after Sasha managed to access the main server room, I figured it was in our best interest to at least be aware of anyone who may be a threat," Grace said calmly, her eyes making a sideways glance at Clive in the bed.

"So, you knew who I was the whole time?" Clive said sheepishly.

"No, I knew what your file said about you," Grace said, sensing Clive's uneasiness at this new information. "I didn't know you until you and I went out for dinner. That's when I met you," she added tenderly.

Clive wasn't entirely sure how he felt about the whole thing, though he suspected that since he'd also been lying about who he was, it was only fair that Grace was able to keep the same secret.

"Fair enough," Clive said, when it was clear the room was waiting for him to say something back to her. He also managed a light squeeze of her hand, which released the last bit of worry that lingered behind her eyes. "How did they take it?"

"As expected, they were a little skeptical at first," Sasha said. "But, like me, once Grace's team showed them the encrypted virus hidden inside the data key, they seemed more open to hearing us out."

"Each of them was given the option to stay onboard after the launch in a couple days or be given a ride home," Grace said calmly.

"You think it's safe to keep them on the ship?" Clive argued.

"I asked the same thing," Danika said, "but Grace seems confident that they should be entitled to the option we have been given." She placed her arm around Sasha's waist.

"You two are going to stay?" Clive asked, surprised.

"Hard to go back knowing we were sent here to die," Sasha said solemnly. "I imagine some of the others feel the same way."

"What about you Clive, you staying or going?" Danika asked.

The question landed heavily on Clive, who had been

avoiding asking himself the same question since he woke up. *How could I ever go home after what happened? Then again, would Commander Hammond ever see justice for what he did if I don't?*

"We can transmit any message you want back home once we have gone under the radar. In fact, I'm told that today we will be testing the main drive components for the city and once we are given the all clear, Dr. Nowak believes we should be ready to launch Atlantis early. There is only one final thing left to do," Grace said passionately.

"And that is?" Clive asked.

"Ask the people what they want."

"You really want to put that kind of power in the hands of the people in this city?" Danika asked.

"If we can't trust the people to do what's right for Atlantis, then we have failed anyway," Grace countered.

Just then the sound of beeps began to play from LUCYs around the room. Everyone perked up.

"What is it?" Clive asked, as Grace's voice filled his head.

We are at a crossroads, as our city and our way of life is being threatened by the outside world. First and foremost, we are and will remain a research facility, but as someone asked me recently, Why have these amazing tools if we are simply going to squirrel them away from the rest of the world? Clive shot Grace a little smirk, and she laughed. *Then what is the point in our work? So, I'm proposing three votes today. The first is whether we should share our technology with the world, create an open-source network for everyone to access. The second is if we feel this network should include work that creators feel could be weaponized. And lastly, Atlantis, unfortunately, has become a target. Our very existence is seen as a threat to the outside world. Because of this, I, along with Dr. Nowak and a team of researchers, have created a device that has the ability to cloak Atlantis from the outside world. It will not be one hundred percent effective, as nothing ever is, but it will give us security. The third vote is whether or not we activate this device during our launch, which has been moved up to forty-eight hours from now. Please take some time to think about your vote, as this will surely dictate the direction we, as a city, decide to go in moving forward. Voting will be for all citizens over the age of thirteen, it will be anonymous, and will be open for the next twenty-four hours. Thank you all.*

The room stayed quiet as each one of their LUCYs lit up with the votes displayed across its screen. Danika and Sasha looked hesitatingly at one another before they clicked through their screens.

"You didn't tell them about the attack?" Clive asked, surprised.

"People don't know the specifics of the attack, but everyone has been informed there was an attempt to hack into the servers. What good does it do to have people making long-term decisions based on fear?" Grace said calmly.

"Sometimes fear isn't a bad thing."

"Sometimes," Grace agreed. "But this isn't one of them."

"Exciting vote today, Ms. Alice," Dr. Kashyap said as he entered the room with his team of doctors. Clive recognized Akima, who was holding a large bowl filled with a familiar thick pink goop. "But if you will all excuse us, we need to see if this adjusted formula will be enough for the depths of Mr. Davies's wounds." He shooed Danika and Sasha away from the door. "This formula will be particularly messy," he added with a chuckle as he put a face shield on over Clive's head. "Trust me, you'll want this." He winked.

"And you're sure we can't just stay and watch a little of it?" Sasha said as she tried to get a better look at the gnarly pink goop.

"Not this time! Mr. Davies should really be resting. I'm sorry, Ms. Alice, but I'm afraid this time it includes you. Mr. Davies needs to sleep. It will be the best way for the medication to work," he said, placing a gentle hand on her arm and guiding her to the door. "He will be awake in eight to twelve hours, and, with any luck, fully healed."

Clive watched as Grace, Danika, and Sasha filed out of the room, leaving him with the team of doctors.

"As exciting as it is to try new formulas, I think it would be prudent to say that you should stop getting hurt like this," Akima said with a laugh as he stirred the mucky contents of the bowl.

"I hope this is the last time, Akima," Clive said wincing as he tried to adjust his position in the bed.

"Unfortunately, with a wound like this, Clive, we will need to sedate you. Any movement will weaken the tissue regeneration," Dr. Kashyap said as he invited one of the doctors over with a prepared sedative. "Are you ready?" he asked calmly.

"Ready," Clive said, as he leaned back and shut his eyes.

The doctor asked Clive to count back from ten, but he was out before he got to four.

When he awoke, Clive had no idea how long he'd been out for. He was surprised when there was no searing pain in his chest as he tried to move. It had been replaced by a new numb sensation and a heavy ache. This didn't stop him from slowly tilting his head to peer around the room. It was empty, the only sounds coming from the various machines humming and beeping around him.

At some point someone had covered his body with a warm blanket, which Clive was grateful for. Bracing himself for further pain, he began to sit himself up. Once again, there were no searing pains, just the tight grip that was pressing down on his sternum. The further he moved, the more the area ached, but it never reached an unbearable level, at least not for him. If anything, he was more surprised by how winded he'd become by such a normally simple task.

Clive looked down to see the bedsheet had fallen from his chest, revealing a blue and white hospital gown. Loosening the strings around his neck as much as he could manage, he pulled the gown forward until he was able to make out the area where days before a knife had been lodged in him. He ran his finger down the thick red scar tissue. It had puffed up more than the one on his leg, but it was much better than being dead.

Footsteps sounded from the doorway, and Clive looked up to find Akima standing there with a tray of food.

He began to speak but stopped when he caught the confused expression on Clive's face.

"Just a minute," Clive said, putting his finger up while he began looking around him. He wasn't wearing the interpreter and realized they must have removed it when they did the operation. He spotted it on the table beside him and reached over to grab it, trying to ignore the tugging in his chest. With some fiddling, he managed to pick it up.

"There, that's better," he said after putting the tiny device in his ear.

"Sorry, I hadn't realized," Akima began, but Clive waved it away.

"No worries. After everything you've done for me, you don't ever need to apologize," Clive said, giving Akima a warm smile.

"Well, you have certainly made things more interesting around here." Akima laughed as he placed the tray in front of Clive, which he now saw was some hot soup and bread.

"Looks amazing. Thank you." He felt his mouth salivating at the sight of food.

Akima examined the scar on Clive's chest.

"Unfortunately, the nerve damage may never recover one hundred percent, and the tissue and the muscle will need to be worked and rehabbed for a while in order to build up your strength. But Dr. Kashyap seemed very happy with the results. Again, it was a rather deep wound, and we were lucky that you managed to not be cut through any major arteries." Akima moved in to take a closer look, but stopped. "May I?" he asked, taking a hesitant step back.

"Of course, you're the doctor," Clive said, as he dunked the bread into his soup. "As long as you don't mind that I eat?"

"Not at all, that's why I brought it," Akima said with a laugh.

"Then examine away!" Clive said, as he put the soup-covered bread into his mouth.

"Just give me a nod if you can feel any of this." Akima pulled out a little metal stick with a rubber end and began moving it along the scar tissue. Clive gave Akima a nod every time he managed to feel something, and the number of nods surprised both him and Akima.

"What's happening with the vote?" Clive asked while Akima began typing some notes into a tablet.

"Not sure yet, but I know some preparations have already started to launch the city," Akima said.

"That was fast." Clive spooned another bit of soup into his mouth. He guessed it was a potato and leek, but he really had no idea. All he knew was that it was delicious.

"Well, once we know, there is no real reason to delay," Akima said, still typing away at the tablet.

"So, you really don't know yet?" Clive laughed, and Akima shook his head and gave Clive an embarrassed smile.

"What's that? I'm sorry, I'm just a little distracted."

"Doing your job is not a distraction," said a soft voice from the doorway. Clive looked over to find Grace standing there. "I'm happy to explain everything to Clive, Akima. Would you mind giving us a moment?" Akima turned and left without another word.

"I think you scare him," Clive said as he finished off the bowl of soup.

"I have that effect on people, I guess." Grace smiled. "How are you feeling?"

"I'm fine. How is the vote going?" Clive said, barreling past her pleasantries.

"Fair enough. Nearly the entire city has voted, and we have overwhelmingly strong support on two of the three votes, both with over eight-five percent acceptance."

"Let me guess, sharing technology and sharing potential weapons," Clive said, his eyes watching hers for a sign that he was right.

"Yes, almost everyone agreed that we should share technology and that anything that could potentially be weaponized should only be shared if the team involved in creating it felt its benefits outweighed the risk of weaponizing it." She seemed pleased with the results.

"That sounds like it's what you were hoping for," Clive said with a smile, and Grace returned it with one of her own.

"It is." She let out a big sigh before taking a seat at the foot of Clive's bed.

"I guess the hiding part isn't as unanimous," Clive said, leaning forward to put his hand closer to Grace. She took it happily.

"I admit I'd like a larger margin than we have, but currently, and unless something dramatic happens, a majority of people agree that we should protect ourselves if we are to keep ourselves safe. I think it's a divide between those who understand what kind of technology we have in Atlantis, and those who don't." Grace squeezed Clive's hand gently.

"Unless you're prepared to share everything with the citizens of the Atlantis, you can't expect them to make informed decisions," Clive said, returning Grace's squeeze.

"You mean tell them about the attempts to destroy the city and everyone in it?"

"You don't think they should know?"

"I think we can't start the existence of Atlantis on fear and anger."

"Sounds like you took a big risk," Clive said, wincing at the pain in his chest as he began to laugh.

"Well, it paid off. Tomorrow at sunrise, we launch Atlantis and activate Blue Crest. This time tomorrow, we will be officially off the grid."

"And me?" Clive asked, as his thumb began caressing the top of Grace's hand. He'd been thinking about this from the moment he got up. What would happen to him now? Was he a fugitive? How could he return to a country and a home that had been so willing to sacrifice him for something they feared?

"Calm down, Clive," Grace said, wrapping his hand, which at some point must have begun to shake, in hers. "You, along with all of the others sent here, will be given a choice to return home or live here as you have been on Atlantis."

"You would trust us?" Clive asked.

"You certainly have more trust than anyone else I've ever met." said a voice from the doorway. Clive hadn't been sure just how long she'd been there, but hearing the Israeli accent, Clive knew it was Talia Vaknin who stood in the doorway before he spotted her. Her eyes landed heavily on Clive. "Sorry, I hadn't realized anyone else would be here." She looked at Grace, who to Clive's joy didn't pull her hand away at the entrance of someone new.

"Come to finish the job?" Clive said, wincing, as he readjusted his position on the bed to sit up further.

"You think I would have anything left to finish if I had wanted you dead?" Talia said, giving Clive a sideways smile.

"Well, I appreciate you not letting me die, and also not destroying the entire city," Clive said, motioning for her to come into the room.

"What you did was stupid."

"It worked."

"Barely."

"Barely *worked* though." Clive laughed, placing a steadying hand on his chest as he did so. "I'm surprised you're still here."

"So am I," Talia said. "I suppose I have you to thank for that?" she added, sharing a look with Grace.

"This city is going to need people like you in it," Grace said as a light flashed across her LUCY. She must have been receiving a message, because she stood up from the bed. "If you'll excuse me, I have to take this. We have shuttles leaving in the next few hours, taking some of the residents who wish to return back to the mainland. After they leave, we will launch the city and activate Blue Crest. I recommend you both come up to the upper deck to witness it." Grace gave Clive's hand one final squeeze before exiting the room, leaving Talia and Clive alone.

"So, I take it you're staying?" Talia asked, giving Clive a cheeky wink.

"I'm not sure," Clive said, ignoring her jest.

"Come on. You're telling me you're going to leave that woman and this place to, what? Go back to Canada?" Talia laughed as she pulled up a chair and sat at the foot of the bed. "At least Israel is hot."

Clive had been trying to ignore the feelings he had for Grace, telling himself that they weren't real, but hearing someone else bring it up had made his skin tingle more than he would ever admit.

"Don't be a fool, Clive. You and I, Danika, Sasha, the rest of the people sent here, we don't have homes to go back to. How do we function in a world we know tried to kill us?" Talia said, shaking her head. "We don't."

"If I don't go home, the truth about why I was sent here may never come out."

"And what truth would that be?" Talia asked, folding her arms and looking impatiently at Clive, who sat uncomfortably in his levi-bed.

"Last year, I was sent to Iran on assignment. It was supposed to be a simple in and out. We had a lead on an organization that was threatening to kill the leader of the Iranian Liberation

Party."

"I remember that. We had similar intel but no one on my end was surprised. Death threats must come with the position."

"They did. But my government wanted to understand how credible the threats were. Having a democratically run Iran would look really good for us, I guess," Clive joked weakly. "Anyways, I was sent to get the intel, and, as it turned out, not only was the threat real, it had already been set in motion by the time I arrived."

"The bombing." Talia sighed quietly. "That was you?" she asked, and Clive nodded gravely.

"The bomber had planned on targeting Leila Ahmadi while she was out giving a speech to her people. A speech that happened to be at an orphanage. When I learned this, I made a request to intercept our suspect and take them out if necessary. When they said no, I reached out to my commanding officer, and when I explained it to him he agreed that I should ignore the intel. I tried to minimise the damage from the blast, but, in addition to the bomber, two others were killed and five wounded."

"What you did saved lives," Talia said quietly.

"What I did took three lives. Two of which were innocent."

"We don't have the luxury of looking at the world through the lens of the innocent and the not so innocent. Just like deciding to go home doesn't do you or anyone else any good. Do you think anyone will care about what you have to say? You disobeyed an order and killed three people to save dozens. Just like you convinced me to disobey my orders to save thousands. Both of our countries were willing to destroy this place to maintain their own power. They treat us like we are the pawns in their game, and we play because we think we are doing it for the greater good. But who is it really good for? Us? We were sent here to die." Talia paused, letting the words sink in. "You think for a second anything you do or say is going to make a difference? If you leave Atlantis, you are going home to nothing. People like you and me don't get the benefit of having the truth on our side."

"So, we give up? We let the people who damned us get away with it?" Clive said, as the beeping from his heart monitor quickened.

"No. We stay here, and we live to fight another day. With the resources of this city at our backs, we can stand up to our countries. Look at everything Grace has done for the world by creating Atlantis. If I had known why I was sent here—" Talia took in a sharp breath and began shaking her head. "The people I—"

"But you didn't."

"But I could have, and I would have. If it wasn't for you."

"But you didn't," Clive insisted again, and Talia began to nod slowly.

"Stay. Here in Atlantis. Me, you, Danika, Sasha, the rest of the agents sent here, together we can tell our truths, let the world know what is going on. Together we can help Atlantis usher in a new era. We can validate all the good Grace and her team have been doing." Talia stood up from her chair and turned to leave.

"Did you come here to try and convince me to stay?"

Talia stopped short of the door and turned to face him.

"No. I just wanted to say thank you. Consider the rest of it a hope." And with that, she was gone, leaving Clive alone in his bed.

It wasn't easy, but the next morning Clive managed to get topside with a little assistance from Akima. He'd been able to get a little rest in, and his injuries appeared to be healing well despite a little pain in his chest. But Dr. Kashyap had insisted he not leave the levi-bed for any reason and definitely not try to stand up.

Clive was happy for the assistance, but it certainly didn't make it any faster trying to maneuver around the city, especially as it appeared that all of Atlantis was also going topside to see the launch of the city. Clive and Akima followed the steady flow of people riding the TOTS until they reached a high section off of the main dome where Clive had been told by Grace to meet her.

Grace had sent the message shortly after she'd left. When he finally managed to reach the spot she'd suggested, he wasn't surprised to see Talia, Danika, and Sasha, along with a few other faces he didn't recognize. Clive suspected they were the other operatives who'd been sent to the city from various countries. His suspicion was confirmed when one of them turned and Clive saw it was Jan, the tall German man who Danika had shot in the arm. His wound must have healed well enough, as did his grudges, because he stood laughing at a joke from none other than Danika, who was standing at his side.

"I think you spend as much time in the medical wing as you do the water," said a familiar voice from behind him. Clive turned the levi-bed around and was excited to see Squints and his family had been invited as well.

"This old thing? Just a little scratch," Clive said, trying to calm the worried look on his friend's face. "I'll be back with you in the water in no time."

"I'm happy to hear that," Squints said, moving in to give his friend a gentle hug. Mia, Ilyana, and Martim weren't as merciful as they swarmed the levi-bed and embraced Clive in a heap. Despite the mild discomfort from his still-tender chest, he found their embrace to be more comforting, although Margarida was quick to give each of her children a swat on their heads.

"Go easy on him," she said as she wrapped Clive in a soft hug. "I'm glad you're safe."

Clive didn't know what they had been told about his injuries, but if they knew anything more, they didn't say it.

"Thank you," Clive said, trying to ignore the tears welling up in his eyes. He quickly wiped them away as he felt a hand land on his shoulder.

"Idiot," Danika said as she stepped in and squeezed his shoulder.

"I think she means, we're happy you're here," Sasha said, swinging around from behind her, letting out a charming laugh as she linked her arm through Danika's.

"No, I mean he's an idiot, and the sooner he realizes this, the safer we all will be," Danika said, her hand relaxing a little on his shoulder.

"It's good to see you too, Danika."

"So, you decided to stay." Danika looked down at one of the Halo choppers, identical to the one that had brought Clive into the city twenty-six days before.

"That's the last one to go, in case you were thinking of changing your mind," Sasha said, also looking down at the helicopter. This received a jab in the gut from Danika.

"I thought about it a lot last night," Clive said, letting out a heavy sigh as he looked around at the people on the deck with him. Most of them he barely knew, and some of them had recently tried to kill him. And yet none of that bothered Clive in the slightest. "Atlantis is my home now, I think."

"Do you think they will regret it?" Danika asked as she leaned over the edge and watched people board the helicopter.

"Who knows what they are going back to? Not everyone is as messed up as we are." Clive laughed, wincing at the fresh wave of pain in his chest.

"Fair enough," Danika said. "But you have to admit this place would be pretty hard to leave."

Clive wasn't about to tell her how close he'd come to leaving. He'd even asked Dr. Kashyap to prepare a travel kit for him to go home with, and he was kind enough to keep those preparations a secret. In the end, Clive knew that going home wasn't going to make a difference. He would just be doing it because of some naïve sense of duty. *No. For once I'm going to do what I want to do, not what I think I should do.*

Clive spun around in his levi-bed, looking around the deck. There had to be hundreds of people on the deck with him, and when he moved closer to the edge and peered over, he could see thousands more scattered throughout the entire topside of Atlantis.

Clive wondered about Aiden, Nick, Kissa and her mom, and even Akmed, who Clive had met on his flight into Atlantis. *Are they all on the decks of the city, waiting to see what is going to happen?*

"She's not here," Sasha said, giving Clive a wink.

"I wasn't—"

"Sure." She smiled.

Just then the last Halo took off, taking the final wave of people with it. As the helicopter lifted off, Clive finally spotted Grace who, as he should have guessed, was down at the landing pads saying good-bye to everyone who had chosen to leave. *Of course she was.*

Clive, along with everyone else around him, heard a ping in his ear, followed by the sound of Grace's voice. She was still standing on the helipad, looking out over as many people as she could see. Clive suspected the entire sky side of the city must be covered with people.

"Citizens of Atlantis. As we say good-bye to the last of our friends who are leaving us today, I'm standing here looking up at this beautiful sunrise, which brings on a glorious new day. Today we set ourselves free. Free to set our own path forward into the future, free to venture into a new horizon. A venture that has been in motion, that some of us have been preparing for, for over eight years now. Atlantis has become our home. It has become a beacon of change in our world, and the decisions we make today will allow us to continue to change and inspire others for years to come. Today, we launch. We release our city from the oceans that surround us and become the first free city on this planet. We will try to leave this world better off than when we arrived, and maybe try to clean some of it along the way." Grace laughed to herself, though Clive and everyone else could hear she was on the brink of tears. But she composed herself quickly. "I wish I was the person who could stand here and give the speech that inspires you all to do wonderful things. But everyone here already is doing those wonderful things. So, most of my work is already done." She let out another laugh, as did some of the people around, including Clive.

Clive couldn't help but wonder if Grace truly didn't understand the impact she had on people, and if maybe that was for the best. If history has taught us anything, it's that power corrupts the mind of everyone unable to separate themselves from their achievements.

A silence fell across the crowd as the ground began to thrum and the engines of Atlantis fired up. What was before a floating city in the middle of the ocean was now a voyager, ready to traverse the oceans, unlike anything the world had seen before.

Clive watched as all around the outer rim of the city, panels of green light flashed, sending a blue-green hue up into the sky as the light slowly encased the city, causing it to vanish into thin air. Blue Crest was activated.

"Today we launched Atlantis. Tomorrow, we change the world."

The End.

Acknowledgment

First of all, I would like to thank you, the reader. If you have managed to get to this point in the book then it means you have finished it. I truly hope you enjoyed reading Atlantis as much as I enjoyed writing it!

If you did enjoy it please feel free to share this story with your friends, review it online or sign up for my email list for upcoming book releases and stories on my website www.jonnyonthepage.com.

Atlantis is the second novel I have chosen to self-publish since beginning this journey last year. I can't express how thrilled I am to be given the opportunity to continue to hone my skill and put new stories out into the ether.

Creating the modern city of Atlantis was fun in so many ways. Trying to understand how something like this could be possible proved to be a lot of fun. I hope your own imaginations were able to explore the city and spark some fresh possibilities in your mind. As always though, none of this would have been possible without the help of so many people.

As is often the case with my writing I need to say thanks to my Mum, who has always been my biggest supporter and the first to read and edit all of my pages. Without her in my corner to help get my stories off the ground I'm not sure any of this would be possible.

To my incredible and supportive partner Hilary, who always reads and provides advice on everything I do. Her patience with me while I work through all of the problem areas is very generous to say the least. She is a constant source of love and positivity and I could not do this without her. Thank you, my love.

I would also like to thank my family for, although not always understanding what I do, always being there for love and support. Especially my Dad, who believes even my early drafts are good enough to publish (which they are not). Much love to you all. JGJSHLRDJLAHBKALLNGKGRHTHDPGRJKC

There have also been many people who are not my direct family who have helped make this book possible and I would like to take this moment to thank them as well. Trista, was my brilliant editor who helped finesse the book into everything you just read. Her attention to detail was just what the book needed to help bring it to a strong finish. I thank you. I have always said, I am a writer and not a speller. So truly this book would be in shambles without the hard work of the editors who assisted me along the way.

My cover artist Robyn, whose work elevates the story and captures the eyes of the reader before you ever turn a page. Her talents do not stop there. Not only is she a gifted artist but also a brilliant architect and wonderful mother. The fact that she carves out a little time in her day to help me with any of this is astounding and mind boggling to me. Robyn, you are a talent! Thank you.

A special thank you to my friend and neighbour Stew who helped talk me through some of the technical aspects of the story, I appreciate you giving me your time and chatting with me.

Lastly, I would like to thank you the reader, once again. A book is not a book without people who want to read it. I hope that it has provided you with some joy and possibly some entertainment. I don't plan on stopping any time soon, and if you enjoyed this book please check out *Ash and Sun* or keep your eyes peeled for my cozy mystery *The Limestone Manor*.

If you enjoyed this story or any of my others, email and let me know at Jonny@jonnyonthepage.com.

Until next time,
  Jonny Thompson

About the Author

Jonny Thompson is an award winning writer and performer living in Ponamogoatitjg/Dartmouth, NS with his partner Hilary and their delightfully entertaining dog Henry. Jonny was born in England and grew up in the traditional lands of the Anishinabewaki and Attiwonderonk nations now St. Marys, Ontario.

Jonny attended Dalhousie University, where he received a BA in Theatre. He's worked professionally in stage and film for over thirteen years, including five extremely exciting years travelling the world as a puppeteer.

Jonny's debut novel *Ash and Sun* was released in October 2022. He has written various novels, novellas and short stories which can be found on his website https://jonnyo nthepage.com/.

He is continuously working through new projects and looks forward to sharing them with you soon. Thank you for reading!

You can connect with me on:

🌐 https://www.jonnyonthepage.com

Also by Jonny Thompson

Ash and Sun

After a 200-day suspension, all that Sergeant Adam Jennings wanted was a win on his return to the Global Investigation Bureau (GIB). But when a simple warehouse fire begins to look more like a homicide investigation, he is forced to watch as the entire case begins to unravel, slowly revealing the dark underbelly of a world that should not exist. Saddled with an unwanted new partner, and a tarnished reputation, Jens is forced to tread a thin line between right and wrong as he tries to discover just what the truth really is.